Birds *of the* Snows

TARANNUM RIYAZ

Translated by the author from the Urdu original

Barf Aashna Parindey

THORNBIRD

NIYOGI
BOOKS

Published by
NIYOGI BOOKS
Block D, Building No. 77,
Okhla Industrial Area, Phase-I,
New Delhi-110 020, INDIA
Tel: 91-11-26816301, 26818960
Email: niyogibooks@gmail.com
Website: www.niyogibooksindia.com

Editor: K.E. Priyamvada
Design: Shashi Bhushan Prasad
Cover design: Misha Oberoi

ISBN: 978-93-91125-28-8
Publication: 2021

Printed at: Niyogi Offset Pvt. Ltd., New Delhi, India

To my daughter

Shabnum Bhat

Contents

Publisher's Note

It is with deep sadness that I write this prefatory note to the English translation titled *Birds of the Snows* of Dr Tarannum Riyaz's original Urdu novel *Barf Aashna Parindey*. Translated by the author, this work is a labour of love that she was keen to see published, as were we at Niyogi Books. However, due to the sudden surge of the pandemic, the author was taken from us in May 2021. The news of her passing hit us like a bolt from the blue. Indeed she left us much too soon.

Tarannumji was a good friend, with whom I often interacted during my days at the Sahitya Akademi. A well-known Urdu poet, she was a regular in many of the Akademi's multi-lingual Poets' Meets. With a mellifluous voice, she recited her poems with enough feeling to carry the audience with her. When I was editing *Indian Literature*, I published English translations of her poems. Thus a friendship based on mutual respect developed between us.

Birds of the Snows evocatively describes childhood in Kashmir, capturing beautiful images of the landscape, the changing seasons, the customs, food and birds of the region. The author has crafted a coming-of-age novel that depicts a young woman's search for fulfilment and the deep humanity she displays in caring for her professor, after he suffers a stroke. The backdrop of Sheba's family and her determination to chart her own course provides the setting for the story, with Kashmir as the larger landscape of the narrative. The use of poetry and references to classical music, as well as observations of nature, birds and trees add subtle touches to the sensitive unfolding of the novel.

When Tarannumji approached me to publish this book, her only request was that the editing should be of 'international standard'. I don't know if we have been able to fulfil her desire but when I contacted her so that she could review the edited files in 'Track changes' mode, she told me her husband Dr Riyaz Punjabi was in an ICU in a Delhi hospital, fighting for his life, and she had neither the time nor inclination to attend to this work. She requested me, 'Teacherji *aap meri taraf se yeh kaam kar dijiye* (you please take care of this on my behalf). Unfortunately, Dr Riyaz Punjabi left this world in April 2021 and in a month's time Tarannumji also succumbed to Covid-19.

Though Tarannumji passed away during the course of the production of this book, and was unable to see the finished work, its completion is our sincere tribute to her memory. We are sure that she will live on through her works, the recordings of her poetry recitations at various literary events that can be viewed online, and her children.

Nirmal Kanti Bhattacharjee

Editorial Director, Niyogi Books

List of Characters

Chowdhury Khuda Baksh Khan: A famous jurist and landowner of Kashmir, who had four sons

Chowdhury Bashir Khan: Elder son of Chowdhury Khuda Baksh Khan and Sakeena Begum, settled in Lahore

Bhai Jaan: The son of Chowdhury Khuda Baksh Khan's third son, called *bhai jaan* by his siblings and cousins. His siblings are his younger brother Qaiser and his younger sister Shaheen

Naaheed: Daughter of the fourth son of Chowdhury Khuda Bakhsh Khan

Nasir: son of the fourth son of Chowdhury Khuda Bakhsh Khan

Chowdhury Najam Khan: Second son of Chowdhury Khuda Baksh Khan and Sakeena Begum

Suraya Begum: wife of Najam Khan; she is called Nanna Jaani by her granddaughter Seemeen

Faheema: eldest daughter of Najam Khan and Suraya Begum; called Baaji by her younger sisters, she is the mother of Seemeen

Seemeen: daughter of Faheema and Mukhtar Ahmed

Farkhanda: second daughter of Najam Khan and Suraya Begum; called Farkhi by her siblings and Aunty Phirki by Seemeen; Farkhanda is married to Zahoor-ud-din and their son is Yasir

Sheba: youngest daughter of Najam Khan and Suraya Begum

Zahoor-ud-din: an engineer, husband of Farkhanda

Yasir: son of Farkhanda and Zahoor-ud-din

Zaheen-ud-din: a businessman and brother of Zahoor-ud-din

Nuzhat: wife of Zaheen-ud-din; she is called Pyaari by her mother-in-law

Aasim: son of Zaheen-ud-din and Nuzhat

Muqim Ehmed: Zaheen-ud-din's uncle

Munazah: Muqim Ehmed's daughter

Azeez Bhat: owner of a grocery shop across the street from the gate of Chowdhury Najam Khan's bungalow

Zarifa and **Hanifa**: daughters of Azeez Bhat

Shahaab-u-din Shairwaani: A university professor and later civil servant, whom Sheba considers marrying

Shams-u-din Shairwaani: brother of Shahaab-u-din Shairwaani

Professor Daanish: A sociology lecturer, and Sheba's guide, whom Sheba looks after, along with her classmates, when he falls ill

Mrs Daanish: Professor Danish's wife, who works in the US and visits occasionally

Mayuri: Sheba's room-mate and best friend in college, who later marries and moves to England

Prashant Patel: Mayuri's husband, who works in England

Saleem Miyaan: Dr Daanish's cook and helper, who also takes care of Sheba

Gulla Bhai (Ghulam Mohammad or **Gull Mohammad):** The cook and helper at Suraya Begum's home in Srinagar

The Walnut Orchards

Behind the plum tree, there was a small mound of brown earth on the soft ground. The birds had scattered half-eaten raw plums like flowers on it. The sun had set a short while ago and the fragrance of walnut peel and leaves wafted across on the cold breeze from the orchards beyond the rather wide but just ankle-deep stream.

A dupatta-clad girl of medium height was walking towards the plum tree, gazing at it with anxious eyes. For many hours her heart had been pounding in a way it never had before, yet the moment she set her teary eyes on the branches, she felt her heart come to rest on some object; but then the object fell to the ground, and her heart fell with it and got lost somewhere too.

Tears flowed down her pale cheeks. Crying without parting her lips, she reached the mound and, kneeling down, buried her face in it. It had dried in the sun during the day, but now her tears were making it wet again.

Patwari uncle had left, leaving her alone there. As the girl heard his steps fading away, her sobs became louder, sounding in rhythm with her trembling body.

That day, Sheba had been reading the story of ancient man; her father was helping her along. Hearing Abbu's heavy breathing and occasional coughing, she felt he was tired, and asked her father if he wanted some water. As she went to the kitchen to get a glass of water, she saw many half-ripe cherries from the cherry tree near the compound wall scattered on the grass—thanks to the birds, especially the parrots. Abbu had said she needn't go so far as he could always drink from the copper surahi on the side table. The surahi had recently been plated with nickel in the month of Ramadan and was shining brightly; the tiny branches with birds and flowers carved on it were now clearly visible. But Sheba wanted to get fresh water from the kitchen for her Abbu.

The distance from the porch of the bungalow to the kitchen was just about 50 steps but she stopped in between to pick a few cherries and even tasted them secretly—the green cherry was hard, the white-and-red one sour. She wanted to taste some more cherries, so that she could know in how many days they would ripen but most of them had been pecked at by the birds…and for many days now, her guess had been wrong. Cherries are very tasty! Also, you can select two pairs from a bunch of cherries and wear them dangling from your ears like big red pearl earrings! Everyone wants to wear such earrings and eat them after some time, and wear them again and eat them again…that's why it is so important to know how much longer the cherries are going to take to ripen fully. She could certainly have shown them to Ammi but then Baaji—her elder sister—would blame her that she ate soiled cherries and made Ammi eat them too. But no one can scold Ammi, and Ammi doesn't in fact eat them! After washing them, she tastes a bit of each and then announces how much time they will take to ripen. She then throws them in the garbage, but Baaji could still hit and scold Sheba on this pretext.

Sheba looked around and walked quickly to the kitchen. Hiding some cherries in her small fist and carrying a glass of water given to her by Noori Nana, the cook, she had already spilled half the water by the time she reached Abbu. But taking the glass in his hand, Abbu smiled pleasantly and gulped it down.

'Want some more?' Sheba asked, nodding her head up and down like Ammi.

'No, *beta* (child). Thank you very much,' Abbu replied, smiling again.

Abbu was sitting in his big chair, checking Farkhi's progress report. She looked at the wooden chair; it was painted deep brown, with flowers, creepers and leaves carved on it in such a way that they easily caught the light. She sat down on the carpet holding the book in her lap, from which she was trying to read, Abbu correcting her now and then.

'Early man lived in caves.' She completed the sentence slowly.

'What is the word for cave in Urdu?' Abbu asked her.

'*Gaar*,' she replied.

Abbu shook his head from right to left. 'It's not *gaar*, it is *ghaar*; you have to say it using the base of your tongue.'

'Yes Abbu...*gaa...r.*'

'No child...*ghaa...ghaa.*' Abbu looked at her but did not smile.

'Yes Abbu...*ga...ga...ghaar.*' Sheba growled a couple of times and, ultimately saying the word right, burst into laughter.

'Yes, there you are!' Abbu laughed too.

'But what is the difference between the two Abbu?'

'A big difference, *beta*, pronunciation is very important. Do you remember what you did yesterday?'

'No Abbu, I don't.'

'You pronounced *qualeen* (carpet) as *kaaleen.*'

'Yes, but afterwards I could say *kaleen*, I mean *qualeen*,' she laughed again in celebration of pronouncing the word properly.

'So, nothing is hard if you really try to do it,' Abbu said smilingly, yet in all seriousness. 'Oh God, this child does not take any interest in her studies!' His forehead was furrowed.

'No, Abbu. I take interest in my studies. I will read all those books you've bought for me.' She looked at Abbu, her head bent down, her eyelids touching her eyebrows, her chin on her chest.

Abbu shook his head again.'Oh no, not you my child! I'm looking at Farkhi's report card. I know you're very good at your studies and love to study as well. And I know, by 3rd grade, you'll be reading these books fluently,' said Abbu.

'Farkhi!' Abbu called out loudly so that Abdul Qayoom would hear him and send Farkhi to him.

'I'll call Farkhi, Abbu!' Sheba said, and ran out to the lawn where Farkhi was playing with her friends from the neighbourhood.

'I'll play for you. Go inside, Abbu wants to speak to you.' She pushed Farkhi from behind, who was sitting in a row of four playing *kho-kho*. Farkhi ran inside.

'What is this report, child? You barely passed these subjects but stood first in games! Had you spent that time on your studies, your grades would have been better. Games were not that important,' Abbu said sternly without looking at Farkhi, turning the pages of the report card while he spoke.

'No Abbu. I couldn't have scored full marks even then,' Farkhi retorted, frowning and shaking off the dust from her hands.

'Really? Why?'Najam Khan raised his head. Farkhanda looked at his face. When Abbu asked something and stopped talking, it meant that he won't ask anything else or scold you, and you could ask him whatever you wanted to and tell him whatever you wished to say.

'I would have kept thinking that if we practised properly, the 4th standard team could not beat us in the finals. So how could I remember what the teacher was saying? I even got this score because I studied right through the nights during the exams. Can I go now Abbu? We were playing *kho-kho* in the backyard when you called. It is evening already and Azeez Bhat will soon be calling Zareefahaneefa (Zarifa, Hanifa) back home,' Farkhi explained, rubbing the mud off her little hands. 'Mehmooda has already gone. Her brother scolded her for being out so long.' Farkhi bent her head sideways helplessly. 'Abbu, if we had a brother, he would scold us all the time for no reason too, isn't it?'

'No *beta*, how could he do that without any reason? And only if he was your elder brother could he do so; and that too, only if you were at fault. Otherwise no one is allowed to raise his voice at my children,' Najam Khan smiled.

Farkhi laughed gleefully. 'May I go now Abbu?'

'Yes, you may.' Najam Khan looked at his nine-year-old daughter. 'Oh yes...' He looked up at the door.

Farkhanda looked back. 'Yes, Abbu?'

'You should call him Azeez *Kaka* (uncle). Everyone calls him *Kaka*. Even I call him Azeez Kaka. And you know that he is much, much older than you.'

'But now he looks shorter than me...' Farkhanda stopped for a while at the entrance and looked at her father again. 'Abbu, when a person sits at one place the whole day, he becomes short. Just some time back, when I went to his shop to buy some candy, my hand wouldn't even reach the counter. Now I've grown bigger because I play, but he is short because he doesn't play. Now, if I stand near the gate I can see him, I mean his head, even when he's sitting inside his shop.' Farkhanda crossed the doorway but turned her head towards her father again. 'Abbu, have you seen Azeez Kaka walking in the street? It seems as if he's still sitting and not walking. That gown-like thing he wears touches his feet.'

'Yes, it's called a pheran. This word is from the Persian word *perhann*.'

'Yes Abbu. Perhann. Pheran. Azeez Kaka's pheran reaches his feet and that's why he looks like he's sitting. And his *khadaons* (wooden slippers) sound different when he walks, like the sound of a child clapping. Isn't it?'

'Is that so?' Najam Khan looked at her round eyes turning rounder still, in her childish enthusiasm.

'You know Abbu, whenever it rains and he walks in his high-platform wooden slippers, there's no sound. That's because he doesn't walk fast, as he can fall; but when it is dry, his flat slippers sound like a child clapping.' Farkhanda clapped and tried to listen to its sound carefully.

'Oh…I see.' Najam Khan nodded.

'Yes, Abbu. And you know,' she began and Najam Khan looked up in apparent concentration, 'it's because his *khadaons* have become thin.'

'Because of long use, much of the wood is rubbed away, making them thin and shorter near the heels. That is why when they touch the soles of his feet, it sounds like clapping. And then it is time to get new ones,' he explained.

'Don't they have long boots, like the pair you gave to Noori Nana for shopping?'

'Not usually, and Azeez Kaka has to walk only from his shop back home or from his home to the shop. How will he pull those heavy boots on and off all the time? So why not wear *khadaons*, take them off in the shop and sit there comfortably, cross-legged inside his cozy pheran?'

'Oh, yes! Who will pull his boots on and off for him, he doesn't even have servants! But Zareefahaneefa can pull them like Sheba and I do, and get one shoe off even before Abdul Qayoom can start pulling the other one off, isn't it Abbu?'

'Yes, and get a tummy ache from pulling them off too!' Najam Khan nodded, laughing pleasantly.

'Oh, we do that on purpose for fun,' Farkhanda flashed her small teeth in a wide smile again.

'Oh, I didn't know that!'

'But to pull boots off shouldn't be so difficult, Abbu. Shouldn't they be slightly loose anyway?'

'If they are loose they wouldn't be that comfortable when the snow is deep and there is an icy wind, as it will find its way into your boots!' Najam Khan explained smilingly, bending his neck slightly towards his shoulder to indicate that the discussion was over.

'Yes…' Farkhanda nodded her head too.

Najam Khan folded the report card. 'Ah, the questions these children ask!' He found himself saying and stood up smiling, to put the report card away with other important papers. Farkhanda saw him doing this and looked at the floor near her feet, then ran to the outer door but suddenly stopped, turning her head back towards her father.

'Did I do very badly, Abbu?' she asked inquiringly.

'No, sweetheart.'

Najam was smiling and surprised at himself, as this was something new for him, with no precedent in previous generations because no child had ever been so bold in the entire family. 'But you should give more time to your studies in future!' he said quickly and started looking at the other papers.

At that time Najam Khan could hardly guess that one day she would take her decisions herself with the same confidence. Najam Khan belonged to a family which believed that working hard was below their dignity. But his father broke away from this tradition and studied Law to become a famous jurist. Ruling over the tenants was their tradition and he, too, followed it but he was considerate and fair-minded. Najam was very intelligent but, like all intelligent people, he couldn't work hard at a job that was not to his liking. His father wanted him to become a lawyer; he wanted to be a doctor, but was not encouraged to do so. Things stopped at graduation. However, in order to fulfill his urge to study medicine, his mother arranged that he learn from their old-fashioned family hakim. Najam Khan continued to study and even learnt flying, but being asthmatic, he had to retire prematurely from his flying career. He mastered different languages, and learnt new techniques of agriculture. He planted 2,500 trees of best quality walnuts called 'Paper Walnut' for their very thin shell and fine quality. But he hardly got to taste one in the coming years.

He became a bodybuilder and learned how to sing different classical ragas, yet the doctor in him was always restless. But by the time his father passed away, he was too old to study medicine.

Finally, he said yes to marriage—something he had put on hold for a long time. But, to save himself further restlessness, he promised himself that all his children would be doctors. He announced this in the *Diwan Khana* (drawing room), in front of the full-size picture of his father, painted using natural colours from vegetables and flowers. Well-built and six feet tall, Chowdhury Sahib, a Lahori Punjabi, wearing a crested turban above his English suit and tie, stared back helplessly at his son from within the frame of the portrait. Looking at his double chin and sharply pointed and twisted moustache, Najam Khan laughed so loudly that his wife, a delicate Kashmiri woman, involuntarily clutched the invisible bulge of her belly and took a step backwards.

After Chowdhury Sahib's death, the responsibility of looking after their vast lands in North Kashmir and the two bungalows in the city passed on to his sons. It was the second-half of the fourth decade of the 20th century. British rule was over. New borders had been drawn. India was divided into two countries.

Najam's elder brother, Chowdhury Bashir Khan, had gone to Lahore to take care of the family property there. He had to stay put there because of the political uncertainty in the two countries, and no one was sure of his return. He never returned. After completing their higher education, his children settled in the West, visiting him only every two or three years. In the first decade of the 21st century, he died in his big house in Lahore. Two country-made cars and an imported one mourned silently in the portico. On the second day, the neighbours found him dead in his bed with the photo album of his family in his hand. They informed his sons; they couldn't make it to the burial in time, so the neighbours had to manage that. The children, however, sent money to meet the expenses for the funeral. Only when they'd come to sell the property would they thank the neighbours personally—after visiting their father's grave and saying *fatiha* (the short first sura of the Koran, used as an essential element of ritual prayer).

Following mutual understanding, Najam Khan took charge of the two bungalows located in the city, each with a large garden around it. He was told that the air pressure in Srinagar was comparatively higher; and so, there was more oxygen in the air as compared to the hills around and, therefore, was better for an asthmatic. The two younger brothers remained in the village to take care of the lands there. And so, the management of the lands was divided but not the property itself. Much later, Najam Khan realized that his younger brothers had conspired to send him away and keep hundreds of *kanals* of land, which was worth a fortune, since the law required that to claim the property one had to have it in one's possession. Although due to the Land Reformation Act feudalism had been abolished, the two brothers showed it as self-cultivated—and not cultivated by tenants—so no land was taken by the government. The illiterate tenants were not aware of the new Act. And no one was there to tell them about it either.

The late Chowdhury Khuda Baksh was not a feudal; his land was not a grant from the Maharaja. He was against the very idea of grant of lands as *jagirs* (estate). He viewed it as an act of great injustice. But he liked to buy land, and he bought it in the beautiful valley of Kashmir. It was not easy though; since he was not born in the valley, he did not have the right to buy property there. So the childless landlord, Mardaan Ali Shah—who wanted to sell his property—legally gifted the land to his adopted sister Sakeena Begum, who was none other than Chowdhury Khuda Baksh's wife. Chowdhury Sahib paid him the price he wanted for that piece of heaven.

Every one of his children had an equal right in the property, Najam Khan would think when his brothers sent him a few bags of corn and walnuts once a year. He would feel very sad and wouldn't go to the village for months together. However, in the harvesting season, during the short vacations in the schools, he would visit the village to offer *fatiha* at his father's grave.

Sitting on a sofa in the corner of the Diwan Khana, Najam Khan looked at his parents' pictures. For a second he felt his mother had called out to him from the lawn, saying Abbaji wanted him downstairs. She called him in a low voice. Mother would always call from inside the house and not coming out to the lawn, whenever she had to call upstairs for some child. And from any floor of the bungalow, or from any corner of the garden, the children would hear her voice because she would stand facing the entrance and call them by name. Although her voice could be heard by no stranger, as no one was around the bungalow for miles, she would still never shout anyone's name, sitting in a chair on the front lawn. Instead, she would always ask the maid to do so or would go into the house if no one was around.

Najam Khan felt he had just heard her voice, saying: 'Tell Najam Khan that Chowdhury Sahib wants to see him,' as if she was addressing a servant. Najam Khan rose from the sofa and went up to the wall. He removed the picture from the wall and held it in his hands. Mother would always call him by his full name, like father who would call Najam Khan's elder brother, who was a few inches taller than him, by his full name.

The camera was an early model. His elder brother, Bashir Khan, held it close to his belly so that he could get Abbaji and *Bebe*, sitting in front of him, well into focus. They finally appeared on the screen after many attempts, sitting on high-seated chairs. Abbaji was tall and well-built, but Bebe was somewhat shorter. Abbaji was wearing a deep blue suit, which looked black in the picture; the blue necktie also appeared to be black, but his crested turban looked white as it was. Bebe's off-white Kashmiri silk sari looked pure white on the screen. The younger children had to jump up to their elder brother's waist to have a glimpse of the screen, but Najam only needed to stand on tiptoe to get a full view.

'I didn't do anything wrong,' Najam complained in his mind to his parents' photograph. 'It was they who left me of their own accord,' he added.

Whenever he went to the village he would complain about his present to the memories of his parents. Mother was not buried in the village; she was taken out of the hospital in the city and buried in the nearby graveyard. In those days, Chowdhury Sahib was posted as *Wazeer-e-Wizaarat* (governor) in far-off Ladakh. There was no telephone there; you could send a telegram, but the arduous journey back to Kashmir would take many days. The decisions could, however, be taken by Haleema Begum, the eldest person in the household, who was a second cousin of their mother and a widow. She did what she thought right, Najam had always believed. The children might not have insisted on having a last look at their dead mother, he thought. He missed and remembered his mother often. His eyes filled with tears and he prayed for the peace of her soul. His thoughts travelled many years back into the past.

Bebe, a beautiful face with kindness appeared in his mind. She was lying tired on her bed. When Bebe delivered her last child, she fell seriously ill and never recovered. In the early years of the 20th century, she was admitted to Srinagar's Rainawari Mission Hospital, and neither the mother nor the baby came out alive. Although only 31 years old, having borne many children, she had grown very weak.

Her cousin had come from Lahore when Sakeena Begam was expecting, ostensibly to look after the household and take care of her pregnant sister who was not well. After Sakeena Begum died, Chowdhury Sahib not only married Haleema Begum but also brought her children from her previous marriage to his home. He might have been impressed by her apparent motherliness for her nephews and nieces, or God knows for what reason, Chowdhury Sahib transferred his whole property to her name. Thus, she was the owner of the property when Chowdhury Sahib died, and only her own children were the legal heirs. But her children transferred it back to their maternal cousins, who were the rightful heirs to the property. Hearing about the imminent partition of India, she went back to Lahore because she feared being neglected by her stepchildren, whom she had never treated well as their stepmother.

After many years, a very old woman visited Chowdhury Najam Khan's wife, Suraya Begum, to tell her something about the death of Sakeena Begum. But Suraya Begum didn't tell Najam Khan anything, as she knew that hearing the truth, he would be devastated.And the truth was that widow Haleema Begum had not come to the Valley out of any love for her cousin, but with a devious plan in her mind. When Sakeena Begum delivered the baby, Haleema Begum, with the help of two nurses, got an ice slab put under Sakeena's head. She had bribed the nurses with 50 rupees each, which was a big amount in those days. One of the nurses was the same old woman who visited Suraya Begum to admit her crime and ask for forgiveness, not wanting to die with the heavy burden of guilt. But Suraya Begum said that it was only God who could pardon her.

There were some more days left for the delivery, but Haleema Begum got Sakeena Begum shifted to the hospital on the pretext of some other illness. That incident was still fresh in Najam Khan's memories.

'You…you, will not cry.' Bebe had opened her eyes slightly, touched his face lovingly, and held his small hand. Najam Khan, too, had held that ice-cold hand in both hands and looked at the words tattooed on it, which he had touched many times before: Unfaithful World.

He touched the words 'Unfaithful World' with his fingertips, least knowing that he would never touch them again. Sakeena Begum had gone to school and was educated. Only a few decades earlier, broad-minded people had come forward for the education of women. Why did Bebe have that tattoo on her hand? Najam would think sometimes. The phrase remained an inseparable part of his memories of his mother.

'Okay?' mother had asked him very softly.

'Why Bebe? I am big now and no one hits me.' His nine-year-old mind could not understand more than that.

'Yes, my child…that's why.' Bebe had bent her head to her left, where Najam sat. A tear rolled down from her left eye and Najam wiped it with his finger.

'What happened Bebe? Does it hurt?'

'Yes, my child…Perhaps…if I die, you will look after your younger brothers. You are the older one…and you will not cry, okay?' And then Bebe had closed her eyes. She was taken to Rainawari Mission Hospital. He wondered if Bebe ever opened her eyes after that again.

Najam Khan's eyes filled with tears. He always remembered how, when Bebe had closed her eyes, a tear had run down Bebe's left eye and rolled towards her ear. Bebe had said, if she did not return, he had to look after his younger brothers, like Bebe herself did.

'I did as you wished, Bebe. It is they who pushed me away! Unfaithful world!'

Najam Khan, sitting on a sofa in the corner of the Diwan Khana, sighed deeply. His eyes could not hold back the tears anymore and rolled down his cheeks. Najam Khan's family was given only two rooms to stay in the grand mansion when they visited the village during his children's vacations. Although he lived in a nice bungalow in the city, Najam Khan always thought of the mansion in the village as his real home. But he still took very good care of the property in the city because he knew it belonged to his two brothers. After the death of his father, all the moveable property was shifted to the village. Suraya Begum had once timidly suggested not to do this. But she was asked not to bother herself with matters between the brothers, as the house in the village was always considered as the real home. Najam Khan was deprived of all that as well. He had been in the city, yet he did not know where all those valuable items had vanished—the silver utensils, big, small and huge copper pots all neatly carved, double blankets of shahtoosh, rolls of pashmina, and Kashmiri and Iranian carpets—they had all disappeared.

Father had built his dream house with a lot of love. It was a Victorian style mansion with eight large rooms and long galleries in the front and back, and on the top was a wide wooden balcony. All the three floors had stairs carved from a single grey rock. It was the only building with a shining metal roof in the vicinity that shone in the sun, and could be seen from miles away.

Najam Khan was standing at the window of a room on the top floor, in the bright, soft moonlight. It was the month of October; he was looking out at the flourishing walnut orchard, his muscular arms resting on the window sill. His broad chest was short of breath though, because his asthma acted up at this high altitude. He was thinking about the past and was worried about the future of his innocent Kashmiri wife and their little daughters, sleeping in the next room.

> *'I had thought I am going home*
> *But this path leads to somewhere else.'*

Najam Khan recalled this couplet.

Six-year-old Sheba's eyes were wide open. In that pin-drop silence, nobody could guess how noisy the rain had been in the evening. But now this magical silence was disturbed by the far-off howling of the jackals and barking of the dogs. When one of the jackals howled, all the other jackals everywhere around started howling too, and then it would be quiet again. All these sounds disturbed Sheba's peace and her heart would start pounding. The intoxicating evening breeze had brought rain and the scent of drying branches scattered on the grass, as well as the unique fragrance of the soft, green peel of the ripe walnuts and their leaves. Her sleep was disturbed further as an apprehension of some unknown peril raised its fearsome head in her little heart. Abbu will get tired standing at the window, she feared, and will fall to the ground. Abbu's chest will burst for lack of breath. And if something happens to Abbu, both uncles will get Sheba and her sisters married to their sons so that they can grab all the property—the same way they had grabbed all the gold bars and other valuables, which grandfather had left in their safekeeping a few days before his death. The gold was in a secret vault under the floor of grandpa's room, and no one had a clue about it. Grandma might have known when she was alive.

Such talk was heard long after grandpa's death but no one had any proof because Abbu's elder brother was in Lahore and Abbu was in the city, and was never informed about the seriousness of grandpa's illness.

Najam Khan could have reached the village when Chowdhury Sahib was dying if he had been informed in time, people would say later.

Sheba saw her uncle's bald head, shining like a new copper coin, on the *khatamband*—the varnished hexagonal decorative woodwork design of the ceiling. It did not look brown in the dark but was grey and reflected the weak rays of moonlight falling on the marble floor. The beautiful ceiling was made of finger-sized wedges of wood joined in a hexagonal pattern, dividing the ceiling in a geometric design. *Chachaa* has a big, carved copper tray before him. This is the tray in which the servant, Abdul Qayoom, and Noori Nana—Noor-u-din the cook—carried *qurbani ka gosht* (the meat from the animals sacrificed on the occasion of Eid-ul-Azha) to distribute in the neighbourhood.

One person holds the tray covered with a white embroidered cloth, while the other hands out the meat in handfuls. The tray in front of Chachaa is filled with halwa and covered with shining silver foil. And everyone knows that delicious halwa is flavoured with saffron and garnished with walnuts, almonds, cashews, pine nuts, pistachios, and raisins. Near the copper tray there is a light green *zehrmohra* (a quarter-plate made of jade-like semi-precious stone) with a heap of gold bars on it. This plate is one from the set that Abbu had brought back from some foreign country. The silver foil is decorated with saffron leaves that read 'Property', in the same way that Noori Nana decorated dishes on Eid, writing '*Eid Mubarak*' on them. But Noori Nana takes a long time doing this in the kitchen. Of course, Noori Nana can write neatly like her school teacher but Sheba, although she's now in the 3rd grade, can't write that well. Chachaa has pulled off the cloth covering the tray of halwa and thrown it aside; he is gobbling up mouthfuls of the sweet dish with one hand, and is biting at the gold bars with the other. Chachaa eats the 'P' of property, then the 'r' and 'o', and then he gulps down the 'per' and 'ty' one after another quickly. He doesn't look at the people around, nor does he share anything with anyone.

But their children are so good; all the cousins are close friends. They wait eagerly the whole year to see each other in the summer. And it was just yesterday when all the children were talking about it while returning from the mill. The sun was about to set and they were walking between the rows of corn planted near the walnut orchards. They were having all the fun—talking, singing, playing, jumping, dancing, somersaulting, and squatting like monkeys and standing up again. The hot topic of discussion, as always, was the same favourite one: how to lengthen the stay of the cousins from the city, when the brief vacations were over. How nice would it be if *Baday Abbu* (Sheba's father) did not have to take his children back to the city for some more days! The setting sun, shining through the walnut leaves on either side of the path, made the tall grass spread its scent all around. The graceful grasshoppers—with long, green legs, bent in sharp angles and dancing merrily—flew here and there; they looked very humble and yet quite important. They looked like little helicopters, as do the dragonflies. The children soon got busy trying to catch some of them. Baaji finally succeeded in catching one. She pulled a thread from the ribbon holding her hair, tied it to its tail, and started flying it like a kite. The poor creature flew just once and then its tail broke off, and gliding less than an inch forward, it nose-dived into the grass.

Baaji got angry when Farkhi asked her for some thread. 'It's not for children! Didn't you see the grasshopper falling down?'

Baaji looked at Farkhanda with an expression as if she felt very sorry for the grasshopper. She, of course, didn't say that the grasshopper had died, meaning, thereby, that she hadn't killed it. And yet, every child knew that any flying insect, when it falls because it is unable to fly, soon dies! After a little while, Baaji, with a new thread from her ribbon, was after another grasshopper. While all this was going on, thick fast-moving dark clouds with lightning and thunder, covered the sky above the walnut trees. The children were passing through the middle of the orchards when it began to rain heavily. They tried to take shelter under the trees but got drenched in minutes. The elder bosses, 13- and 14-year-old Baaji and *Bhai Jaan* (elder brother), were also scared. Bhai Jaan was their elder uncle's first son, and was as old as Baaji. He was also her foster brother because his mother had breast-fed Baaji too. Both of them lorded it over the other children.

When the first showers and strong winds drenched 10-year-old Naaheed's 7-year-old brother Nasir's neck, and a walnut fell on his head with a thud, he started crying loudly and clung to the walnut tree. Seeing this, the others laughed at him. But seeing them laughing at him, Sheba went and stood by his side near the trunk of the tree. It was meant to convey that he had not done anything wrong by crying, and that she, too, was about to cry. Getting this silent message, Nasir smiled through his tears. The other children—apart from Farkhi—were Bhai Jaan's younger brother Qaiser, and his younger sister Shaheen. They were shivering with cold and afraid of being laughed at, but walked after the teenagers with their heads held high.

They had no servant with them; they used to come back home on their own every evening. But that evening, the way home seemed to have changed. Not a house or a landmark could be seen anywhere around. There were a few farmers' huts in that area, but the downpour had been so heavy and the clouds so low and near the ground, that those small mud huts were lost to sight. And the impudent walnuts, tossed here and there by the wind, certainly didn't have the sense to distinguish between a tenant's and a landlord's head! Frowning and turning her nose upward, Baaji sternly looked up at the walnut branches. But to escape from the torrents of water coming down from the branches, she had to quickly close her eyes and bend her head low. The wind began to pick up. And so, the lost caravan had to take shelter under the very trees that were pelting big walnuts on their heads. Yet, the innocent joy and excitement of collecting the windfall was so great that no other pleasure could be compared to it.

In the sudden cold brought on by the rain, every new walnut picked up had a warming effect and the sobs soon changed to smiles. The number of nuts gathered, was compared! They had been thrust into pockets and collected in the skirts of their dresses too. And yet, despite all the fun, an unknown fear gnawed at their hearts.

Bhai Jaan suddenly announced that there was nothing to worry, as he had recalled that on the left side of the dried and fallen (or perhaps fallen and dried up) walnut tree, the stony path led to the tenant Mohammad Lone's hut, and getting there would take hardly 10 minutes. 'If we start courageously now, we'll soon be there because staying here longer can be dangerous.' Hearing this, Baaji said that it was dangerous anyway as lightning could strike anytime as well. Hearing that, Shaheen screamed loudly and started crying, and Farkhi had to hug her close to comfort her.

Like Sheba, in future these incidents would be the best part of everyone's memories. How eternal each moment seemed to be, but they were, of course, temporary like everything else—every one of the caravan had to part from the others in their life later.

When the adventurers, loaded with walnuts, began to walk back to their left, they found that the stony path had changed into a raging stream; it had earlier been a stream, and had turned into a path only after it had dried up. The children, disappointed but curious, were astonished at the fresh and noisy stream, with its pleasant scent of the drenched earth—when the sun suddenly reappeared, spreading its golden rays, and the rain stopped. Sheba, though, still in the grip of some unknown fear, didn't like the rain stopping so suddenly.

She did not know why! Maybe, just like that! Or maybe because a few minutes ago all was movement and activity. The rain was falling hard from the sky and the trees were also splattering them with big water drops. The wind was blowing fast.The water was flowing here and there noisily. The leaves hugged each other, and seemed to be talking to each other urgently about the sudden rain. The branches fell on one another. Drenched in the rain, the fragrance of the soft green peel of the walnuts, leaves of the trees and the corn plants had become more intense.

And now? It was as if everything had come to a standstill somehow. Sheba looked around. The wind seemed to push away the low clouds, which were like a thick fog. A huge rainbow arched like a bow in a cloud-free stretch of the blue sky.

At a distance, they could see smoke rising from a hole in the roof of a small hut. In a tacit agreement, four bigger feet headed in that direction—the smaller feet following them as fast as they could. After crossing the small slope, the mansion could be seen but it was still far away.

Under their wet clothes, their tiny shivering bones and chattering teeth—between 20 and 28 and thus lacking wisdom—were seeking some warmth, which could only be found under the roof of the hut made of uneven stones and mud with a fireplace inside it.

That was the Pahari tenant Ibrahim Waar's hut. Ibrahim Baba was very happy at seeing the young and older masters in his house. He spread his new *loyee* (woollen shawl)—which had been dyed orange with crushed walnut peel, for his guests. When Gulabo Bibi, his wife, pulled the husk off the corn cobs and buried them in the soft, smouldering coals and hot ashes in the *choolha* (the traditional wood burning stove), the fragrance sleeping in the corn was awakened. She reached for a big basket made with the thin branches of some wild bush, took out some walnuts and broke them with a small stone on a slab lying near the hearth. It was customary during the rains in the hills that the roasted cobs of corn were served and eaten with the season's fresh walnuts. As a courtesy, the children also offered to sacrifice the nuts they had collected, but it was politely declined. The basket was made of the same kind of branches which were used for weaving a framework to hold and cover a terracotta bowl, a kangri, with smouldering coals for warmth in winter.

Otherwise, without the framework, one cannot hold the bowl as it is very hot. Sheba touched the kangri nearby out of curiosity. Seeing this, Faheema slapped her head.

'Children shouldn't touch a kangri, don't you know?' Faheema said in an admonishing tone, glancing at the people sitting around. Gulabo Bibi was pulling the hot embers from the hearth with a long-handled iron ladle to replace the ash already covering the corn cobs to hasten the roasting, as there were some live coals in them. She quickly turned to face the children.

'There is little heat left in it…I had filled it in the morning, so it must not be hot anymore. There would only be ash in it by now,' she said placatingly.

'I was only touching the handle,' Sheba said, looking down at the floor and feeling the slap burning near her temple. She was trying hard to control her tears and stop sobbing. 'Just to see if the basket is made of branches of the same kind of bush that are woven around the kangri,' she said in a tearful voice, raising her head and looking at Nasir's face. Nasir looked back at her with the same expression which said that if he were to speak, his voice would also sound tearful like Sheba's.

'Is this a question you have to answer in your exams?' Baaji shouted in a voice louder than the sound of the slap she had given Sheba.

Though not included in the exam, only Sheba knew how important it was for her, and Baaji did not know anything about it at all. She looked sheepishly at the other children and found the same expression on their faces as Nasir's. Only the older ones were trying to look mature, drawing long faces. The younger children knew this very well.

The heady aroma of roasted corn announced that the treat was ready. Gulabo Bibi held each cob in long iron tongs, knocking off the ash from it by hitting it lightly against the wall of the hearth, and wiped off any remaining ash with her hands. All cold and shame vanished when all the cobs were served, laid invitingly on a thick-edged, round and unglazed terracotta tray. It was a feast for all the children, big and small, happy and innocent.

The Noisy Brook

About a kilometer away from the mansion there was a small valley with a two-storey wooden house called the 'Mill'. It was only called that but was not actually a mill. It was not an old structure, and had been constructed recently by *Badey Chachaa* (elder uncle) and *Chhotey Chachaa* (younger uncle). It was not very far from home, nor was it so close that household matters would interfere in its business. Otherwise, this building could have been built anywhere, as the estate around the house was so vast that if you tried to go around its boundaries riding a horse, you would still not be able to see all of it.

Business matters were discussed at the Mill and *Munshiji* (the clerk) also looked after the accounts there. He also taught the children in his leisure time, and in the long winter vacations the children spent school hours in the Mill.

The hunting guns were also kept at the Mill. There was no Animal Act till then, and hunting was not illegal yet. Only the two old guns, with very long barrels and not used anymore, were kept hanging diagonally on a wall in the Diwan Khana. The hunted animals were skinned and cleaned at the Mill and then sent to the home. They hunted birds, water fowl, rabbits, deer and some other animals. Leopards, bears and foxes were mounted and displayed in the verandas or galleries of the mansion. If it was only the head and the neck, it was fixed on the wall; and if the skin was not damaged much, the animal was carefully mounted and fixed—standing on a wooden board. Decorated with painted dry grass and tree branches, it looked like a live animal. The men of the family participated in carving its features, as every member of the family had some artistic talent.

Cotton wool and *multaani mitti* (Fuller's earth) were beaten together and kneaded. It was used in shaping the beast's nose, jaws and so on, and became stone-hard when it became dry. Then it was painted with a special paint, to which certain chemicals were added in order to protect the mounted figure from termites and silver fish. Bhai Jaan was also allowed in the team working on mounting, painting and decorating it.

Expensive items, brought from the city or another state, were checked at the Mill first. Womenfolk of the *kashtkars* (tenants), sitting in long rows, would peel and shell the walnuts in the open space in front of the Mill. They had to do it carefully to avoid breaking or otherwise damaging the fragile kernels. They were happy getting a little money in return for their labour. Their slender fingers turned orange with the walnut peel, and it seemed as if they had painted them with henna, which turned even darker after working many hours at the job.

The walnut kernels were dried in the sun for many days, packed in wooden boxes, and then sent to other cities and states. Rice and corn was also traded, besides the dry fruit.

After Abbu moved to the house in the city, *Chachaa* was considered to be the *Nambardaar* (the village elder), being the eldest person in the family there. Sundry small complaints, disputes and other matters were also heard and decided at the Mill.

The children once had the chance to see an interesting hunt when Najam Khan killed a man-eating snow leopard. The leopard would enter the village at night and kill cattle and dogs. One night when Zaitoon's father, hearing the goats bleating loudly, went out of his house to check on them, the leopard ambushed him and carried him off into the jungle. His screams awakened the whole neighbourhood. The loud barking of the landlord's dogs woke up everyone in the house. The safety of *kashtkars* was also one of the traditional duties of the landlord.

The elders went out with loaded guns, accompanied by servants with gas lamps. The children felt that the biggest dog, Dabbu, had the loudest bark. Dabbu was like a friend to all the children in the house. He seemed to be saying '*hanh-hanh-hanh*' thrice, and then '*hunh-hunh*' twice. When Zaitoon's screams were heard, the young children also started screaming and clinging to their mothers; the older ones were also crying and trembling with fear, and clung to their siblings under the warm cotton wool quilts. Sheba's heart was beating hard. While wandering through the orchards, children would often see Zaitoon walking barefoot, laughing and running on the grass. She did not mind the thorns which could prick her little, darkish feet. She lived closer to the jungle, a short distance further away from the Mill, where there were many pine and cedar trees. Monkeys hung upside down on the branches; some of them sat grooming each other, and some looked for lice in the fur of their young ones. They did not scare the children, nor were the children afraid of them. Even parrots were not scared of the monkeys. They flew about happily and fearlessly in the trees.

The trap in which the leopard was caught, stood near the jungle for many years, entertaining visitors and children alike. The four-by-eight rectangular wooden box had iron rods fixed in the centre, dividing it into two parts. Dabbu was led into one portion on the right, with his dinner. The children were not allowed to see anything after that; the others also returned home. Early next morning, two gunshots were heard from afar. Later, the children found out that the first bullet had hit the leopard's paw, making him growl loudly. Abbu then fired another bullet straight at its forehead, and it died. Sheba felt so sad seeing the leopard lying dead on the trap floor, looking at her with its half-open, unmoving and stony eyes.

The greedy leopard had entered the box to eat the dog, which closed like a rat trap. Had it not been so greedy, it would not have been caught in it—nor would it have died.

The leopard was mounted like some other animals, and the family members were photographed standing beside it.

But Abbu chose to wear a pistol around his neck and not the gun with which he had killed it. In that old picture, Sheba is sitting in front of its open jaws holding a bunch of marigolds. Farkhanda is sitting on the leopard smilingly, as if riding it. She, too, has flowers in her hand. Baaji is standing near Abbu and looking keenly at the bunch of flowers she is holding. Ammi is not in that picture, as she believed it a sin to be photographed. Abbu tried to convince her but she held fast to her firm conviction.

It might have been in the late summer when marigolds are in bloom. Who knows whether the trap is still there or if years of snows and the rains have caused it to fall apart! Abbu, too, is no more. Many long years have passed. Pictures, too, like works of art, become important with the passage of time. Sheba often thought about these things in later years.

There was not a single picture of Ammi in it, but there were many other interesting pictures in the family album. The first page had a picture of the Hazratbal shrine in the Naseem Bagh area. Its pagoda-like architecture looks like the shrine of Hazrat Khawaja Naqshband Sahib. Like many other shrines built in the region, it has a wide square roof covering the whole building. There is a smaller square roof on top of it, which is covered with still another smaller one like that. This beautiful series of roofs continues, and the last one has a short minaret on top of it in the centre. The first roof has excellently carved wooden ornamentation attached to it in all the four corners. They look like lotus flowers hanging upside down.

Abbu said that before reaching other places, Buddhism had reached the Kashmir valley first and flourished there. Kashmiri Nagas accepted the creed, along with their previous symbol of a dragon as they had been worshippers of Naga—the serpent. From Kashmir, Buddhism spread to Gilgit Baltistan, Kashghar, and the kingdom of Khotan. The ancient kingdom of Khotan was located on a branch of the Silk Road, running along the southern edge of the Taklamakan Desert in the Tarim Basin—the southern area of present-day Xingiang. Buddhism continued further on to China, Korea, Japan, Thailand, and other countries from one side of the Kashmir valley, and to Ladakh, Tibet, Nepal and other Himalayan states from the other; and the pagoda architecture spread far and wide along with it. But it was also thought that the pagoda architecture can be traced to the older Nepalese stupas, which was adopted in Southeast and East Asia on the one hand, and to the Kashmir valley through the Ladakh region on the other. Whatever the origin, the style is still very popular in Kashmir. Abbu had once told Sheba that it greatly influenced handicrafts in the Valley, with its fire-spewing dragons, chinar leaves, nightingales, flowers and creepers painted delicately on the papier mâché items in vibrant colours, and also carved painstakingly on wooden artefacts.

The new building in Hazratbal on the bank of the Dal Lake was modelled on the holy shrine in Madina. The Azan from the magnificent minaret next to the green dome seems to be coming from all corners of the sky. Six-year-old Sheba closed her eyes in devotion, the way Ammi did for the prayers after namaz. The previous scene returned to her eyes once again.

The room became very dark, probably because some lingering clouds from the storm last evening covered the moon. Sheba stared at the ceiling which was almost invisible in the darkness with wide open eyes. The sound of Abbu's breath was barely audible now. It resembled the sound of the air passing through the swing, hanging from the walnut tree in the backyard, as it begins to stop. She was hearing Abbu breathing continuously, as the sound travelled directly from Abbu's window to her. A short while ago she had heard it growing faint; and now, she just could not hear it. Is Abbu dead? She thought in terror and felt as if the rope of the swing had broken and she herself was dying, having fallen to the ground. She sat up in the bed. Her sister Faheema, older by seven years, poked her in the ribs. 'Can't you sleep peacefully?' she asked irritably and, changing her side, went back to sleep. Baaji's bony elbow felt like the joint of the divider in her geometry box. She wanted to tell Baaji that Abbu had died but choking on her own pain, she could not utter a word. She started crying silently and slowly rose from her bed. She glanced at Ammi's bed; Farkhanda was fast asleep with Ammi's arm under her neck like a pillow. Sheba sobbed silently. Whenever she slept with Baaji, she made her cry on some pretext or another. In her imagination, Sheba moved a step back, picked up Baaji along with her bed, and threw her down from the window.

But the next moment, she saw her sleeping peacefully as before. She was enraged, but also laughed at this absurd thought.

A strong gust of wind hit her face as she walked carefully to Abbu's room. Sleeping on his huge bed peacefully, Abbu's huge chest moved slowly up and down, and his nose blew out the same sound as the rope-swing when it's just about to stop. A smile spread on her lips and she returned to her room. She held Ammi's left hand very softly, spread it and put her neck on it. She didn't disturb Ammi's sleep at all; Ammi pulled her right arm out from under Farkhanda's neck and put it on Sheba's waist. Sheba laughed softly and closed her eyes.

The next morning, the children woke up to such an interesting day that no game could be equal to all the fun. Early in the morning, when their devout parents got up to offer their *Fajr* (dawn prayer), the carefree children woke up too—but only to go right back to sleep, as it had started raining heavily. But the walnut-pelting rain and clouds which had been forcefully driven away by the strong winds last evening had given a thorough soaking in the night to all the hills and valleys around, before making a comeback. The waters cascading down the slopes had transformed the dry bed by the side of the house into a wide, noisy stream. By morning, it had almost reached the backyard, and had covered the path the children took to go to the Mill every day. Small particles sparkled like myriads of tiny suns between the countless big and small round stones and pebbles in the bed of the stream. These particles must be gold or silver, the children thought. But the elders had explained that it was not so, that they were of some other metal, or mica. Actually, it was not a regular path but the bed of the stream, like the one going to Mohammad Lone Chaacha's hut.

On waking up, the children heard a rumble, like that of a big truck being driven on a dirt track but seemingly not going anywhere, as the noise neither faded nor stopped. There were no paved roads around, and only the trucks would ply on the dirt tracks. Which meant that the stuff in the trucks—the wood, the stone slabs, and charcoal, when jolted about on the uneven track did not get hurt, Sheba thought drowsily and then turned on to her other side.

The buses from the city came only up to the area of Sogaam. The five miles further to the house were covered by tonga. But the local people—who were mostly *kashtkars*—would not take a tonga or a horse, and just walked instead. They would run along the tonga happily, getting out of breath, relating the latest news about the village to the travellers. After a few years the buses started going those five miles also, but then the journey became somewhat sad and incomplete. However, only the children, coming from the city to spend their brief holidays in the village, could feel that.

Sitting near the tonga driver, they felt that the horse was not driven by him, but by the one sitting beside. The horse would blink its big, long-lashed, blinkered eyes of its own accord and happily jingle the bells around its neck as it trotted on. Its long, silky mane shone in the sun; or even without the sunshine, when it moved its neck softly from side to side and swished its tail—which looked like a waterfall, but from right to left and not to-and-fro like the waterfall.

The stream was very noisy. Who was making so much noise? Everyone in the house was making much noise. The stream was so close to the mansion that they had to speak louder than usual in order to hear each other.

By the time the children had had their bath and came out of the house, the sun was shining brightly. Only Baaji and Bhai Jaan knew that small fish were hiding behind the stones, which appeared and disappeared in the water. They knew it was not difficult to catch them but they announced that the water was running very fast in the stream, and the younger children were not allowed to enter into it, as they could be carried away by the strong current and drown. In spite of the bright sun, the water was still ice cold. They declared authoritatively that when the water flow would slow down in the afternoon, then there would be no danger.

So, the poor children sat on the bank in a row, watching the fish longingly. They knew very well that the two selfish elders wanted to catch all the fish for themselves; that there was no real danger for younger ones at all!

The turbid, earth-scented water of the stream became white with foam when it flowed over the bigger stones. Baaji and Bhai Jaan, looking for the fish in the knee-deep water, did not venture any further and remained near the bank.

Baaji would move a stone and Bhai Jaan, bringing his palms together to make a bowl, would put it in front of it. The fish would be washed into his hands with the flow of the water and in a fraction of a second, Bhai Jaan would join his thumbs and fingers together. And then the trapped fish would be carefully transferred into Baaji's dupatta, which she had laid in water like a net with its two ends under a stone. The dupatta would swell in the water and the poor fish wouldn't even know it had been caught. It was Ammi's dupatta and not Baaji's, but she insisted on wearing it. Looking at Baaji from the bank, Sheba thought that when Ammi wears it, the beautiful net dupatta looks so nice on her, but Baaji just spreads it plainly from her shoulders across her stomach. It looks as if the dupatta is draped across a *takhti* (the small wooden board to practice writing).

And Baaji tries to scold children like Ammi does, without any reason. After some time, Bhai Jaan allowed the children to enter the stream as well, and they promptly waded in, shouting merrily. The children did not come in when called for lunch, even though their mothers went out after them to bring them back home. The whole day's labour was finally handed over to the mothers. About a kilo of tiny fish had been caught. When they were passed on to the cook, the children felt very happy. Every child was sure that his or her father felt the same way while handing over the hunted deer to the cook. But on seeing the fish, the usually amicable face of the cook turned wary. He knew that cleaning them would take the whole day.

'You have really done much hard work today!' the cook said smilingly, but as soon as he turned his head, his smile disappeared. That's how Sheba knew he was not happy.

Coming in from the heat of the sun, and upon entering the house and placing one's feet one after the other on the cool stone steps felt so good that Sheba would never forget the feeling her entire life. She was sure that others, too, never forgot the blissful feeling either. The vacations came to an end, and the children cried at parting from each other.

Everyone in Najam Khan's house knew about the unjust division of their ancestral property. His wife, the doe-eyed pretty lady from the *chakdaars* (the affluent land owners) of North Kashmir, the senior household domestics, and even the children knew about it. Along with the topic of education, this subject also often found its way into the conversation somehow. Earlier, the kids would find this quite a serious matter, but later on they got bored; so if anybody broached the topic, the others would promptly try to change it.

'Ammi, you speak Kashmiri and Abbu speaks Punjabi, did you not talk to each other early in your marriage? You still can't speak Punjabi fluently!' raising her tired head after doing a lesson from her history book, Farkhanda looked at her mother and asked. Ammi was standing near the fence of the balcony opening at the lawn, and was teaching Noori Nana's idler son Inaayatullah to cut a chicken into 12 pieces. He didn't, however, understand, so Ammi asked him to come up. He climbed up the six steps carrying the chicken and a knife in a large nickel-plated copper tray. After slaughtering it in the prescribed Halal way, its feathers had been pulled off and the soft down seared on the fire. But despite having been told repeatedly that he should not burn its fat, he had still been careless as always.

A little while ago, when they were trying to catch the rooster, its shrill cries were heard all around in the house and the two little children, leaving their books, had run down towards the kitchen garden. But seeing the swing hanging from a thick branch of the mulberry tree right in front of the kitchen, they forgot everything and decided to have some fun. The cries of the ill-fated rooster had also stopped. Suddenly remembering their homework, as well as the cries of the rooster, they ran to the kitchen. The feathers of the chicken had been pulled off, and its skin looked fair, and was very soft to touch. But now, its skin was scorched dark, and lying in the tray with its wings and legs stretched open—it looked like a baby crying for milk. The good-looking *kashtkar* women would lay down their babies on their old, torn sheets before getting to work. The babies, crying and stretching their tiny arms and legs, looked exactly like the chicken. Holding a pencil between her teeth, Sheba stood looking at the chicken for a while.

When Farkhanda had put the question to Ammi, Inaayatullah had just entered the balcony and Ammi looked at her daughter, somewhat surprised. Seeing Inaayatullah, she told him to put the tray on the floor, and asking him to hold the wings of the chicken, she began to cut it into pieces—telling him that it was not mutton to be cut into regular pieces, and be done with it. One has to carefully divide a chicken into proper pieces by separating it at its joints! She did not answer Farkhanda, and perhaps did not want to answer either, as the children saw no such expression on her face. Though all the three sisters were curious to know the answer. Baaji was apparently busy solving a math problem, but Sheba had seen her stealthily casting a quick glance at Ammi. Baaji abruptly changed her expression, as if wanting to know whether Farkhanda and Sheba were taking interest in their homework. Whenever Baaji tried to show that she was controlling her anger, her face would look all the more odd.

Baaji hardly smiled. She would burst into a loud laugh occasionally, and that would bring tears to her eyes. This was strange, as tears appeared in Sheba's and Farkhanda's eyes only when they would laugh continuously for quite some time, but Baaji would have tears as soon as she started to laugh. Baaji's mouth was rather wide, and when she wanted to beat you up on the pretence of examining if your teeth were clean, she would show her teeth to you and ask you to do the same to make sure if you had brushed them properly. Everyone's teeth that Sheba had seen looked like her own, with the upper and lower teeth joined with each other. But Baaji would not join them as the whole world did. And only years later did Sheba realize that Baaji could not close her teeth tight. When she closed her jaws, her back teeth would join but there was still a gap between her front teeth. That is why when she laughed, one could see her gums too.

Baaji wanted to sing sometimes, but trying to copy one of the three girls who led the morning devotional song in school, she would sound ridiculous. However, if Sheba recited a line, which she would sing in tune, Baaji would scold her and later, when the singing session was over, beat her as well. Because hitting her while singing would ruin her own singing mood as well, which she counted as a serious crime, deserving punishment.

Baaji had a small face and a triangular chin; her chin was so small that it looked like her face was joined to her throat, with the chin hardly visible. Sheba never gave a serious thought to these things. But once, when she revealed what she had observed, she got a scolding in the presence of the elders for talking nonsense while studying. At times, she got a beating as well, in private or in Farkhi's presence. Farkhi knew that Sheba was not to blame for this, as she had just blurted out what she saw. But she would always wear such an expression as if to confirm that Baaji was justified in hitting Sheba. At that time, Sheba's soul would hurt much more than the punishment given to her body. She felt a burning sensation at the tender spot slightly above her stomach, and her heart would beat faster—like it did once while coming down the stairs, when she thought she was going to fall, just four steps from the ground.

Sitting in the balcony, Sheba wanted to finish her homework as soon as possible because Abbu had brought some new books that day. One of those was about the Stone Age man; another had big pages with many colourful pictures of birds. She planned to read the one about ancient man first, who resembled a gorilla with his bent body, and had hair all over like a bear.

Sheba had the chance to read a book other than her school books only when Baaji would occasionally be playing with Zarifa and Hamida, the older sisters of Haneefa and Mehmooda. She would get the lucky chance only if Abbu was around, otherwise Baaji would not even let her touch them. That day, there was a great chance of reading them as Baaji was to attend their dolls' wedding function. Baaji did not seem to have agreed to the function readily, but Sheba knew that she was actually keen to attend it but was only acting up to show her importance to others.

Sheba found playing with dolls pointless make-believe. They exchanged their dolls and the bride's supposed mother would put up an act of crying for the bride leaving her house. Farkhanda would really start crying; although she knew very well that next time, she was going to get the same doll back as the bride for her boy doll. All this looked childish and nothing but a waste of time to Sheba, something like cheating on oneself. The expressionless dolls did not look at all human, as the groom would not smile while bringing his bride to his home, nor would the bride cry when she left her parents' home. That was unlike Sheba's eldest cousin who, before taking her place beside her husband sitting in the car, had cried copiously, while the groom kept smiling at Sheba and others around. And somewhat shorter Shameem Baaji's head, while sitting in the back seat of the huge '58

Dodge, would bob up so high with her sobs that even Sheba, standing amongst the others, could easily spot it.

But while marrying her doll off, Farkhanda would cry without any reason. Sheba never expected such foolishness from her. But then, there were so many fools around who, while pretending a fake situation was real, would try to look happy or sad. Sheba would get so put off by these acts that her nose would look weird, as one of her nostrils would invariably flare upwards. She knew this because, one day, put off by all this nonsense, she came into the house from the lawn, while thinking about the whole pretense, and happened to look at her face in the mirror. Seeing this, she started bending her nose, eyebrows and lips at different angles, sometimes with her hands, sometimes without, and eventually went off into fits of laughter.

The dolls' house was just a few inches high, and Sheba always thought that the little, stiff bride and groom looked like corpses. Her heart would be filled with an inexplicable and unpleasant feeling. It was as if they had built a castle in the air for themselves, with fear and foolishness, and artificiality and self-delusion, which no one other than the people who lived in this deception could see.

Sheba, however, always enjoyed playing cooking games. Though the portions were miniscule, it was something real—and the cooked food was eaten too. Noori Nana was told to give them mutton, rice, vegetables and spices, as well as some small pieces of firewood. They would make a hearth with small stones in a corner of the backyard, and cook there. Then it was served on a tray with tiny plates and presented to Ammi, who would taste it joyfully. Hanifa was an expert in digging the hearth in the ground. She was important as such, because when you cook in a fireplace made of clay, one felt as if they were cooking under Noori Nana's supervision. Sheba, too, tried to make a hearth in the ground, but upon putting the pieces of wood in it for the fire—no matter how carefully—it always broke down.

Zarifa and Hanifa were coming over to play with them that day. They were the daughters of Azeez Bhat, who had a grocery shop across the street from the gate of their bungalow. No Punjabi family lived near them in the city. Families that stayed far away could only be visited if accompanied by Abbu and Ammi. People living around belonged to the working class. They would feel happy sending their children to play, as it was better to play in the Chowdhury family's lawns than on the streets. They respected this family because Chowdhury Sahib was a good person. Whenever anybody needed his help he was always there, and was very kind and friendly. In an earthquake, people—including young women who did not come out of their houses because of purdah—took shelter in the lawns of Chowdhury's House. They would feel safe in the bungalow's upper storeys if there were floods. They knew they would be taken care of. It was late Chowdhury Sahib—Najam Khan's father—who allowed a 20-feet wide and a mile-long path along the edge of his property for the people of the area to cut short their long walk to the mosque for offering their prayers.

The children came to know about all this when they grew up and had to deal with *patwaaris* (revenue staff), and needed maps and old records to settle some matters regarding the property.

When the servant left with the chicken, Farkhanda looked at her mother again. Ammi also knew that Farkhanda would not sit in peace, and nor would she let her do so till she got an answer.

'I could speak a little Urdu and your Abbu knew that. My father, Sheikh Gulam Mohammad, spoke Urdu, Persian, Arabic and English remarkably well—like your father. And then I learnt Punjabi at my in-laws,' Ammi said, looking at her children one by one.

'It is like, although you kids know a little Kashmiri, but you can play with Zarifa, Hanifa, Mehmooda and Hamida…You will learn this language by and by like this… You were born in a place where people speak it, so why can't you speak it fluently? This is because it's not spoken in your home. One easily learns the language spoken in one's home. Now you should get back to your studies!' Ammi said, and got up smiling and went inside. On reaching the door, she turned her head back and looked at her children. She remembered a couplet:

Children, do not know a pearl from a shell.
These flowers may ask for the moon as well.

She saw tiny necks bent over their books. But some more questions were arising in their little heads, to be asked later at some other time.

Abbu had been out of town that day. The children came to sleep in their parents' room. They stayed up and talked till late at night.

'The name of Ammi's father was Sheikh Gulam Mohammad because her grandfather's name was Sheikh Gulam Ahmad, whose father was Sheikh Abdul Qadir, who was the son of Sheikh Aabid, and his father was Sheikh Alam,' Sheba told Farkhi excitedly the next evening while they were doing their homework. 'You didn't understand, right?' They had the friendly relations of siblings, just a year-and-a-half apart in age.

'No. But there's nothing much to understand about it. Actually, it seems foolish and meaningless,' Farkhi retorted.

'No. It is something very interesting. You went to sleep soon, and I heard it all for you, and now you call me foolish?'

'All right, I will not say anything like that anymore, I promise.'

'The word Sheikh is used as a surname by those who converted to Islam.'

'Oh! Is that so?' Farkhanda exclaimed, and Sheba recalled the expression on Ammi's face while talking about it.

'The most interesting thing is that my great-great-grandfather Sheikh Alam's parents were Hindu Rajputs,' Ammi had shyly said, smiling in a very different and lovely way. Sheba told Farkhanda about the interesting topic.

Ammi's father, our *Nanna Jaan's* property was also grabbed by his uncles. His grandfather's famous gardens, named after him—Sheikh Qadir Gardens—actually belonged to Nanna Jaan, as he had already given his other sons their share of the property. But they deviously got the gardens transferred to their names. There were some more lands as well. Nanna Jaan went to his hometown, Peshawar, for business, and being disillusioned, he stayed put over there. A British customer once visited his shop. He spoke only English and was overjoyed talking to Nanna Jaan, who knew his language. Knowing the ruler's language has always been an asset throughout history!

Nanna Jaan knew other languages as well. They became good friends. Nanna Jaan learnt that Mr Lawrence was going to be posted as an important officer in Kashmir. He invited Nanna Jaan to accompany him. Nanna Jaan told him the whole story; Mr Lawrence promised Nanna Jaan that when they got there, he would make sure that Nanna Jaan gets his property back. Mr Lawrence kept his promise and Nanna Jaan got back his ancestral property. Some of his mother's relatives had shifted to Burma (present-day Myanmar), and some to Punjab. Nanna Jaan settled down in Kashmir again. He married *Naani Jaan* (maternal grandmother). Ammi and her siblings were born and everything was fine.

When the children grew up, they came to know that the garden in the south-east of the Kashmir Valley was still known as Sheikh Qadir's Garden. But after Mr Lawrence left, a minister named Subhraam had grabbed that garden through filing a false claim in the court and getting a decision in his favour.

The next day, when the children went to sleep in their parents' room once again, something even more interesting was awaiting them.

Ammaan—mother, would pray till midnight. While she was praying, Ubaid went out of the house. The creaking of the doors awakened Habeeb too, even though Zeba asleep nearby, kept sleeping soundly. He stealthily followed Ubaid, who was walking fast and straight, as if somebody was leading him in a certain direction holding his hand. He did not look left nor right, neither did he look down at the ground. Perhaps he didn't care about being pursued, or was not aware of it. He had a white woollen blanket wrapped around himself. However, his left shoulder and arm were not covered. His right hand was under the blanket and his left hand swung to and fro while walking. He walked along the fruit trees near the bank of a branch of the river Jhelum. Habeeb quickly guessed that Ubaid was going to cross the river.

Although it was summer, it was a cool night. The air was filled with the scent of fruits and flowers. The waning half-moon was sinking beyond the river. Near the Chinar tree in the *chakk* (landed estate), the dark-haired, tall and young man went down the five or six steps to the river. It was the Sheikh family's wharf, which was in their own *chakk*. A few boats were tied near the willows on the bank.

Ubaid chose a small boat, untied it and picked up an oar. The elder brother Habeeb hid behind a peach tree. When

Ubaid got his right hand out of his woollen shawl to row the boat, Habeeb saw that he was holding a rosary in his hand that shone brightly in the dim moonlight.

From that day onwards, no one at home asked or said anything about the matter to Ubaid. He would usually remain silent when spoken to, as he did earlier as well. Only Ammaan would brush his hair from his forehead with her fingers and kiss it, murmuring blessings and prayers. Ammaan's eyes would be wet and filled with a multitude of emotions—affection, helplessness and peace, all at the same time. It was like the clouds suddenly disappearing from a part of the sky while raining, and the sun emerging. The rainbow appears on one side while it continues to rain on the other side—like fine droplets that fly around while drying a dupatta, with two people holding its two ends. Ubaid sometimes did not come home for many days. Ammaan, while serving *mushkbudij* (a type of naturally scented rice, and which has almost vanished now, as nobody grows it anymore because of its low yield) from the big copper pot with a long-handled wooden ladle onto copper plates, would let a tear drop on to the edge of the plate, while heaving a deep, sad sigh.

'God only knows where is my *darvesh* (one who has renounced the world),' Ammaan would cry silently.

Ubaid had tried to change his previous lifestyle and spend more time with Noorjahaan, but he did not succeed at it. Noorjahaan never asked him why he went out at night, nor did she complain or protest about it. She would accompany him silently to the river and return home alone.

She remained steadfast in her love, or perhaps devotion, for her husband.

In the centre of the garden, near the riverbank, there was a very old walnut tree on a small, green hillock. Noorjahaan had the ground under the tree levelled, and a platform made there, and planted some rose bushes with ruby red flowers around it. Ubaid liked that place and spent much of his time there, and even the other members of the family would go there to meet him.

Suraya Begum heaved a deep sigh and did not speak for some time. The children didn't talk either, as Ammi had told them that they should listen to something, without talking.

Suraya Begum also told her children sadly that when Ammaa fell ill, Ubaid was somewhere away; he returned only after her death. He spent that night hugging his mother's grave and left in the morning, never to return again. He went to a deserted place to live, miles away from his home town.

If Sheba asked Ammi what happened after that, Baaji would scold her, and like always, would ask Ammi herself instead. Sheba cleared her throat and looked at Farkhanda, who was also awake. 'What happened after that Ammi?'

Baaji, who lay on Abbu's bed, with her elbow on a pillow and resting her cheek on her palm, looked expectantly atAmmi. In the next story, the children were introduced to an interesting character.

When people came to know that Ubaid had returned and was staying at home, they began to visit him there. Ubaid hardly spoke to anyone, and was mostly lost in deep meditation; but he would open his eyes sometimes, look at the audience and smile. People would sit and wait for hours in the hope of being rewarded with a smile from the mystic.

Salted pink Kashmiri tea and *qehwa* (a traditional preparation, made by boiling green tea leaves with saffron strands, cinnamon, cardamom, and occasionally Kashmiri roses to add a great aroma) in a carved copper samovar, along with a willow basket full of *baqarkhanees* (a thick, spiced flatbread that originated in modern-day Bangladesh during the Mughal period) and *kulchaas* (a mildly leavened flatbread) were taken to the platform at intervals the whole day long.

The samovar is a kettle-like pot with an upright metal tube in its centre; smouldering coals are put into the tube to keep the tea hot. Boiling hot tea was flowing the whole day long. The servants would take the empty samovar back to the kitchen and bring a full one in.

To change the routine, *Badee Bahu* (elder daughter-in-law), who was Sheikh Habeeb's wife, fixed morning hours for the visitors.

Ammi described an important senior domestic so vividly that the children felt they could see him there before them.

'Abdul Ghaffar, come here.'

Badee Bhaabi, Ammi's elder sister-in-law Zeba, entered the kitchen and looked out of the window.

'Get another hookah to the Diwan Khana. Sheikh Sahib is waiting for it, and there is a guest too. Put the mild tobacco in it,' she instructed a servant and turned back towards the kitchen.

'Thank God, Sheikh Sahib has at last shifted from strong to mild tobacco,' she murmured to herself. The servant was carrying a pile of split wood to the kitchen for the fire. While passing the kitchen he heard his name being called, asking him to get the hookah. He threw the wood on the ground in the kitchen and rushed to the cabinet with the hookah, as he loved to smoke from the special, carved copper hookah. When the scented, heavy tobacco smoke passing through the water and the tube reached his lungs, he would feel that all the day's fatigue had disappeared. But hearing about the mild tobacco, his enthusiasm vanished. He was a hookah addict. Every half an hour, he needed almost two ounces of tobacco! It was a normal thing for the servants to have a few puffs from the hookah, to make sure that it was perfect, before presenting it to the master. The hookah pipe was held carefully with the lips folding inwards, to avoid wetting it with the spit. He was not happy with the mild tobacco used for many days by now. He had thought that he was asked to be quick because there was some hookah-loving guest like himself that had come. But that wasn't the case.

He opened the closet and took out the freshly nickel-plated, long-necked, carved copper hookah and a hookah bowl, with a marked lack of interest. Both had chinar leaves carved on them. The hookah had bigger designs on it and the fire bowl had smaller ones. On the stems near the leaves there were crowned nightingales, similarly bigger on the hookah and smaller on the fire bowl. Abdul Ghaffar held them in his hands and went to the backyard. A noisy stream, flowing down from the high hills nearby and crossing the meadows, meandered through the villages. The long stem of a cedar tree, split along the width and hollowed out like a pipe, had been placed near the back door of the kitchen in order to bring water from the brook for use in the house.

Abdul Ghaffar separated the hookah tube from the tube binder and washed them. Then he filled the hookah with fresh water and attached the tube and binder to it once again. When he held the pipe in his lips and inhaled, some water got into his mouth. He detached the pipe once again and poured out some of the water from the hookah. Then he put the pipe back in it and inhaled again. No water reached his mouth this time; it made a low, rumbling noise but it still did not sound right, and he shook his head. Now, instead of pulling the air in, he blew it out a couple of times; some water came out like a small fountain from the opening of the other pipe of the hookah. Then he drew in the air through the pipe once again and a satisfied expression came to his face, as this time a soft, perfect rumble sounded through the hookah.

Taking long strides, he went to the side room of the kitchen. Being the senior servant, Abdul Ghaffar was like a family member. He would smoke marijuana mixed with his tobacco. He would not work much but was good at supervising other servants. There was no restriction on this harmless, old pot addict entering the area of the house reserved for the women folk. Reaching inside, he opened the door of the closet and took out a bottle of scented water. He pulled the pipe out of the hookah, and putting his thumb on one end of it, poured a few drops of the perfume in it. He then blocked the pipe's mouth with a wooden stopper, and after removing his thumb, stuck another stopper into its another end. He put the pipe aside for some time and sat down near the fireplace. Holding the fire bowl in his hand, he put some tobacco from the wooden tobacco box with two compartments; from the other compartment, he added some coal to it. There were forceps tied to the neck of the bowl to pick live coals with it. He took out some embers from the hearth with a small shovel—kept for this purpose in the kitchen, and put them on to the tobacco. He added some live coals to his kangri also. He picked up the scented pipe and fixed it back on the hookah. Taking a few puffs and grimacing, which meant he did not like its taste—but the next moment, holding the hookah in one hand and his kangri in the other, he headed towards the Diwan Khana, humming a tune.

Expecting a handsome baksheesh, he smiled broadly and bowed, offering his greetings. When he entered the Diwan Khana, Sheikh Sahib gestured to him to place the hookah on the floor. The guest returned his greetings with a nod and smiled back. Abdul Ghaffar looked surprised when he saw that the guest was smoking a cigar and had a tie around his neck; wearing a coat and pants like an Englishman, he had placed his hat on a short-legged table nearby. The table was carved from a single block of a walnut tree. Its legs had many chinar leaves and nightingales carved on it, and they were in the shape of a lion's paw. 'Thank God I cleaned a two-day old spot of tea off its surface in the morning,' he thought. He had done it with a very light hand so that its varnish would not get damaged. The Sheikhs, his masters, wore long shirts and pajamas with waistcoats and a *qaraquli* (semi-rectangular cap of fur). Abdul Ghaffar looked at the guest for some time with great interest. They were not sitting on the carpet but on the designed, walnut wood low sofa.

Abdul Ghaffar placed the hookah on the floor and handed over its long tube to Sheikh Sahib who held it in his hand without looking at Abdul Ghaffar. 'Thank God I had selected a long tube for the hookah that can reach the other side of the room where the sofa is!' Abdul Ghaffar thought to himself, heaved a silent sigh of relief and sat down on the floor near the hookah. With a little iron spoon tied to the kangri, he stirred the fire in it because otherwise the embers would just die. When Sheikh Sahib, lost in conversation, forgot to puff on the hookah for a while, the coals in the fire bowl would die too, he brooded.

The guest who visited the Sheikh family that day was none other than Chowdhury Najam Ahmed Khan, who had made friends with Sheikh Habeeb while shopping in Srinagar, as both of them had liked the same shade of *kashmira* (a cloth of pashmina). There being only one roll in the shop, they had to share it. And while talking to each other, they had found that they had one more thing in common—a fondness for writing poetry.

When Bhaabi Zeba had called Abdul Ghaffar's name through the kitchen window, which opened onto the backyard, Suraya also peeped through her window from upstairs. That was because she had just heard the unfamiliar neighing of a horse; the members of the family recognized their horses from their neighing. Although this was the inside of the house, yet because of purdah it was not considered appropriate for ladies to look out of windows openly. Womenfolk of the tenants did not observe purdah though.

The stable was in the east side of the backyard. Kareem Joo, the syce and an expert in training horses, was pulling at the bridle of a white mare, trying to lead it to the stable. But the mare was resisting, moving its head from side to side.

Ammi imitated the mare for her children, moving her head the way she moved it, usually to say 'no'. Her earrings moved from right to left and back, and the small blue and red pearls attached to them touched Ammi's neck some four times.

Suddenly, Suraya saw a strong, brown hand with a golden watch strapped on its hairy wrist close to the white cuff buttoned with a golden cufflink; it was patting the mare on its back. Ammi had seen a wristwatch for the first time in her life. Her brother Habeeb used a pocket watch tied to his waistcoat's button-hole with a thin chain, and kept it in his upper pocket; the younger brother Ubaid had nothing to do with things like watches. Suraya quickly drew back but the next moment, when she peeped out stealthily again, the guest was not there and the white mare was walking obediently with Kareem Joo, the horse-keeper, who had rather dark skin.

Only God knows what Abbu had said to the mare to make her understand the situation, Sheba had thought.

'So, you had not seen Abbu's face?' Farkhanda asked, looking at Ammi.

'That was the custom…the would-be bride and groom did not see each other, but I saw your father's hand at least!' Ammi said with a little laugh. 'And you know, brides were not supposed to eat for two days before departing to their in-laws' house. There were no cars those days. The *baraat* (bridegroom's wedding procession) would arrive with the bridegroom and the relatives on horseback or in a big boat, and return with the bride in a palanquin carried by *kahaars* (the bearers). Naturally, there was no bathroom attached to the sedan chair, so the poor bride reached her new home starved and half-dead!'

'I would never starve my daughters like that,' Ammi said smilingly. Ammi rubbed Sheba's cheek gently, and caressed her hair. Her hand smelled of the quince jam which she had made that day. She had made plum jam as well, but that had a light aroma and it did not reach the children's study. Some half-ripe plums were left on the tree.

'Ammi, had Abbu not seen you either?' Farkhanda asked. Suraya Begum looked at her face.

'People see their brides secretly before getting married, isn't that so?' she asked again, and Suraya Begum's eyes grew wider.

'The brother of *Chhoti Chachee* (younger aunt) had secretly seen Rabia Baaji in the dargah. Bhai jaan had told this to Baaji, and she also knows this.'

Farkhanda's round eyes betrayed no surprise and Sheba thought that Baaji would now surely beat Farkhanda on some pretext. But when Ammi laughed suddenly, Sheba felt Baaji will not beat Farkhi after all.

'Yes, my child, he had not seen me secretly but just by chance,' Ammi said between the pauses. To Faheema, that incident sounded very interesting but Ammi did not go into the details.

On Abbu's arrival, the children enthusiastically told him what Ammi had told them while he was away. But they were very disappointed when they found that Abbu already knew all that. Najam Khan even remembered something more that he did not share with his children.

It was early morning. The cool air was very pleasant. In addition to Sheikh Chakdar's chickens in the coop, many other birds also added their music to the morning concert. A melodious bird sang continuously. Some other bird, at a distance, was chirping at regular intervals. It was as if the scent of the river bed's wet earth and the fragrance of flowers had enchanted the surroundings.

Suraya would herself take the tea for her brother Ubaid to the platform in the mornings, as purdah was not a problem that early in the day. Even though these were Chakdar's own orchards, there could be a tenant around if she went a little later. She held a small samovar by the chain fixed between the ewer and its handle. Looking down at the ground, she walked fast. Suddenly, she felt that someone ahead of her was standing near a tree, humming a tune. She was sure it was the guest who had come to visit them the previous evening. She hid behind an apricot tree to wait: if he went back to the house soon, she would take the tea to her brother Ubaid, but if he lingered or decided to take a stroll, she would go back and send a servant out with the tea.

When the guest heard the slight ring of the chain of the samovar, he looked about without a thought. While going behind the tree, the morning breeze blew Suraya's dupatta for a second. The guest, taking it for the wing of some water bird, reached the other side of the tree without wasting a moment.

After putting the boiling samovar down, Suraya just stood there when she sensed some movement. Najam Khan had never, ever, seen a beauty like her, though she tried to cover herself by pulling her dupatta over her face, head and shoulders. The guest was ashamed for the intrusion, and quickly moved to the other side. But an enchanting glimpse still remained with him. Such graceful almond eyes and yellowish-brown pupils were something he had seen for the first time.He also learnt that an oval face can be a most beautiful face. If the nose is sharp, the nostrils look like the petals of the little white flowers that grow in the grass in the summers. If the skin is white and not red, the beauty becomes divine. And hands that look like white doves are not an impossibility. And also, that although the common Kashmiris living on the lake or on the land could be fair or less fair, but girls from the upper class, who stay in *purdah*, are prettier than Mughal princesses. And entering into a relationship with their family could be a matter of pride for Punjabi Chowdhurys.

Chowdhry Najam Khan never regretted it his entire life, after learning this. In fact, that day Abbu told his children some more details about Ammi's Rajput ancestors. New converts to Islam were given the honorific of Sheikh. Some Sheikh families were descendants of those who converted to Islam when Hazrat Shah-i-Hamdan arrived in the Valley in the 11th century, along with a number of Sayyids. Their shrines are located in different areas of the Valley, including Srinagar. Ammi sent halwa-roti and *qehwa-baqarkhanee* on Mondays and Thursdays—as well as in the holy month of Ramadan—to those holy places.

Many others also converted after that. Before that, people would satisfy their spiritual urges by following their own traditions. Various beliefs alternated in the region. Sometimes the Nagas who worshipped *Naags* (serpents) were a majority, and at other times it was *Pisachs* (Tantric Hindus) or the Buddhists. It is important to know that in the 1st century, during the reign of the Kushan King Kanishka, the Fourth World Buddhist Council was conducted at the famous resort of Harwan, near Srinagar. The Fourth World Buddhist Council was also previously held in Sri Lanka, during the reign of King Wang Mani in Tambapanni. The Bodh doctrine was recorded for the first time ever in that council, on *Bhoj Pattar*, which was obtained from the bark of the birch tree. In Kashmir, Buddhism remained confined to Ladakh and the areas around it; the believers of some sects of Hinduism, as well as the number of believers in Islam also increased.

That day, Abbu talked about some other pleasant and important things too, and called the Valley a heaven. Coming home for a short vacation, Sheba felt a wave of pride and kept looking at the changing views from the window of the vehicle. My great land. My Kashmir. The land of soft-spoken, humble, handsome people: of intellectuals, artists and craftsmen; the land of silk, pashmina, saffron and lush green meadows. The home of mountains, valleys and waters. A paradise on earth with a 5000-year-old documented history that has few parallels in the world. One of the oldest languages and civilizations on earth. The Kashmir of saints and sufis. Sheikh-ul-Alam's and Lal Ded's Kashmir. Shakhya Muni's prediction, Buddhism's cradle, Kashmir; Kashyap Rishi's and Parvarsen's Kashmir; Lalitaditya's and Suyya's Kashmir; Ashoka's, Kanishka's, Kalhana's and Badshah's Kashmir; Habba Khatoon's and Arnimal's Kashmir.

Or perhaps Moses' and Jesus' chosen place for eternal rest, maybe, who knows? A land which has many symbols of its grand past displayed in the whole region; its ruins and figures of carved stone have the perfection of Egyptian architecture and the perfection of Roman statues. The sacred region that King Kanishka selected from the vast country of India to be the secret repository of Buddhism's greatest documents. Being a follower of one of the Bodh sects, he called a conference to remove the confusion among the followers of Buddhism, and wrote a new *Tripitaka* carved on copper plates. That sealed treasure is still buried in this land, or is being passed from one heart to the other through Buddhist monks and intellectuals, to this day. Or perhaps, as they say, like the secret of Jesus Christ's holy bloodline, which is transferred from one generation to another of a particular Christian sect secretly. Some even say it included intellectuals and artists like Sir Isaac Newton and Leonardo da Vinci, and will be made public at the right time.

When Faheema passed 8th grade, her father advised her to go in for sciences. She suddenly gained importance in the family. She could now call upon anyone who was playing or studying, to answer any of her important or unimportant queries. After passing the 9th grade, she could call even an elder like Ammi for that.

She would play with the other children only if she was winning. The moment she began to lose, she would become very upset and start crying. Then, however, she would somehow stop crying and, leaving the game, would announce that it was time for her studies. If she lost in the beginning, she would blame one or the other sister and stop playing. If both of them protested, then it was difficult to blame them at the same time, and she would complain to Ammi. She would tell her with tearful eyes that they were interrupting her studies and get them scolded. She would often make Farkhanda take her side, and that would make Sheba feel lonely. The girls who came to their house to play did not go to school. Sheba could not speak Kashmiri very well and they could not speak Urdu fluently, and certainly not a word of Punjabi. After playing for a while, both parties would stop because they not only needed to play kho-kho, 'I spy' or build small houses, but after getting tired, they needed to talk too.

In those intervals, Sheba would sit on the swing without swinging. It would be painful for her and she would bitterly think that the loneliness and pain was caused by her own sisters. And that would bring tears to her eyes.

When Faheema passed 10th grade, Najam Khan was sure she would now become a doctor—and she was even surer of this than him. She would always appear with a book under her arm.But in 11th standard, she failed in Physics. While preparing for her compartment exam, she would be annoyed all the time without any reason. She did not grow very tall, was lean like before and walked with a habitual stoop. Wearing a dupatta would still make her look like a wooden board.

Farkhanda was younger than Baaji by four years but only an inch shorter, and even had her own dupatta. Being physically weak, Faheema was sure that she had a right to all the favours, as well as all the love and attention from her parents. Waiting for her results, she offered to take on the responsibility of teaching her two younger sisters. Since beating students was not considered a violation of human rights in those days, it was also naturally included in Faheema's duties. Farkhanda would always agree with what she said. But she would do what she wanted to, simply because saying 'yes' to Faheema was more important than acting upon it. That would give her an upper hand in the presence of other siblings.

Sheba would agree only on what she felt was sound from every angle but would not agree if it did not. Agreeing to something that her conscience did not approve of was self-deception to her, even if it meant a beating from her elder sister. She would get beaten and sob, but she would stick to her decision. No one could prevent her from doing that. As a punishment for refusing to obey Faheema's orders, Sheba's long pigtail was pulled with a sharp jerk and she would also get a hard slap, and only that would satisfy Baaji's ire.

To get a seat in medical college, it was necessary to clear the pre-medical exams with high marks. But Faheema did not get good grades, and barely passed. In those days, there were no entrance tests for different professional admissions. After crying a lot, she finally announced it confidently that she would graduate in sciences and go for higher studies to become a scientist. Najam Khan believed this, and his mind was at peace. But Faheema would still remain tense. Besides this, there was another set-back she had to face…and being the eldest daughter, she could not even share it with anyone. When she reached 12th grade, everyone in the house was saying that Sheba was growing taller than her.

Faheema was averse to Sheba's slender-fingered hands, long hair, light-brown almond eyes, and her intelligence and quick wit. Because she knew that a girl who preferred to read novels instead of taking an interest in her school books could understand things other than her studies. Her plump figure and growing taller was a sign of her being less hard-working, and in the future that could cause Sheba's failure and disgrace. And so, she had to be 'set-right'.

Fixing Sheba was very important for Faheema, and so was inventing new allegations and following them up, to prove herself caring and far-sighted—and to prove Sheba wrong. To inform Ammi about these matters became her duty. Like the reason Sheba's hair came undone repeatedly was not because of her thick hair but because she deliberately made a loose braid of it, though it seemingly looked tight and firm.That Sheba did not touch her school books, but would finish a novel in a single night. She would encourage Sheba to put on lipstick and then complain to Ammi under the oath of secrecy and get her caught red-handed. To tear up Sheba's books and hide her notebooks, and recover them from behind the bed, under the carpet or other such places, and get appreciation for herself and punishment for Sheba. Watching the screaming helplessness in Sheba's light-brown eyes was a source of consolation to Faheema for not getting a place in medical college, and it would give her a strange sort of peace.

Sheba had inherited those light-brown almond eyes from her mother. Ammi had very fair skin, and Abbu had a wheatish complexion. Faheema's complexion was fair like Ammi's and she was proud of it, but her nose was bigger, like Abbu's. She had rather wide lips, but a triangular face like her paternal aunts; her eyes were roundish, black and big, and her short hair was thick and curly, like them.

'She has taken after my sisters!' Abbu would say with great affection. Farkhanda, who was born after her, had the same features as her. Her complexion was fair like Ammi's but had a rosy tinge as well, and she was slightly shorter than Faheema. Sheba had an angular face, like no one else in the family; she also had a cleft chin like Abbu's, and the cleft would disappear when she smiled. Her nose was sharp like Ammi's, and her skin, golden-white—a mixture of her parents' complexion. She had long, thick hair, like no one knew who. She wanted to read everything like her grandfather, and was keen and curious about everything. And Faheema disliked seeing all this, and even listening to all about these things.

Faheema graduated and Ammi wanted to marry her off. She was not very interested in continuing her studies either. Her marriage was fixed and the boy was an engineer, not a doctor. He had been living in a hostel for a long time, in another city, and wanted to come home now. The date for Faheema's wedding was fixed, when they unexpectedly received a proposal for Farkhanda as well.

Farkhanda was only in 11th grade, but marrying off girls of that age was a common occurrence in those days. The proposal for Farkhanda's marriage had come from a family of somewhat lower social status—something that was not acceptable to Najam Khan's family. Farkhanda had no objection to the proposal; although her objection or acquiescence would not have been of any consequence, she protested in a peculiar way by becoming abruptly silent.

Suraya Begum had to intercede on her behalf, and convince her father in her favour. Najam Khan was aware of her lack of interest in her studies and, and being a broad-minded and liberal person, he finally agreed to the proposal for the happiness of their daughter.

Later, it came to light that she would have agreed to this proposal only. In her parents' generation no one could know when and how she had seen her future husband, Zahoor-ud-din. Younger siblings and cousins of her age only knew that the young man was a good football player. But among the next generation, the secret went around that Farkhanda—the maternal aunt, the paternal aunt, the maternal aunt-in-law or the paternal aunt-in-law, had…a love marriage! That was considered sensational in those days, as even imagining it signified revolt.

Hope and Home

When Zaheen-ud-din's (the brother of Zahoor-ud-din, Farkhanda's husband) family got him married to Nuzhat, they did not seem to be compatible at first. 'She is a very intelligent girl. My son will soon recognize her merit,' his mother would say.

'They are not compatible because Pyaari is more intelligent than Zaheen-ud-din,' the younger generation of the joint family thought. People also said that he wanted to marry his paternal cousin but she did not want to marry him.'

Everybody said Pyaari was not at fault, and Zaheen-ud-din, spurned by his cousin, was a drunkard and a chain smoker who suffered from an inferiority complex. To satisfy his ego, he became defensive, and was unable to commit himself to anyone, and assumed pretentions to be a great person. Some people said that his attitude towards Nuzhat was like this because he was apprehensive of being rejected again. So, if she ever wanted to break up with him, he could say that he never liked her.

Zaheen-ud-din was proud of his good looks but his vanity far exceeded what his looks actually merited. He had been very sure that since he was known for his attractive personality in the whole family, his financially weak uncle Muqim Ehmed's round nosed, thin lipped, but big-eyed daughter Munazah would not only like him, she would actually be proud of her good fortune. But Munazah did not show any interest in him, and on the contrary, accepted the proposal for an average-looking, good-natured son of a colleague of her father.

To Munazah, it was not an issue as to why she liked Zafarullah and rejected Zaheen-ud-din. But if asked, she said that first of all, her family members, who didn't insist on marrying her off within the family, would not object to her decision. Though they did not know that marriage between close relations could be a danger for the next generation's mental health. Secondly, she had always thought that Zaheen-ud-din was a narcissist. His attitude always seemed to give one message: 'Look, I am so handsome!' For example, when with his first and second cousins, he would always sit or stand motionless, as if he was some famous film actor or model posing for the paparazzi. Then, he would narrow his eyes and look at someone's face, and after favouring the person with an artificial smile, he would turn his head and the smile would disappear from his face in a flash as if it was not a smile but charity.

Thirdly, he always—consciously or subconsciously—wanted every girl he came across to like him. If it took some time to get the girl's attention, he would try hard till she showed an interest in him. But the moment he got it, it was over! And he was ready to go after another girl, and so on, endlessly.

Fourthly, Zaheen-ud-din was a smoker since his college days; and by the time he became a showroom owner, he had become an alcoholic too, returning home every evening hours after closing down his business.

The fifth and most important point was that Zaheen-ud-din didn't seem to be aware of any of this, and it was as if he just did not know what others were saying about him. And if some cousin tried to tell him what people thought, he would have nothing but contempt for the person and his or her opinions. This clearly showed that he did not want to improve and become a better person.

This five-point index was an integral part of his personality. Zaheen-ud-din would only talk to Nuzhat as if he was ordering her, he neglected his household responsibilities—leaving every job half done or putting it off to some other time. He would also show no response, as if he was stone deaf, to any question or query about it by her. 'Not looking into my eyes is perhaps because of the newness of the relationship and would pass slowly,' Nuzhat thought. On her part, she would meet the demands of the relationship with sincerity and selflessness, and sacrificing all. If both of them were in the same room, he would pick up the newspaper and sit with his face to the wall, close to it. It must be because of the light coming from the window, Nuzhat thought. And yet the room was always bright, as it had four windows, and sitting with his back to the wall could possibly let more light on the paper. What could be the reason otherwise, she often wondered.When Nuzhat couldn't find any reason for all this even with the passage of time, she would be sad. It must be some psychological problem, she would think in later days.

If she was busy doing something for somebody else in the household, he would murmur something with an unpleasant expression on his face, as if conveying to her that she wasn't doing it right. Looking at his expression, Nuzhat would also think she might have actually done something wrong, and consequently, her confidence would be undermined. In fact, she could have lost it altogether if her mother-in-law didn't show a great deal of trust in her. Nuzhat would be astonished to see him muttering to himself while she carried out any chore. There was a peculiar touch, a unique sensibility in everything she did, and everyone in the household appreciated it. But Zaheen-ud-din would always show anger without any apparent reason. Earlier, Nuzhat thought that he was full of anger for everyone, but later she realized that he was indulging in a deliberate anger at her. For example, if his after-shave lotion was hidden behind another bottle on the dressing table, he would shout at her and say things like he had seen it before he went for his bath but it wasn't there any longer, and where could it have disappeared? No, she must have put it somewhere else! If she pointed out that she had no reason to do something like that, as she did not have any use for it, he would start hurling abuses at her, and if some other family member entered their room at that time, he would move other things on the dressing table and finally find the missing bottle. Nuzhat would be taken aback by such antics.

Even more agonizing for Nuzhat was the realization that he was unfaithful to her from the very beginning. Sometimes, one of the relatives or some visitor would tell her that he was seen with a girl sitting in his car. The same girl would be seen with him for some months, and then it would be some other. Earlier, when Nuzhat would ask him about this with an aching heart and swollen eyes, he would deny it on oath, but even this denial was hurtful. He would say that if he was wrong, may God's curse fall on him or upon her—whoever was lying. Nuzhat would think she might have been informed wrongly as he was so angry, but he could have said it without using harsh words, which kept her eyes moist for many hours. However, one day, the truth became evident to everyone at home, and she cried her heart out. She could not even speak a word because of the grief and anger she was feeling. And Zaheen-ud-din, instead of consoling her, said that all her crying was an act, and that a decent woman could not even entertain such abominable thoughts about her husband. Girls from honourable families do not get carried away by what others say, they do not blame their husbands, and that she must have loose morals herself if she can say such things. That day, Nuzhat's tears never ceased to flow even though she kept herself busy the whole time. She imagined her future and grief filled her heart, as she loved her husband Zaheen-ud-din sincerely, and she had always relished her dreams about her future home at her in-laws, and earnestly wished them to come true.

Zaheen-ud-din fell ill and decided to move to their flat in Delhi, because he wanted to have the best treatment, even though the doctors had not advised him to do so. Nuzhat looked after him like a dutiful nurse, and one whom no other nurse would relieve at the change of shift. The servant, not used to the heat in Delhi, had left to go back to the Valley.

One day, she had a fever. In the afternoon, she took some medicine and lay down at the foot of her husband's bed. Seeing this, he abruptly stood up and started packing his bag. Nuzhat, tired and weak, was surprised and got up too.

'If the wife rests, who will look after the ailing husband?' he taunted, looking away. 'I'm going to some hospital. A hospital is far better than a home like this, there's no fruit at home for juice even! I'll grow weaker by the day.' He headed towards the door.

'No…no…I was not resting…I felt feverish…and just lay down to relax for a little while as I had nothing to do, and also because Aasim is also sleeping…and I couldn't go to buy any fruit as the shops are closed in the hot afternoon. We still have some fruit at home. I know because Aasim did not want to eat, and I gave him some fruit instead. But I'll go and get some more!' Nuzhat quickly added, and somehow made him sit down on the bed.

'Some shops may be open,' she said, going quickly to the door.

It was a holiday, and there were not many people on the streets in the hot afternoon. The newly wed son of the next door neighbour was about to go somewhere on his scooter.

Nuzhat asked him for a ride. She had never sat with anyone like this before, and would have never done so in normal circumstances. But she wasn't herself, and the agony, sadness, tiredness, tension and loneliness had been too much for her to make proper decisions.

She did not sense anything wrong at first but when he bent his body backwards and tried to touch her chest with his back, she felt so helpless, ashamed and humiliated. She wanted to jump off the scooter and let a speeding vehicle crush her.

Nuzhat developed a fever that did not leave her for a long time. Zaheen-ud-din had come to Delhi seeking treatment for some small kidney stones, a minor problem which could have been treated at home by drinking more water or other fluids, and did not need any special consultation or surgery. Nuzhat took good care of him, and he was fine. And finally, when Nuzhat became so weak that she could not look after Aasim properly, Zaheen-ud-din took her to the doctor. There was no apparent reason for her fever, and she was advised some blood tests. Zaheen-ud-din found the whole thing very interesting.

Nuzhat had felt that Zaheen-ud-din, being an addict, had lost his attractiveness to a great extent. His baggy eyes were now prominent on his face. He had gained much weight, and looking at his face, his ears would be hidden behind his puffy cheeks—and his head, behind all that. The hair, once framing his face handsomely, could hardly be seen from the front. And whenever he had a haircut, his cheeks looked swollen like a frog's.

Nuzhat knew that he was aware that he had no attraction for the opposite sex anymore, but his defiant, self-centred mind, wanted to satisfy his urge of being liked at any cost. So he became very appreciative of the magical skills of a South Indian nurse, who would fill her syringe with blood from a blue vein on Nuzhat's long inner arm with her hands in an instant. He would look down upon Nuzhat, as if saying that to get a syringe of blood from someone's vein was the finest skill in the world and which was something Nuzhat could never do. Zaheen-ud-din had many tests done unnecessarily for himself too.

There was no serious cause for Nuzhat's fever. It had lingered on because she was not getting proper rest and running around in the heat and the sun. The stubborn fever left her only after tormenting her body for three long weeks.

Earlier, Zaheen-ud-din would not insult her openly, but after his father died, he would scold her in the presence of others as well. Her mother-in-law would call her with a voice filled with love at that time. 'Pyaari!'—she had given Nuzhat the name 'Pyaari', which meant 'the sweet one'—'please come here my daughter, I can't find my glasses…please look for them in the bathroom for me, my child!'

Nuzhat, though busy with some household chore, would enter the room, look here and there, find them near where her mother-in-law sat, and hand them over to her. She knew this was just a ruse her mother-in-law had devised for comforting her, and her mother-in-law also knew that Nuzhat was aware of it too, but neither of them acknowledged it.

When her little son was growing up, he would get scared and start crying at seeing his father yell and shout in anger. His light-brown eyes would become red. Whenever he cried, the father scolded Nuzhat for not taking care of the child properly. This anger and agony affected the child adversely and, when he grew a little older, his father would sometimes slap him for his screaming too.

'Aasim is an irritating child,' the family members would say. 'No, it is because of his father's behaviour that he is ill-tempered,' Nuzhat would helplessly try to convince them. Despite all this, Nuzhat was always discussed like an important person amongst her relatives, as she always had a dignity about her that attracted everyone's attention.

Zaheen-ud-din had made Nuzhat quit her job. Before she got married, she had been teaching in a good school in the city for two years. She had felt extremely upset about this. A pretty and intelligent teacher, friendly and full of motherliness, 'Miss Nuzhat Madam' was very popular amongst the staff and the children alike. The children wished their teacher would go on leave, and Miss Nuzhat Madam would take them up for a class or two. Staff members would be happy sitting by her side during the lunch break. The colours she wore were unique and defied categorizing as any particular shade. She used kohl with such a fine line that others could not be sure whether she had really put any. She wore it close to her upper eyelashes, a line so thin that it disappeared when she closed her eyes, and so neat on the open eye that it did not look artificial.

She wore lipstick only slightly darker than the real shade of her lips so that, once again, one wondered whether she wore it at all. Her nails were neatly trimmed, with colourless nail polish on them, which just made them shine and look very natural. This refinement and charm were aspects of Nuzhat's personality which she lost by and by. When her husband made Nuzhat quit her job, on the pretext that she should devote more time to her home, she was very upset. Because she knew the reason was something else, something of which a wife's faithful and fair heart, while thinking of blaming her husband, would not approve.

Her sensitive mind would keep thinking about these things and, in the little disturbed sleep she got, she would see strange dreams—Zaheen-ud-din pursuing her and she, reaching a desolate place, falling on the ground. Leaving her there, Zaheen-ud-din begins to go back and, seeing this, Nuzhat walks towards him. Zaheen-ud-din then stares at her with his bloodshot eyes—she would wake up from such dreadful dreams. But sometimes she had sweet dreams of her childhood too—her mother combing her hair, baba gifting her a big colourful box of six pieces of chocolates on her standing first in class. Leaving her mother, she runs to baba and asks for more sweets and toys, which baba, by some magic trick, gets for her instantaneously. Sometimes baba brings her favourite nut chocolates, which she wants to share with her brother, who, however, snatches away the whole box from her and she, calling out to baba in her dream, would wake up.

Sometimes she dreamt she was at school, preparing a date-sheet for the examinations with her fellow teachers. A teacher asks her to accompany her to the cafeteria. When she gets up, she sees that the skirt of her dress has huge ink stains on it. The fellow teacher still insists affectionately that she accompany her to the cafeteria and she, hiding her tears, is about to go when the second teacher looks at her and whispers something to the other teachers sitting close to her. The second teacher was the same one, who was jealous of her popularity with the children and the staff, and disliked her. On waking up, she would sob for a long time, aware of the bitter reality behind these dreams.

Soon after Aasim started school, there were complaints about his bullying and hitting the younger children of his class. Then there were letters asking the parents to come to the school to discuss the problem. But his father would not go, saying that he could not spare any time from his business, and so his mother had to go instead. The teachers and his mother would warn Aasim to stop his bad behaviour, and some days would pass peacefully after that.

When Aasim was eight or nine years old, he almost stopped listening to his mother. She complained about this to his father, but he was silent as usual, and never asked his son to mend his ways. Zaheen-ud-din, perhaps, wanted to attribute this as the reason for his own attitude to Nuzhat. He had observed the expression of disapproval of his family members, and the child being rude to his mother could be put up as a proof that she was wrong and he was right. He did not even think about the possibility of his child being spoilt by his petty politicking.

Nuzhat had thought that Zaheen-ud-din might be rude to her, but he would not like his son misbehaving with his mother in his presence because it would harm the child morally, and be very bad for the development of his personality. But Zaheen-ud-din did not realize this at all. Nuzhat was shocked, because she thought that her husband was intelligent. She was shattered, and was convinced that drinking had affected his brain so badly that he could neither evaluate things properly nor was he capable of judging them objectively. In addition to all that, the realization that she had an unruly son would make her wonder what should she live for now? As this suffering was the most painful thing in her life, worse than all the agonies she had suffered so far. More painful than the anguish of that night when, carrying Aasim—smaller then her closed fist inside her—tired of standing before the sink in the washroom and vomiting for almost an hour, she had returned to the bedroom. She had pulled her cold shivering body under the quilt. It was freezing cold as it had snowed heavily, and she felt as if the blood in her veins had also frozen, like the frozen water droplets on the glasses of the small ventilator. Zaheen-ud-din spent the greater part of his evenings in bars and frequently going to the toilet. Chain-smoking had turned his teeth to a dirty yellow. He would get into bed with stinking breath, his yellowish teeth reeking with the unpleasant smell of liquor, which had become a part of his personality for many years by now. He would grab sleeping Nuzhat's soft, warm shoulders in his ice-cold hands and try to teach her the meaning of relationships, in God knows what language. But dragged from the valley of dreams and woken up suddenly, Nuzhat never ever let him know of the revulsion she felt. Being an expecting mother, the heightened sense of smell would turn something upside down in her stomach. In place of the sweet sleep snatched away by the cruel claws of an unknown monster, she would try to control her nausea. Tears would appear in her eyes, as she felt that instead of a loving relationship, she found herself in the clutches of a man-eating demon, who demanded a human sacrifice every night. But that day, when Nuzhat happened to touch her small cold feet to those of Zaheen-ud-din's warm feet, he quickly pulled them away. Nuzhat immediately folded her legs, and her knees touched her stomach. A wave of pain moved through in her womb because feelings travel speedily to a sensitive organ of the body, and Nuzhat had become very sensitive those days. She had a light brown-eyed, curly-haired, tiny little body growing towards its completion inside her. She shivered with cold in the bed for a long time. Finally, she gathered the strength to get up and fetch a hot water bottle from the kitchen as the servants had already gone to sleep by then. It was so hard for her to get out of the bed at that time, to balance the heaviness of her tired body, to walk with shivering, cold feet and keep her helpless shoulders upright.But when she reached the bed, Zaheen-ud-din turned to her side with his warm palms which had long invisible thorns on them that pricked straight into her very soul. Why didn't Zaheen-ud-din's hands feel cold as his feet did that time? Nuzhat kept searching for the answer to this question.

Aasim began to behave with his mother as he did with his father, rather both of them would blame Nuzhat for something at the same time. Nuzhat would look at them astonished with her wide-open eyes, amazed and speechless.

'How things were taking shape,' she thought. She had begun her new life with great hopes. She loved Zaheen-ud-din unconditionally. For a long time, she blamed herself for his attitude. She suffered lack of sleep, drowsiness and heart palpitations for many years, trying to get accustomed to his loud snores and stinking breath but never thought about the real reasons for her troubles. For a long time, she was sure that Zaheen-ud-din would acknowledge her love and selfless sacrifices one day, get rid of his addiction, be able to judge things properly and stop using harsh and abusive language. Things would be fine soon and remain so ever after. But nothing like that ever happened. She then tried to live without such vain hopes. But now her child's behaviour was even more heart-breaking for her.

'He will be fine when he grows up,' her mother-in-law would say, trying to comfort her. 'Children are closer to their mothers. His stupid father does not understand this.' She would look at her daughter-in-law with eyes full of love.

'The child knows that his mother always belongs to him but to get something from the father, he has to humour him,' her mother-in-law would add.

Aasim had observed that when his grandmother said these kind words to his mother, she tried to hold her tears back; and looking around with her swollen red eyes, she would make herself busy at some chore. Aasim also observed that Pyaari sniffled repeatedly, and pretending to wipe the sweat from her face, would actually wipe her tears. At such times, Aasim would silently follow her wherever she went in the house. Then one day, Aasim was suspended from his school as there were far too many complaints against him: he answers his teachers back, he tears up the books of everyone who sits near him in the class, he throws the duster for cleaning the board out of the window, etc. He had been repeatedly warned to stop his bad behaviour. Ultimately, he was suspended from school till a final decision was taken, as his attitude could adversely affect other children too. The parents were summoned to see the class teacher and the teachers' representative.

That day, Nuzhat observed the tension on Zaheen-ud-din's face: he had always been an egotistic man, but his face no more looked the way it did when blaming Nuzhat. He was not holding his head so high that his two extra chins could appear. There were wrinkles on his forehead, and his eyes looked away furtively. Sitting in front of the teachers along with his wife, he looked like a worried father.

'Normal kids do not behave like him,' the teachers' representative said, looking at the two other teachers. 'The school rusticates such children, and his behaviour is getting worse day by day. We have already warned you many times.'

'Please excuse him this one last time. He will not repeat it in future.' The father looked at his son's face and then at the teacher's. Aasim was standing straight with his head slightly bent and eyes raised. He was looking at the teacher. His hair was spread evenly on his forehead.

'How many instances are you going to reassure for, Mr Khan? Our school employs the latest teaching methods. Kids can be mischievous, and intelligent kids are often so, but there is a difference between being mischievous and indisciplined. And how will a child behave who has not been taught this difference? We have no personal grudge against any child. We have a counsellor in our school too, we try to solve problems on our own, but this child has a different problem. He does not know how to respect teachers! Our school psychiatrist says that, that...' the teacher looked at Nuzhat. Zaheen-ud-din looked at his wife sternly too. Nuzhat felt as if, in the blazing noon, the man sitting on the scooter had pushed his body back to such an extent that she was about to fall off. 'He is not respectful to his mother at home either, I am sure,' the teacher said, looking directly at Zaheen-ud-din. Aasim suddenly looked at his teacher for a moment. Pyaari was saved from falling off the scooter. Tears filled her eyes.

'Mr Khan, a person who does not teach this basic thing to his child destroys his character forever. This must be the case, otherwise he would certainly respect his teachers. A teacher told him that he had not learnt anything all these days, and he retorted loudly that she had not taught him anything! Answering his elders back and not respecting the one who has borne him will make him disrespectful to his father as well when he grows up. He picks a fight with everyone but he is not to blame for this, rather he is not to blame at all. The environment in which he has been brought up is responsible for all this. To train a young and delicate mind, one has to become a role model himself, and only then will the child try to take after that role model. The mother should have full authority to raise her child. Someone must have challenged Mrs Khan's authority to develop this attitude in the child. Something went wrong somewhere, Mr Khan, you need to think about it.'

The teacher looked around the room. Some moments earlier, when Nuzhat's eyes were moist, she kept looking at her feet for some time, and then she looked at Aasim. The nine-year-old child had fixed his gaze on the children playing and running about in the playground. Her face was expressionless. When Aasim heard the low sound of Nuzhat sniffling, he looked at her and she shifted her glance to the teacher. Aasim raised his eyes towards the teacher's face. The teacher wore her hair trimmed short, it fell on her forehead every now and then exactly like Aasim's own hair, and she would brush it towards her ear with her fingers with their slightly grown, neat nails. She was wearing just a single pearl in each ear.

'Please give us a last chance madam, he will not repeat it again, if...' Nuzhat looked at her husband's face after looking at the teacher. 'Yes madam, last chance please,' said Zaheen-ud-din in a meek voice.

'I will talk to the principal and let you know, but even if he agrees this would really be the last chance. For now, he will not attend school for one week, and please do not waste this time. Teach him to behave. And you should know that this is not home but a school,' said his class teacher rudely. 'There is no place for unruly children here,' she added firmly and, before looking back at the notebooks in her lap, she gave Aasim a stern look. Aasim shifted his gaze from the teachers' representative to his class teacher, and an expression of helplessness appeared on his innocent face. Seeing this, Nuzhat's face also saddened.

Kids need a stable home and loving parents. How can a child feel relaxed in this atmosphere of anger and neglect? This is his school and that is his home…my poor child, Nuzhat thought helplessly. Zaheen-ud-din also felt the rudeness of the class teacher's voice, and a wave of depression swept over him.

'What a way of understanding the psychology of a child. He is just a child and needs only love! They say they have a psychiatrist in the school. She counsels them.' Zaheen-ud-din's heart was filled with love for his child. While returning home, Zaheen-ud-din looked at Aasim in the rear-view mirror, who was looking at the changing scenery through his window. 'God knows how the school staff counsels them!' looking at the road with his hands on the steering-wheel, Zaheen-ud-din thought.

'They are right. Children need an environment of love. How can he be happy if his home environment is not peaceful?

If the harshness of the surroundings is destroying the peace, it will certainly have a negative effect on an innocent mind, there is nothing strange about it,' Nuzhat said in a low voice, looking out through her window.

'Oh, now you are going to lecture me about where he lacks love too!' Zaheen-ud-din said sharply, adding, 'You do not know anything.' Nuzhat was not surprised by his attitude. Because she knew Zaheen-ud-din might be good at his business but he lacked common sense. God knows how he deals with important matters of the business, Nuzhat had thought earlier too, because to every sensible statement that Nuzhat would make, Zaheen-ud-din's reaction always suggested that she had said something wrong, and he would insist on proving her wrong. But Nuzhat was always right, as God had blessed her with intelligence, which all the family, other than her son, knew well. His innocent mind would get confused between right and wrong. When the belief he had in everything his mother said and did was weakened, he gradually stopped listening to her—and then to others as well, including his teachers.

Accepting the fact that she was the wife, Nuzhat would let him prevail, thinking that it was caused by a difference of perspective. But by and by, as she came to the realization that he actually felt insecure because of her intelligence, she would not talk to him except when it was absolutely necessary.

Perhaps it was just by chance that the Khan brothers decided to go for a week's holiday, a venture that had been put off for long. The health resort in the hills, being off the beaten track, made every member of the family relaxed and happy. And Aasim also tried hard not to anger Abba, as otherwise he had threatened to break his legs. He believed Abba always did what he said. He started taking interest in games. But most of his games included bullying someone else, whether playing at home, with his cousins or at school. He did not enjoy the game unless he brought whoever he was playing with to tears. Then he would glance at the poor victim like his father, and bend his head slightly, looking away at the ground and enjoying, keeping his neck rigid, and thus making two little folds under his little chin.But at times, he would feel compassion towards his victim and feel his pain in his heart. Then, he would rub his eyes red and, looking around him, sniffle like Nuzhat—with tears rolling down his cheeks too.

At the health resort, he was looking for some games he would enjoy. And in that one week he not only acquired a very obedient disciple but also found that they both had a liking for the same games. These games included cricket, running and climbing trees. The disciple was Yasir, who was younger Aunt Farkhanda's son. Yasir was also very happy to discover that brother Aasim, with whom he had always wanted to play but who always left the game in the middle and hit him on some minor pretext and spoiling the game totally, would not hit him anymore. This friendship lasted many years, mutually sharing each other's little secrets, but finally one of them had to part with the other, leaving only his memories behind.

After returning from the seven-day vacation, the whole family was happy for some time, except for Zaheen-ud-din. There was no change in him—neither in the manner that he had recently adopted towards Aasim, nor in his behaviour towards Nuzhat. When Aasim perceived this, he sat at his study desk for many hours and, taking a compass out of his geometry box, made a number of scratches on the top of his table. He greatly desired to burn his school bag filled with books, but having family members around, put it off to some other time. Aasim and Yasir would also go outside to play cricket or football in the playground. Aasim made friends with other boys, and he started spending some time outside of his home.

No complaints were received from the school either. At home, he spent much of his time at Farkhanda's apartment, which was a portion of the same family house.While ironing his own clothes, Uncle Zahoor would iron Aunt Farkhanda's dresses as well. Aunt Farkhanda would play with him and Yasir. Uncle never scolded her for anything. After some time Zahoor-ud-din had to move to another area as the ancestral house did not have enough space for the growing family. Aasim also wanted to go to their home and live with them.

When they were busy with packing their stuff, Aasim would follow them everywhere, sniffling and wiping his tears. His father scolded him, and even hit him. He had fine hair on his slender legs that were still growing. Abba suddenly picked up a slipper from the edge of the carpet and threw it hard at his legs. He ran to his room enraged, and in retaliation broke four window panes with his cricket bat and then ran out of the house. Before running away, however, he couldn't resist casting a glance at the floor of his room. The sharp shards of broken glass, scattered all over on the carpet, looked so nice. This brought a smile of success to his innocent face but he knew he would not be able to enjoy the wonderful scene for long because, hearing the sound of breaking glass, people in the house would start looking in the room for the reason. He had to disappear before they reached there. With the marvellous sight of broken glass shards in his eyes and welts on his calves, he slipped out to the street through the back gate.

When Nuzhat could not find Aasim anywhere in the house, she cried her heart out. She yelled at her husband in the presence of everyone saying that if anything happened to Aasim, she would burn the house and kill herself—and that she had endured the abuse and torture all these years only because of Aasim, otherwise she would not have tolerated a callous-hearted, cruel person like him for a single day. But Zaheen-ud-din just kept silent, and she went to the kitchen, crying. She unexpectedly saw Yasir stuffing the wheat parathas—made of two joined loaves greased with ghee, that were kept in the willow basket for evening tea—into the small pockets of his jacket. Nuzhat's tearful face broke into a smile upon seeing this.

'Let me put a little more butter on them,' she suddenly said with a lot of love in her voice. Yasir looked at her apprehensively, but the smile on her face showed that she was happy sharing his secret. Blinking his eyes, he smiled and extended the parathas towards her.

Nuzhat put some butter on each of them, made them into a roll, and put them in a polythene bag. Yasir unzipped his jacket and put the packet carefully in his inner pocket. Flattening it with his hand, he zipped up his jacket again.

'It would have stained your jacket otherwise!' said Nuzhat, kissing his cheeks. He gave her a broad smile, wiping off the wet seal of spit from her motherly kiss from his cheeks—which looked like the red *maharaji* apples, which are picked from the trees when green and stored from autumn to winter, during which they turn red.

He looked around stealthily and ran towards the gate. Zaheen-ud-din came out of his room and went to the garage. While crossing the veranda, he spotted Yasir heading towards the gate, repeatedly looking behind him. He noticed a slight bulge on the left side of Yasir's jacket, wondering what it could be. Yasir quickened his pace when he saw his uncle in the veranda. Zaheen-ud-din looked at the collar of the red jacket near his thin neck and proceeded to the garage. Aasim wore the same jacket till two years back, but it was small on him now and no longer fit him, thought Zaheen-ud-din. Taking small steps with his little feet, Yasir looked exactly like Aasim did a couple of years ago.

When the trucks were loaded, Farkhanda confided in Nuzhat that Aasim was going with them; Nuzhat smiled sweetly in approval.

When aunty and uncle got into the car, Aasim looked at Yasir with tearful eyes. 'Nuzhat must be crying,' he said, adding, 'I want to go home.' He started crying and looked at the driver with resentful eyes.

'No, my child, we have already told your mother,' his aunt said, smiling. Aasim's tearful eyes abruptly shone and he burst into loud laughter. Listening to his loud, happy laughter, everyone started laughing too.

The time spent in his uncle's house then, and after that, was filled with the most cherished memories of Aasim's life. After spending some days with his uncle's family, when Aasim returned home, a dreadful piece of news was awaiting him; it was something he had feared for some time. The family members had found out that although he left home regularly for school every day, he was not going to school, but instead spent his time playing with other dropouts.There was no notice from his school either about that. Aasim wondered what he would do if Abba hit him, but Abba neither hit him nor spoke to him.

'If Abba beats me, I will go to uncle's place,' Aasim said innocently, raising his head while eating and looking at his mother's face. 'Abba will not hit you, my child. You are a big boy now, no one hits grown-ups because they are responsible people, and you have to think about yourself,' Nuzhat said reassuringly.

Sheba was offered a scholarship for higher studies from an out-of-state university, and Abbu had allowed her to go. When Faheema heard it at her in-laws' home, she burned with envy and felt like a fish out of water.

After getting a job as an engineer in the electricity department, Mukhtar Ahmed had spent many years at various construction sites for dams, far away from home. Life there was only wires, water, rocks and cement, and there was no place for anything, or anyone else. Those days, there were no women in the technical field; so, like a soldier posted at the borders for a long period, when Mukhtar Ahmed did not see a woman even once and realized this time and again, he suddenly came to the realization that he had reached marriageable age for quite some time by now.

A girl from a prestigious family was chosen for him. She looked even younger than her real age as she was rather skinny, and the somewhat over-age groom liked this all the more. He was a man of medium build, average qualities and ordinary thinking. He relied on God in most matters, and thus, would remain happy. He had sparse hair on his arms and hardly a beard on his Mongolian face, though he did have some hair around his chin, making a smallish circle that matched his thin moustache. He had high cheek bones, and a fair and pink complexion.

The more Faheema disliked her own scrawny figure, the more she liked Mukhtar Ahmed's plump figure, and they had a happy married life.

Seeing Faheema upset, Mukhtar Ahmed sent her to see her parents. She reached her parents' home in an agitated state of mind. She wanted to convince her father in the name of her honour, as well as for her apprehensions of the orthodox in-laws' taunts, to not allow Sheba to go to another state for studies.

Sheba had always suspected Faheema's hand in her being caught red-handed by her mother while reading a novel or wearing lipstick, her books being torn and her notebooks disappearing behind the bed, but never openly blamed her sister because of her strong belief in the sanctity of close relationships. Now she listened to her sister's reaction in stunned silence. It dawned upon her that Baaji, who always tried to shut her up by telling her that she was wrong, was really herself a liar, because the reasons she gave Abbu for not sending her to study out of state were baseless. A sudden wave of abhorrence swept over Sheba's mind and she felt that she had destroyed a part of her own being. She stood shocked against the wall for some time. Everything Baaji said had no logic.

'Abbu, please think of my prestige, I am sick of being taunted all the time.' Baaji had tried hard to look sad but the expression on her face was the same she had on putting a morsel of tasteless, salt-less food when Ammi, fasting herself, would sometimes ask Baaji to taste some special dish she had prepared for Abbu during Ramadan.

'What taunts, my child?! Enjoy your tea. There is nothing to be taunted about in this,' Abbu said, taking a sip from his cup.

'No girl from their family has ever been sent to a distant place like this, and especially for studying—and to top it all, all by herself!' Baaji lightly pushed away the cup of tea in front of her. Some tea spilled into the saucer of the cup of light blue china, but luckily none onto the table.

'No girl in their family might have been interested in going for higher studies; maybe no one received such an offer on merit,' Abbu answered serenely, before eating the piece of *baqarkhanee* that he had broken from his plate and was taking to his mouth.

'But she did not get a degree graduating in Sciences! It is only something related to Humanities!' Hearing her father's answer, she perhaps forgot the topic. She shook her head and looked towards the window, gazing at something in the garden. Sheba also looked out. The sun was about to set and its rays rested on the tops of poplar trees. Birds were flitting around, searching for a nice perch to settle down for the night. A mynah sitting on the branch of an apricot tree was continuously chirping in a shrill voice.The sun's rays, falling on the dining table and the carpet, had changed their colour passing through the rainbow-coloured ventilator glasses. In the centre of the green carpet there was a big, blue circle with orange flowers, which looked green in the blue light coming through the blue glass, and the blue circle looked purple in the light passing through the red glass.

The angry expression on Baaji's face would always terrify Sheba and scare her out of her wits till some years ago, and she would cry her heart out. Seeing the anger and dislike in Ammi's eyes because of Faheema's false complaints against her, she would be tormented by overwhelming sadness for hours, even days—and on top of all that, Baaji would slap her without her being at fault.

'She selected the topic all by herself without any guidance from her teachers, got approval from her principal, participated in an international competition and was successful! She did her college, city and country proud. This is surely more important than any degree, isn't it? You should encourage your sister, but on the contrary, you...'

'What about the reputation and honour of our family?' Faheema interrupted.

'She has already enhanced the prestige and honour of the family, and as far as women's education is concerned, our mother was educated even in the old times. I am in favour of women's education—remind your in-laws of this, and if they still don't understand, to hell with them!' Abbu raised his voice. Pushing her chair away, and leaving the dining table, Baaji suddenly burst into tears.

'Yes, I know I could not become a doctor; I did not have the capabilities, so how could I?' Baaji started sobbing, just like she used to do—with her face fuming red upon losing in a game to her sisters, who were some six or seven years younger than her.

Ammi came up to her and caressed her hair gently. Sheba watched silently, standing near the wall. Baaji was wearing a magenta salwar kameez of Kashmiri silk. Listening to Abbu's answer, she fixed her gaze at the hem of Baaji's kameez. The poor silkworms weave a cocoon around them to grow, which turns into the death cell of a prison for them. Strands of silk come from those cocoons. The mulberry tree, with the swinging rope hanging by its thick branch, is denuded of its leaves every spring by the silkworm farmers. The leafless tree looks like a stump and not like a tree anymore. But it is the law in the Valley that no one can stop the farmers from chopping off the small branches and leaves for the silkworms. The government has planted nurseries for this purpose and the small trees there have even bigger leaves, but they still do not spare the tree with a swinging rope hanging by one of its limbs.

Sheba thought of the poor little worms and the soft silk. Some decades ago, the Srinagar Silk Factory was the biggest silk factory in the world. It could still well be so. Had Baaji's suit been deep blue, brown or black, or some other darker shade, it would have looked even better, Sheba brooded. The magenta kameez was embroidered with turquoise blue thread all over it. Sheba never liked parrot green, turquoise and lemon shades, but many of her outfits had these shades only because they had been selected by Baaji. Looking at these shades, Baaji's usually angry face would shine for some moments, a sign of her being in an agreeable mood, and thus saving Sheba from some unfair scolding and punishment. Sheba's subconscious, therefore, always made her say yes to clothes of those colours, although she was not consciously aware of it. The day she got the opportunity to select clothing in the colours of her own choice for the first time by herself, she had still picked up a piece of turquoise-coloured fabric, but then she abruptly put it back. The gleam on Baaji's face appeared in her mind, standing beside her own insignificant figure. She looked at the rolls of cloth of colours that were jarring to her—like parrot green and lemon yellow—but then she put her golden hand on a roll of black cloth instead, and her heart was filled with peace, and her face, relaxed.

How could a stubborn Baaji accept this defeat? She would surely vent this anger on her in some dreadful way. But then, she soon came to the realization that she was not at Baaji's mercy anymore. She heaved a sigh of relief and stood there as if witnessing the climax of a melodrama. Then she calmly smiled at Baaji and turned towards her room.

Faheema stared at her. Sheba had fastened her hair with a black pin at the nape of her neck, with her thick long hair flowing lose and rippling about her back. In the centre of the black pin was a single white pearl, shining dimly. Faheema was overtaken by a great urge to suddenly pull all her hair out from the roots, but the next moment she thought that if her pin had been parrot green instead, a white pearl would have looked much more beautiful on it.

'Ammi, she has gone totally out of control!'

Listening to her voice, Sheba turned her head and saw Faheema's face, combining expressions of hatred and contempt at the same time. Faheema had pursed her lips, twisted her nose upwards, and had many furrows on her forehead.

Leaving tears in Ammi and Abbu's eyes as well as smiles on their faces, Sheba left for another state to study further.

***

When Seemeen saw herself standing near Nanna Huzur in the picture in an album in Nanna Jani's house, she tried hard with her seven-year-old mind to remember but could not recall that mamma had ever dressed her in a salwar kameez, and let her hair grow so long that she could twist them into two thick braids, and got her photographed. She was such an expert in braiding hair that she could even braid mamma's short hair. But mamma had Seemeen's hair trimmed every month. And she had never worn earrings...how could she?

Holding the album in her hands, she bent her head and spread the fingers of her right hand; the album almost closed shut. She had never got her ears pierced. Seemeen held the album carefully in her hands again. Only one thing was right in the picture—the two story books she had in her hands. But she also had many other story books; apart from *The Adventures of Huckleberry Finn* and *Robinson Crusoe*, she had *Moby Dick*, *Aladdin* and a recent edition of *The Three Musketeers*.

Holding the album in her hands and looking at the pictures keenly, she went towards Nanna Jaani's room. Walking without looking at the ground, she tripped at the threshold, and fell. She dropped the album; she had bruised her knee. She picked up the album to see whether it was intact and pulled up her long, frilly frock slightly. While examining her knee, she silently shed some tears. Wiping the tears from her angular golden face left a couple of dirty streaks on her cheeks. She wiped her eyes but her upper eyelashes were still wet. Nanna Jaani was busy in her namaz. Seemeen watched her, standing near the door.

Nanna Jaani sits up after the second prostration, and pays homage to the angels sitting on her shoulders, one by one. She then joins her hands in the shape of an open book for the final supplication to God before getting up. And only then does she talk to whoever is waiting for her.

'Nanna Jaani!' Seemeen called in a tiny voice, with its muffled pain from the mishap near the threshold.

'What is it Baby?' grandmother asked, looking at the door. Seemeen had crossed her arms diagonally on her chest, holding the album under them carefully.

'My dolly wants to see the album!' grandmother said, rising from the prayer mat, and went to have a closer look. She looked at her face carefully to ascertain the cause of stains on her face as well as her sadness, not asking directly lest she starts crying. She caressed her hair, drawing her into the room.

'Nanna Jaani, I look so good in the picture. If I had long braids earlier, why does mamma get my hair trimmed? I will not let my hair be trimmed anymore, and where is this dress of mine?' Seemeen asked, looking upset.

'It isn't you, my child, it's Aunty Sheba,' Suraya Begum said, patting her cheeks.

'Is that Aunty Sheba?' the voice suddenly sounded happy with curiosity.

'Yes, my doll, this is your Aunty Sheba. She looked exactly like you when she was your age. Her hair was like yours, her eyes like yours, and…'

'I want to go to Aunty Sheba,' Seemeen said, putting her finger on Sheba's picture.

'Your Aunty is in a faraway place; she has gone there to study and can only come back in the holidays, during the summer vacation.'

'When will we have summer here?'

'In just a month…when we can easily see the little green almonds hidden behind the blossoms, the summer will be here.' Suraya Begum pointed with her finger towards the garden and Seemeen also looked out. In the garden, the half-open buds, some of them in bloom as well as the pink—light pink-and-white blossoms—on the grey branches of the almond tree looked like tiny flowers. Exactly above the crown of the tree, a huge, pure white cloud stood like a mountain touching the blue sky.

'Look Nanna Jaani, so many colours—white, pink, grey, blue and, and that's all!' She counted four colours on her fingers; she had put the little finger of her right hand on her left thumb, and was lost in thoughts.

'Who did Aunty Sheba's hair?'

'I did it, who else?'

'Mamma does not know it, oh, but I can make braids, Nanna Jaani!' Seemeen wanted to say something more but heard her mother's voice and stood up.

'Mamma has come to take me back home, Nanna Jaani, but I want to sleep here with you. I want to go to Aunty Sheba. Don't tell mamma that I'm here.' Seemeen hid behind the bed. Faheema had heard her voice and stopped at the door.

The decades-old bed of walnut wood had many figures and words drawn on it in blue, green and red. There was a cat but it had no moustache, and a dog with very short tail, and many other funny figures. There was other interesting stuff as well—flowers, the letter alif, jeem, the numbers one, two, three, etc. And all that meant that this place had been used for hiding earlier too. Seemeen smiled silently.

Najam Khan had, at one point, reserved this biggest room on the first floor as his three daughters' study room; and children, as Seemeen also understood, do not only study while at their books. It is important to play as well—be it getting up suddenly with a pen in hand and going behind the bed to play hide and seek, or stealthily draw lines, circles and images in the books and the notebooks, even when elders were around. This was the source of some respite from burdensome studies, and carried a big bonus of fun as well.

Seemeen raised her head slightly to look at her mother. Mamma was coming towards her, laughing. When she sat down and opened her arms, Seemeen came out from behind the bed and hugged her mother.

'I want to go to Aunty Sheba,' Seemeen said to her mother's shoulder. But Faheema, making an unpleasant face, pushed her away lightly and stood up.

'She is such a nice person, Mamma, and Nanna Jaani says that I look extremely like her. I want to go to Aunty Sheba.'

Suraya Begum laughed, 'It isn't extremely my child, but exactly.'

Faheema looked at them expressionlessly. 'We will talk about that later, but for now, we are going home,' she said.

'And I want to grow my hair longer to make two braids like her. You don't trim your hair, and your hair does not grow long. From now on I won't let my hair be trimmed, I will make them into braids, like Aunty Sheba. I will do it myself, you don't know how to, that's why.'

Faheema frowned and looked at her daughter. Her eyes were wide with surprise. She pursed her lips, pulled Seemeen by her arm and left the room.

'Nanna Jaani!' Seemeen screamed.

Suraya Begum got up. 'Faheema, don't be so harsh, my daughter,' Suraya Begum called loudly, leaving the room as well. 'It's time now for *Ishaa* prayers (one of the five mandatory Islamic prayers, this is usually observed as the second prayer after sunset). Only God knows how Gulla has cooked the dinner! Everything changed since the day Miyaan Noori left...everything changed. Now, how much can poor Gullaa do by himself?' Suraya Begum murmured and went down the stairs to the kitchen.

Sheba was busy with her studies. She had done her M.Phil. in Sociology and was working on her doctorate now. She felt so proud of herself when she was approved to complete her doctorate under the guidance of a brilliant sociologist. Professor Daanish was the epitome of knowledge: the books written by him had been a part of the curriculum of every college and university for the last two decades. His articles had ensured increased sales for newspapers and magazines publishing them. He was not only famous in his field in the country, but abroad as well. After his retirement, universities would vie with each other to get him to be a part of their faculty. Sheba was working hard at her studies.

When she visited her hometown once or twice a year, Faheema would never come to see her—even if she was sent for by her parents. Sheba, too, never went to her.

Farkhanda would come to see her younger sister though. Her young son Yasir had made good friends with Sheba, and the friendship deepened with the passing years. Sheba had seen Faheema's daughter only when she was a tiny baby. The topic, that Seemeen had not only the looks of her Aunt Sheba but also behaved like her, was fondly talked about in the family.

'Seemeen is your true copy, she will grow tall like you; her eyes, face—everything,' Farkhanda told Sheba. An affectionate smile spread over Sheba's face.

'Is that so?'

'Yes Sheba, she is your Xerox copy; you'll be surprised to see her.'

'And how does Baaji treat her?'

'It can't be the way she used to treat you, of course. After all, she is her daughter. But you know, when she observes her resemblance to you—in looks and habits—you should see her helplessness!'

'Such as?'

'Like she wants her hair loose. You pin up your hair, she leaves hers loose, and it looks as beautiful on her as it looked on you. A couple of years ago, when she saw your picture, she insisted on having braids like you. Baaji wanted to get her hair trimmed but she put her foot down. Now, when Baaji looks at her long, undone hair, she irritably says that her daughter is going to break Sheba's records,' Farkhanda laughed.

A green leaf danced down from the tree and fell on Sheba's dupatta. She held it by its stem between her thumb and fingertips, and started rotating it. They were sitting on chairs under the fig tree.

'What had Sheba done, Farkhanda?' Sheba asked, looking at Farkhanda's face, 'What record had Sheba set?' Sheba raised her head a little and looked at the grape vine. She suddenly sounded gloomy. The palm-shaped, pentagonal leaves had tiny bunches of grapes hanging near many stems, but they were still very small. Some other branches still had tiny little creepers hanging from them, which looked like the yarn of an unravelled, old green sweater. 'Do you remember? We would take them for paan (betel) leaves when we were kids…' Sheba's voice suddenly rang out.

'Yes, we would put one leaf on top of the other, add salt to them and try to fold them into small packets. And we could never really fold them!' They laughed the way they would in their childhood.

'That tasted delicious, sour leaves with a pinch of salt.'

Tea was served in the lawn—pink salted tea with *baqarkhanees* especially brought from the south of the Valley. Sheba noticed that the cup in which she had been served the tea was the same in which she used to have her tea before she went to the hostel. It was gleaming as always, placed on a carved copper tray. A smile spread over Sheba's lips.

'Is Ammi back home?' Sheba asked Ghulam Mohammad, the cook who was like a member of the family for many years now. He liked to be called Gulla because it was his pet name at home. Najam Khan and Suraya Begum called him Gulla, and the children addressed him as Gulla Bhai.

'No, not yet, I have got your cup out of the pantry. Begum Saahiba must be on her way,' replied Gulla Bhai, nodding while serving the delicacies from the tray on the table. He put the half-empty glasses of water in the tray and turned to leave.

'Thank you, Gulla Bhai!'

Sheba had reached home in the afternoon. The family members were away somewhere. She called up Farkhanda, and she came soon to see her sister.

'Ammi, perhaps, had to go to Faheema's place; her mother-in-law is back after her Haj pilgrimage,' Farkhanda said, picking up the teapot.

'Nobody is picking up the phone there.'

Sheba held her cup in her hand. It was a small mug, gifted to her in school for winning a debate. It was a thick, white china mug which had sustained many bumps hitting the tap when being washed, but it never broke. It had a beautiful picture on it. A blue-feathered little bird was sitting on a branch with many flowers on it. The bird's beak was half open, as if it was chirping.

Sheba heard the sound of the small door fixed in the main gate opening, and turned towards it. She saw Ammi coming towards them. She had two more people with her. Sheba got up and hugged her mother. Ammi held her close for many moments. Sheba was surprised to see her childhood peering across Ammi's shoulder. Behind Seemeen, she saw Faheema.

'Seemeen!'

Sheba shouted her name and Ammi broke the circle of her arms and let Sheba go to Seemeen.

'When you grow up, you will look like her,' Ammi said, looking at Seemeen; and Sheba, too, stood there for some moments to look at her. Seemeen ran to Sheba.

'Aunty Sheba!' Seemeen shouted, recognizing her suddenly. She hardly reached up to Sheba's waist. Sheba thought it was as if the little Sheba of past years had come to meet the grown-up Sheba, and the little Sheba was no more scared of Baaji.

'*Assalam-u-Alaikum,*' Sheba said, looking at Faheema.

'*Wa Alaikum-assalam,*' Faheema answered her greeting, and looking at Sheba's face keenly, reached for a chair. She had an expression on her face as if to suggest that she had seen something strange. Sheba knew that Baaji was deliberately making a face suggesting that she had seen something negative.

'Sheba, you look old!' Baaji said in a voice that successfully combined apprehension with insult, but also wore an expression of astonishment. 'There is always a time for getting married, ageing robs beauty,' Faheema looked at Farkhanda's face for affirmation. Farkhanda, however, did not let any expression show on her face.

'She is not so old, but that is the reason I have called my loving child for a longer vacation this time,' Suraya Begum said, smiling, looking at Sheba. My daughter will very soon be a bride, InshAllah,' she said.

Sheba smiled back and Farkhanda smiled too. Seemeen laughed loudly.

'Oh, really, Nanna Jaani! Will Aunty Sheba be a bride?' Seemeen asked.

'But Ammi, you never said so before,' Faheema said. The expression she had on her face a short while ago had disappeared.

Sheba smiled at her and Faheema thought she was insulting her. 'But where Ammi? Which family?' Farkhanda asked in a happy, curious voice.

'Or is it that you have found someone yourself, I suppose?' Faheema said in a tone which had both aversion and belief in it.

Sheba continued, looking at her with a smiling face. 'I had thought Baaji must have grown up with the years but our Baaji is still a girl of yesteryears! Our Baaji's mind has stayed in her childhood,' Sheba said smiling, looking at Baaji and then at Farkhanda, and got up to go inside. Farkhanda did not let any expression appear on her face this time either.

'Of course, we acknowledge her abilities, if there even is something like that. I suppose her Abbu will have no objection to her decision either,' Ammi said, looking at them one by one. 'You are her sisters, you may ask her,' she said, picking up a raw fig from the ground. 'Oh, you greedy birds! Let the fruit ripen,' Suraya Begum said smilingly and collected the cups and tea set in a tray. 'I am going for a quick bath.'

Sheba stood up and Seemeen got up even before her, and started walking a step ahead of Sheba. After a little while they both held each other's hands, and ran to the house. Seemeen's childish laughter echoed in the lawn.

'Please send Gulla Bhai here, my child.' Suraya Begum's voice overflowed with love for her daughter who had returned after many days, and Seemeen's smiles added more sweetness to it.

Though tired, Sheba could not sleep well that night. Why did Baaji behave like this with her? The question that would bruise her heart, though softened somewhat in intensity while away from home, it still raised its ugly head, taking away her peace for the whole night. She kept staring at the silhouette of the unlighted bulbs.

Baaji would be deep in sleep, forgetting everything like always—but here she was, awake, recalling everything like always. Seemeen desperately wanted to sleep over at Nanna Jaani's place for that night but Faheema, scolding her, had taken her away with her.

She recalled Seemeen's innocent face. She heard a rooster crowing from some distant place. It was early dawn. Sheba took a deep breath and closed her eyes, changing her side. After a short while she drifted off to asleep. The relations, as well as matches for her, started coming to their house as they learnt that Sheba had come for some days. But…

There were still many days till the end of vacations. It had been a long time since Sheba had sat on her study chair facing the garden where she could see three Indian horse-chestnut trees, which would lose their leaves in the long autumn only for a few days, unlike other trees that remain leafless for months in the hilly areas. And on moonlit nights, when birds sat on its branches, Sheba could see their shadows on her bed. She would go to the window to look at them. Against the backdrop of the vast sky, it looked as if someone had drawn a picture with blackish-blue paint on a grey canvas. Buds could be seen on these three trees the very day after they had lost their last leaf. And the day after that, the horse-chestnut trees would start growing tiny shoots. Growing bigger day by day, they would begin to sprout leaves, increasing with every day, as in the plains. This only happened with the horse-chestnut trees, and not with other trees in the hills. But the autumn was still far away. Their leaves looked like walnut leaves, and had a pungent smell peculiar to them.

Sheba had not added more to her treasure-trove of her parents' love—neither had she played with Seemeen to her heart's content, nor had she sat on the swing hanging on the thickest branch of the mulberry tree without swinging, and thinking long and deep about some matter (the swing would slowly move about on its own), when she suddenly had to leave. That day, the newspaper headline was about the famous sociologist, Dr Daanish. He had suffered an attack of paralysis. Sheba was deeply perturbed. She was not doing her Ph.D. just to fill in a blank on a form; she wanted to do much work. She had plans to read a lot of books, and write many papers yet. She had enrolled in this course two years ago. The paper said that when Dr Daanish did not come out of his room till noon that day, his domestic help knocked and found him on his bed, moaning. He was on his bed but his lower limbs were on the floor. His wife, who taught at a college abroad, was informed. Dr Daanish was admitted in the Intensive Care Unit (ICU) of the hospital in a semi-conscious state. He was paralyzed on the right side of his body. For the time being, nothing could be said definitely about his condition.

Holding the newspaper in her hands, Sheba was lost in her thoughts without even sitting in the swing. 'When will Daanish sir recover?' She had never seen any such patient recover fully. 'What if he doesn't recover?' she brooded.

The department would arrange for another guide for her. But who knows how the new guide would be? And what would his style of working be? What if he sent her shopping with his wife, for carrying her packages—like her previous room-mate, Garima had to do? How would he guide her in using the material she had collected under Dr Daanish's supervision? What if like her ex-Head, he was jealous of Dr Daanish too? Then he would make her suffer as well. The story of the ex-Head's jealousy towards Dr Daanish was well known at the university, and it sometimes affected innocent students too.

Suraya Begum had planned for Sheba to get engaged this year and marry during the next vacation, as she would be through with her studies by then. The only pre-condition was that the boy should be understanding and appreciate her desire to study further. But she had not talked about this with Sheba as yet. Hearing her decision to go back, Suraya Begum was much perturbed. She looked at her with an upset expression on her face.

'Can't you stay for some more days, my child?' Suraya Begum asked, caressing her long, braided hair.

'No Ammi, if I go now, I will be able to return soon. Otherwise things will get complicated for me. Otherwise, I didn't want to go so soon either,' Sheba replied, looking at some faraway place in the lawn. The wall joining the passage to the mosque had a somewhat higher platform. Abbu had thrown some corn for the pigeons on it early that morning and the birds were still pecking at it.

The tray in front of her had a number of delicacies on it—wheat parathas with a thin layer of ghee joining them, that would, however, separate the layers when baked on a flat iron griddle; oven-baked thick *girda* (a tandoor bread from Kashmir, made with dough that's fermented overnight) bread with poppy seeds on its thicker edges. *Sheermals* (a mildly sweet naan made out of refined flour, leavened with yeast, and baked in a tandoor; the flour is kneaded with warm milk sweetened with sugar and flavoured with saffron and cardamom), which are usually eaten after being softened by soaking in a cup of tea, were served on round trays. All these savouries emitted an appetizing aroma. A short while ago Gulla Bhai had brought *tsochwour* (a small and round Kashmiri bread) made somewhat later in the day. Sheba had once seen exactly the same *tsochwours* spreading the same aroma on an educational tour to north-west China, in eastern Xinjiang's capital, Urumchi (Urumqi). She was very happy to see them there. God knows what the Chinese called them in their language. She had even seen *girda* there. Sheba wanted to know their local names but while she was looking at all those breads of different sizes and shapes, the lady interpreter had gone quite far. She learnt that these delicacies were taken from this area to her Valley. That day, Sheba related the whole story to Mayuri.

Salt tea had been boiling in the samovar since morning. The more it is boiled, the tastier it gets. The servant keeps adding more tea to the kettle and taking out some live coals from the kangri with tongs, adds them to the iron tube and then shakes it carefully in a certain manner so that the tea does not spill—it looks as if the samovar is shivering, and the ashes drop to the bottom, making space for more burning coals in the tube.

The copper samovar and plates had flowers, leaves and branches carved on them; the cups and saucers were all white. The traditional Chinese cups without handles, which looked like small soup bowls, were not used in the household because no one except Suraya Begum knew how to eat the soaked bread from the cup without a spoon. In the western corner of the garden, there was a woodpecker sitting on a branch of an apricot tree. After constantly tapping on the hard bark, it was heard calling. In the lulls in the conversation, the sound of this constant tapping was trying to reduce the sadness on her leaving in the silent morning. The outer balcony was only used in the spring, and the spring was in full bloom. It was such an enchanting season that there was none like it in the whole world. It was such a beautiful spring that no one would want to leave it and go to the plains; a spring of such colours and scents that one would never tire of looking at, even forgetting one's hunger and thirst. The spring of lakes, mountains and moonlit nights, bulbuls and water birds, the spring of flowers, trees and fruits, and of fresh corn and walnuts in their green peel.

Sheba's room in the hostel appeared before her eyes. It would never look good, no matter how it was decorated. It had an iron cupboard, a wooden table, dirty-looking grey cement floor, many books and a damp bathroom. The mirror was hazy, and had been like that for a long time as the seniors had confirmed, and the walls with white distemper were soggy. The leakage from the joints of the water pipe in the wall separating the next room (number six) and its attached bathroom, in which Diljeet and her two roommates—Dolema from Ladakh and Srilata from Madurai—lived, had made many different patterns on the walls. One of those designs looked like a three-horned cow. There was a lamp shade and the dim 40-watt bulb hanging in the high ceiling of the room. It made the shadow of the showerhead look like an inverted umbrella, and covered most of the floor. The single ventilator could not provide enough light, and sometimes one would crush some small bug under one's foot.

'What are you thinking, child?' she heard the sad voice of Ammi. Sheba looked at her, and then bending her head down, started looking at her cup of tea. What stuff are mothers made of? They send away their children, from whom they do not want to take their eyes off, to a distant place for a better chance in future and life for them, and then live unhappily ever after.

'I will wind up everything, and will be back soon,' Sheba said, bending down and looking at her mother with a pleasant expression.

'Right!'

Sheba did not understand in what tone her mother said the word 'right'; did she agree with what Sheba had said or did she want to know something more?

'All right, my child, eat some breakfast, we will think it over later.' Suraya Begum broke a paratha into small pieces and put it in Sheba's cup.

Professor Daanish was allowed to leave the hospital. He was in the ICU for the first three days. There was no improvement in his condition, except that he had regained consciousness. He was shifted to another room next to the ward, and kept under observation for some more days. There was still no improvement in his condition and finally, his wife—who had come from abroad—and his students brought him back to his residence at the university.

Leaving her luggage in her room, Sheba rushed to see Dr Daanish. He was in the lawn, lying in an easy chair. His domestic help was pressing his right foot alternating his hands, and his whole upper body was swaying rhythmically with its movement. The skin of his foot was shining as his help had put some oil on it. Professor Daanish looked at Sheba with a faint smile on his face, and showed a glimpse of recognition too. His face looked pale.

'Be…seated…She…ba.' Professor pointed to a chair with his left hand. Sheba sat down silently on the edge of the chair. Dr Daanish had completed his sentence in broken words and could not say Sheba; instead, he said 'Shih- - -ba'. Sheba was looking at his face.

'How do you feel now, sir?' Sheba tried to smile. She stood up seeing Mrs Daanish coming to the lawn from the house.

'Please be seated!' Mrs Daanish said, sitting down in a chair near her husband. She was a tall, bony woman, with her hair trimmed short.

'Thank you, madam…What do the doctors think?' Sheba asked, sitting down again.

'His doctors are not giving a satisfactory answer. My leave will be over in a few days. Sometimes they say it can take six months, but the other day they said that they could say nothing for sure yet.'

'Madam, can't you extend your leave?' Sheba asked abruptly.

Mrs Daanish looked at her. 'I want to make all the necessary arrangements before leaving, lest I keep worrying over there. Yes, I can extend my leave by some days, but how long? A week at the most…and for what hope? If he does not recover and the leave is also wasted, what would I do then? I had planned this vacation for winter like every year…we do not have much time there. Daanish knows my schedule…

it is too hot here…it is unbearable.' Mrs Daanish shook her shoulders and spread her hands. Rounding her lips, as if whistling, she put the fingers of both her hands together and looked at the back side of her hands, one by one.

Listening to her, Sheba's face took on an expression of distaste. Mrs Daanish would purse her lips after every sentence, and she had pronounced the word schedule in a different way. Earlier, the word was pronounced in the British way, but now the accent was American. Skedule, schedule—does it matter? Madam is working in another country. She is a foreign government employee and is proud of it. Although she was born, educated and got married in another country, now she is proud of her links with the new country and not her motherland anymore.

'One has to go even if one does not want to…what can I do? A job is a job…I am at a senior position there and am expecting a promotion after six months, isn't that so, Daanish?' Mrs Shehla Daanish looked smilingly at her husband's face. Sheba felt that it was a fake smile. An artificial smile, where the lips are broadened but no smile shows on the rest of the face—just two arches around the corners of the lips or the lines near the corners of the eyes. Sheba looked at Mrs Daanish's face more keenly for some moments.

Dr Daanish stared at Shehla Daanish silently. His face wore a blank expression—he was not smiling, but it did not look like he wasn't smiling either.

'He was not…smiling…But it did not…look like he wasn't…smiling either.' Sheba considered the funny sentence, relishing it for a few moments, as she did in her childhood when she would break a sentence and make it up again in reverse. But sadness engulfed her again. She heard some voices at the gate and turned her head. Diljeet and Mayuri, looking for Sheba, were at the gate. They had planned to come with her but Sheba had left alone without meeting anyone. Some other students had also arrived. Aaftab Aalam and Saagar had a nurse with them whom Mrs Daanish had sent for. Seeing the nurse, her face lit up.

'By the rules I should be relieved of the tension now, but…' said Mrs Daanish, lowering her head. She had a couple of vertical lines on her brow and was looking at her feet, as if she had dropped something there. Sheba also looked down to find what she was searching for, but seeing nothing there, she thought this must be the way Mrs Daanish gave a problem special consideration.

There was a strong gust of wind, and the dry leaves were heard dropping down to the ground in the silence of the campus. Sheba raised her head and looked up at the sky, not knowing why.

'And I am still worried…but what can I do anyway?' Shehla Daanish said and exhaled deeply. 'Now, I will be able to work there peacefully at least, because Daanish will be looked after properly. Otherwise it would have been very difficult.' She smiled and looked about, not at the nurse and Professor Daanish, but only at the students.

Sheba observed that Aaftab Aalam and Saagar were looking at her face like dunces. Diljeet and Mayuri had expressions of near hatred on their faces. And Sheba was looking at everything expressionlessly. Shehla Daanish had also noticed these expressions, but she kept smiling; and this, too, was noticed by Sheba.

After a while, the students got up, one by one. When they came out of the garden, Sheba stopped near the small door at the gate. She looked at the upper edge of the door and smiled sadly. On the green painted wood, there was a faded patch. Many days ago, Aaftab had written '*Daanish Kadah*'—The House of Wisdom—on the door with his beige highlighter. All the five students were there when Aaftab had written these two words. They all stopped when they saw Sheba looking at it.

'Is this the end of Daanish Kadah?' Sheba spoke in a low voice, as if to herself, but it was heard by everyone around.

'I hope not,' Saagar said and released a deep, sad breath.

'Yes, it will be ruined, I can see that,' Diljeet said with a gloomy face.

'Be positive, can't you?' Mayuri said, looking at their faces one by one. 'Sir will be fine by the grace of God,' she added softly.

'Oh, come on! I have seen your God, okay!' Saagar said angrily and shook his head. 'The world gets to see such an intellectual only once in centuries. What had he done to your God that…' Saagar looked up at the sky.

'Stop talking like that, you atheist!' Mayuri too shook her head.

'Don't you believe in God?' Sheba asked, looking at Saagar's face.

'Let's ask Diljeet.' Aaftab Aalam set his eyes on Diljeet's face.

'Hey you pretty *sardarni* (sikh woman), have you seen God, I mean *Wah-i-Guru*?!'

'I don't really know guys,' Diljeet said.

'Mrs Daanish did not even give us any tea,' Aaftab Aalam sighed deeply.

'I wonder if she even gives sir anything to eat?' Diljeet said; there was loud laughter this time too.

All of them moved as one towards the cafeteria. When they came out of the cafeteria after tea and snacks, the peacocks on the trees of the vast campus were about to tuck their bills under their wings. Small bats were already out, flying about in the sky to hunt small insects. They were on their way to the hostels. It was the boys' hostel first and then, a little further away, was the girls' hostel building. When the girls got there, it was almost dark.

'We are late,' Mayuri said, looking at the sky; everyone else looked up too.

'Hey, where is this kite going so late?' Diljeet asked, surprised.

'It may have an appointment with someone!' Mayuri retorted laughingly.

'It isn't a kite, it's a bat, you wise ladies!' Sheba said smiling.

'Bat?'

'Yes ma'am!'

'Oh no, my dear it's a kite. Bats aren't so big…look at it, it's certainly a kite!'

'They are big, even bigger than that. Kites are in their nests by this time. And see, they fly differently. Look at them properly; see how many of them are in the sky now, like a rally. There is a difference in the way the birds and bats fly. Birds move their wings in a circular motion and bats just move them up and down. Actually, these are not their wings, it is the skin joined to their arms. If you look at them against the background of the sky, you can see it is brown, not black like we always think. The skin is so thin that light passes through it and it looks brown.'

'Yes, these are bats indeed! They have no tail!' Mayuri clapped loudly and joined her hands. 'We do not have such big bats in our Valley; they are small in size. But these bats are also very dangerous, they suck the blood of animals… even humans,' Sheba added seriously.

'What is so special about sucking blood? If we are late by another few minutes, the warden will suck our blood too; run, let's run!' Diljeet said, and all three girls started running, laughing out loud.

Reaching the hostel gate, Sheba saw a small owlet peeping through the hollow of a dried mulberry tree and moving its dotted feathers, chirping. There were big owls in her Valley, and they never chirped but only hooted. Sheba looked at it for some moments and smiled. It sounded as if someone had rung a bell made in imitation of the call of a bulbul. Hearing it, the girls had another hearty laugh and stopped, gasping for air as they had been running and laughing. The tiny bird, with its small round head and pointed slender ears, looked at them with its half-open big, round eyes. In the dim light of the evening, he looked like a little round man in an overcoat with his hands in the pockets, deep in thought, contemplating some intense issue.

Dr Daanish was looked after by these five students, who nursed him together, or one by one. Aaftab Aalam was in charge of the salary of the nurse and the domestic help. The rations for the month and the everyday menu were Diljeet's duty. Consulting the doctor and giving the patient his medicines was Sheba's job. Mayuri and Saagar looked after everyday arrangements, advised the nurse and the helper, and kept an eye on the cleanliness of the house.

Sheba's new guide was also Professor Daanish's fan. She was very kind to her students, and was worried about his health like them.

Dr Daanish had been unwell for almost a year. There was no improvement in his condition.A few years ago, he had retired from a university, but they gave him an extension for another two years. After that, he was employed at this university but for the last one year, he was unwell. He could neither teach, nor read or write anything. He would just look around blankly. Now, for some days, he looked quite weak. Though his students cared for him to the best of their abilities, still, they thought that they could not look after him properly—and were sad that their inexperience might be the cause of the professor's ill health. They often discussed this sadly. Their new guide, Dr (Ms) Mumtaz Aalam, would try to cheer them up.

'Please do not blame yourself for this; it is such an illness that one is almost helpless. No one can do better than the way you all look after him.'

'But madam, he has almost stopped eating,' Diljeet said. She hardly ever looked as serious as she looked now. 'I ask him so often to eat something, but he hardly listens to me,' she added.

'Will he be all right madam? Or…' Saagar asked gloomily and Mayuri interrupted him, 'Don't you have faith in God?'

'The doctor keeps saying we have to wait for some more days, but I don't see any signs of recovery and…' Sheba was interrupted by the doorbell.There was a letter from the Vice-Chancellor's office.

'Madam,' Aaftab said, extending his hand with the letter towards Ms Mumtaz Aalam. He looked shocked. 'This… this…' he looked at the other students. 'Sir to vacate this residence, madam?' Aaftab asked in a low tone, and all the innocent faces looked even more sad and worried. Ms Aalam was about to say something when the phone started ringing. The nurse answered the call; Mrs Daanish was on the line. She told the nurse that she will not be granted any leave this year. No one was surprised to hear this, neither the patient nor the attendants. Ms Aalam quickly took the phone from the nurse.

'Actually, Mrs Daanish, his deputation is over and he has to vacate the flat,' Ms Aalam told her.

'Sorry, I beg your pardon, what did you say?' the voice on the phone asked loudly.

'His term is over and he has to vacate the flat...' Ms Mumtaz Aalam looked at the people around her. She sounded quite low.

'Under such conditions...can't he get any concession as a special case madam?' the voice on the phone was heard saying.

'We are trying our best but we are not sure...'

'You must make some alternative arrangements, madam! How can I help you, being so far away?! Please make some arrangements for the time being. When I come there, I will bring him here, and I will be sending money till I get some days off. Do not worry on that account. OK then, thanks! Talk to you later,' Mrs Daanish said and the line was disconnected. The speaker was off but she was easily heard in the whole room.

Ms Mumtaz Aalam stood still with the receiver in her hand for some moments. Then she put it back on the cradle and returned to her chair. So many faces were waiting for her reaction. These students did not look like young people at a university. They seemed like immature primary school children with blank expressions, and looked very perturbed and unsure of themselves. Ms Aalam felt her heart overflowing with motherly feelings for them. This hot blood is so innocent, thought Ms Aalam, but these broad shoulders and firm jaws are actually soft, like kneaded clay...that's why they can be moulded in any shape, and one can win their confidence, and make or break them. She looked at Aaftab's and Saagar's face, and then towards the girls. Diljeet had tears in her eyes. Mayuri looked at the sky through the window and Sheba glanced at Ms Aalam's face with questions in her sad eyes, as if waiting for something.

'Come what may…we will not let sir go anywhere in such a condition,' Aaftab Aalam said with determination.

'Even if madam…we…have to go on a strike, strike!' Saagar said in a protesting tone and Ms Aalam shook her head.

'No, no…things would not go to that extent, babies, we will do something…everything will be all right.'

She looked at their faces.

'Please, madam!' the girls said. They had a gleam of hope on their faces.

A long letter was written to the Vice-Chancellor signed by many students and teachers, seeking to reverse the decision. It worked and the decision was withdrawn till further orders.

Dr Mumtaz Aalam stopped near the library when she spotted Sheba, and called out to her. Sheba ran over to her. 'We have a one-year extension now, at least,' said Ms Aalam.

'Thank God, madam! This is very good news, but…' Sheba said, walking alongside Ms Aalam.

'Do you have any apprehensions?' Ms Aalam asked and stopped.

'Madam, I was wondering…where will sir go after that?' asked Sheba, looking at Ms Aalam's face, and then turned her eyes elsewhere.

'His wife will come and take him with her,' Ms Aalam said and began to walk again. Sheba also walked along.

'No, madam, I do not think so. She is very career-minded…she is least bothered about his health,' Sheba said.

'Oh, is that so? But why…and what about the children?'

'They don't have any.'

'But Mrs Daanish went abroad recently, isn't that so?'

'No madam, she has been there for many years now—she has a job there, and comes over here only during the Christmas holidays; and this, year she is not coming at all. Earlier, sir would also visit her there, but...'

'Oh, then, but maybe she would live with him again because of his ill-health?'

'Yes maybe, but…'

'But?'

'If that does not happen, then who will take care of him?'

'We are all here. We will manage.'

'But how long?' Sheba said, stopping near a gulmohur tree.

'Yes, what else can be done? But doesn't he have any other relatives?' Ms Aalam asked, sitting down stunned on an iron bench fixed to the trunk of the tree. The bench was painted brown. She was wearing a sari of the same shade. She was a 50-year-old woman with a kind face, who looked younger than her years, and had attractive features. Seeing the fair face in the brown background, Sheba smiled.

'Do sit down, Sheba! Oh, I am so tired.'

'Yes madam.'

'Yes…what were you saying?' Ms Aalam asked. Sheba also sat down on the same bench at a little distance and looked at her for a moment; she appreciated the nice feeling of being invited in a friendly manner by her guide. At this stage of university education, teachers and students sometimes become really good friends, Sheba thought affectionately.

'Yes madam, he has an older sister. She is a widow and stays in her hometown, living on her garden and some land. She, too, doesn't have any children. But that is a remote area. Looking after him and arranging for the medicines will be very difficult for her. She had come to see Daanish sir once, bringing some fruit from her orchard. She thanked us profusely, and then left. And she is too old, madam; it must be very difficult for her to even look after herself,' Sheba explained.

'You are right. When are you appearing for your viva, is it the next month or after the vacations?'

'Yes madam, after the vacations.'

'Our Head of the Department praised that project you had worked on. By the way, what are your plans after your doctorate?'

'I am not sure madam. My family is going to marry me off, but I want to pursue my career…wish to do my D.Lit. after this as well…Society faces new challenges… our generation too…the whole world is confused…This globalization…some people trying to alter the very many different civilizations and turn them all into one global culture…not to forget these increasing nuclear forces and capitalists' pressures on politics around the world. Where are humans going? Where? When I think about all this, it drives me crazy...We have to...our generation has to do something, otherwise no one knows what the result of all this greed will be. I also want to look for a solution to all this...I will write on this, perhaps go abroad to study these topics as well.'

'Won't you go for a job?' Ms Aalam asked, looking at her face. A cool breeze blew and orange petals of the gulmohur flowers began to fall on the hair of the women sitting on the bench.

'No madam, I will not be able to concentrate on my studies then,' Sheba answered, picking up a tiny branch of gulmohur and looking at its leaves keenly.

'Oh yes, that's true! If you're bound to a desk job, your priorities will be taken over by responsibilities. Anyway, I wish you luck!' Ms Aalam said, getting up.

'Thank you, madam!' Sheba also stood up.

Ms Mumtaz Aalam had already taken a right turn to the faculty residential area.

The Sleeping Moonlight

That evening when Sheba received a phone call from home, Seemeen also spoke to her. 'Aunty, tell me who I am!'

Sheba heard the voice and recognized it. Yasir also had a girlish voice, but a little heavier. 'Yes, you are…I know Yasir cannot have such a sweet voice.'

'Then who am I?' the voice on the phone became chirpy.

'Two people can call me aunty in this world and both have sweet voices, so I am sure that you are my little, sweet, precious, darling Seemeen, isn't it so?'

The laughter of a child like the tinkling of *paazeb* (an anklet) was heard on the phone. Hearing this, Sheba was all love. 'I miss you so much, my little doll!' she said.

'I miss you too Aunty Sheba, that's why I stayed back at Nanna Jaani's house. Nanna Jaani told me today that she would call you in the evening, so I…'

Sheba heard her laughter again. 'So, you…you what?' Sheba asked smiling.

'So, I was sure mamma would not allow me to…Yasir and brother Aasim are also here today, with Aunty Phirki!'

(Seemeen called Farkhanda *Phirki*—a spool—instead of Farkhi, ever since she was a child. After that, Suraya Begum also lovingly called her Phirki occasionally). So, I told mamma that my leg hurt…and everybody knows Nanna Jaani has a massage oil. But when Nanna Jaani came with the bottle of oil, I told her I have no pain,' Seemeen said laughingly. 'When are you coming Aunty Sheba? I have to talk to you about so many things, do my hair like you and study like you. I want to become like you,' she said in her innocent voice, which had a genuine seriousness in it. A smile appeared on Sheba's lips.

'All right, fine…the vacations are close by. I will be there with you the very next day of the vacations!'

'Please let me know about the time and the flight number the day you make the reservation, because we have to make many arrangements for the vacations.'

'Yes, my doll…I will sure do as you say.' That evening, when Sheba went to bed, she missed home badly. 'Cute children of our household,' she said softly. Aasim was also one of them as Farkhanda loved him like her own son Yasir, and Ammi also treated him like Farkhanda's child.

Missing Aasim made Sheba think about Nuzhat, too. Her patience was sometimes discussed at Sheba's home. This time, she would meet Nuzhat and talk to her for a long time, Sheba thought. But the vacations seemed still so far away. How she herself eagerly waited for the vacations when she was a child! She would spend the few days of the summer vacations on the family estate with her cousins. Sheba suddenly felt as if she was smelling the magic fragrance of the peel of ripening walnuts and their leaves. Red poppies, black at the centre, which grew wild on the sides of the fields appeared before her eyes. She remembered the backyard of the village bungalow where the fragrance of marigolds made the surroundings magical. Sometimes, when she went there and moved from one flowerbed to another all by herself and sat in the eastern corner on a big stone slab under the plum tree, it would give her immense pleasure—as if the whole world belonged to her. And when, in those silent surroundings, some child would call her name and reach there to intrude in her domain, she would be awakened from her reveries. She would then be lost in another day dream, in which there were holidays and cousins, plenty of servants who would act upon their every wish, many silken-haired young lambs and kids, the big horses and the small colts and ponies—including the one the children were allowed to ride on, though only if the horseman was there. A smile appeared on Sheba's lips. She remembered the son of KamaalJoo, the syce. The word 'Joo' was used after the name of working-class elders as a mark of respect.

Abbu used to say that the word 'Joo' had reached the Valley with the Jews, who travelled with Alexander the Great to this land. People living in the hills of Kashmir still like to name their sons Israel, the land of the Jews; and the names of many places in Kashmir resemble the names of places in Israel. People belonging to the Kashmiri Pundit race have a marked resemblance to Israelis.

The syce's son had dark skin, long teeth, a big nose and broad nostrils. When he ran with some riding child, his hair fell over his forehead and he, too, looked like a horse. But Sheba had never told this to any other child as they would have made fun of him for this, whereas Sheba liked his face because of his features, or in spite of his features, as he looked very innocent.

Abbu had once said his mare was taller than the tallest black horse in the present lot of horses. She belonged to the real Gael race. She was pure white and her sweat had a pleasant smell. When Abbu offered her a ball of butter on his palm, the mare would lick it up at one go. Whenever Abbu related this event, he held his palm before him as if it still had a lump of butter on it. And when they went to the village in their new jeep, Abbu had declared that his mare was faster than the jeep. So, a driver was arranged from the city. Next day both the uncles in the jeep and Abbu on his mare went on a round of their lands and in between, wherever they had to stop—like at a spring or by a stream, a particular tree or hillock where lunch, supper, buttermilk or tea was served—Abbu reached first, even though it was a level dirt road to drive the jeep on. When Abbu spoke about the mare's death, his eyes filled with tears but before they could fall, he wiped them off pretending to rub his eyes.

The paternal aunts who lived there wore similar clothes, though they had different temperaments.The elder uncle had married a farmer's daughter as his second wife, whose skin was milk white. But her teeth looked dirty, like overripe grains of yellow maize. Whereas his first wife's smile would show her gleaming white, beautifully spaced and even teeth, like milky corn. But the brown-skinned first aunt would hardly smile. Some years ago Sheba had once said to the second aunt, looking at her face intently for some time, that the first aunt had better teeth than her, and the second aunt had looked at Sheba's face in astonishment for some moments hearing this. Lying on her hostel bed, Sheba remembered her second aunt's surprised reaction and burst into laughter.

But the first aunt always enjoyed the right of being the first lady in the family. She was the one whose decisions were followed by everyone, and all the keys were tied to a corner of *her* dupatta. When the elder uncle bought Bhai Jaan a bicycle, he taught his second wife to ride it too. He had made a statue of his younger wife which he had fixed in a cabinet in a corner of his bedroom wall behind a glass screen that could not be moved from its place, and could not be touched without breaking the glass. Sheba had often tried hard to move the glass with her thumb and first finger but with no success.

The dresses for the aunts were cut and stitched at home from the same length of cloth. The children's clothes were also sewn by the tailor at home, or bought in the city or some other state, which Sheba's parents usually brought to the village.

And there was a sketch of Uncle Benazeer near the western entrance of the bungalow, carved on one of the big stone slabs forming the base of the building. He did it before committing suicide, after he was deceived in love. In the beginning, the people of the household were probably saddened looking at it; but for Sheba's generation, the whole account was a mysterious story, as it had no emotional value for them anymore. But the story was related frequently by them and everyone listened to it with great interest. Sheba, while passing by the door, would always look at the picture keenly.

Sheba thought of all her cousins. There was little Zaitoon, who was always smiling, walking around barefoot, and the thorns would not prick her delicate feet. Zaitoon would be grown up by now. God knows who she would be married to. God knows if she had a pair of chappals now, Sheba mused.All the cousins who were living in different places by now—some in the city, some in another state, and some in other countries, at a college or university. Lying on her bed in the hostel, Sheba sighed deeply. Last time, Abbu had said he would move to the village after marrying Sheba off because he missed the place very much. He said he wanted to be buried in the village. 'May God bless Abbu with a long life!' Sheba said to herself.

Sheba changed her side towards the window. There were stars in the black sky, but not as many as she could see from her lawn in Srinagar or in the vast sky over the village bungalow. Here, they were very few, dimly peeping from the polluted sky. Sheba's sleep had vanished. She pulled the bedside table drawer open and took out a book, switched on the lamp on the table by her bed and started reading its last pages again; it was Shakespeare's *Othello*. And after some time, the book was lying upside down on her chest and she was deep in sleep.

Next evening, Sheba was told on the phone that Abbu had gone to the village in connection with his claim for his share of the property and had fallen ill there. The day before, elder uncle had called them at home and everyone there was going to the village. Ammi was trying to hide her choked voice on the phone. Shocked, Sheba almost collapsed on her bed. My poor Abbu! He should not have gone to that hilly area, no one needs any land, but everyone needs Abbu. Ammi needs him, and the children too. How weird her uncles had been, wanting to justify ownership over the hundreds of kanals of land, valuing it as equal to a single bungalow in the city, whereas they had already sold the other bungalow in the city saying it was their share, and Abbu had never disputed that. They were so sure of this justification that they told Abbu to file a case in the District Court of the area when Abbu asked for his share from the vast estate. As the case related to property in the village, it could not be contested in any other city court. Abbu never wanted to take family matters to the court but the wrongful claims of his brothers finally compelled him to do so.

Friends saw Sheba off, promising her that they will pay greater attention to looking after Dr Daanish. No one had really realized as to when Sheba had taken charge of Daanish Kadah, with others just following her instructions.

The flight to her city seemed to be very long that day, and she was exhausted when she finally reached home. Looking at her weak, tired mother, she found some strength in herself but felt that her mother became weaker when she saw her. Suraya Begum kept looking at her pretty daughter who had come home after one long year, and whose Abbu was not there to receive her at the airport. Her mother's expressions gave her a helpless feeling of insecurity; she hugged her and cried. No, she did not cry—hugging her mother, she wiped her tears silently and placed her arm behind her mother's shoulder. Her mother had approached her with open arms and she felt like crying though.

The journey to the village had always been her favourite journey but today, waves of sadness washed over her mind time and again. She occasionally looked at the reflections of Ammi, Baaji and Farkhanda in the rear-view mirror. Baaji's husband was driving and no one talked to anyone. Farkhi felt nauseous like always. She always had this problem even as a child. It was as if Sheba had returned to her childhood. At that time, when the clean window of the bus got stained and Farkhi began to stink, Sheba would shift to some other seat as many seats became vacant while reaching the village because the border area started soon after the surrounding area of their village. It was rumoured that the tunnel-like, difficult and almost unapproachable path on the east of their village reached to the border of Russia.

Sheba would then sit on different seats in the bus, one by one, till Baaji would scold her for jumping around. When she would leave Farkhi and go to another seat, Farkhi would look at her in a strange way, and then she would try not to look into Farkhi's eyes. And it was very difficult to make Farkhi understand that even mentioning the word 'vomit' would make Sheba nauseous too. Farkhi was not steadfast in many matters either, as she would also sometimes join Baaji in the false complaints against her. And that too for just a piece of chocolate or a slice of pickle from Baaji, as the jars were placed on the uppermost shelf in the kitchen and only Baaji could reach up there. And sometimes Sheba, after getting a beating from Baaji—even without having done anything wrong—would forget the pain, and would not complain to Ammi, for a few slices of carrot pickle. How foolish, what a stupid girl she was!

Sitting at the back, Sheba caught a glimpse of her face in the rear-view mirror and turned her face towards the window. That little, frightened, stupid girl….No, no, no…no self-pity! I must not succumb to self-pity.

'To remember your past miseries means to sadden your present and undermine the future,' Daanish sir had once said.

I must not dwell on these thoughts and weaken myself, Sheba thought to herself, shook her head and, turning away from the car window, unconsciously looked at Baaji sitting in the front seat with her husband. She was fast asleep. Sheba again turned her face towards the window. Baaji could sleep anywhere, even if it was noisy. But Sheba could not go to sleep unless she had her own bed or some temporary arrangement especially made for her. Sheba tried to look at Baaji's reflection in the rear-view mirror but she could not see it. However, she could easily imagine Baaji sleeping as her eyes were always half open, with a trickle of saliva always flowing out from the side of her mouth towards her ear. And if she had a hand under her cheek, the saliva would smear her hand too. That looked so gross! Just as while eating a cherry, one unknowingly chews on an insect in the cherry, which feels like grit between the teeth, and which Sheba would spit out immediately and then keep rinsing her mouth again and again!

The car hit something on the road and everyone felt the jolt. Ammi, who sat near Sheba, looked around and turned her tired eyes towards the road. Baaji coughed and cleared her throat, rubbed her nose with the back of her right hand, and went back to sleep. It was a speed breaker which, being higher than usual, had hit the front bumper of the car. Farkhanda had her head on Ammi's shoulder and was deep in thought. Ammi had also rested her cheek on Farkhanda's head.

The road had been widened and bituminised. It looked black and shiny, and was level and smooth now. As soon as they saw the hills, they could see many big and small monkeys, but the broad and noisy stream which flowed by the side of the jungle was nowhere to be seen now. There were dull stones in its place. The colourful stones, which would once shine like silver at the bottom of the stream in the crystal-clear water, looked dull and colourless now. When a bus would drive through it, the spray of the water would be splashed up to the windows, and the children screamed and shouted in excitement. They would hang out of the windows, and get soundly scolded for that. Sometimes, they would spot a driver or his helper in the stream, with his trousers rolled up above the knees, washing his truck. At that time, the children would feel a strong urge to jump out of the bus and get into the water up to their knees and vigorously throw buckets of water on the truck.

Even sleeping children would wake up, listening to the singular and exciting sound of the bus crossing the stony waterway. The jeep would not make as much noise as the bus would; still, it was quite loud. Though Abbu could have stopped the jeep at any place he wished, he never stopped it at the stream. He said that the water was very cold and the children would have aching feet till who knows when. But even without getting into the water, the legs of all the three children would hurt every now and then, and Ammi would get tired, massaging their calves.

A school bus with students singing loudly on their way to a picnic passed their car, and Sheba recalled that it was the same hymn that was sung in her school too. Sheba was one of the three girls who sang it—standing on the stage, facing the other children—every morning. But after many years, when she came to know that the line '*lappeaatihaidua banketamannameri*' was actually '*lab pe aati hai dua ban ke tamanna meri*' (my heart's desire comes to my lips as my prayer), a smile appeared on her lips.

Abbu should be fine, dear God! She prayed from the bottom of her heart. The weather played hide and seek throughout the journey. It would rain heavily sometimes, and sometimes it would be a light downpour. It started snowing when they reached the hills, in big and small flakes. The small flakes were so tiny that they were like some insects even smaller than mosquitoes flying around. But soon, they were falling hard and thick.

The further they went, the more heavily it snowed. The car bumped against some small rock again. Sheba began to worry again for her Abbu. He was not well. It was almost evening by the time they reached the village. Ice cold winds welcomed them the moment they stepped out of the car. It was *very* cold. Abbu was lying almost unconscious in a semi-dark room. His brothers were away somewhere. The aunts told Ammi that the doctor had visited him, and had said that he would regain consciousness very soon.

When the crowd moved away from comatose Abbu's bed, it was Sheba's turn to go to him. She put her hand on his forehead, and he opened his eyes for a second, looked at her and closed them again. Abbu's big eyes were the same, and he looked at her as he would while playing with his children, and it seemed as if he would open his eyes wide and smilingly say 'I'm absolutely fine, I was just kidding'. But Abbu's broad chest, on which he used to have his three children lie together, and tell them a story, was shrunken. And it was not that soft now. Ammi once said that sometimes, when she was busy with household work, Abbu would comfort a child for some moments by cheating it with his breast. Sheba once again put her hand on Abbu's forehead and, seeing this, the others also tried, but Abbu did not open his eyes.

Everyone had left Abbu's room, except for Ammi and Sheba. When Ammi—after her *wudu* (ritual cleansing before prayers)—spread her prayer mat in a corner, Sheba went out of the room too. Abbu was not his usual self, and Sheba felt that a very sad night was approaching. It was not Abbu but someone else—weak and thin, lying on the bed helplessly, who could not even open his eyes. When he had opened his eyes earlier, it was without wanting to…it was just a reflex action, the body's reaction to a sudden touch.

Sheba was going to think about this the whole night. She was probably going to cry as well, as she was very restless. She went to Abbu's room again and again, and came back after a glance but she could not go far from the room as her childhood, holding a treasure of memories in its arms, was knocking at her heart. On such evenings the children would return home singing and jumping, collecting walnuts, and suddenly running fast in an attempt to catch a bird pecking on the grass. Bowls of cream would await them to be mixed in their salted tea, the aroma of corn and wheat parathas with fresh butter on them would spread far and wide, and pull in the children fast with invisible chains of appetizing smells.

Abbu had not eaten anything for two days. It was not an asthma attack because he was breathing normally, but the illness had begun with an attack. After that the doctor had given him some medicine and his breathing was better, but since then, he was just lying unconscious.

The next day, Sheba was awakened by the sound of Abbu coughing; it was late in the morning. Some of the young children in the big house were still asleep. She ran to Abbu's room. He was sitting on his bed, and Ammi was feeding him something with a spoon. Sheba shouted Abbu's name smiling excitedly. She went to him and he looked at her smiling. 'How is my Abbu?' she asked, nestling her head in Abbu's lap, but Abbu did not caress her. When Sheba placed his hand on her head, Abbu gently stroked her hair just once and opened his mouth to await a spoonful of bread soaked in tea, as Ammi had asked him to. Sheba suddenly sat up. Ammi's face was clouded with gloom but she had a sad smile on her lips.

'Ammi, Abbu is not very well…isn't it so?' Sheba asked, looking at her parents.

'He will be all right, InshAllah! Today, he has regained consciousness,' Ammi said in a depressed voice.

'He…he does not talk. Does he recognize any one?'

'He asked for his morning tea earlier, and then told Farkhi she had lost weight and looked weak.'

'And?'

'And nothing else…sometimes I feel he wants to say something but then he closes his half-open mouth and is silent. He's done it again and again since morning.' Ammi turned to him with another spoonful but he kept looking at her without opening his mouth.

'Please open your mouth and eat something. You have grown so weak…you…you…' Suraya Begum said in a tearful voice but Najam Khan kept looking at her face without any expression.

'Abbu, please eat something,' Sheba pleaded in a trembling voice. Tears appeared in her eyes and rolled down her cheeks. Suraya Begum gestured to her not to cry although her own eyes were full of tears.

'It means...that...Abbu...Ammi...Abbu...now...'

'No, my child...Abbu will be fine.' Ammi wiped her eyes with her soft dupatta and Abbu looked at them in turn, with a look of astonishment on his face.

'Yes,' Abbu said in a soft voice, 'do not cry.' He smiled too. Ammi offered him a spoon again but he shook his head.

'No...no...' Abbu said, like an annoyed child, and looked at the door.

'That...that...' he said again.

'What, Abbu...who?' asked Sheba.

'That...that...that...'

'Tell me please...what is it? Who are you asking for?' Suraya Begum asked, looking at his face keenly, but he did not utter another word.

Sheba's heart was pounding hard. She felt as if someone was ripping her soul out of her body, and she wriggled restlessly. The thought kept coming to her mind every now and then that Abbu would not survive. She rushed out of the room and ran to the backyard.

The big stone slab near the base of the plum tree close to the broad trunk of the walnut tree was now clear, as the snow had melted away. Being wet, the light green stone of the slab looked dark green. In the morning light, the plum tree's autumn-stricken branches were casting their weak shadows on it. Sheba sat down on the ice-cold slab, put her head on her drawn-up knees and began to sob. After some time, she heard a child crying loudly and raised her head from her knees. The sky was clouded over again. There were no marigold plants near the compound wall as they die in the cold winter. The flowerbeds were filled with the water from melted snow.

Many of her cousins were not at home. Bhai Jaan was in another state; his younger sister lived with her husband at another place. The brother younger than her was away, studying in a distant state. The first uncle, who had married a second wife in his middle age, had three children by her; two were asleep and the third one was crying noisily.

When Abbu's condition remained stable for some three or four days, the married daughters decided to leave. Ammi wanted to move Abbu to the city but uncle assured her that he could be treated very well in the village too, as it was not like the old days and all the new treatments were now available there as well. So, Ammi decided to stay back.

'You should also leave, my child' she said, looking at Sheba, who was sitting near Abbu's feet on the bed.

'No, Ammi. We will all go together.'

'Why don't we take Abbu with us to the city?' Sheba asked, looking at Abbu's expressionless face, which had a childlike innocence on it. He did not know what they were talking about but looked at everyone's face silently.

'No, my dear, he will be given the same treatment here too. The medicines and good food…here, he can get comparatively purer food stuff. I, too, can stay here with him; if we admit him to a hospital there, they may not allow an attendant with him,' Suraya Begum explained.

'Abbu! Let's go home...would you like to come to the city, Abbu?' Sheba asked, looking at her father's face as she sat before him.

'That...that...that...' Abbu said again, and did not say anything comprehensible after that.

Farkhanda entered the room. Abbu looked at her keenly. She had trimmed her hair short. 'When did you trim your hair, my child?' Najam Khan asked, and everyone's face shone with happiness.

'Abbu! You are fine, now we will go home...' Sheba said quickly and Najam Khan looked at her face.

'That...that...that...that,' Najam Khan said once again, and looked towards the window from where he could see the lines of trees in the fruit gardens. He did not say a word after that, and closed his lips.

'He will be fine...you should go home now,' Ammi said, looking at her daughters.

'But Ammi!' Sheba remonstrated, looking at her mother helplessly.

'My presence is enough for him here. I am fine and there are so many people around. People come to see him from distant villages, there is nothing wrong in staying here. You, too, shall leave with your sisters, Sheba. God has been kind to us as he can walk, and he's talking too. He will be better within a few days, and then we will also come, Allah. Isn't that right? You will have your vacations then as well, so do not waste your time, my child!' Suraya Begum said, and Sheba looked at her face silently.

'And you also go and look after your home,' Suraya Begum said, looking at Faheema who had just entered the room, and looked towards the other window. She could see the scene outside through its half-drawn curtain.

The snow from the last few days had melted away in the morning sun, and some patches of ground looked dry. In the fields, the roots and the cut off stems of the corn plants from the last season looked like big thorns, and there was not a leaf on the walnut trees. But now the whole sky was white. It looked as if it was going to snow again.

Suraya Begum kept looking towards the window. Many moments passed silently. 'Oh yes, it could be difficult to drive later. The roads will be bad because of the snow, Ammi is right,' Faheema broke the silence and everyone's thoughts returned to the room, as if from some strange journey. 'Yes Baaji, we must get ready,' Farkhanda said, shaking her head, and stood up.

Sheba arrived at the hostel with sad eyes and a pale face. Mayuri was not in the room. Being tired, she lay down on the bed without taking a bath. She should have slept as she was worn-out, but God alone knew where her sleep had gone. It was already evening and the silence of the hostel was broken by the sounds of other students talking, but her mind was not able to understand anything. She could only see the white ceiling of the room—all else was dark. She took a deep breath and just dozed off. But after a few minutes, she was awakened by a scary dream. She sat up on the bed. Her heart was beating fast.

'Where are you Mayuri?' Sheba murmured to herself.

'I am here, Sheba. I was quiet lest I woke you up,' Mayuri said, and switched on the lights.

'How is Abbu?' Mayuri asked, sitting on the edge of Sheba's bed.

'Slightly better. But I'm scared...I don't know what's in store for us, I'm really worried.'

'No, everything will be fine. You should be brave! There are some letters for you, would you like to have a look?' Mayuri said and went to the table. She got some envelopes out of the drawer.

'See this, I got a letter like this as well, it's an interesting offer...and this too.'

'Yes, I remember. We had applied for the fellowship in Canada, and now, after one year...' Sheba said, cutting the envelope open.

'They have agreed; it is a very good offer, Sheba. We will go.'

'I don't know...but you must go. I will think about it later.'

'We won't get such an opportunity again. I thought we both would go together, and remain together like always.'

'How can we two remain together, Mayuri? Abbu's condition is uncertain. And you? Your folks want to see you settled, they want a Non-Resident Indian (NRI) for you. And there, you can have this chance too, isn't that so?'

'Yes, that's true but...'

'But we are no longer children now. We've grown up, we are grown-ups! We have to understand our responsibilities.'

'Oh yes, that reminds me. We have a seminar, Sheba, in Aligarh...will you come? Sir wants us to go as well.'

'Oh...how is he?'

'He is better! Absolutely fit mentally—understands everything but cannot speak properly. Sometimes, he only remembers when we prompt him. But he has not suffered any memory loss, it's just that he cannot articulate some words at times, otherwise he knows everything. But poor soul has become physically handicapped, and that is the...'

'Yes; that is a tragedy, a healthy mind but an unhealthy body. It is better if a person does not know at all what he is going through and becomes like a child again—simple and innocent,' Sheba said. Her voice had become very low. She took a deep breath and opened another envelope.

'It is a two-day conference. We will go Sheba! Please don't say no...it will be a good change, and it will also give you a well-deserved break. Please, will you come?'

'Alright,' Sheba softly responded.

'Hurrah, thank you!' Mayuri cried and, jumping from the bed, stood in front of Sheba. 'And you know, the topic is so interesting! "Influence of the Electronic Media on Society", and I am loaded with that, and you too!' Mayuri said, and after taking a full round of the room, sat down on Sheba's bed again.

'How?'

'I had the same topic in my M.Phil. "Media and Society", we could draw upon all that, right?'

'Yes, and my topic was "Common Customs in Different Societies", Sheba promptly said. A smile had already appeared on her face when Mayuri shouted 'Hurrah'. She shared Mayuri's high spirits.

'May Bhagwan bless everyone with a friend like you,' Mayuri said, putting her arms around Sheba's neck. She kissed her forehead and went to her study table quickly.

'But Allah should not give a friend like you to anyone,' Sheba said in a serious tone.

'O God…what have I done?' Mayuri also asked seriously.

'Ruined my sad mood,' Sheba countered smilingly.

'Thank you Sheba, I jumped for joy to see you smiling. I just cannot see you unhappy and depressed! Now get up and take a bath. We will walk up to Daanish Kadah. Man is mortal, child, why waste life? This moment is fine, so why should we worry about, what is next?' Mayuri said, laughing.

'You keep saying that one should always think positively. This positivity straightens everything out and we must respect our soul, given to us by Bhagwan. Why torture our souls by remaining sad?' she added.

'Yes, you're right. I was ungrateful, giving way to negative thoughts, whereas there are many positive things to look forward to…but thank you, my dear, you are a good friend, Mayuri!'

'Great! Now get up,' Mayuri shouted, laughing. Sheba walked towards the bathroom.

There had been a very welcome new development in Professor Daanish's household. One of his old servants, hearing the news of his illness, had returned after five years. Actually, after the death of his wife, his daughter-in-law started acting as the master of the home. She was childless, and was annoyed with him without any reason. He was a quiet, honest man who would usually feel content with whatever little he had, and did not want to complain to his son and cause any trouble. On the pretext of a few days' visit to the city, he left his village forever. He knew his Sahib's household, and the word had reached him that his master needed him badly in his illness; and he, too, was in need of a job. He was, therefore, sure that his master would allow him to stay in his house.

Things turned out as he had hoped for. And from the day he returned to Daanish Kadah, the whole house looked tidy. Though taking time off from their busy schedule, the five students used to get confused. Sometimes, one of them would think that the nurse might have forgotten to give the professor his medicine—and that no other student would have got there either—and so, they would rush to Daanish Kadah, and the others would also think the same and reach there! The nurse would get very confused by all this and threaten to leave in bewilderment, but was somehow always entreated to stay back. Sometimes, the doctor was called twice a day; and sometimes, Professor Daanish's face was washed two—even three times a day! Professor also did not refuse his loving and kind students. He would not tell a student that the other one had already done that, and when students learnt this by any chance, they would feel embarrassed. Other things were also looked after in an orderly manner now. The students would often wonder how an aged, feeble villager could play such important role in an intellectual's life.

On seeing his old domestic help in his home again after all these years, a smile appeared on Professor Daanish's face; and Saleem Miyaan started sobbing.

Habitually nostalgic about old and new things, Sheba would always get lost in thoughts when lying in her bed at night. Last holidays, Farkhanda's children Yasir and Aasim—as Farkhanda took Aasim as her own child too—insisted that Sheba should spend some time at Aasim's home.

After much pleading, Ammi had allowed Sheba to stay there for one day, as it wasn't considered appropriate that a younger sister stay at her sister in-law's place without any reason. Furthermore, there was no other girl of Sheba's age there, and her sister Farkhanda also stayed in a separate house.

That night, the children and their aunt slept in the children's room. She shared Yasir's bed and across the centre table, Aasim lay in his own bed. They chatted for a long time, sang some songs and at last, Sheba sang them some lullabies and put them to sleep. She missed Seemeen a lot, but the little girl had not been allowed by Faheema to go with them. Seemeen had cried a lot and Sheba knew she must have cried for a long time and finally, exhausted, would have fallen asleep. Or maybe the innocent soul was still crying?Why is Baaji like that?

Lying on her bed, Sheba shook her head but did not shift her gaze from the night lamp giving a blue light.God knows how Daanish sir is doing; Diljeet, Mayuri and Saagar have also not called for many days. Tomorrow morning, rather early in the morning, I would call that pretty Sikh girl with a changed voice and surprise her, Sheba thought to herself. A smile appeared on her lips. She looked at the wall clock. Its radiant hands shone gently in the blue light of the night bulb. It was 2 am. Not disturbing Yasir, she got out of bed softly and went to the bathroom.While crossing the window, she happened to look at the magical view of the garden and stopped involuntarily. The tranquil moonlight peacefully rested on the green grass and colourful flowers. She suddenly felt like going to the lawn, sitting on the grass and becoming a part of the serenity. Be one with it. Be lost in its silence.Think about its cause and source. Be connected to its source and know from where this silence comes and where it will go, get connected with only this and break free of everything else. Just for this silence? Yes. But she had thought like this once before as well. When there was no silence. It had been an enormous, screaming noise but probably only she had heard it, and that was when Daanish sir was ill and Mrs Daanish was leaving for America. That time, Sheba happened to look at him. He looked at every face, one by one; he had no expression on his face but had a grave silence in his eyes, a screaming silence, and Sheba could see this silence shouting and crying in his one half-closed eye which was affected by the paralytic stroke. That day, Sheba desperately wanted to run away to a place where she would never see such a sight again, and where there would be no one to talk to—a desolate place, a jungle, a desert, a graveyard. What was the common link between the crying silence of Daanish sir's house and the singing silence of Aasim's home, that both inspired one to break all relations with everything?

Understanding something and not understanding many things, Sheba's feet were frozen near the window for some moments before she entered the washroom. Near the exhaust fan ventilator, she could hear sounds of people talking. The fan was off.

'Who could be awake this time of the night?' she thought for a second. She knew there was another bathroom adjacent to the next room, and the door between the two might have been left open—which is why she was hearing voices. Sheba was about to leave the bathroom when she heard someone sobbing; she could not take a step forward. It was a woman.

'Stop this drama now, I want to sleep!' said a male voice.

'I was sleeping too! You ruined my sleep and now say things which make one's heart bleed! You…you are not even …You have no fear of God!'

'Why don't you like me touching you? You would like someone else to do this…I know…' the man retorted with a strange laugh.

'Hold your tongue! You try to push me to the bedroom in everyone's presence when you are drunk…in such a shameful manner! I…' the woman said between sobs and the man shouted back, 'Stop this nonsense! I do it because

I do not want them to know that…that,' the man coughed loudly, 'and you spoiled my sleep! If you had any attraction, I would have slept peacefully by now! Like an insipid sin…I…unnecessarily…to my own self…without any reason…as if…'

'You should be ashamed of these shameless words… you…' the woman's pained voice was heard.

'Me, ashamed? Why? Look at her, how brazen she is! She has lost every bit of appeal…all my desire disappears when I go near her! And…she…' the man laughed again, tauntingly.

'Keep quiet now! You…yourself…yourself…you…'

'What? What has gone wrong with me? What do you mean? Oh…you are…you are very experienced with men! How do you know that…I…you whore…how you know… that…that…I…' the man shouted.

'Do not use abusive language! And do not test my patience, I…I…' the woman said, crying. The pitch of voice was quite high now. 'With constant drinking you have turned into a beast, and you are half mad…if you do not hold your dirty tongue…I…I swear…I will wake up mother and…'

'Yes, why should you care about her health and rest… the woman sleeping only after taking a pill is not your mother! She is my mother…and thinks of you as her daughter, and you…'

'What do you know of respect for relations…she is ill because of your bad habits and you certainly do not care for her! And…if, God forbid, your brother-in-law does this to your sister…would you tolerate this! Would you?'

'How dare you drag my sister in our family matters? Do not even dare to mention my sister's name!' the man shouted, and the sound of a slap was heard. The sobs changed into screams.

Sheba was shocked and just stood still there, looking at the ventilator. She had never been through something like this before. She could only understand that a man was insulting a woman, and that the woman seemed to be weak and utterly helpless.

She looked at the ventilator helplessly. Suddenly, she heard a faint noise behind her and on turning around, found Aasim sitting on his bed. His lips were drawn and he was looking at Sheba.

'Father is fighting with Pyaari,' Aasim said when his eyes met Sheba's.

'What?' Sheba was horrified. She looked at him and, shutting the bathroom door behind her, went to his bed.

'Abbu will hit Pyaari. Pyaari's ear was bleeding last week too…and Pyaari did not know about it. I told her about it.' He was crying and sobbing. Pearly tears dropping from his eyelashes and flowing down his flowery cheeks.

'You know, Aunty Sheba, I don't annoy Pyaari now. You can ask anybody…I am grown-up now.' He looked at Sheba for affirmation. Sheba nodded.

'Only Abbu hurts Pyaari. None other than him,' he continued helplessly and his voice rose. Yasir was breathing rhythmically in his sleep. The sound of his breathing died away and Aasim abruptly stopped talking, looking at him, alarmed. Yasir changed his side and began to breathe again as before.

'What should I do? Abbu is a bad person...' Turning his gaze from Yasir, Aasim looked at the bathroom door helplessly and kept crying.

'No child, please don't cry...everything will be fine,' Sheba said, reassuringly running her fingers through his hair. Her voice was choked.

'But you know, Aunty Sheba, I am not afraid of Abbu!' He abruptly wiped his tears and tried to control his sobbing. He was growing taller and thinner too. Trying to stop his sobbing, his thin ribs under his blue-bordered sky-blue night suit could be seen jerking in the light of the night bulb. His sky-blue suit looked white, and the blue edges at the end of his sleeves and pajama hems looked black.

'He is not scolding her anymore, they are sleeping now,' Sheba kissed his forehead and stroked his hair till he went to sleep again. While returning to her bed Sheba looked at the calm moonlight in the lawns once again, and then lay down. Her sleep had vanished. Her mind was in distress.

Many thoughts came to her mind, such as: humans are worse than beasts; and these men...man looks human... but man is not a human...made of some weird stuff... different from every living being...who has nothing to do with humanity, among others. Sheba restlessly looked towards Aasim's bed. The tears on his cheeks had dried but his eyelashes were still wet. (Inside Sheba's thinking brain, another brain of another Sheba was thinking). He can lie for his ego…and man is all ego, he relates everything to his ego. He can go to any extent to satisfy his ego…and a woman is a mere body for a man. But to a woman, the concept of relationships is related to the wholeness of the home and its social worth…and it is there till she loses her patience.

Sheba put her palm on Aasim's cheek and looked at the light-yellow, cup-shaped, canvas lampshade. One could see the delicately painted nightingales on it in the day but they were not visible now, as if they had flown away, thought the other Sheba's other brain again.

And…*this* is the weakness of women; after every bad experience she tries to begin anew in the hope of some peaceful moments again. And man thinks that she is scared and weak, and that he is strong—otherwise why would an educated and intelligent woman like Nuzhat take this continued abuse? And it is the bitter truth that an unfortunate majority of women in the world are the most helpless creatures…and within these abusive relationships that they endure, the language used by the perpetrator is such that it can pierce the victim's eardrums, and their hearing ability itself, and any other listener's ears too—like my ears. And who knows till how long these shameful words will reverberate in my mind and hurt my whole being. Sheba thought all this with closed eyes, but opened them again and looked at the ceiling bathed in blue light. Sound is the enemy of peace. She exhaled deeply and her eyes were filled with tears.

'Why not go to the grave now…to have…to have the blessing of silence…the calm of the grave is incomparable,' she thought ardently. There will be no voice…it will be her own self and her own silence—nature's actual gift, silence… motionless silence.Her heart calmed down by these thoughts. The same calm she had experienced some time ago when she had looked at the peaceful moonlight. Her sleepy eyes began to close but she opened them again.The gift of life is given to a person only once…she had to live…she had to work a lot…she had to live for her work…she had to live and work…she would live.

She closed her eyes and extended her arm to touch Yasir's forehead tenderly. The chubby little fellow had a layer of fat on his forehead, inside Sheba's thinking brain, the other Sheba's brain thought smilingly. All men are not alike…there are some who are full of humaneness, affection and motherliness; that's why the world still exists.

She turned to Yasir's side. 'Won't you be a nice man?' She softly kissed the cheeks of the six- or seven-year-old little man who slept beside her, and a smile came flying like a butterfly and alighted on her lips. She was about to sleep.

Lying on her hostel bed, Sheba remembered the softness of Yasir's forehead and a smile appeared on her lips. She closed her eyes, took a deep breath and went to sleep.

The university was closed for a fortnight by the authorities because of an agitation. Sheba went on a trip to her hometown. She even went to the village along with Farkhi's family. Abbu was like before, and so was the situation there. But Ammi seemed to be less sad and more hopeful. Abbu behaved like a peaceful child. And Sheba cried her heart out secretly at times.The 20-day vacation was over very soon. Sheba returned to the hostel and found it the same as she had left it. But Professor Daanish looked healthy; he had gained some weight. Saleem Miyaan looked after him well and the positive thing was that instead of two helpers, Daanish now walked with just Saleem Miyaan's help. Saleem Miyaan was sure that very soon, his beloved master would walk with the help of a stick—and that later he would not need even a stick.

His students were going to celebrate this—when suddenly, one fine morning, they realized that the dream of seeing Professor Daanish healthy again was not going to come true so soon. It was the day the department was holding a seminar titled 'New Global Challenges'. The students were getting him ready to take him to the event. All the four students were there, except Saagar. Dr Daanish obeyed them like a child. The girls selected a deep-blue suit for him from his wardrobe. When they selected a tie to match, there was disagreement about it between the students. Aaftab liked a tie which had red blocks on a blue background, but the girls liked a blue tie with diagonal black stripes. In the early days of his illness, Dr Daanish would smile at his students when the boys wanted him to relax in a lawn chair and the girls wanted him to take a walk. He would make a comment, though he could not speak the words properly, and address his pupils by their names. When Saagar entered the room, the argument was at its peak. He greeted his favourite professor and enquired about his health, but Dr Daanish looked at him blankly. The expression of familiarity that would appear on his face upon seeing his students was not there. When Saagar saw that his question did not bring any expression Dr Daanish's face, he was shocked; the other students were alarmed too.

Professor Daanish seemed to be deep in thought. They were talking to him like always, sometimes about the topic to be discussed at the seminar and sometimes about his health.

'Sir, what happened?' Mayuri asked, distraught.

But Dr Danish just kept looking at her face without any expression. It was then that they realized that although they had been there for the last one hour, he had not spoken a single word. He would look at his bookshelf repeatedly. When Sheba saw him looking towards his books, she understood the whole thing and was sad.

Sheba remembered when she was a child, tongas plied on the city roads. At a little distance from her home, there was a garden called Gol Bagh, and she once saw a big black horse sitting there. It looked bigger than the other horses, even when it was not standing. When Sheba's tonga passed by the garden she saw that looking at the horses harnessed to the tongas running, the huge black horse with a shining coat and healthy build would helplessly try to stand up but would end up just moving his neck from side to side. The horse would try again and again to stand, but to no avail.

The next day, Sheba went to see him in the park and saw that he had fractured his right hind leg, but his eyes were still set on the moving tongas and she saw the pain and sadness in his lovely, long-lashed big eyes. She sat down and cried bitterly.

Ammi had sadly told her that the fractured bone of a horse does not mend. That's why his master had abandoned him at Gol Bagh. Listening to this, Sheba had cried again, thinking that his cruel master had left him there to die—or maybe that the helpless owner had to abandon him there as he was not able to pull the tonga anymore, and the poor man just could not feed him any longer.

Abbu had explained that horses had no muscles below their knees, they had thick bones, and the blood circulation in them was very slow. He had also said that even a hairline fracture is a big problem for a horse, as it carries its almost 500-kilogram body weight on its four legs, and cannot support it on only three legs. A leg without muscles does not have proper blood circulation and the healing process is so slow that the wound gets infected.

Then after some days, Sheba saw that one of the eyes of the horse was missing. Ammi did not say anything to her, but told the servant that he should not take or bring children back by that road.

Gulla Bhai had said that some predator must have pulled out the horse's eye. Sheba had asked him what a predator was and Gulla Bhai had said 'one who preys on other animals or eats carrion, like a kite or a vulture'. Sheba had asked him what carrion was and Gulla Bhai had replied that it was a dead animal. After that, she did not eat anything and was ill for many days.When Sheba had recovered, she found that the horse was gone from the park.

Then Gulla Bhai told her that it might have died because of hunger or illness, or it may have been shot dead by the municipality and the carcass carried away, and Sheba had been down with fever for three more days. That incident took place decades ago but made Sheba sad even now.

Dr Daanish was looking at the same row of his bookshelf where there were two volumes of a book written by him on new global challenges, published just last year. Sheba looked at his eyes and saw them full of tears.

Dr Daanish did not speak for many days after that. His healthy brain in an ailing body had become a prison for him. The students had never seen his eyes teary, not even on the day when he suffered the stroke. They kept wondering and looking at each other.

There was even more bad news awaiting Sheba that evening. The moment she reached her hostel, there was a call for her from home saying that her father's illness had taken a turn for the worse, and that all her family were going to the village. All the flights for the next day were already booked as it was spring, when many tourists throng the Valley. She had to take a bus. It would take 24 hours to get there; fortunately for her, a very kind family was also travelling with her. When she reached her city, everyone had already left and there was no one at home. She took a bus again, and left for the village.

Sitting on a seat near the window she relaxed somewhat, thinking that she would be able to see her Abbu in the evening, as well as her Ammi and other members of the family. Half-way to the village, a peasant from their lands in the village also got on the bus. Sheba recognized him and was somewhat relieved that in the dark of the evening, she would have someone known to her around.

He was one of the people who used to bring bags of grain from their lands to the house in the town. When the feudal system was over, they would still come to the city to get some work, and would stay in the servants' quarters in the backyard of Sheba's father's bungalow. Though they no longer enjoyed the patronage of the landlord, it actually continued for decades even after the Land Reforms Act. After working outside at their job, they would offer to do some domestic chores in the evenings like chopping the wood for the wood-burning stove and *bukhaari* (the wood-burning heaters for the house). Sometimes Abbu would ask them to trim the branches of the trees and clean the garden, and give then them a tip. They cooked their food in the basement and sometimes, if they saw children around the kitchen, told them stories too. Sheba had always experienced this ambience of respect at home.

The seat on which Sheba sat was meant for two. She had put her large bag next to her so that no one would sit there, though if some lady wanted a seat, she would remove her bag for her to sit there. The seat for three people across the aisle was vacant till Noor-ud-deen, whom the children called 'Noordeen', sat down on it. Sheba saw that he, too, recognized her but did not greet her as he used to do when she was a child—the way his ancestors had done to the landlord for generations. Noordeen did not sit on the seat the proper way.

Because two more places were vacant on that seat, he put his bag against the window and sat on the seat with his legs folded inside his pheran.

'How are you?' he asked her loudly. Sheba nodded, and then started looking out of the window once again.

'How is everything at home?' he asked again in a louder voice. Some people from the seat nearby looked at him. Sheba nodded again. At the next stop, many passengers got off the bus, and many others got on to it; many of them knew Sheba.

'The elder Pathan's youngest daughter…' Noor-ud-deen smiled, looking around him—a smile which meant that all were equal now. And a commoner did not have to stand in front of the landlords any more but could sit on his seat with folded legs, and address the members of the landlord's family in a loud voice. Sheba did not like the way he spoke to her. She decided not to turn her head towards him if he spoke to her again.Why did she feel like this? Because, till some days ago, this man would salute her family members along with everyone in his family. But she favoured equality amongst all human beings, and he was older than her as well, so what was wrong in addressing her the way he did? But shouldn't he have greeted her? Yes, but being younger in age, she could have greeted him too. Did she not favour equality for all human beings? She was a hypocrite, actually. No, the truth was that she disliked his boorish behaviour. Why? Was he her slave? He was a citizen of a democratic country. Still, sitting with folded legs on a seat was not good behaviour. What was that to her? He could sit the way he liked to. He talked to her because he wanted to. She could have chosen not to answer if she didn't want to. She was not used to this kind of behaviour. She could accept this behaviour from others but not from this man. That meant that the feudal in her was still very much alive. No, the feudal had never been there. She had always been a humble and friendly person, compassionate to every living being. She never liked discriminating amongst people. What kind of reaction was this then? It was the shock of the changing values; it meant she was shocked…Yes, she was, and there was nothing strange about feeling like that.

Sheba, deep in thought and almost fighting with her own self, was not looking at the beauty of the meadows and orchards on the way. The bus stopped for a while once again, and her chain of thoughts was broken. She missed her Abbu badly. Some people got off the bus. Others got on. She spotted another farmer. He wished her good evening, and she responded too. He sat down on a seat ahead of her and looked back at her.'When did you hear the news? People say you were out of town…It is very sad…'

Sheba's heart began to sink. 'My Abbu…is my Abbu alright?' she asked so softly that even she could not hear her own voice, but she did not say a word to anyone and, turning her face to the window, looked out.

Soon, the whole bus was discussing her Abbu's death two days ago. She covered her face with her dupatta in a way that the right side of her face could not be seen in the bus; she had angled it towards the window pane. Her frail figure began to tremble.

'He had been ill for many days,' someone said in a louder voice.

'Yes. He was waiting for the spring.' This voice seemed to be of an old man.

'Is that so?' The new voice was somewhat younger.

'Yes, he was ill since winter…then improved slightly and was partly in his senses but could not recover fully. He would only stroll sometimes…would not talk much at all…And the hakims said he was waiting for the spring blossoms; the doctor said he could die at any time.'

'He was the last virtuous member of this dynasty…'

'He had such a glow on his face…when the body was given a bath, the snow-white beard on his face had grown longer…He wore a beard during the last years of his life, he was clean shaven before that…a man looks saintly with a beard.'

'And what about the property case? Who takes anything along with him when he leaves this world…everything will be left here only.'

'His brothers were very cruel to people at one time. Thankfully, times changed…but the elder Pathan was like his father, Chowdhury Khuda Baksh Khan. I remember how they would distribute food on Eid-ul-Fitr and Bakr-Eid…a number of goats and sheep were slaughtered so that every household in all the villages around would get some meat. Begum Sahiba, the elder Pathan's mother, was also a very kind lady…and a very brave woman too. When Chowdhury Sahib went to Punjab or to his job in Ladakh, she would put his turban on her head, wear his gun around her shoulder and take a round of the lands! No one knew this...people would think Chowdhury Sahib had not gone to Punjab. My mother saw this by chance once when my father was sick. Mother wanted to take the cattle for grazing and entered the bungalow to tell them about Baba's illness, and Begum Sahiba had just taken her turban off from her head and was hanging the gun on the wall. She told my mother not to mention this to anyone, and gave her some baksheesh as well.'

'But she did not have the good fortune to find a couple of yards in this ground...died in a city hospital and was buried there too; her children were quite young at that time.'

'Nothing remains but Allah,' said a voice in a low tone. There was pin drop silence in the bus.

The bus became noisy while crossing through the turbulent stream. The stream had some water because of better snowfall that winter. Sheba looked at the stream with her inflamed eyes and covered her head, neck and half of her face with another fold of her dupatta.After this, there was an area called Sogam, which was once covered on horseback... Abbu would answer her countless questions during that trek. Abbu could always be heard breathing slightly louder than normal, and with a different sound—like the swing hanging on the mulberry tree in their city house, when the swing is about to stop and ropes make soft sounds, moving slowly. Now, no one was there to sway the swing to make that sound. She put her dupatta on her eyes and left it there for some time. The sun was about to set.

Getting out of the bus, she saw some women going towards her bungalow.

'How are you, little Begum Sheba?'

Oh…they wanted to know whether she knew about her father's death or not.

'My Abbu is unwell…' she said quickly and ran towards the bungalow.

In the dim evening light, no one saw her when she entered the gate. She climbed the first staircase and ran towards her father's room but there was no one inside. Abbu's bed was empty; the other family members were also not there. Abbu's walking stick stood silently near the huge bookshelf. The eyes in the peacock-shaped handle in the stick were not shining. There was none of the smell in the room that belonged to her Abbu. She ran out towards the other side. She completed one round of the mansion breathlessly, but did not see anyone. When she ran towards the entrance again, she spotted *patwari* (an official who visits agricultural lands and maintains records of their ownership and tilling) uncle entering the gate. He stopped when he saw her running. 'Where are you going child?'

'Abbu…Abbu…where is Abbu?' she asked breathlessly with a great effort, but without crying.

'Come…come with me, I will show you…'

The patwari headed towards a corner of the front lawn, where there was a plum tree at a little distance behind a huge walnut tree. A mound of brown earth was raised from the ground and birds had scattered red and green fruit, like flowers, on it.

'This was his wish…to be buried here. He passed away the day before and was buried before anyone could arrive from the city,' the patwari said softly. In the blue of the evening, Sheba bent her head, looked at the mound of earth and then at patwari uncle. He quickly went back towards the entrance of the bungalow. Sheba turned her head towards the grave and fell on her knees, burying her face in the earth. Now her wailing could be heard even from afar.

After burying Chowdhury Najam Khan in his land, Suraya Begum came back to the city. Faheema and Farkhanda were also leaving for their homes. Sheba also had to leave for her hostel after some days but she did not have the courage to go so far from home, leaving her mother all alone. She made Farkhi stay for some more days before she left. And then, only Suraya Begum remained all alone in her bungalow with the huge garden around it.

When Sheba was leaving, Suraya Begum hugged her and cried for some time. She also wished Farkhanda happiness in her house when she sought her leave. After that, she entered her room for her evening prayers.The sound of dishes being washed could be heard from the kitchen.When she passed Sheba's room, she felt as if someone had pierced her heart with a sharp, pointed object. On the portrait hanging on Sheba's closed door, a sparrow was feeding her baby in the nest with an open beak. Her little birdie was so far away… who knew when she would come back again? Farkhanda and Faheema would visit in a month or so…but Sheba? Her eyes were so red…my doll had cried a lot by herself!

Suraya Begum touched the portrait softly with her fingertips and began to cry. Sheba's voice echoed in her ears.'Why do you miss me so much, Ammi?'

'Why shouldn't I miss you, my child?' Suraya Begum opened the door and looked at the neat, silent room.

'Hadn't you cried a lot when I was born?'

'Yes, my child.'

'You had composed a poem in Kashmiri too, which meant:

The first daughter is all made of gold,
The second, too, can be accepted somehow,
And the third is like a hammer on the head.
God! You did not answer my prayers.

Suraya Begum touched the chinar leaves embroidered with brown thread in fine needlework on the white bed cover. 'Yes, my child. Your father also wanted an heir for his property. Girls have to leave their parents' homes. But our love for our daughters was never less than it would have been for a son!'

'Yes, you loved us very dearly, Ammi! I love you too. Please do not be so sad missing me like this!'

'I am too lonely, my doll…the home is empty, baby… Farkhi and Yasir have gone…your Abbu will never come back…the house is huge—and this emptiness, many times more huge.' Suraya Begum's face was wet with tears as if she had just washed it. Earlier, when Najam Khan was there, Suraya Begum would not miss Sheba so much. She would sometimes cry secretly, hiding it from all. Now, she was not scared of anyone who could hear her cry in the upper storey.

The entrance near the garden led to a long gallery, connecting the kitchen to the bungalow. Gull Mohammad was not heard washing the dishes. He must have gone to his room, but he had to come to the kitchen again to cook the dinner. Suraya Begum felt that Gull Mohammad was not around. She stood there for some moments and entered Farkhanda's room. Yasir's school tie was lying on the floor in a corner. When she picked it up and hung it on a hook inside the door of his cupboard, she felt someone had torn her soul out of her body. She put her hand on her heart, sat on the edge of the bed and cried bitterly.

After some moments, she rose and went to her room. A big portrait of Najam Khan, hanging on the wall, was smiling at her. Suraya Begum wiped her tearful eyes with her dupatta and stood on her *janamaz* (prayer rug), then abruptly sat on it and bent her head to the floor, crying uncontrollably. She could not understand why she was crying so much. She had been crying for so many days, but why was she crying so much now? The children had always been away from home. She was all by herself in her room since she had returned from the village, then why was she feeling that the baby sparrow flapping its wings was not able to fold them closer to its body...nor was the mother sparrow able to feed him with her beak, and that both were dead tired? And why did she feel that Yasir's tie had slipped from the bed in Farkhanda's room because Farkhanda or Yasir had not been there to pick it up? And why did she feel that Najam Khan's smiling picture hanging on the wall for many years, which would peacefully smile till then, actually had a very sad smile today?

Suraya Begum lifted her head from the *janamaz* and looked around with red eyes. And why did she feel that the cupboards in her room and the doors of all the rooms and all the windows, all the tables and all the objects on the tables were very lonely and sad? Why did she feel that every nook and corner of her house was angry with her, and that there was a dreadful silence which was refusing to own her? So where could she go, where? Suraya Begum wiped her tears and looked at the window.

'Here, listen!' Gazing outside the window, she moved her lips. There was a fig branch swinging downwards in the wind. 'Listen…here…no one lives here now…' she murmured.'Here, here…listen, nobody lives here now…no one…' Suraya Begum said, now more loudly. 'No one lives here now, there is only a dreadful silence here!' she shouted loudly and screamed, and began to cry as she knew that it was all silent around and that the servants' quarters were far away in the east of the compound, at the end of the garden.

She kept crying. She missed Najam Khan badly. She was missing her children too. She missed her children's friends. She missed their nanny, Aziz Bhat's wife. She missed the dresses they wore when they were young. She was missing them clad in their school uniforms, their innocent faces and heads bent over their books, Najam Khan examining their progress reports, their broken writing on the back of the huge wooden bed in the study room…She missed those precious moments when they followed her with their tiny feet—like chicks trying to keep pace with the mother hen, and turned when she turned and moved when she moved—as now those precious movements would never return because children have their own lives and Najam Khan, who would enquire every evening on returning home about their well-being and phone calls, was not there anymore.

Now nobody lives here. Suraya Begum also does not live here. A woman resembling Suraya Begum, resembling a once pretty woman…Suraya Begum, a middle-aged woman, is seen in the house; who has her children's childhood, her husband's love and her youth living inside her. She lives in her private world where there are young parents and three little daughters smiling and sometimes fighting, and Suraya Begum, taking them from Najam Khan's arms or cuddling them, kissing them many times on their cheeks, wiping their tears with her dupatta and not letting them out of her sight, and sharing everything related to them with Najam Khan, and laughing with him or talking to some of her children. But she does not live in the house, she is just…in the house.

Suraya Begum was seen in the garden at that time. She had just returned after touching the swing in the semi-dark garden. There was no food scattered for the birds on the wooden platform around the apricot tree across the swing for many days now. Suraya Begum was thinking about something while returning towards the entrance. 'What would these birds be thinking?' she thought. Suraya Begum suddenly stopped. How can she go so far every morning to give the food to the birds? It's much too cold at that time. But she could make a bird bath near the outer wall of the kitchen where the water pipes entered the house. And she could make a small cemented platform there. When she would scatter bread crumbs there every morning, the sparrows would come and chirp. And they would come there in the evenings also, have a wash in the bird bath and drink water too. A faint smile appeared on Suraya Begum's face, but feeling the smile, more tears came to her eyes, which she stopped by closing her eyes. Before entering, she looked towards the kitchen and wiped her face with her dupatta. She touched her face with her fingertips. It was not wet but her eyes were filled with fresh tears once again, and those were the tears that would always flow because of loneliness—the eternal enemy of this social animal, the cream of all creation. And which will end only with her life as there is nothing like companionship. The urge for togetherness is the biggest weakness of a living being. Togetherness is an unparalleled security, as to have company is the biggest symbol of a human being's strength. To lead life with one's self needs divine strength. Then, a person becomes one of the Sufis and hermits in his aloneness—only after a great toil, of course.

Suraya Begum drew in a deep breath and entered the house, as there was still some time left for the evening prayers.

Heemaal and Naagraye

When Sheba returned to her hostel after many days, Mayuri ran to her and hugged her. The paleness of Sheba's face was not very visible in the dim evening light. She had shed a lot of tears for many days. She looked silently at the books lying on the table across Mayuri's shoulder, resting her chin there, nestling close to her.

'How is sir?' she asked in a feeble voice.

'Thank God, he is fine…we make him do some exercises nowadays!' Mayuri said softly.

Sheba talked about her father till late at night. But when they reached Daanish Kadah the next morning, she was quite composed.

'How are you, sir?' she asked smilingly, looking at Dr Daanish. 'Sir, exercises now, isn't it?

'That…is true…' Daanish said in a low voice. Saagar looked at him with a smile on his face.

'And how do you feel now, sir?' Sheba asked quickly.

'I feel…I feel…I…cannot…cannot say…' he lowered his head.

'You feel better, yes?' asked Mayuri.

'Yes...but I wanted to...to...' Once again he did not complete the sentence.

'You wanted to say so yourself...isn't that so, sir?'

Daanish nodded pleasantly.

The following day, he was quiet again.That evening, the students were sad again because of Daanish's deteriorating health. They talked about it outside the Daanish Kadah, and shared their concern before leaving for their rooms with heavy hearts.

Sheba suffered spells of depression every now and then. One day she sat on her bed with her head on her knees, playing with the hem of her salwar, shedding tears silently. Mayuri looked at her helplessly.

'Have you really forsworn to take care of yourself?' Mayuri rose from her bed and went across to her.

'No Mayuri, but I can't help thinking of Ammi all the time...how would she be spending her time...how will she survive?' Sheba did not let her voice get tearful even though the tears flowed fast and thick.

'Can you solve any problem by crying?' Mayuri said in a pained voice; and Sheba, wiping her tears, got up to drink some water.

The next day, Sheba and Mayuri had to go to Chandigarh to attend a seminar. When they returned on Sunday evening, they went straight to Daanish Kadah. Saleem Miyaan was sitting against a pillar of the veranda, crying silently. He stood up when he saw them.

'Sir...master...the master is not going to live anymore, madam...' said Saleem Miyaan, wiping his tears.

'No Saleem Miyaan...this can't happen! We will call the doctor right now...Didn't the others visit all these days?' one of them asked.

'They did...the doctor came in the morning and emptied a big bottle of glucose in him intravenously...' Saleem Miyaan said, showing how long the bottle had been, measuring it along his hand and the elbow.

'But master felt very cold after that. He did not say anything, madam...I saw him shivering, gave him a hot water bottle and tried to make him drink some tea but he kept moving his face away...I am very upset, I have no one except for him...' sobbed Saleem Miyaan, walking behind Sheba and Mayuri with quick steps.

'Good evening, sir!'

Professor Daanish was sitting in his easy chair with his eyes closed. He opened his eyes and looked at them pleasantly.

'Sir, please eat something light, like oats or *khichri* (a soft porridge made of rice and lentils)...Mayuri and I have only just returned. We want some tea, do have some with us,' Sheba said smilingly and turned towards Saleem Miyaan.

'What have you prepared for us, Saleem Miyaan?' Sheba looked at Daanish sir again, who was looking at Saleem Miyaan expressionlessly.

'I will get some juice...and tea too,' said Saleem Miyaan, and Dr Daanish nodded slightly.

'Toast...some...some bread for...for them...' he said, and Saleem Miyaan nodded his head a couple of times quickly. 'Yes master...I was also thinking the same!' he said with a broad smile on his face.

'Yes; that is right, Saleem Miyaan...and get some tea for sir also. We will have tea together after so many days...I mean after two days,' Sheba smiled, and pulling a coaster towards Dr Daanish, sat down beside him. Mayuri went to the kitchen with Saleem Miyaan and brought over a glass of juice.

'Didn't these boys come over, sir?' asked Mayuri as she entered the room. 'I don't know where they keep loitering about all the time...' Mayuri said, as if talking to herself. She handed over the glass of juice to Sheba.

'Because they are a little free now!' Sheba held up the glass to Professor Daanish's mouth.

'You know, sir, when I quoted you in my paper, there was a loud clapping for a long time! Please drink this juice, sir. We'll have tea after some time.'

Mayuri also sat down nearby.'You know sir, you wrote in the chapter 'America's Influence on Central Asia' in your book *America and Developing Countries*, that the media can fake reality for decades,' Sheba said enthusiastically. Professor Daanish looked at her keenly for a second, and then shifted his gaze outside the window. He moved his lips again.

'Yes...the media can propagate falsehood for realities for decades,' he said in a single sentence. 'And the people are not even aware of that,' he continued, looking at the window.

Sheba and Mayuri looked at each other in surprise. There was a sudden glow of delight on their faces. Saleem Miyaan came with the tea. Sheba made Professor Daanish drink all the juice.

'I'll make the tea, sir.' She rose and went to the table.

'I'll help her, sir,' Mayuri said, and got up. Professor Daanish kept looking out of the window. Sheba took a second to reach the table.

'Mayuri! Didn't I tell you…that…Mayuri, this is a wonderful sign! You don't realize what this means!' Sheba chirped like a bird in her excitement and joy.

'I know Sheba! Sir will be fine now, isn't that so?' Mayuri looked at Sheba with shining eyes.

'Yes Mayuri! Sir's memory is perfectly alright! He has regained his ability to speak, so he will be fine within days now…and by the grace of God Almighty, he will also walk without any help soon!' she whispered.

'Bhagwan is so merciful…isn't it so?' Mayuri whispered back.

'Yes, that's why they say Allah is kind and merciful!' She turned her head towards Dr Daanish.

'Sir, sugar?' But he didn't answer, and kept looking out the window. Sheba knew that he took half a teaspoon of sugar in his tea but she didn't know why she had still asked him. She made the tea and took it to him. He looked at her eyes. His lips moved again.

'For decades…and to counter these falsehoods we must have…We…we…' The girls were giving him full attention, listening to him repeat his famous quotation, but he could not complete the sentence.

'We...we...must have...' he couldn't finish the sentence, and looked at Sheba.

'We must have an honest media,' Sheba said quickly, and Professor Daanish nodded enthusiastically. But the next moment he began to cough, and got a hiccup while coughing. He coughed again; his eyes watered. When the cough stopped, he looked at each of them, exhausted and out of breath.

'Yes...but...I can't...I just can't...' While trying to speak fast he shook his head many times, and then broke down. Mayuri also started sobbing, and Saleem Miyaan tried to wipe away his tears.

'It's not like that, sir...you will soon be able to speak properly again,' said Sheba, sniffling, and collected the dishes to hand them over to Saleem Miyaan.

Saleem Miyaan looked at Professor Daanish repeatedly, and then around him, before turning towards the kitchen. Sheba and Mayuri got themselves busy for some time tidying up Professor Daanish's room.

In the evening, when Saleem Miyaan brought some soup for Professor Daanish, he shook his head and refused to eat it. Saleem Miyaan quickly headed for the hostel.

'What does this mean, sir? Your speech has been affected a bit and your body too, but I...we know, sir, you are absolutely fit mentally! Why...why should you punish yourself by refusing to eat, sir? When you can eat for our happiness in our presence then why don't you try to become healthy again for us, sir? Why don't you cooperate with your dear students? Do not do this, please...' Sheba sat down on the floor. 'We want to see you healthy again, please sir! You will become weak if you don't eat; the doctor said that you will be fine again...but you should eat, sir ...Some protein...and if the body does not get enough carbohydrates too, what can be done then?' said Mayuri, and sat down near the easy chair.

'Doc...tor...lies...I will not...be...I...cannot be...' Professor Daanish said slowly, looking at his hands.

'You will be, sir...I promise...trust me, you only have to eat properly. Just for one month...for our sake, eat regularly for just one month...please, sir.'

Looking at four tearful eyes, Dr Daanish's eyes filled with tears too. He turned away. 'Salee...eem Miyaan...' he called, and Saleem Miyaan quickly reached him with a bowl of soup.

'Thank you, sir!' said one of the girls, and the other smiled.

***

'These holidays will be spent discussing the same topic again—who I would marry,' Sheba often thought.

When she entered the gate of her home after so many months, Suraya Begum was sitting in a chair near the grapevine in the garden, separating *haak* (collard greens) leaves from their stems. At first glance, Sheba saw that the grapevine had grown thicker and looked stronger. The grapevine had grown bigger, like Sheba, but Sheba didn't feel strong like it. And that means Sheba was weak, unlike the grapevine, un-grapevine-like…'un-grapevine-like', she thought—the way she would think as a child. A smile appeared on her lips but disappeared the next moment, as there was something in the way her mother was sitting, which made her feel that Suraya Begum was very lonely. When the fallen leaves crackled under Sheba's feet, Suraya Begum turned around. Sheba observed that Ammi's dull face brightened upon seeing her. She ran to her mother and hugged her; within that embrace, Sheba realized her mother had lost much weight. She was about to say something when she felt her mother's body trembling. After a moment they separated from each other, wiping their tears, and smiles appeared on their faces. Sheba sat on the thick stem of the grapevine, shaped like the number four written in Urdu, and it began to swing like a cradle. The leaves of the trees were making a whispering noise in the pleasant sunshine of the hills. Two birds flew around the branches of an apricot tree, and a sparrow also chirped somewhere in the tree. Gulla Bhai was doing the dishes in the kitchen; he cleared his throat a couple of times.

'I will ask him to bring another chair…' Suraya Begum said and got up again.

'No, no Ammi! I am so tired of sitting,' said Sheba. She had always seen some five, six chairs in the garden. She hurriedly turned her head towards the other side as if to get rid of this thought but her attention was drawn to the swing hanging from a thick branch of the mulberry tree. Nobody had thrown any food around for the birds as Abbu used to do every morning. While having his breakfast, he would trim the edges of rotis and break them into small pieces with his fingers for the birds. That was when Abbu would also discuss matters for the day—which of the children needed what, whose function was to be attended, what was to be bought and what would be cooked for dinner…and other things besides that, which he had forgotten to mention the night before.

Sheba took a deep breath. Ammi looked at a big *haak* leaf, turning it upside down a couple of times. Sheba knew that Ammi's eyes were full of tears and the leaf looked hazy to her. She broadened her lips into a smile.

'Ammi, don't search for those tiny insects so much. Let them cook in the spinach—they are all protein!' she said jokingly. Suraya Begum smiled without raising her head. Gull Mohammad had heard them talking and had brought a chair for Sheba.

'*Assalam-u-Alaikum*' he greeted her and touched her forehead with his fingers, bowing his head while going towards her suitcase.

'*Wa Alaikum-Assalam* Gulla Bhai! How are you?' Sheba said kindly. Suraya Begum raised her head and looked at her for some moments.

'Your face looks so dull, my child…are you alright?' she asked her, craning her neck to appraise her better.

'Yes, I'm fine...only a little tired.' Sheba got down from the bent grapevine and sat in the chair. She picked up some *haak* leaves in her hand and began to look at them.

'I will do it; it is not your work. Wash your face and hands. Okay, yes...you can clean some to have a little practice. After all, how long do daughters stay?'

'Let things take their course, Ammi...Who am I or you to interfere? God knows best, and He does what he wishes to do.'

'Yes, my child. You know Faheema's brother-in-law? The younger one...you've seen him.'

'Yes, I saw him many years ago when he stood first in the 10th standard. What about him?'

'He's now a senior police officer.'

Suraya Begum kept cleaning the greens. Sheba felt her Ammi's nose had grown longer; and also, that her reddish nose was very sad. She took a deep breath and released it slowly as if she had not sighed at all.

Suraya Begum peeled a purplish root of *haak* and, slicing it, offered it to Sheba.

'It is sweet...' the tip of her red nose smiled. Sheba bit off a small part of it with her front teeth.

'My child, I was saying...we will go to their house or invite them here one day...as you...'

'I don't like all this, Ammi...Do whatever you think is proper...as you wish,' Sheba said, picked up the *haak* root from the basket which was woven out of willow branches sliced into halves, and bit another small piece from it.

'One has to do all this in life...Faheema said that Seemeen wants to celebrate her birthday here. Usually the others also come along too...'

'How is Seemeen? She must have grown tall...'

'Yes...but very thin, like her mother.'

'But she's just a child...only in 6th standard!'

'Yes, and her habits are exactly like yours—everything, the colours you like, things you would spend your time doing...'

'My little doll...I miss her so much! And how is Yasir? I so much wish to see them...' Sheba's voice sounded earnest. 'When will they come? Oh, do call them this week, Ammi!'

'Yes, my child. Farkhanda was waiting for you...she will be coming over tomorrow.'

'Yes, she will...but I want to meet Yasir more than her!'

'Yes, yes, everyone will be here.' A smile appeared on Suraya Begum's face, which made Sheba peaceful; she had been watching her mother's face intently the whole the time. Is loneliness an enemy that has been wringing out the moments of peace from her face? 'Does Ammi smile only once in a while? Baaji and Farkhi are busy in their own worlds; I, too, am away,' Sheba thought to herself.

She looked away at the cherry tree and the blue sky above it. A thin white cloud drifted across it. The door of the gallery opened and Gulla Bhai appeared.

'What else to cook for dinner ma'am,' he asked, stopping at a distance. '*Bitiya* (affectionate term for daughter) is also here today...how about the red rooster?'

'Yes! Sheba dear, tell him what you would like to have for dinner. We do not cook much now; I do not eat rich, spicy food anymore…'

'That's good…spices are not good for health, though there is no harm in using them occasionally. We will have whatever Gulla Bhai wants today, but what has that poor red bird done to you, Gulla Bhai?'

'Please leave that to me madam!' Gulla Bhai bent to pick up the nickel-plated copper tray with the peelings of *haak* roots and stems, and his cap dropped into the tray. Gulla Bhai had shaved his head clean and his hair had grown back a little around his ears and on the neck only. When had Gulla Bhai become bald? Sheba thought seriously. Most of his hair that had grown recently was grey. While picking up his cap, Sheba saw many lines and squares appear and disappear in the lines on the back of his neck. His cap had grown loose on his head. When he put it back and stood up, it just slid down on his head. Why did he buy a loose cap when he had to shave his head? But he had no hair. He might have thought of shaving his head afterwards. In hilly areas, people rarely wear round caps made of netting; they wear them more often in the plains.

Sheba glanced at Gulla Bhai when he turned to go inside. Actually, those diagonal and horizontal rectangles reminded Sheba of her childhood days when Baba Sahib, the cotton-fluffer, would come to their place and stay in the room next to Gulla Bhai's. He had similar lines on his neck that could easily be seen by the children who stood near the well-built Baba Sahib sitting on the floor. The children even touched those lines with their fingers sometimes but quickly pulled them away, making sure that Baba Sahib would not feel them at all. And when he turned towards them, the child touching his neck would move aside and, wearing an innocent look on his little face, would request Baba Sahib to complete his story. The children spent a lot of time with him. There were so many interesting memories connected with Baba Sahib.

Baba Sahib's daughter also accompanied him. She called him '*Baabe Saeb*' which the children would pronounce 'Baab Saab'. She was some eight years older than the children. Baab Saab looked like most people his age. He wore a triangular cap on his head, a semi-circular piece of cloth folded and sewn on one side, with some embroidery at the border. The dignified-looking pointed top of his cap added to his stature, making him look taller. The lines made many figures on his neck which appeared and disappeared on his ruddy skin, at the edge of his cap. He called those lines wrinkles as he grew older. The figures were square, rectangular and triangular, and sometimes the lines reached straight to the ear and then disappeared behind it. But when Baab Saab bent his head slightly they reappeared in different shapes, leaving the children amazed.He also told them stories in Gulla Bhai's hookah room while smoking when he was free.

'I will tell you a new story today,' Baab Saab would say, taking a deep puff from the hookah and looking at the children with smiling eyes—who were busy exploring Gulla

Bhai's room for all the interesting things they would find, and they quickly crowded around him.

'*Bitiya*, leave the blade alone…you might cut your finger accidently,' gently admonished Gulla Bhai when Sheba was about to go to Baab Saab with the blade of Gulla Bhai's safety razor in her hand. God knows where Gulla Bhai hid those blades after that, as none was ever seen in his room again.

'Whose story, *Baabe Saeb*?' Gulla Bhai asked. The children would also try to call him *Baabe Saeb* like Gulla Bhai in a Kashmiri accent but could not say it correctly.

'Whose story, Baabe Saahib?' Sheba said with a great effort.

'Today humm…gurh…gurh…gurh…Humm…' he would take another deep puff from the hookah, sounding gurh…gurh…gurh, and clear his throat. 'Yes…humm… humm…' Baba Sahib took a few more puffs and appeared to be deep in thought. The children looked at him with their tiny chins raised in anticipation. 'The story of Yousuf Zulekha,' Baab Saab smiled, taking the pipe of the hookah away from his lips and holding it there. He could even talk with the pipe tucked in the corner of his mouth. Baab Saab had deep green eyes and many lines extending to his temples from their corners, where his cap would cover them. He had a salt and pepper beard, somewhat more grey than black, trimmed exactly in the pointy shape of his cap. The children sat in front of him, silently admiring every action of his for hours on end—Baaji, Farkhi and Sheba as well as any cousins visiting from the village.

'Will it be over by 1 o'clock Baab Saab?' Baaji enquired assuming an air of responsibility.

'Yes, we will finish it before lunch,' answered Baba Sahib, putting his hookah aside, and looking at the children one by one.

'But you will complete the story, Baab Saab?' Sheba asked anxiously.

'Yes…the complete story!' Baab Saab would purse his lips tightly and hum a tune for a few moments. The children looked at him earnestly. He would begin telling the story in the traditional way it was told in the Valley and would, at some point, stop and sing some lines included in it. Gulla Bhai accompanied him in the song.

The children were not allowed to go into the room where Baab Saab was fluffing the cotton. The rhythmic sound of '*dhun*' would reach their ears and the little heads bent over their books would become alert. Once, Sheba, though scared of being discovered by someone—especially by Baaji—peeped through the small gap in the slightly open door, nevertheless. The room seemed full of smoke, just like their cook's lazy son would make the kitchen look by feeding the fire in the hearth or stove carelessly with firewood that was not dry yet. Actually, it wasn't smoke in the room but tiny wisps of cotton floating around and filling it like mist, and if you looked hard for Baab Saab, you would finally see his arms in his orange woollen pheran with the raw walnut peel. He would be holding a bow-like device, making the music of *dhun*, hidden behind that screen of cotton suspended in the air like dust. It was such an interesting scene that day, but it ended with a painful jerk when Baaji suddenly came from behind and pulled at her thick, long braid. Sheba's heart kept pounding hard for a long time after that.

Lost in her thoughts, Sheba's heart beat fast again for some moments. Every story Baba Sahib told was very interesting. Baba Sahib would have a huge quilt spread before him. It was like a big bag made with two sheets of cloth, with a layer of fluffed cotton in between, and sewn up on all four sides. He would repeatedly beat the quilt hard with a long, supple stick. Sometimes, the children were also allowed to beat at it. The stick was a branch of some tree stripped of its leaves, which had become very smooth and slippery with repeated use; and it looked as if a carpenter had run a plane on it to make it so. But every joint of the stick, somewhat thick like a finger joint, made it evident that it was not the work of a carpenter's plane, because each one of them bulged out a little. It was so interesting to beat the cotton-filled quilt to spread the cotton wool evenly inside the cover. Baba Sahib would then thread a thick, long needle and cross-stitch the quilt again and again. At that time, he would tell the story all smiles but, sometimes, he would become sad too.

'Tears would roll down the eyes of Hazrat-e-Yaqub *Alaihesslaam* (peace be upon him)…he would ask his other sons…' Baab Saab would stick the needle in the quilt, and leaving it there for a while, reach for the hookah. At this point the children would desperately want to make stitches in the quilt like him. Sheba once tried and had lost the needle in the cotton wool in a trice. Baba Sahib then had to search for it, pressing the quilt many times at different places to find it.

'What happened then?' one of the children would ask anxiously.

'Hazrat-e-Yaqub would cry and curse the moment... When...do you remember children...I told you...didn't I?' Baba Sahib would say, and get some fresh tobacco from the tobacco box, which had two sections in it.

Sheba recalled that the tobacco smelled somewhat like tamarind. Once Phirki put a pinch of tobacco in her mouth, and Baaji, threatening her with dire consequences if it was reported to the elders, blackmailed Farkhanda to work for herself for a long time. But Baaji should not have done that, as after a few years, when Phirki was caught smoking and got scolded by everyone, Baaji had to face the ignominy too.

Baab Saab would add some soft charcoal from one section of the tobacco box, with the small tongs tied to his kangri, to the *chilm* (the fire bowl of a hookah). Then he would add some live embers from the kangri on top of the charcoal in the fire bowl so it would start smouldering sooner. One of the children usually filled his or her tiny lungs with air and offered the services of her puffed-up cheeks to blow into the hookah bowl, which was usually not accepted because none of them could blow in a light, smooth manner, the way Baab Saab could. Because when the children blew at it, they would scatter the ash out of the bowl—and sometimes, even a small live coal or two, and that could be dangerous as it could start a fire.To fill the fire bowl was a kind of interval when the children just stood or sat close by.

'Yes, we remember Baab Saab!' one of them would answer, and Baba Sahib would move his head, holding the fire bowl in his hand. The children even standing were almost as tall as the seated tall and strong Baab Saab. Some more lines would appear on his neck. Baab Saab would stroke his beard, remove his cap and put it on the quilt spread in front of them and then pat his head before scratching it and beginning to hum.'*Humm...humm...hoooon...*'

The children looked at him curiously and he started singing properly.

'*Haa Baabeh Saebo... Yousuf chhoowadaan...asenemone Dall Shikaarye...*' Baab Saab sang, moving his head in rhythm, and then explained the meaning to the children. 'Hazrat-e-Yousuf's jealous brothers said..."Baba Jaan, Yousuf is crying...we will take him with us for a picnic to the Dal Lake."' Baab Saab's eyes filled with tears. 'Those cruel brothers were Yousuf's enemies...they wanted to get rid of him,' Baab Saab would say in a gloomy voice choking with emotions.

'Did they have a Dal Lake...a Dal Lake there also, Baab Saab?' Sheba had asked that day.

God knows what Baab Saab had replied. How the stories and folk tales are localized by the people of a particular area! They do it according to what they are familiar with, moulding them in the way they can easily communicate it to others, Sheba thought to herself smilingly, lost deep in her reverie.

Baab Saab had a daughter. Sheba had always found her very pretty. She had a lovely pink complexion, and was tall like Baab Saab. Her eyes were also green like her father. She would come with him to the city. Her name was Heemaal. When Baab Saab introduced her to the children, she also spoke out her name at the same moment. Listening to this, the children burst into laughter and Baab Sahib laughed too.

'You remember the story of Heemaal-Naagraye... Naagraye, the Baadshah of the serpents?'

'Yes, yes, Baab Saab, the Baadshah of the snakes...the snake that lives to be a 100 years, and becomes the king of the snakes! Isn't it, Baab Saab?' one of the children answered.

'Yes...Naagraye had also lived a 100 years, and had acquired the special power...which power was that?'

'He could change himself into a human being,' some other child replied.

'Do you remember what happened after that?'

'Yes, Baab Saab...But if you tell us again, we will remember the whole account better!'

'Is this a school lesson?' Baaji said, flaring her nostrils angrily but nevertheless looking at Baab Saab's face as eagerly as the others, awaiting the story.

Baab Saab recounted the already told story with renewed enthusiasm and the children also listened to it with equally deep attention, as to hear a story repeated was a sheer delight.

'So, won't we listen to a new story today? All right, fine. But only when we have finished this...we can then start a new story, but only if we still have the time,' Baab Saab smiled with his green eyes.

'Where did Naagraye live?' Sheba asked quickly, making it clear that the story had begun and soon the specifics would be related—something Sheba loved listening to.

'Naagraye lived in *Paataal*...Where did he live?'

'He lived in *Paataal*!'

'In the deepest reaches of the earth, in the netherworld... And that, too, at the bottom of a lake...He changed his appearance soon after he came out of the water and transformed himself into a handsome young man. Heemaal was a princess there...What does Heemaal mean? I had told you, remember?'

'We've forgotten, Baab Saab...' a tiny, innocent voice said.

'I remember, Baab Saab...' another tiny voice piped. '*Hee* is a bushy plant, very common in our Valley...It has yellow-white and sweet-smelling flowers, very much like jasmine... And *maal* means garland.'

Sheba remembered that all the children had looked at Heemaal, making her blush and smile shyly. The children saw that her temples reddened exactly like the creases on Baab Saab's neck when he turned his neck towards the children while stitching the quilt.

Baab Saab's daughter always looked very pretty to Sheba, and especially so when she once came along with Baab Saab unexpectedly on a soft and pleasant sunny day. Little Sheba had a big surprise that day. Heemaal seemed to have suddenly grown taller, almost like Baab Saab. She did not have a runny nose like before, nor did she run around barefoot without any purpose in the garden—and her clean and tidy feet looked nice. Her hands were also neat. She was older than all the children there, but she would still dig the ground with them, using a dry branch, to make the small house in the garden with the twigs scattered around on the grass, and did not need to blow the dust off her hands. Sheba, on the other hand, always carefully dusted her hands but they would get covered with dirt in a short while again. Heemaal's nails were also clean now. They weren't tidy and long, and had not been neatly trimmed after growing a little as Baaji's were, although Baaji was younger than her by a year. Perhaps it was because that was a practice in Heemaal's village. She now lowered her head every now and then, especially when she laughed, God knows why, and her eyes, which looked like Baab Saab's before, now looked far more attractive than his as they had no lines in the corners. While smiling, her eyelids appeared puffy around her eyelashes, like egg-shaped circles laid down to rest. Her green eyes almost disappeared behind her eyelids and could barely be seen under them, shining beautifully, though not as black eyes, as they shine more than green eyes; but though green eyes may not shine much they look more beautiful. Like the green ink shining in the inkpot even if the sun's rays filtering through the branches did not reach the inkpot directly, when during the examinations the whole class came out of their classrooms to sit in lines on the ground, in the kind and soft sunshine. And Heemaal's neck was slimmer than Baab Saab's, and only a single line appeared on it when she turned her head to right or left. No figures made of any lines appeared on her neck, rather one would see two bones at the nape of her neck when she moved it at a particular angle, one smaller than the other, and those looked very beautiful too.That day, telling the story of Heemaal and Naagraye, Baba Sahib had called Heemaal his little princess.

'But Naagraye was yet to become a king, isn't that so?' a little listener asked.

'Yes, he came out of the deep waters to this world. The king here was looking hard for a suitable groom for his princess as she just did not want to marry any of the suitors who had asked her hand in marriage. However, the princess was very happy upon meeting Naagraye, and the king made arrangements for Naagraye to stay in the royal guest house. Naagraye and the princess became friends, and fell in deep love; he declared that he could not live without her and she said she would die if she would not become his!'

'She would die if she would not become his? What does that mean?' not understanding anything, Farkhanda asked him.

'That means the princess said that if she couldn't be with Naagraye, she would…' a cousin tried to make Farkhi understand.

'No…that means that if Naagraye did not marry her, they would…' Baaji left the sentence incomplete.

'Then the princess would swallow a diamond!' said Sheba.

'Shut up! Baab Saab did not say this…' said Baaji, raising her voice.

'Yes, I did say that…I said it last time,' Baab Saab smiled. 'She would swallow a diamond…' Baab Saab turned to his hookah and Baaji bent her head to lick the stone in the ring on her finger, as the princess might have done, and looked around to make sure she was not seen by anyone. Sheba wrinkled her little nose and quickly looked away.

'But there was a problem …' Baab Saab reached for the kangri with the tongs which were tied to the hookah bowl. 'Rather, there were two problems. Now, what were those two problems?' He began to pick small embers from the kangri and put them into the hookah bowl.

'Two problems?' a child asked.

'Which two?' Baab Saab asked, as serious as a school teacher.

'That he was really not a human being,' another child said.

'But he looked like one…' yet another voice declared.

'But that was cheating,' said Sheba.

'Yes…because the truth had not yet come out in the open…' said Baab Saab. 'But he loved the princess very much.'

'Why didn't he tell her that he wasn't a human?'

'Because he did not want to lose her…or maybe he wanted to tell her when the time was right. But the truth was, after all, the truth. And there was one more thing…he had seven wives in *Paataal* (the netherworld)…' Baab Saab drew deeply on the hookah. 'And, perturbed by his absence for so many days, the whole of his kingdom had started looking for him.'

'Oh no!' exclaimed a cousin anxiously. He was older than every listener there but was listening to the story for the first time.

Baab Saab had the hookah tube tucked in a corner of his mouth. 'And after that...all his queens,' Baab Saab said, and in the same instant a loud roll of thunder was heard outside.

Ammi called Gulla Bhai urgently. 'Get the tray of tomatoes inside...it's about to rain!'

The tomatoes were divided into fours, without peeling the skin, and had been put out in the sun to dry. Ammi's worrying tone about the tomatoes getting wet sounded exactly like cousin Mansoor Bhaiye Jaan's 'Oh no!' to Sheba. The clouds made another thunderous clap. It seemed they had reached down to the room where the cotton was fluffed, and it started getting dark quickly.

'We will do rest of the work tomorrow...' Baab Saab put the hookah aside and inserted the needle into the big ball of thick thread.

'And what about the story?' a child asked, but there was no eagerness in his voice because firstly, the story was being repeated and secondly, some of the children had already stood up, as the weather outside was perfect for them to run around in the rain and have fun. By the time the children got to their shoes and slippers, it had already started raining cats and dogs, like it happens sometimes with the summer rain. By the time Ammi called the children back inside—because of Gulla Bhai's complaints—they were already drenched, shouting, screaming and making merry running around in the garden. The rain stopped suddenly. The sun's rays could be seen emerging from behind the clouds again, making the well-washed grass and plants shine. Just like Ammi's green Kashmiri silk dupatta which had *muqaish* (tiny pieces of shiny metal) sewn on it here and there, and which would shine like numerous tiny suns whenever Ammi moved her hand even slightly.

A parrot screamed from somewhere above on the grape vine, and Sheba raised her head to look up, returning from her childhood. The clear blue sky looked so tranquil in the background of the vine, except for a huge grayish cloud near the horizon.

Gulla Bhai was frying parathas in the kitchen. He was humming some sad tune in a low tone. The delicious aroma of the parathas reached the garden. Kashmiri salt tea must be boiling on the other stove, thought Sheba immediately. Was the tune sad or did she feel it was sad? She shook her head and took a deep breath. Ammi must be offering her namaz; she would call her over when she was done with it. She would walk around in the garden till then.Those were lovely days, she thought, and a smile spread over her face.

When Baab Saab married Heemaal off, her husband would also visit them as there was no work in the winters because everything was either covered with snow or under a dirty opaque sheet of ice. People preferred to stay indoors as the government offices were shifted to the winter capital of the Valley, and the schools and colleges were also closed. Sometimes, these labourers would go across the tunnel in the Pir Panjal range to the Punjab: before Partition to the Punjab that was now across the border, and after that, to the Punjab on this side of the border.

Sheba remembered that no child liked Heemaal's husband, even though he had chopped a huge tree trunk into small pieces within no time on the very first day of his arrival and made a big heap of firewood for the bukharis and the hearth, upon which Ammi remarked that he was a hard-working boy. He was not slim like Heemaal, but had only a fair complexion like her. He was always seen with his mouth half-open, and his tongue resting on his lower teeth. When the children discussed this topic, Mansoor Bhaiye Jaan said that he probably always had a bad cold and because of the blocked nose, he had to breathe through his open mouth. When he wasn't chopping wood, he would sit next to the wall, his pheran wrapped around him. Although he was a woodcutter, he was too lazy to go out and find work. The skin of his hands looked rough, and Sheba found it was very rough indeed when she once touched it, whereas Heemaal's hands were soft like flower petals.

For two years, he visited them with Baab Saab and Heemaal. But one morning he left, telling Baab Saab and Heemaal that he was going to see his mother for a few days, and never came back. Ammi had given Heemaal some very nice dresses, and also some not-so-nice ones. She wore them under her pheran and looked very pretty in them. But soon, her lovely eyes were swollen when she waited and cried for him. After a few weeks, Baab Saab went to his village looking for him, leaving Heemaal with Ammi, but found that his son-in-law had stayed in the village for only two days. He had also told the people in the village that he did not want to return as he had been married for two years but they still didn't have a child. The children did not know about this.

Baab Saab searched for him at many places because he wanted to confirm this directly from him. Then someone told him that he had gone to his maternal grandparents' house. However, when Baab Saab got there, he found that he had already left. Baab Saab returned, much perturbed and very unhappy, having also found that his son-in-law had always wanted to marry his maternal cousin.

Later, following a serious discussion between Mansoor Bhaiye Jaan and Baaji, which the children hardly understood, all of them were agreed on one point: that his cousin must also be used to sitting against the wall with her tongue resting on her lower teeth, and that this common trait must have been the source of attraction between the two.

After finishing his work, when Baab Saab left for the village again, he made Heemaal stay with Ammi once again, as he had heard that his son in-law was getting married to some other girl. Heemaal was usually busy grinding spices, and with swollen eyes she would ask Ammi, 'What was my fault, Begum Sahiba? All this was the will of God Almighty.'

It seemed that Baab Saab had forgotten all his yarns and tales. When the children asked him, he would speak for some moments and then fall silent.

Strolling alone in the garden, when Sheba reached the compound wall, she saw that two bricks near its base were falling out. When Sheba turned towards the entrance crying, Heemaal's reddened green eyes suddenly appeared before her again.Why had Baab Saab got his princess married to that snake? In those days too, the children asked themselves why Baab Saab had named his daughter Heemaal when he knew that the story of Heemaal and Naagraye had ended in a tragedy. But Naagraye was not like him. When he did not return to *Paataal*, his queens came up from the netherworld to look for him in the woods and the fields. When they finally found him, they told the king all about him and also claimed that they could prove it. The king and the princess agreed to this. Naagraye repeatedly said that by trying to find the truth, the princess would lose him forever. However, she did not listen to him and in the end, his seven queens took him back with them to *Paataal*, and she became miserable. But this did not happen with Heemaal.

In the next season, after the harvesting of the crops, the woodcutter appeared unexpectedly, and cried before Ammi, saying his wife had died in childbirth, and that he had come back to take Heemaal with him. Heemaal was sitting in the other room, softly scratching her toes as if she had a rash which makes your skin swell and itch, and which only goes away with soaking your feet in water boiled with dried turnips.

When Ammi asked him if he had spoken to Baab Saab, he replied that Baab Saab had told him to ask Heemaal.

Ammi asked Heemaal but she did not reply. She just kept pressing her toes one by one. The children saw that the woodcutter also went to the kitchen following Ammi but stopped at the door.

'Will you go with me, Heemaal?' he asked her, seeing that she didn't answer Ammi.

Listening to the woodcutter's sad voice, Heemaal looked at him with her green eyes that had turned red from crying. All the children were praying that Heemaal would scold the woodcutter and ask him to get lost, but Heemaal nodded in assent. She moved her head so quickly that her big, round earrings touched her cheeks, and the silver coins on the tassels stitched to the black neck of her pheran jingled pleasantly.

The Mourning Doves

Having done his M.Sc. in Geology, but still preferring to become a police officer, the young man was tall and fair with eyes neither too big nor too small. His eyes and hair were black, but the hair had a bluish tinge. He had a longish, plump face with bulging cheeks, and some four or five moles around his big nose, which were the same colour as his hair and the eyes. His nose curved in the centre and its tip bent forward towards his lips, like the beak of a predatory bird. He forced out short bursts of air through his nose again and again, making an unpleasant sound, which could easily be heard by a person near him, and even by those sitting a little further away.

When he left the dining table to attend to a phone call, the clatter of his steps was rather too loud. His skull had no curve at all and made a straight line from the base of his neck to the top of his head. The thick skin of his neck between the khaki collar of his shirt and the bluish black line of his hair was rather prominent. He was tall in a peculiar manner too, as his torso was longer than his legs. His wide brown belt above his heavy hips and his brown boots, and the short legs taking big strides would give one the impression that he was undisciplined and careless. One felt that the weight of his personality impacted too heavily on his surroundings, and that gave the impression of him being cruel and uncouth.

When he rose to attend the phone, he looked across the table at Sheba once, who was sitting in a corner chair eating and talking to Seemeen. When he returned and sat down, Sheba heard the sound '*khund*' coming from his nose. He pulled a dish of soft, delicious and aromatic red *Rista* (meat balls made of mutton beaten on a stone slab with a broad wooden hammer to a spongy texture, and cooked with spices and saffron) towards him, occasionally glancing at Sheba. For a second she felt something like helplessness inside her, but the next moment she was quite composed. She looked at the others present there. Ammi, too, looked at Sheba every now and then. Farkhi and Faheema were talking to each other, almost whispering. Seemeen was thinking about something, holding a spoon in her hand, eating slowly. Sheba looked at her with affection when she suddenly heard a noisy rattle. She bent her head to her plate and raised her eyes towards Raahat Ali Khan, who was hurriedly gulping down his food in big mouthfuls and making a clatter with his spoon and the plate. Sheba felt like leaving the table and sitting on the sofa with her plate. What a din Police Officer Mr Raahat Ali Khan was making! 'Raahat' literally meant peacefulness, but there was nothing of the sort in his actions, she thought.

'Our Raahat Miyaan is a very busy man…' said Faheema to Farkhanda, looking at Raahat Ali Khan smilingly.

'Oh yes, this police life is like that...'

'*Chaachoo*, why are you eating so hurriedly?' Seemeen asked innocently.

'Because he has to go,' Faheema looked at Seemeen sternly.

'No mamma, he always eats like this...hurriedly! I know it in my room when I hear the sound of spoons and plates,' said Seemeen as if informing the others, but this made Sheba laugh.

'Like someone doing the dishes...' Sheba bent her head towards Seemeen's ear, and said in a whisper. Seemeen burst out laughing.

'Pay attention to your food,' said Faheema. Trying to control the impish glint in her eyes by blinking her eyelashes quickly, Seemeen put her tiny finger on her lips. But everyone, except for Faheema, had a smile on their faces, even Raahat Ali Khan.

'OK, OK, I will eat slowly now...' said Raahat Ali, looking at Seemeen.

'And *Bhaabi* (sister-in-law), her hair looks untidy...get it trimmed.'

'No!' Seemeen shook her head. 'I want to grow my hair like Sheba *Khala* (elder sister),' Seemeen said quickly.

'And leave it loose like her too?' asked Faheema in a threatening tone.

'No, Khala has a pony tail...' Sheba said hurriedly.

'Girls must not leave their hair loose, and simplicity is their biggest ornament!' said Faheema, stressing each word.

'I know, mamma, why you said that...' said Seemeen, and Faheema thought she was supporting her.

'Tell me why,' said Faheema, pausing with her spoon midway to her mouth, looking directly at Seemeen.

'Because you have very short hair. It looks like a brush!' Seemeen laughed loudly and Suraya Begum cleared her throat.

'The food is delicious...isn't it Seemeen?'

'Yes, Nanna Jaani.'

When they were leaving, Seemeen cried a lot, insisting that she wanted to stay back with Nanna Jaani. But Faheema did not allow that, like always.

When Sheba reached her room, she picked out one of her favourite books from the bookrack and lay down on the bed, looking at the pages of the book with pictures of birds. She wanted to have a look through the window but the curtain was drawn. She got up to draw it aside a little and returned to her bed. Across the gate, on the other side of the pathway, the greyish white sky was spread out behind many branches of autumnal chinar trees. All was deathly silent. She took a deep breath and laid her head against her pillow, opening the book at its centre. There was a picture of a nightingale on the right page. It had delicate white feathers under its brownish eyes, and a half-open tiny beak, as if chirping. The name under it read White-cheeked Bulbul, or White-cheeked Nightingale. A smile of affection appeared on Sheba's face as Seemeen's innocent and intelligent face appeared before her eyes. 'My little white-cheeked Bulbul' she said slowly to herself, and switched off the table lamp.

Sheba opened her eyes when she felt a dim light reflected from the ceiling on her closed eyelids. She looked at the ceiling. The varnish of the pentagon-shaped *Khatamband* ceiling (the art of joining together geometrical shaped wood to construct a ceiling) was reflecting rays of light to the bed. Perhaps some wedding procession passing along the road across the garden was sending up those beams of light. She heard wedding songs coming from a distance too. Women made two rows of six, seven or eight, holding each other's waists and, singing these wedding songs, simultaneously shifting the weight of their bodies from one foot to the other. They would make two rows or sometimes four like that, to sing at the occasion of receiving the groom or seeing off the bride. The women of the Valley are born poets who create poetry, set it to a tune and sing it, suiting the occasion.

A smile appeared on Sheba's lips. She heard the songs being sung at the wedding, with claps accompanying the fast tune, which meant that the bride had been seen off. She closed her eyes again. She could clearly hear the rhythmic loud clapping of the women accompanying the songs. Then the sounds began to fade away, which meant that the bridal palanquin had departed, or that the groom had taken his bride away in a car.

Sheba saw herself in a wedding dress, behind her closed eyes. She looked very pretty but who was the person sitting next to her? It was Raahat Ali. She abruptly opened her eyes. 'O Allah, not that!' she whispered and closed her eyes. Now, there were no sounds anymore. Tired of all the trials and tribulations of a marriage, people would be sleeping peacefully now, and the home would appear sad and empty. And what if the bride's mother lived alone in the house? Sheba's eyes were open again. She felt a wave of pain in her heart. 'May God keep Ammi's simple heart always happy!' she said to herself and closed her eyes again.

Once again, she saw herself in a bridal dress and, hearing the sound of '*khund*', she peeped out from behind her *ghoonghat* (the traditional veil) at the groom sitting next to her—whose face was hidden behind a flowery *sehra* (a headdress worn by the groom), with his protruding nose peeping through the garlands of flowers like the muzzle of Abbu's pistol. Sheba laughed at this image without opening her eyes and tried to sleep again. In her imagination, she saw herself in a bridal dress and smelled the fragrance of jasmine and roses reaching her from someone sitting next to her. Sheba stealthily peeped out of her *ghoonghat*. This was a handsome, dark guy looking at Sheba, raising half his *sehra* and smiling on catching Sheba looking at him, and enjoying it too. But who was he? She had never seen him, Sheba thought, half asleep. But he was a nice guy. She smiled a little, and finally went to sleep.

Next morning, when Gulla Bhai brought her tea, she got up. She had got into the habit of taking bed tea in the hostel. Gulla Bhai made a cup of tea quickly and, stirring it with a teaspoon, placed it on the side table by the lamp. Gulla Bhai never made any clinking sound while stirring the tea. She smiled.

'Thank you, Gulla Bhai,' she said softly, and picking up the bird book, took a deep breath to take in the fragrance of the tea. This time the page that opened had a picture of an owl with its fluffy wings, staring at the camera with his round, black and white eyes in its big head. He looked angry with those who had played a trick upon him in the dark, using an infrared camera to take his picture without his permission, and seemed to be ogling at Sheba. The name under it read Himalayan Wood Owl. Sheba looked at the picture for some seconds and then burst into laughter. Then she was suddenly surprised at how she had laughed loudly all by herself. Ammi entered the room, calling her name; Sheba wished her good morning.

'You should not drink tea on empty stomach, baby...and you should have offered your namaz first...' Ammi drew the curtains away fully. There was no sun, and the sky looked colourless and dull.

'Faheema called in the morning,' Ammi was looking through the window at some distant object. 'She asked why you were wearing those long pendant-like ear ornaments...Raahat Ali does not like jewellery...' Ammi kept looking outside.

'Ammi,' Sheba called her in a chirpy voice and her mother looked back at her.

'Yes, my child?'

'Please come here...I want to show you something.'

Ammi came over to her. Her face was sad like the colourless sky when she had turned towards her, but looking at her most intelligent daughter laughing, she smiled too. 'What is it?' She sat down on the edge of the bed.

'This…Raahat Ali!' Sheba opened the book with the picture of the owl before her and burst into laughter.

'I, too, did not like him, my child…' said Ammi, after she, too, had had a good laugh, and caressed Sheba's hair. 'But I was only concerned about your growing age…'

'What age, Ammi? Also, at least you should like the boy…and I am not that old…let me finish my studies!' Sheba held her mother's hand and rested her cheek on it. 'Isn't that right, Ammi?'

'Yes, sweetheart…we will all like the person destined for you.'

'We also have a part of destiny with us…here in our heads,' Sheba touched her forehead with Ammi's fingers. 'You know, Ammi…I think the brain should be named "destiny"!'

'Is that so? Then may God bless your destiny with some wisdom!' Ammi smiled, drew some round unseen figures with her index finger on Sheba's temple and looked out of the window again.

Looking out through the double-paned plastic window of the airplane, Sheba's eyes filled with tears. Lonely Ammi in the big house, the silent Gulla Bhai, the garden with the dying grass, the swing with the wooden seat hanging by thick ropes swaying sadly by itself—why had all this happened? Sheba's heart beat fast for a few moments. Should she have come away, leaving so many sad things at home? How sad had everything become with her not being there. And Ammi had grown so thin…

Sheba looked down at the ground. There were roads and narrow pathways leading to small towns. Such a scene was seen at intervals, and would hide again behind piles of clouds. Sometimes, the plane seemed to be just sitting on the clouds. The blue sky and the brilliant sunshine above the clouds looked beautiful. After some time, when there were no clouds, the Pir Panjal range appeared with its many peaks and countless trees. One face of the mountains had dense forests with thick snow caught between the trunks of the trees, but the other side had fewer trees—which were spaced well apart from each other, and had no snow near their trunks. Why so? Sheba thought. Maybe it was because the sun's rays passing easily through the sparse trees would melt away the snow, whereas on the other side it would not melt it so readily, thus retaining the moisture and helping the trees and the greenery to grow in abundance.

The next moment, the clouds disappeared. There were wide roads now, and big rivers with houses on the banks.

She could now see big buildings with huge water tanks on their terraces, the stadiums and railway lines. This was the other side of the tunnel. The small well-planned cities and towns—Jammu, Pathankot, Ludhiana and Kapurthala. The screen in front of her seat showed some places across the border to indicate the present position of the plane as well. There were some areas of Afghanistan—Kabul, Mazar-e-Shareef, some cities of Pakistan—Jhelum, Quetta,

Rawalpindi and Gujranwala, indicated with arrows, and even some areas of Central Asia like Samarkand, Dushanbe and Tashkent. After a while, some coastal areas also appeared on the map—Karachi, Mumbai and Colombo. The wide roads along the big rivers, and the smaller roads by the side of the long roads leading to the cities made straight lines, circles and squares. Had there been no clouds, the traffic plying on the roads would also be visible. They can also be seen at night, she thought. When you fly over big cities you can see lines of red and white lights—which are actually the headlights and taillights of vehicles, and look like rivers of light: the white river for the approaching ones and the red river for the ones going in the opposite direction. While travelling across the sea, one could sometimes spot ships in the ocean too.

The announcement by the stewardess broke Sheba's chain of thought. She advised the passengers to fasten their safety belts again because of the expected bad weather. Sheba had not undone the belt around her small waist to begin with.

One of Farkhanda's distant relatives from her in-laws side had also sent a proposal, asking for Sheba's hand, but on the condition that Sheba would not work after marriage. Suraya Begum answered it with silence.

Everything appeared white through the transparent plastic. Clouds flew in different directions. Suraya Begum's helpless face appeared against the white background.

'But she wants to work after finishing her studies, Farkhi.'

'She wants to, not you...If you want, Ammi, this could be the best proposal!' Farkhanda had replied, looking at Sheba.

'Why should you work, Sheba? The amount of money you will earn in a whole year, they donate every month to the poor and the mosques! You'll want for nothing!' Farkhanda had tried to make Sheba understand while Suraya Begum kept helplessly looking at both their faces alternately. Sheba was astonished to hear this, and moved her gaze from Farkhanda's face to the window. But she realized she had to join the conversation, Some pigeons were looking for shelter on the sill of the closed window. It had been snowing since morning; it was light earlier, and the tiny snowflakes melted on reaching the ground. But for some time now, it had been snowing more heavily, and the snowflakes were like white blossoms or fluffy cotton-wool open bolls—like the wings of wild pigeons, like the feathers of water birds or wild ducks. The roofs and the lamp posts were wet. The trees were wet. 'Where could the poor pigeons sit?' thought Sheba. And she looked at Farkhanda again.

'Phirki, is this really you talking? I want to do something in life…on my own. Something of my own choice…a job, some teaching and more research. He wants a housewife…A working woman can also be a good homemaker but if he lays down pre-conditions, there will be no chance of any compromise!' Sheba bent her head slightly and looked at the flowery design of the carpet.

'We are not that modern yet, Sheba …good families still don't like their women going out for work…Like this, you will never get someone from a good family to marry!'

'No Farkhi, these families are not good, my child! Even common families always had their daughters educated about the worldly affairs as well as about religion…These families aren't of noble descent…they only want to appear upper-class and noble. In our religion too, we have best examples of working women!' Suraya Begum said all this in one go, and was quiet again. Sheba raised her head.

'So, should I say no to them then?' getting no answer, Farkhanda asked in a low voice.

'Yes, baby…there is no other way. If our child is not happy, we are not happy either.'

Sheba relaxed listening to this, and the expression of relief was there on her face even when Farkhanda had left. Ammi also seemed to be at peace. The pigeons were perched on the window sill. Two crows were sitting on top of the entrance gate, letting their feathers get wet. They were mountain crows, a little smaller, and with black necks. There was no snow on them. It may have been because the heat of their little bodies had melted the snow sooner or they had just shaken it off their feathers, she thought. Or perhaps they had water-resistant feathers like ducks and swans. These birds, while they appeared to be sitting idly, actually keep preening and oiling their feathers. They have an oily substance in their skin at the base of their tail feathers. They peck at it and rub it all over their wings with their beaks.

'It may be because all the sheltered perches were occupied by the other birds or maybe they do not feel any cold, or maybe they love the snow…yes, that must be the case,' Sheba thought. She remembered that whenever there was snow, these crows cawed even at night.

Staying away from her Valley, Sheba sometimes had to tax her memory to remember all the intricate details of nature there, but she always succeeded. Shifting her gaze from some crows that she had been looking at intently, she concentrated on the falling snow. It fell in an interesting way. No, it was falling just the way it always fell. Only, when you looked at it in a different way, it looked like it was falling differently. For instance, if one looked at it slightly raising the head, the snowflakes looked scattered in the sky, coming dancing down towards the earth. If one looked at them straight, it felt that they were coming down from the sky straight in a very regular manner, and if one looked straight up from below, it would feel as if there was a huge white ocean cascading down from the sky right onto the roof tops.

Sheba thought about these things with a strange feeling, which combined a sacred bond with her motherland with the pain of having to stay far away, along with her sad feelings for her mother's loneliness, her desire to do something while living in the hostel, and her happiness at meeting Mayuri—all at the same time. She could see the clear sky beyond the transparent plastic window again. Ammi has great trust in her, Sheba thought with confidence. But Ammi would now be living about sadly in that huge house once again. Sheba, too, was sad. She pulled out a parrot feather from the book she held in her lap, which she had kept there as a bookmark, and put it between some other pages. She tried to fix her gaze at the writing on the page again. During the last vacation, this feather had danced down to the ground in front of her when she was sitting in the garden reading her book. She quickly rose to pick it up and felt very happy. She had smiled and looked at the sky with a feeling that the parrot had thrown down the feather especially for her. She had laughed that day at this quaint thought.

What a din these parrots make! They are not peaceful even while flying. In her childhood too, their screaming would give away the fact that the parrots were flying in the sky, and the children busy with their studies would raise their necks up and get so engrossed in looking at them that they would just forget to look back at their books. But then, resting the head on the back of the neck was so relaxing for the children, who otherwise had to look down at their books continuously. Their necks could get tired too, but none of the elders ever appreciated it—neither at school nor at home. If they looked around even for a second, someone was sure to shout, 'Get back to your book!' without considering the fact as to how long could a child keep his or her neck down; and also, that one had to look up once in a while too! And the children knew that those birds that look like a plus sign while flying, but with one line longer and more streamlined than the other, and who keep changing their places as if pursuing each other, making a lot of noise, are parrots. Even though one could not clearly see the colour of the birds against the blue background of the sky when one looks up at them. And those that are shorter than the parrots but thicker and fly silently, beating their bigger wings like eyelashes, are pigeons. And the ones with huge wings, that look like white clouds, with long necks and beaks, and their long legs extended beyond their tail, were water birds. God had made their legs long so that when they catch a fish or some insect with their long bills, standing at the banks of the water bodies and bending their snake-like long necks, they do not wet their necks or the legs. There are many other birds too, but they are not easily seen flying like these. Sheba smiled, and leaving the little Sheba of her imagination looking at the birds in the sky, returned to her seat in the airplane.

Fire crackers had been set-off the night before, along with the music of the band. In such situations, birds get scared even in the day time—mostly the ringed doves, which are also called turtle doves and pigeons. The doves do not open their beaks while cooing, and they fly straight upwards, not from one branch to another, as birds usually do, but straight upwards without looking at the sky, as if they were puppets and someone had jerked their strings towards the sky. But hearing a cracker blast, they get so scared that they just fly off in any direction, even though they may come back to the same place after flying around a little, making a mysterious whispering sound with their whitish wings while flying. The evening before too, a dove had darted into the branches of an apricot tree at hearing a cracker blast to hide itself. And when it heard another, it burst out of the branches, and flew in a different direction. It tried to sit on an electric wire but slipped from it, and quickly balancing itself for a second, flew to the other side, Sheba remembered.

Before the songs of the women, a very sad tune had been played by the band. One group of the band played a piece of a composition in higher notes and the other repeated it in lower notes, as if in the first one had shared some sad moment with the other and the other one had played it, enquiring about it in sympathy. Last night, Sheba had shut the bird book and closed her eyes when she heard the band. In the dark silence of the night, the band playing at some far-off unknown place had made her sad. But why? At that moment she also thought about Ammi saying that girls have to get married, and Baaji saying that she had started looking overage. And what about her? She had not thought about herself at all. But everyone else wanted the same; and the relatives, friends—all of them, even Ammi, were eager to get her married.

Lost in her thoughts, Sheba had a book open in front of her. She tried to concentrate on the content: 'At last, after furious plunges, he wrenched himself free. His tormentors set off towards Jones Road, laughing and jeering at him, while he, half blinded with tears, stumbled on, clenching his fists madly and sobbing.' She took a deep breath and closed the book. Her favourite writer sometimes depicted such bitter realities of life in his writing that a mind looking for peace would become sad and agitated instead. But the sadness brought by art has a strange magical power in it, which compels you to experience the same sadness again, the same way that you are attracted by its pleasant passages. 'James, you're a magician!' she said to herself, and put the parrot feather back between the pages that had made her so sad.

The exams were close by and everyone in the hostel was busy. Sheba also got busy with her studies but often had episodes of sadness. Then she tried to console herself. Mayuri had gone to her hometown. She could have helped her cheer up if she had been there, but she was not around. Sheba appeared for her exam papers one by one. Being very tired, she would fall in deep sleep, and thus be spared the chain of thoughts which had now become a part of her life. Still, the moment she lay down, many thoughts rushed to her mind—which would sometimes bring sleep, and at other times, tears to her eyes. 'Why had God made me so sensitive?' She sometimes thought, shaking her head.

That night she received a phone call from Farkhanda, who sounded very sad. 'Pyaari is no more, Sheba...' said Farkhanda immediately after hearing Sheba's voice.

'What? You mean...Pyaari...Pyaari...'

'Yes, Sheba...Pyaari died...and Aasim has run away from home.'

'Oh no! What are you saying?'

'Yes Sheba, it's true. And because your vacations are near, I thought I better tell you all this now. Nobody called you from home earlier because they did not want to distract you...but then, you would have been shocked to know this on reaching home.'

But Sheba was already stupefied. Hearing the sad news, far away from home in a depressing room like that was no less than a major shock to her.

'But how is this possible Farkhi? So many things at the same time,' Sheba's voice rose.

'Not at the same time…many days have passed by now.'

What Sheba heard after that was no less than any tragedy. Yasir had spent a night at Aasim's place. When he returned in the morning he was very disturbed, as he had gone through great mental torture. Loud sounds at the dead of night had woken Aasim up, as they were sleeping in the next room; Yasir also got up because of the commotion. Taaya Abbu was drunk, and was hurling curses at Nuzhat. Yasir rose to go to the next room and Aasim joined him, nervous and agitated; both wanted to see what was wrong with the man. The children saw Pyaari sitting in a chair a little distance from Zaheen-ud-din, who was bent before her with his hands on his knees, spitting at Pyaari's clothes and yelling 'Shame! Shame!' at her. Aasim shouted at him, asking him what he was doing, and Zaheen-ud-din also shouted back.

'Ask this shameless slut who was the lover she was talking to in the morning…I was in a hurry then…ask her to whom she was asking how the matters will go if he did not come over, and that she had been waiting for him for three days…She was smiling, asking him if she had to send a car to bring him over…That she had just taken a bath and her hair was wet! Ask this old whore! I had gone to the balcony to smoke a cigarette; I came inside suddenly and caught her red handed! Ask this bitch! Shame on you!' Zaheen-ud-din spat again on the floor in front of her. 'I was shocked to see that… had I not been in a hurry I would have kicked her out of the house! I spit on her face…I do not need her!' stinking foam flew from Zaheen-ud-din's mouth as he spewed all this. The floor of the room was bespattered with his spit.

After the incident, people at home thought that because of excessive drinking over the years, Zaheen-ud-din was losing his mind; and by now, after drinking, he behaved like a total idiot. In the morning of that day he might have thought that he should not think about his wife this way. But when he remembered it after drinking, he became aggressive and the liquor gave him the courage to create a scene as usual.

Pyaari's face reddened, and her eyes were burning upon listening to the abuse. She looked at both of them one by one.

'Who was he, Pyaari?' Aasim looked at Pyaari and Pyaari looked back at him, shocked.

'What will this prostitute say! I will tell you…she was always like that. When I married her, many people had told me that they were going to marry her but I had upstaged them! She was always like this…shameless bitch!'

Yasir did not ask anyone what the words 'whore' and 'prostitute' meant. But finally, he asked Gulla Bhai, who told him he would think about it. And Gulla Bhai's thinking never came to an end.

Aasim interrupted and shouted at his father again. 'Please keep quiet! Let me talk to Pyaari…' He went close to Pyaari. 'Who was he?'

Pyaari's face turned dark, and her lips quivered. She looked at her son, at his father and at Yasir with wide, red eyes. 'What are you saying? This...this...I...you are asking... me...me...' Pyaari's whole body trembled.

'Who was it, Pyaari?' Aasim looked at Pyaari's face. Pyaari did not expect this question from Aasim.

Afterwards, it was discussed at home and they thought that Aasim should have tried to stop his father behaving so shamefully rather than asking Pyaari that question since he, after all, was not under the influence of liquor. How could he ask his mother a question like that? But he was only a child. Woken up suddenly at midnight by all that noise in the next room, how could he understand so soon what was happening? But in the presence of the adolescent children, in front of growing children, Pyaari could not have borne it, and she did not.

'I...I had a bath...the drain was getting clogged and the bathroom was filled...water up to my ankles,' she said, trying to control her sobs. 'For the last three days...the water has stayed there...It takes hours to flow out...I phoned the plumber...he had been promising for three days that he would come over. I was calling him every day...' Pyaari said this with great pain, as if she had been made to ride a scooter without her clothes on, and the driver had tried to touch his back against her and she, trying to escape, had moved so far back that she had finally fallen from the scooter and been crushed to death by a speeding vehicle. But her nude body remained where it was, and people stared at her in obscene curiosity while she bled from every pore, as sometimes her face was white and sometimes dark, sometimes pale and sometimes red.

Pyaari got a fever after that and had a constant pain in her left side. She lost her hunger but still kept herself busy with work. No one took any notice of her condition, neither did she tell anything to anyone. She only mentioned it casually once to Aasim, but he didn't think that it was something serious either. He thought that since despite the quarrels at night Pyaari looked almost normal the next day, she must be fine. But no one knew that Pyaari had got very scared, as she had lost all her expectations of a good life that night, and she had nothing to hope for now. Zaheen-ud-din, who talked like a half-wit during the day and acted like a total idiot at night, had now become completely irresponsible and wild with no norms or etiquette left. A senseless person like him could repeat such episodes ad nauseam, putting her honour and prestige at stake. And life did not have such value for her that she would want to live anymore, only to be disgraced all the more. Whenever Zaheen-ud-din came before her, she closed her eyes. Her mind and heart were in a strange state of loss. She wanted to go away forever but had nowhere to go. She thought of going to her brother's place but she knew that she would be sent back soon. And Zaheen-ud-din's presence at home would make her feel insulted, hurt and pained. She was a stranger in the house, and felt as if the elders, children and the servants looked at her with suspicion. When, for a complete week, she could not escape this constant mental torture, nature helped her out and relieved her of all her misery. Nuzhat went to bed that night and didn't wake up the next morning. She was seen lying on her bed on a wet pillow, with her face turned to the ceiling. Mother-in-law's dear one, Pyaari, had become Allah's Pyaari—the dear one of God; and thankfully, her mother in-law wasn't alive to see this tragedy.

When Pyaari was found dead on her bed, everyone was surprised at how she could have died so suddenly. But Pyaari was not alive to tell them that this had not happened suddenly. When the female relatives almost pulled Pyaari's head away from Aasim's lap to give her the last ritual bath, Aasim had struck his head against the wall and let the blood flow. He pushed away everyone who tried to come near him. Finally, his father approached him but he stopped him with his open palm.

'Don't even touch me!' he screamed with the full force of his lungs.

After burying his mother, no one knew where Aasim went—no one knew where he vanished after leaving the graveyard.

Farkhanda told Sheba that a month had already passed since. Sheba could not sleep that night. She cried till late at night and couldn't sleep even then. She cried for many days secretly and appeared sad in class, but away in the Valley, among the high peaks in a home filled with love, no one knew about her grief.

On Saturday evening, Sheba felt some heaviness in her head and did not go to the library. Lying in her bed, she kept looking at the ceiling, her eyes wet with never-ending tears. She rose and sat on the bed, and picking up a book from the side table, opened it to the page she had read some days ago, and now wanted to read again.

> *EMILIA: Oh, the more Angel she, and you the blacker Devil.*
> *OTHELLO: She turned to folly, and she was a whore.*
> *EMILIA: Thou dost belie her, and thou art a devil.*
> *OTHELLO: She was false as water.*
> *EMILIA: Thou art rash as fire, to say that she was false. She was heavenly true.*

Sheba let out a painful sigh. She covered her face with her hands and sobbed uncontrollably. She had been trying to forget this tragedy for many days now, but could not.

The vacations had been postponed. When Farkhanda called after a few days, Sheba hoped that she would hear some good news about Aasim, but there was none. 'Any news about Aasim, Farkhi?' she asked immediately without even saying hello.

'No…No news. Yasir is so sad, he has gone very quiet…' Farkhanda sobbed.

Sheba's eyes filled with tears too. 'It's now one month, Farkhi…Who knows…maybe he has…'

'Yes, Sheba. We all have apprehensions about just that…Now we are waiting for these three months to pass, maybe he really has gone for training…He was spending his time with school dropouts…somebody could have brainwashed him…'

'Oh no…what a tragedy for a poor little soul like him! Who knows what he's doing, carrying that mountain of agony in his breast…His life will be ruined…Oh, how can this happen Farkhi?'

'Zaheen-ud-din looks devastated now.'

'He deserves it…you know that. Proud, shallow and jealous jerk!'

'Yes, he was jealous indeed…And God knows why he suffered from a strange type of insecurity. He spoiled his son himself. I remember long ago, it was a Sunday…Aasim was about nine years old; when he woke up around 11 am and Nuzhat told him that there would not be any lunch for a late riser who had his breakfast late, disturbing the routine, and that evening tea would be served soon. Nuzhat told the servants this as well. You will be surprised, Sheba, when you hear what that man did! He ordered food from a restaurant at 1 pm and made his son eat with him too!'

'Yes, he laid the foundations for his son's bad behaviour.'

'Yes, and when Nuzhat talked to him about this, he said, "My child cannot starve while I'm around!" Who could tell that stupid fellow that a mother cannot let her child go hungry, that she definitely would have given him something to eat in the afternoon. But his ill-conceived action must have made the child think that his mother's reprimand was not important, and he began to misbehave…On top of that, he was non-existent as a father.'

'He spoilt his own son for the sake of his ego.'

'Yes. Everyone knows this.'

'But he might not have realized he was misguiding the child.'

'He's a total mental case!'

'Oh, absolutely!'

'He could not bear the whole household praising Nuzhat…And I am sure he must have been picking fights with her, creating unnecessary issues because he was jealous of her.'

'Yes, but why?'

'Because alcohol robs you of your senses and causes permanent damage to the brain as well…Poor Nuzhat would not have been able to make him understand anything. Oh, yes…she had said that his IQ had gone down almost to the level of a child, and that she had to tell him repeatedly something that just needed common sense to understand. Poor Pyaari…and he became angry seeing that everything Pyaari had been saying was true. You know, Sheba, Pyaari was a very loving person…she always put the happiness of her husband and the family before her own. When she talked to me, she gave me the feeling that a very intelligent person—a pure and pious soul—was before me, and it was hard to believe that she was married to such a monster and lived in the same house with him…Her soul was virgin, only her body would bear the brunt of this relationship; she did not get any satisfaction and pleasure from her marital life... It was as if she was caught by a man-eater and being eaten in portions to inflict wounds on the body and soul...' Farkhi's voice was filled with agony.

Sheba had turned to stone.

'He was never a good man, Sheba. He gained some measure of importance when his business suddenly flourished, but he was never faithful to Pyaari. Everybody knew that he had created a position in his office, not really necessary for the business, employing girls only. Some of them stayed just for six months, and then were replaced by another one soon. He was seeing other women too. I remember when he was newly-married, I went to his showroom along with Pyaari once; she was not very well and our mother-in-law had told him that morning to take her to the doctor in the evening...Well, there was a haggard-looking woman sitting with him and they were having tea with many goodies. I was at the door when Pyaari went into his office, and he told her that he was busy and that she had come before the scheduled time, but if she wanted to sit and wait he had no objection. Pyaari quickly said that she would come back later and left the room...Can anyone be so mean, Sheba?'

'No...no one can...But some other girl would not have given up so easily, she had every right to sit there!'

'What else could she do? She had been newly married, just for a month...He was a shameless man, how could she stay there! But you are right, one should pay such a brazen person like him in the same coin.'

'Yes, you are right.'

'I tell you Sheba, if he had behaved like that with me, I would have just left his house...But...'

'You are absolutely right Farkhi...If Pyaari had any sympathy from her parents' household or had any place to go, she would not have died...She would have left home, and this brute would have possibly come to his senses. At least she would have been alive...'

'Yes, the stone-hearted man, without a conscience... So cruel to the one who was his life's companion. It was he who was jealous of that innocent soul...And such a sudden death...Sheba, pray to God to take care of Aasim.' Listening to Farkhanda's motherly apprehensions, Sheba's heart became restless. '*Ameen*...he will be fine, Farkhi. Please do not be sad, it will affect Yasir badly.'

'Yasir is not eating properly. Tears come to his eyes every now and then...I am so worried, Sheba, lest he falls ill,' cried Farkhi; the cheeks like flowers and the soft forehead appeared before Sheba's eyes.

Sheba could not sleep that night. Besides what Farkhanda said, there were other things that took her sleep away—some things she'd heard in the past, and some other things she had thought about at that time. She tried to look at the ceiling in the dark and took a deep breath. The night was colder than the day in the plains but her breath was still somewhat hot. Sheba's subconscious thought was that had she been at home, this long breath would have been cool. Her mind was lost again in thinking about Nuzhat and all her suffering. It is said that the saintly Ghaus-e-Pak Hazrat Miraan Sahib had learnt the verses of the holy Quran in his mother's belly, and science has proved that everything the expectant mother goes through—psychologically, physically, emotionally or in her environment, her moods, and patterns of activity and rest—affects the mental and physical health of the new life growing inside her. Aasim's growth was badly affected, and the consequences were clearly visible in his personality. Nuzhat knew that her innocent child was an indirect victim of all that she had faced during pregnancy—and continued to face until she died. Aasim did not have the opportunity to learn any values; he wasn't to blame. Suffering and tense always, she could not concentrate on her child properly. When she was expecting him, Zaheen-ud-din's carelessness would make her sensitive heart ache. When her child was born, Nuzhat had something to live for at least, but Zaheen-ud-din took this emotional security away by constantly harassing her for no reason. And this continuous suffering was too much for her child's psyche.

When others disliked Aasim for his unruly and impulsive behaviour, his mother blamed the bad home environment, as he was the living proof of being brought up in an adverse, abusive atmosphere. And in trying to conceal the torture he suffered, he had become aggressive. His proud and senseless father was happy encouraging him to be disobedient and disrespectful towards his mother.

Why couldn't he understand that a child is always closer to his mother, and thinks of her as a close companion and the most precious being around? That becoming disobedient to her would make him sad unconsciously—and that in turn would make him disgruntled, leading to his immature mind making more mistakes. How the wrongs done by a single man become a curse for many. Why did this happen?

Sheba recalled the aggressive voice poisoning the magical silence of the moonlit night, and the helpless sobbing. Aasim's innocent, tearful face appeared in her mind…her eyes got flooded with tears, and her sleep drowned in them. Many nights, weeks and months passed but there was no news of Aasim. Whenever she received a phone call from home, her first question was about him. Her mind would race trying to figure out what might have happened, how and where Aasim was, and whether she would ever see him again or not…

The Long Autumn in the Chinars

Sheba was deeply perturbed by the questions that appeared and disappeared in her mind. This time, however, the ominous clouds of destruction were so thick that not a single ray of light pierced through them. It was very hard to say who was behind the bloodshed of this militancy working in the garb of 'Struggle for Freedom'. There were surely some other realities behind the apparent truths of the borders, religious polarization and unemployment, none of which were easy to comprehend. Some horrendous reality, backed perhaps by the vast resources of Capitalism, the clout of which exceeded many times all the wealth of the people on the list of the rich in the world. One truth, for instance, could be the greed for mineral wealth and the diamond mines, and letting the children grow for that purpose to an age when they could carry a gun and fight for them, killing people and becoming criminals. Places where the hands of the people are chopped off to stop them from casting their vote. How can political activity stand up in the face of such huge wealth? The weak countries will look farcical before the powers backed by the Capitalists. What is there to hope for when they are least concerned about the adverse consequences of their evil designs and nefarious plans for those poor countries, and do not care even if the rest of the world is pushed to the brink of destruction? There could be other grounds as well, but what outcome can be expected, if efforts to stop the violence apparently seem to be based upon an impulsive approach, thoughtless measures and partisan bias? In other words, the rulers acted in haste without any consideration of the consequences, or were so drunk with power that they just thought the human lives were of no consequence...

These questions stormed into Sheba's head when she went to bed. Her sleep would vanish. What about the peaceful majority who only want to carry on with their quiet lives? And then there are the ones who are blinded by the lure of rewards from unknown quarters, and have become so selfish that they are putting the lives of their own people at stake by providing them with arms and ammunition, misleading them with violent and hateful speeches and prompting them to this bloodshed? They, too, will have to answer for their heinous crimes someday. Had the rulers been a little lenient and compassionate, and had showed their concern in approaching these newly brainwashed youngsters, the situation would not have come to this stage. Agreed that if the safety and security of the country is at stake, the authorities will try to restore peace and order at any cost, but then these are the times when the mettle and foresight of the leaders is tested. They should ensure that the peaceful people are not treated as suspects, lest they, too, turn against the authorities. Sheba suddenly felt suffocated with the rush of these frightful thoughts. How much longer can these peace-loving, innocent people, who have been crushed between the uniformed and non-uniformed gunmen, endure these atrocities? What tortures their bodies have suffered, and how much pain their psyches have borne!

Once when Sheba was going to the airport from her house, she saw people cleaning the blood on the road with brooms of a certain bush. These broom-like bushes that grow in the wild in the Valley are considered pure and clean, and are used to clean the premises for holy rites—like offering *Nazr Niyaz* (making offerings to God and the saints). The blood had been shed last evening, when terrorists had opened fire on a funeral procession. It was the funeral of the eminent dignitary Mirwaiz Moulvi Mohammad Farooq. Sheba's heart had skipped some beats when she saw the picture in the newspapers in the plane. The angelic, noble face bore bullet marks; the bullets had been fired at the funeral procession, at living human beings. The bullet holes in that saintly face made Sheba feel as if they had gone through her own heart.

She covered her eyes with her hands. Why didn't these rulers learn from the great King of Kashmir, Sultan Zain-ul-Aabideen Buddshah? There is no one with such a caring heart for Kashmir—a paradise on earth,

'They want their sky on your soil,
They destroy your roots and want to build nests
in your branches.

Who will care for you in these adverse times?
O my Valley, who will put some soothing balm
on your wounds?'

'Who will dress your wounds, O my dear Valley?' Sheba whispered, sighed, and closed her eyes.

She decided to spend the short winter vacation in her hometown that year and left for the Valley. Those were the early years of the ninth decade of the 20th century. On the short way home from the airport, she saw two school buildings which had been torched, and her eyes filled with tears. Why should the militants burn the schools of their children? Only an enemy would do so. She had read some days ago in a newspaper that a restaurant on one of the two islands on the Dal Lake called Chaar Chinaari had been burnt to ashes. Why should Kashmiris destroy their tourism industry? A huge section of their economy depended on it. Who will buy the unique handiworks of their talented artisans if there were no tourists? If, because of curfews, the fresh and the dry fruit could be sent out of the state only sporadically, whose loss would that be? If the lovers of the Mughal Gardens, lakes and hills were not to visit, there wouldn't be any tourist industry left. And that was exactly what was happening. Whenever Sheba called home she heard such news. No one had any answers.

Mother was very happy to see her daughter home unexpectedly. Though the people of this land had an apprehension of something sinister befalling every moment of their temporary happiness, yet they had learnt to live even under such circumstances, as one gets to live only once. Things had completely changed there. People going for work in the morning would take leave of each other as if they would never return to meet again. The wounded hearts had reconciled painfully with the circumstances but had to pay almost with their lives, as many of them—especially the women—had heart trouble; and many men suffered psychological problems. People who had lost their dear ones looked stone-faced. The ones shot by the security forces for no fault of theirs just vanished, while others stopped using their good senses and went underground and took to guns, influenced by so-called leaders. Thus, leaving their near and dear ones in the limbo between hope and hopelessness, waiting for any information if they were alive and would come home or, if dead, could at least be given a solemn burial. But the 'information' never came forth. There were a few fortunate ones, too, whose unclaimed bodies were found on some road. On the other hand, there were many who were arrested on mere suspicion—never to return, nor was any word heard about them. Their parents stood at the doors of their homes shivering with cold, waiting for them during the curfew hours, or shedding tears wandering on the roads as if they had lost their senses when there was no curfew. Sometimes, believing the reassurances given by the authorities, they relaxed for a while but only to return to the same perturbed state of mind soon. Anyone could disappear at any time. The newspapers were full of such news, and also with advertisements by people seeking information about their loved ones.

Sheba was tense, and felt helpless in the midst of all that. She became anxious and agitated if she heard the sound of a gun from even afar. She felt like running away, closing off her ears with cotton wool, losing consciousness or finally dying, as that bullet had pierced someone's chest too.

There was yet another, and far worse, disaster lying in wait on top of these terrible happenings. That day the sun shone full, not a single shred of a cloud blocking its rays. The snow melted into small droplets from the roofs, the dry branches and autumn-stricken plants.

Sheba sat in the sun near the grape vine in its autumnal garb. The snow had melted from the wooden swing hanging by a thick branch of the mulberry tree, near the autumn-scarred apricot tree in the far corner. It was cold, and would become even colder if one were to swing. Still, if it was dry, Sheba would have gone for a couple of swings because she had not sat on it for a long time, mulling over something, as she once used to do. She looked above at the screaming mynahs sitting on the tree. Four of them came down with a thud as if they had just dropped off from the tree.

'Oh, these quarrelsome birds!' Sheba said and smiled. They were so lost in fighting that if she were to throw Ammi's dupatta on them suddenly, they would be caught unawares. Sheba smiled again. She thought seriously, like she used to do years ago.The mynahs were busy quarrelling. They did not care about the wet ground and the cold; the cold cannot reach their bodies through the feathers, and that is why you hear them chirp in every season. Just a step away, a crow eyed the quarrelling birds keenly. When one of the mynahs, after a short flight, would return to join the fight, the crow would also move a little and start looking at them again. He was actually looking for his chance: when the winner birds would fly away, he would grab the wounded mynah in its blood-thirsty beak and tear it apart with the nail-like sharp point on it the Creator had given him.

'*Cheenkrum...cheenkrum...cheenkrum...*' Sheba heard someone mimicking the mynahs and turned her head. Yasir was about to run towards the fighting birds, imitating them, to stop their fight. But before he reached them, all of them flew away, with just one left behind. The last one could not support itself on its unsteady feet when it would try to stand up, and the crow was about to reach and grab it when Yasir, stomping on the ground, ran to it to scare the crow away.

'No, Yasir! Wait...the mynah will get scared!' Sheba said quickly, and Yasir stopped smiling and laughing. The crow had flown away. The mynah recovered, limped for a few steps and then it flew away too. A happy smile appeared on their faces.Yasir had come to Nanna Jaani's place after his tuition class. There was news of a blast on the road to his home, because of which the security forces had blocked the way. He was ruddy-faced because of the cold. Although he was only 13 years old, he had grown quite tall.

'*Asalaam-ul-alikum* Khala Jaani!' Still far away, he extended his hand before reaching Sheba.

'Khala Jaani's *jaan* (life of Khala Jaani), you will stay here tonight?' Sheba returned his salaam and kissed his forehead without getting up. Yasir had to bend quite low.

'Yes Sheba Khala, I had planned to, but let us see what mamma says. There is some disturbance in our area…they might impose curfew before I can get home. Okay, let me call mamma first.'

He went inside, leaving behind his long-strapped, zip-less cloth bag with a few books on the stone table. Sheba pulled out a notebook peeping out of the bag, and a colourful magazine also slipped out along with it. She picked it up and started looking through it. It was a religious magazine which had some advice about praying and fasting, and some information about good and bad deeds in its editorial, besides asking the readers to read some special articles included in it. Sheba opened the magazine to one of those articles. But as soon as she started reading it, her heart started pounding. An article like that could easily guide an innocent mind to the darkness of death. It was especially addressed to adolescents. It read that they should not go to hill stations this summer. Instead, they should go for some training which would benefit their religion, as doing so was in accordance with the principles of their religion; that it would also add to the virtuous deeds of their parents, and that it would open up the doors of paradise for them.

Sheba observed that there were no reasons given for anything. There were some farewell messages from the ones proceeding for the holy struggle addressed to their parents and newly-wed brides, telling them not to grieve for them as their course of action was for the benefit of their near and dear ones, and also for themselves—in this world as well as in the hereafter.'What is this in Yasir's bag? O Allah, Farkhi, your world is going to end! Our world is going to end!' Sheba moaned, distraught. She was trembling. She felt as if flames were leaping from an inferno ablaze in her head.

Yasir came out after making the phone call and turned pale upon seeing the magazine in her hands.'Khala...did you...have you read it?' he stammered.

'Yes, Yasir. Where did you get it from?' she asked.

'You won't tell anyone Sheba Khala, will you?'

'No...but only if you tell me the whole truth! You know very well that this is not the right path.'

'Yes, Sheba Khala...Ammi and Abbu have told me everything, but I will go...' he said in a resigned tone, bowing his head.

'Where will you go?' Sheba felt the earth slipping from under her feet. 'We will all die here...this would be the death of us all, Yasir!' she said with a trembling voice.

'To look for Aasim Bhaiye...' He raised his bent head and looked at Sheba. Tears rolled down his cheeks.

Sheba kept looking at him in utter bewilderment, her mouth half open. She caressed his head.'Do you think he is still...' she said, looking into his eyes.

'Yes, Sheba Khala. One of my schoolmates was told he is alive...He is wounded, and is in a hospital. I will find him and bring him back.'

'How will you get there?'

'The way Aasim Bhaiye went.'

'You mean, in an unlawful manner.'

'Yes. There is no other way.'

'And if, God forbid, something happens to you?'

'Nothing will happen to me. Someone will take me there.'

'Who? Some other misled person?'

'No, he is a guide.'

'Then he is a misguided one and might not know this, but how can I make you understand…'

'No, Sheba Khala, he is not like that. He is a man of truth.'

'But who knows the truth?! Someone may have misguided him too, someone might have bought him. It is not just the borders nearby but a global conspiracy—for the land of oil, the diamond mines and the minerals resources…for the land of jewels. Every such place is being poisoned. And to prove themselves true, all over the lands of these people, they set their traps as per the size of the prey—big bait for the big fish and small for the small ones. And then these big fish catch the smaller ones but everyone is a victim in the end—some are victims of greed and some of their blind faith, as this great religion is being misinterpreted by these predators to suit their own benefit. And the followers are put to blame; they interpret this religion wrongly, declaring the prohibited as unprohibited. But while it is only some selfish people propagating it, innocent and illiterate people get trapped—depriving a people of knowledge on purpose and keeping them uneducated is also a tactic in this game of selfish greed after all.' Sheba's heart was beating fast. She was oblivious of the fact that her listener was just a 13-year-old child. But the listener was not all that naive, and the truth had started to dawn upon him. He was getting to know the reality.

'So, is all this wrong, Sheba Khala?'

'Yes Yasir, this is wrong! And there are so many innocent people who think that this is the righteous path, and they have no realization whatsoever that they are going in the wrong direction!'

'But he is a decent person. It could be that he is of those who do not know that they are wrong. He says that he will bear all the expenses because he also wants Aasim Bhaiye to come back home.'

'Maybe…But what if he isn't as good as you think, and doesn't let you come back—what then?' Sheba said with great hope, trying to hide the dreadful thoughts in her mind.

'Then?'

Yasir began to think. 'No, he is a good man. He had asked me to join earlier too, but I had said no because I knew my mother will cry for me. He tried to convince me, and also said that he will give me the best gun. He had said that it would be a very good job, and that Aasim Bhaiye is an important person there. But I did not listen to him. He then offered to take me there, and bring me back as well.'

'No, no, my child. You…' Sheba choked.

'I am not going forever. I am just going to bring Aasim Bhaiye back, and that is all.'

'Will he be prepared to come with you?'

'I will make him come with me, Sheba Khala. I will convince him no matter what.'

'And what if he does not let even you come back?' Sheba asked urgently and he burst out laughing.

'No, Sheba Khala! Do you think Aasim Bhaiye will force me to stay there?'

'That is possible, otherwise he would have returned by now…he would not have been angry for this long. Also, if he was angry with his father, why punish the whole family? He would not have been away from home for so long. So what if Pyari is no longer with us? Farkhi is, I am, and so are you! He might have been brainwashed completely by now, and he might try to pull you on to the same path that he is on.'

Yasir looked at his shoes; they were muddy. When he bent his head, his silken hair fell all over his forehead and Sheba's heart was suddenly overwhelmed by motherly feelings for him. She could not contain herself anymore and started to cry. 'Farkhi will die, Yasir! Your Nanna Jaani will not be able to bear this shock in old age…Please drop this idea! Do not kill us like this, it would be a living death for all of us!' she said, and started sobbing uncontrollably. Yasir looked at her for a moment, and then he started crying as well.

'Sheba Khala, in that case, Aasim Bhaiye will never come back…'

'But he is not going to change his path for you either! So don't risk your life, child,' she said, wiping the tears flowing down Yasir's cheeks. 'We can't do anything for him unless he himself wants to…' She wiped her tears with the corner of the triangular scarf she was wearing, with its ends hanging down like the long ears of a goat. 'If you go, may God protect you from all evil because many lives are connected with yours,' she added.

'No, Sheba Khala. I won't go anywhere...I will not go,' he said, shaking his head.

'Make a solemn promise to me!'

'Yes, I do. But you, too, have to promise me one thing.'

'What, sweetheart?'

'That you will not tell anyone about this conversation at all.'

'You also promise me that you will not talk to that man, who wanted you to go with him, ever again.'

'Never...I will stop taking the street I do and will change my route to school from tomorrow onwards.'

'And to no one like him either...who would encourage such things.'

'OK, I will not talk to anyone like him. Never ever.'

'And we will not cry!' Sheba said and smiled.

They hadn't even realized that the sun had set. Their teeth began to chatter because of the cold. They got in quickly and went to the kitchen; the kitchen and the living room were divided into two parts by a four-foot high wall. A longish *dasterkhan* (the traditional cloth to set food upon) was spread in the living room with a samovar full of pink salt tea in it. The steam coming out of its spout was spreading the aroma of the tea not just in the kitchen but all over the whole ground floor.

The other people of the household, such as Farkhi and Seemeen, who were supposed to meet Sheba, were still to reach the *dasterkhan*. In the cooking area, Gulla Bhai was making thin parathas of fine wheat flour with ghee spread on them. Bringing them over to the *dasterkhan*, he was talking to himself and glancing around.

'What happened, Gulla Bhai?' Sheba asked, diverting her attention from looking at the flowers printed on the *dasterkhan*. She knew that when Gulla Bhai was upset about something he would talk to himself, like senior domestics do, to make others listen to them in their own peculiar way.

'Now they will all have cold parathas! Such cold weather… everyone knows that 4 o'clock is the time for evening tea but still…' He put the tray on the *dasterkhan*, spread his hands and moved back to the kitchen.

'Naush-e-jaan isko kijiye, Sahib!
Chai hazir hai; lijiye, Sahib!'

'Drink it, O Worthy One!
The tea is served, O Worthy One!'

Yasir read the verse carved on the brass tray loudly, and quickly turned to the door as if in a somersault. 'I will call everyone, Gulla Bhai!'

Sheba's eyes followed him to the door. After a second or two when she moved her eyes away from the door, she heard his voice coming from the first floor, which meant that he had jumped up two or three steps at a time with his growing legs, otherwise how could he reach the first floor so quickly? A smile appeared on her lips.

'No, never mind! But when you warm them up a second time they don't taste as good!' Gulla Bhai said grumpily, spreading another paratha on the hot plate and shaking his head.

'Gulla Bhai, if you keep these parathas in the casserole from tomorrow and the tea in the thermos flask, nothing will get cold; and to keep the tea hot you would not need to put any coals in the samovar again and again,' Sheba said.

'I could do that, Bibi, but neither would the parathas be crisp then, and nor would the aroma of the tea spread through the house.'

'Oh, is that so?' Sheba smiled.

'Had it been summer, it would not have mattered much. In the winter, no one even sits at the dining table because everyone prefers to eat in the kitchen. I also like it; they chat here, we work here—everyone gathers around here. All is so lively…otherwise, ever since Aasim left, Chhoti Baaji and Begum Sahiba are so subdued as if, God forbid, someone from the home itself has departed. Although the happiness we had in our Kashmir has turned its fair face away from us. Only God knows what has happened…The people who open fire do not know anything…and the people hit with the bullets are also completely confounded. Someone has cast an evil eye on our Kashmir, Bibi,' Gulla Bhai kept shaking his head. Sheba looked at him quietly.

A few days after Sheba had returned to her hostel, Farkhanda called her to say that Zaheen-ud-din had suffered a heart attack and was in the hospital.

'Why, is he all right? Any news about Aasim.'

'Yes, after he heard about him.'

'Is he all right Farkhi? Where is he?'

'Only God knows, but someone told us that the security forces had thrown a truckload of bodies of the young men killed in an encounter—on the roads here and there. One of the injured whom they thought was dead, said that there was a boy resembling Aasim who was injured but was still alive, and whom they had thrown at a crossing. And if he had survived the cold night, he would still be alive...'

'So, did anyone look for him there?'

'They went there but found no one at the crossing. Hearing this, Zaheen-ud-din had a heart attack; he's in the Intensive Care Unit in Soura hospital.'

'Oh no! And Aasim? Where is Aasim then?'

'Only God knows where he is...May God bless him! My heart was pounding so hard that day until they came back after looking for him in vain. I was stuck between life and death, Sheba. Nuzhat is lucky not to have lived to see this day after all,' Farkhanda's voice was heavy.

'No, Farkhi. God will keep him under His protection. You take care of yourself.'

***

After his evening tea, Abbu spent some time before dinner with the children in the living room adjacent to the kitchen, and talked about spiritual and worldly matters with them. The children would be there doing their homework. Abbu would have his tea after the children as he came home later. By then the children would have had their *baqarkhanee*s and *kulcha*s with tea. It was black tea but boiled with a pinch of baking soda that turned its purple colour to pink upon adding milk. That was the customary fare for the breakfast and the afternoon tea in the Valley.

Sheba looked at her hands. Those little hands of hers had grown now. Her fingers were so long, rather too long, but looked good as a slight movement of the hand made a beautiful curve in every joint. Sheba smiled at her hands. In fact, Mayuri had told her that her hands were *very* pretty—like a lotus bud, and Sheba had returned her compliment saying that she had beautiful hands too. Then Mayuri placed her palm on Sheba's palm, showing her that she had even longer fingers than her.

God has created every person differently, and has also given him/her the freedom to choose their own path in life. It's not fair if someone thinks too highly of himself or herself and looks down upon others. Sultan Zain-ul-Aabideen, who was lovingly called and is even still called Badshah—the great king—invited the Kashmiri Hindus who had left Kashmir and settled them in the Valley again. A similar example of such consideration for human values and a benign political approach like this cannot be found in history.

The aroma of tea filled the room. She poured herself a mugful, and filled her lungs with fresh air on reaching the window. The bluish morning was beautiful. 'So where have I been, my dear Valley? Yes, but…' a smile spread on her lips and then disappeared.

Sheba took a sip of tea and looked into the cup. She smiled as if she had seen something in the cup.

Autumn brings rouge from the skies for my beautiful Valley; the green of the chinars turns to crimson and orange, which looks like some yet unseen part of heaven against the background of the blue sky. Snowbirds with soft feathers of vibrant colours visit to bless it with the pride and pleasure of being their host. When the snows accompanying the bluish clouds come to its many valleys, hills and waters, its rivers and springs dance and its lakes sparkle like quicksilver.

Sheba smiled, thinking about her Valley, when suddenly the memory of a weird event came to her mind and the smile vanished.

There was black snow once, after the Gulf War. In Kashmiri, the language of her Valley—the mother tongue of her mother, and the beloved Kashmiri language of hers too, which she spoke fluently for many years now, the phrase 'black snowfall' was used to refer to something impossible. And no one had ever imagined that this phrase would actually come true one day.

She took another sip of tea, smiled again, and resumed her previous chain of thoughts.

Yes, and then there comes a hand with henna on it, holding a magical brush from some unknown world to colour its gardens in shades of heavenly hews, and hands it over to the realm of fragrances. Then the beauty of the different-coloured birds, leaves and flowers reaches its peak.

After that, soft, warm winds tickle the paddies, whisper to the wheat fields, bless the mustard and sesame with spring, and become red in apples, yellow in apricots and purple in plums. The rains carry the scent of ripening walnuts to the dainty, green, silky tresses of corn cobs, and trickle down as fragrant drops, turning the simple folk into poets.

Sheba's eyes searched for something far away, and in a flash she went to her childhood and then returned. After having lavished the bountiful cornucopia of corn cobs, although the maize plants look like sticks standing in the fields, yet they are not all like wood. They are juicy and sweet like sugarcane. However, one needs to be strong to pull them off in the field, which is hard work for children, but all the same it is great to bite and chew on them like sugarcane. But yes, after cutting the plants away, the stumps prick the soles of one's feet like huge thorns while walking in the fields, even if one is wearing very soft slippers. The unique and unparalleled beauty of the Valley is a blessing of God Almighty, as well as a bounty of the hard work of its own people.

Their lives are not protected from the harshness of the elements to enjoy the beauty of the winters from behind closed doors, as the fortunate people of developed countries can. Neither do their harsh working conditions permit them to escape the vagaries of the weather. When the artisan prematurely loses his eyesight caused by straining his eyes through the magnifying glass in embroidering the shawls, he is face to face with the question of how to earn his livelihood. This unfortunate craftsman might have lost this art too. The carpet-weaver was born with colour-sensitive fingers and was undoubtedly amongst the most skillful artisans in the world, but was also the one who could not get anything for himself.

Doctor Sir Muhammad Iqbal wrote,

Baresham qabakh wajaaz mehnat-e-oo
Naseeb-e-tanash jamah-e-taar tare!

(The silk robe that the Honoured One wears, is the fruit of the labour
Of the one who himself is destined to be clad in rags!)

The craftsmen of my Valley give life to the love story of Gul-o-Bulbul—the nightingale and the blossom—on wood, and draw the legends and events in colour with their brushes on papier-mâché, making it look magical. But their humility does not realize the value of their art, and this unique and exclusive art sells for next to nothing. These miraculous artists are famous for the delightful products of their skills for centuries the world over. Their calligraphy, rifle-making, cloth-weaving and other arts and crafts had no parallel in the world in the past either. Sheba closed her eyes to welcome a gentle gust of breeze. Innocent and simple, the Kashmiri craftsman does not know his worth yet. He is content with whatever little he has. But when this artist with a golden hand will wake up, he will change his destiny, as underrating this genius and intelligent race is no more acceptable. 'No more!' said Sheba to herself, shaking her head. The heavy yoke of slavery for which he was condemned for centuries did not allow him to get an education. And therefore, he did not realize the designs of his exploiters, but now he will change his destiny. No one can exploit him anymore, nor neglect his inherent wisdom. His natural intelligence will not let him be a victim of barbarism and inhumanity. The beautiful and genial women, blessed with a poetic genius who compose songs on the fly and sing them on the occasions of marriages and happy events may not be aware of their talent, but they know the language of peace. Their peaceful nature will not tolerate the injustices any more, nor will it let others mislead their dear sons. Their daughters will not grow old alone because their bridegrooms have gone to sleep in their graves, and the would-be brides, longing for henna to colour their hands, would not have nowhere to go. Sheba's eyes filled with tears.

A renowned intellectual, a friend of Professor Daanish, had once provided a very satisfactory answer in his speech to the distressing questions arising in Sheba's mind. Mayuri was also listening to him with full attention, as becoming friends with Sheba, she had developed a great interest in the political affairs of Kashmir too. That day, Sheba had burst into laughter upon seeing Mayuri listen so keenly to the talk by Professor Sameer Ghosh.

The world-renowned professor had delivered a speech on the subject in the university's auditorium. Hundreds of fans from inside and outside the university had crowded to hear him. Sheba and Mayuri sat in the first two chairs of the second row. Sheba turned to Mayuri to say something but had burst into sudden laughter upon seeing Mayuri totally lost in listening to the lecture with her mouth half open as if in a trance.

'Do you listen to a lecture with your ears or the mouth?' Sheba whispered.

'Shut up!' retorted Mayuri without looking at her and punched Sheba in her leg with her smallish fist.

'Why are you looking at the professor with your mouth wide open?' Sheba whispered again, and Mayuri also started laughing.

'Is that so? Well, I am an expert on Kashmir affairs!' she said softly and resumed looking at the stage.

'Yes, it's for the company of a genius like me...' Sheba nodded.

'As if I have no interest in the subject!'

'Oh yes, of course, you do.'

Professor Ghosh looked at the balcony in the auditorium. 'This was the only Muslim majority state that had joined the Indian Federation on its own. It had been accorded a special status in the Federation, and had its own Prime Minister as well as President. It was the only state in India and Pakistan that had the right to adopt its own Constitution for internal affairs; the state had its own flag, which flew alongside the Tricolour.'

Professor Ghosh smiled. Two flags fluttered in Sheba's mind.

Lehra a Kashmir ke jhande
(Keep flying O' banner of Kashmir)
Tifl-o-jawan o pirke jhande
(The banner of the young and the old)
Hardam lehra, har pal lehra
(Keep flying, all the time)
Ta bah qayamat pai hamm lehra
(Keep flying till the end of time)
Halwale dil girke jhande
(The banner of the heavy-hearted tiller)
Lehra a Kashmir ke jhande
(Keep flying O' banner of Kashmir)

'Sher-e-Kashmir had returned the land to the tillers. In the whole of North Asia, it was a unique program of land reforms in which not a single drop of blood was shed.'

A peaceful smile appeared on Sheba's lips.'

Lehra a Kashmir ke jhande.

Dr Daanish had said that Professor Sameer Ghosh belonged to the Left in Indian politics. Everyone was aware of this but he was respected as a great scholar because of his consideration for human values, his strong advocacy for human rights and his compassion for the minorities. Sheba considered his lectures and columns to be of great importance.

Professor Ghosh said that the Leftists had played an important role in Sheikh Abdullah's arrest, but in the 1960s they pressurized the Central government into a reconciliation with him.

'Three wars were fought between India and Pakistan over Kashmir.'

If the Kargil conflict was also counted as a war, then the total number of wars was four, thought Sheba.

'Ladies and Gentlemen…' Sameer Ghosh spoke excellent Urdu, Persian and Sanskrit. Even though he was a Bengali, his pronunciation in all these languages was impeccable.

After he had left, Mayuri and Sheba went to the cafeteria where some of their fellow students were already busy in animated discussions. Later that night back in her room, Sheba turned her head and looked out at some distant object and then glanced at her room restlessly, shaking her head in negation.

A despairing look took over Sheba's face, and her eyes watered. She raised her head and tried to look out again. She could not see anything but darkness since it was still early dawn. She closed her eyes again. A tear rolled down towards her ear and a sob escaped her lips. Mayuri changed her side, turning towards the wall. Her breath could be heard in the room; but the very next moment, her breathing stopped, and then after a little while she inhaled deeply.

'Why are you awake? And you were crying just now, weren't you?' Mayuri said in a sleepy voice.

'Sorry dear, I woke you up too.'

'No, you have not, I woke up by myself. Now tell me, what is it? What is the matter? Missing home?'

'Yes, I was thinking about my home. I was thinking why all this is happening to us…What will happen to my Valley?'

'Everything will be fine, go to sleep now.' Mayuri tried to look at her face in the dim light, coming from the veranda through the ventilator, to know whether she wanted to sleep or not.

'Nothing will be fine Mayuri. It is not such a simple problem. Its roots go back centuries, and no one knows how far its branches, void of all fruit, will spread,' Sheba said in a sad tone.

'OK. If you do not want to sleep, would you like some tea?'

Sheba yawned.

'Shall I make some?'

'Have you had enough sleep?'

'Yes, I am fine. I went to bed early last night, you know. And when you are upset and are not sleeping, how will I be able to? We could just talk.

'No, we are not talking about anything. You will blame me later for not letting you sleep,' Sheba said softly in a blaming tone.

'I will not! Oh God, one cannot even be nice to others in these times,' Mayuri said in a chirpy voice and Sheba smiled.

'Yes, it must have some basis.'

'Not basis, Mayuri, it is ill treatment.'

'But it has always been like that. Every nation has tried to exploit other nations, countries, and people to its advantage, and it will always be the same.'

'But where can we go? We have no peace within our land, nor do we have it without. So much destruction has been wrought, which never benefitted anyone, and has only occasioned much harm.'

'Yes, that is very tragic.'

'And it still continues. But it is now plain that what happened was not right. It is time for the people who claim to be pacifists to come forward and make efforts for reconciliation and rapprochement with the people of the Valley. This is the time to commiserate with them and heal their wounds. Otherwise, there is a danger that these peace-loving victims will have no faith left in anyone, and will lose trust in them forever. The torching of houses, rapes, killings without any provocation, arrests without any grounds—could one ever forget all these horrors?'

'But why do you forget, that this is what happens in such circumstances? Some people have a certain perspective on the situation while others view it differently. What are you thinking about so intently?' Mayuri asked, looking at her and raising her eyebrows.

'Nothing, Mayuri. I was just thinking that though almost all has been lost, and the peace and security of life has been vandalized, there is still a little left that can be salvaged. This devastated land can still be recovered.'

'Yes, all possible efforts should be made towards a new start.'

'Look through the eyes of the victims at the horrendous times they have gone through, and it becomes clear why a fair approach was necessary in the first place so that these innocent people could not be exploited by the evil mongers.'

Mayuri nodded. 'You are right, my intellectual friend,' Mayuri remarked in a gentle voice, and Sheba suddenly laughed.

'I am making some tea. You rid your mind of these serious thoughts and relax for a while. Let me freshen up and then I will get you a nice cup of tea.'

Mayuri got up and went to the bathroom.

Sheba's heart sank into agonizing thoughts again. Close to the window, a bird chirped loudly. She sighed and looked towards the window; it was almost dawn.

Mayuri came with the tea.

Sheba said, 'It was the message of love and brotherhood preached by the Sufi saints that the people came to the religion. It was because of the spirituality of Chishti and Nizam that people followed them, got it?'

'Yes, a little…err, quite a bit!'

'Had they been forced, everyone would have been converted during the long Mughal period. It is documented in historical accounts that the non-Muslims were equally respected throughout the centuries of Mughal rule.

'But we love you, dear! Are Saagar, Diljeet and I different from you?' Mayuri said, pretending to be angry with her.

'No, my dear friend, I am not saying that at all! I am talking about the political strategies, about those who incite violence in people for their political gains and cause such havoc. All this has to do with politics, and all their benefits depend on what these people are personally interested in… some can even be bought and sold! It is all related to greed of some kind or other and, in general, the common people are not even aware of it.'

'But, we are also among those common people, and we are your well-wishers, isn't that so?' Mayuri said, taking a sip of tea. 'Do you like the tea?' she smiled and asked.

'Yes, it's very good indeed! Look Mayuri, there has always been one true language in this world: the language of love. Those Sufi saints...they truly loved the people, and they all spoke the same language to preach the message of love to the ones shackled by their selfishness. When people living thousands of miles apart and least aware of each other's thoughts can think the same way, why can't they similarly have faith in love? In the last decades of the 19th century when women in Europe and America started a movement for their rights, the women here also created similar protest literature.'

'Yes...it is indeed strange that two people living in different corners of the world, speaking different languages and living in different cultures, produced similar writings.

And it has happened many times…in almost every century. It happened even in those days when, to reach another place, one had to travel for months or years across the oceans. During those times, books and translations must have travelled at the same slow pace too, as there were no airplanes, phones, television or the internet. You know this *Shruk* by the Sufi saint Hazrat Sheikh Noorud-din-Noorani?' asked Sheba raising her eyebrows.

'What is a *shruk*?' Mayuri asked with her eyes wide open.

'You are forgetting again! The poetry written by Sufi saint and poetess Lalladed is called *Lalla Waakh*; and similarly, the verses of Sheikh-ul-alam are known as *Sheikh Shruk*. This is actually derived from the Sanskrit word '*shlok*', which translated as '*shruk*' in Kashmiri.'

'Yes, I remember now! You had told me about it,' Mayuri smiled.

'He had said:

Paraankhaely parrgaye
Kharrgaye kitaab baeryheth
Yimdileh nishe baa khaber gaye
Tim narrgaye taartarith kith

(Reading all those books—the flight in the realm of
book knowledge has tied my wings instead,
The donkeys loaded with books went their way,
But only those who looked into their heart,
Went across and reached the yonder bank far away!)

'What does that mean?'

'That is what I am saying! In exactly the same way, Sant Kabir has said,

Pothiparhi jag muwa
Pandit bhayaana koye
Dhaayee akhsharr prem ke
Parhey so pandit hoye

(Many spent their lives in wasteful reading of the tracts,
They never attained enlightenment.
But the ones who read through just two-and-a-half words of love,
Were rewarded with divine wisdom!)

'Got it?' Sheba stared at Mayuri and smiled.

'Yes ma'am!'

'And do you know why we people are here? Why we did not move across the border, and why many of us returned?'

'Why?'

'Because people like you also live here. Otherwise why would some 15 crore Muslims live with 80 crore Hindus? Isn't that only because of love?'

Sheba looked at her cup of tea fondly. Mayuri's face also wore the same tenderness but in the next moment, a mischievous smile danced on her lips.

'Oh, you have these thoughts only because you are enjoying your tea so much!' said Mayuri, and ran towards the door holding her cup of tea and laughing. Sheba burst into laughter. The sip of tea choked her and, coughing helplessly, she left the cup and ran after her.

'I will kill you today!'

Mayuri saw Sheba getting up from her the bed. She put the cup on the window sill and ran out into the lawn. When the laughter glided across the grass wet with dew and reached the other rooms in the hostel, spreading like fragrance, some of the other girls peeped out from their windows and doors smiling, and the morning took on a lovely mood. Both of them were trying to gain the upper hand over the other in this affectionate scuffle, laughing hard. They finally lay down on the grass, trying to catch their breath but the discussion resumed for almost another hour when they got back to their room. Sheba made the tea this time.

Sheba was mostly happy throughout day, but something unknown made her mind restless at times. She would try to find what it was, but then would get busy with something else. The night came only to snatch away her peace again. She kept looking at the ceiling with her eyes wide open. The ceiling seemed darker than usual as the bulb outside in the gallery had blown out, and no light came through the ventilator.

Sheba's face wore an expression of pride. The next moment, she smiled as a different thought came to her mind. How this Valley must have looked during those days, she wondered. Oh, she should have lived in the time when the waters from the enormous lake Satisar flowed out and the

Valley appeared! She would have lived on its highest peak in a small hut all by herself, coming from some unknown land, and with no human beings or animals around. She would look at the far away trees, plants and birds from the lofty heights of the white, snow-covered peaks of the Himalayas. She would be happy, as well as scared at times for being all alone. And she would look silently at the sky lying under a tree, and drift off to sleep. Sheba thought of sharing her reverie with Mayuri. But then she thought of Mayuri's response. She would say that looking at the trees, plants and birds, and gazing at the sky lost in her thoughts, Sheba would live happily on grass and insects. Sheba laughed thinking of this.

She wanted to look at Mayuri and turned her head in the semi-dark room. Mayuri was deep in sleep. The rhythmic sound of her breathing made Sheba sleepy too, and she changed her side. She took a deep breath and closed her eyes. She thought she was going to sleep but under her closed eyelids, the graceful Satisar Lake appeared in all its grandeur and beauty. And returning to her fancy, she continued thinking that she would have seen the Valley filled with beauty of divine grace, with fruits and flowers, grains and dry fruit, metals and minerals, woods and mountains, rains and snows, lakes and brooks, birds and animals, and human beings—the most noble of all creation. She would have enjoyed seeing all this from the beginning. She opened her eyes and tried to see Mayuri again. 'Oh, most noble of all creation, wake up!' she said in a somewhat loud voice.

Mayuri took a deep breath and changed her side. Sheba looked at the ceiling in the dark and smiled, a strange sense of peace came to her mind, as if she was looking at the sky. This peace had come to her after many hours, and it had come with the recollections of the fragrant peel of walnuts and quince fruit. She laughed softly. The fragrance of ripe walnut peel was a part of her childhood memories.

And Bihidana (quince seed), which was her endearing nickname in childhood for important occasions like Ammi combing her hair. Ammi would sometimes call her Bihidana in her childhood as her complexion was like the quince fruit—same as her Ammi—which looks like an apple but is not red, and is somewhat golden yellow, like the golden apple. Ammi washed her daughters' hair with the water in which its seeds had been soaked overnight. Sheba's hair benefited from this more than anyone else's—as unlike Baaji and Farkhi, her hair was not curly but straight, and grew fast. While combing her hair, Ammi would lovingly call her 'My Bihidana'. Sheba unknowingly caressed her hair like Ammi would do while calling her Bihidana. It makes a refreshing, cool drink when mixed with some sugar and water. Used as qehwa, it is helpful in severe colds. The fruit is cooked as a vegetable, and its jam is very delicious and full of vitamins.

Ammi used to cook a delicious dish of quince fruit and mutton. When could she go home? Sheba felt quite homesick. When the water had flowed out of the lake, wouldn't the fish have lost their homes? No, no...they would not have lost their homes as there were many other springs, ponds, streams and brooks. Many depressions and pits must have appeared or would have been created when the water had moved out. It might have rained and snowed all the time on those mountains and dense forests, and many lakes would have appeared. But there are not as many of them anymore, and their pristine purity has been contaminated. Sheba felt another pang of agony in her heart.

There are floating gardens in Dal Lake. The weeds growing in the lake are knit into mats and then some mud is spread on them. Their corners are tied to long poles driven into the bottom of the lake to make a floating garden. In case they are to be taken to another place, the poles are pulled up from the bottom and the garden is rowed just like a boat, or towed behind it. Mexico also had such gardens at one time. In earlier times, canals had been dug out of the Dal to make waterways for transportation, and probably that is why Srinagar was called 'Venice of the East'. The lakes of the Valley have become polluted...

The Dal Lake, situated near the foot of Koh-e Zabarwan (the Zabarwan hills) in front of the Mughal gardens, which was famous for its crystal-clear waters for centuries, is polluted now. The Mughal Prince Daara Shikoh had constructed a royal palace on Zabarwan. A lover of astronomy, the prince would observe the movements of the stars from this palace which was called Pari Mahal—the Fairy Palace. He must have fondly enjoyed the reflection of moon and the lights in the waters of this lake. But now, everything reflected in its turbid waters looks dull and dirty. The pretty Queen of the King Zabarwan is dying. Oh, someone come to set right the fate of my lakes, the future of the waters of my Valley, the destiny of my river Lidder which is getting polluted, the future of my muddying river Jhelum—the fate of the waters of my Valley and my innocent lakes. There are so many problems, verging almost on the mysterious, faced by my innocent lakes. So many issues are connected to the solutions of these problems. Dr Daanish also tried to explain to his students this incomprehensible puzzle once. No conferences, committees and councils have been able to solve it because the number of selfish people is ever increasing.

Professor Daanish, the sociologist, who has an objective point of view and considers the whole world as his brotherhood, says that Kashmiris have been content and affable because they subconsciously value their great historic and cultural heritage. They were artists, artisans and cultivators, were born creatives as such, and their peace-loving and hospitable nature made them respect and trust others as well. This land was encircled by insurmountable mountains, and could only be approached through difficult passes. It was a perfect castle, divinely created, and the invaders were attracted to it as it was such a secure haven. He had said that though intruders began to enter the Valley since the day the art-loving king, Yousuf Shaah-e-Chakk, was arrested in 1586 through deception, these outsiders were still respected by the people till their insidious designs were exposed. But by that time, the intruders had become powerful rulers and the people were completely vanquished.

Akbar purposefully made them wear loose garments instead of their smart outfits in order to make them lazy. On the other hand, history also shows that these peace-loving people were formidable warriors in battle, and very well knew how to defend their land. Sultan Mehmood of Gazni had conquered the whole of North India, but could not set foot on the soil of Kashmir as the Kashmiris inflicted an ignominious defeat on his forces. Mehmood of Gazni suffered such a huge loss of wealth and men that he felt safe only in making good his escape. These realities are documented honestly only by those historians who wrote their accounts objectively, and without any sense of being above the masses and without any bigotry. It is important that the author must belong to the soil and have an open mind and a broad perspective. These traits are not found in any other historian except Kalhana. Although his book is strictly a scientific observation and abounds in myths and folk-lore, yet the truth in many of its episodes cannot be doubted. Other historians coming from Europe, China and Central Asia stayed here for a short time and wrote without good knowledge of many of the important aspects. Thus, they could not produce any writings which could be considered trustworthy or authentic. Only a few of them stayed here for a considerable amount of time and succeeded in getting a grasp of the land and its history, which enabled them to feel the spirit of its people with empathy and honesty, and were thus able to portray the beauty of this land on the pages of their accounts to some extent. But since they did not know the language of this land very well, even they could not grasp many important insights.

How easily Professor Daanish was able to give his students a thorough grasp of complex issues! On this subject as well, he offered a quotation and then elaborated it in a detailed manner: 'A destructive mind can destroy a whole society; and all the same, a constructive mind can build a whole nation.' Who knows how many destructive minds are after my Valley?

Dr Daanish is a genius. Sheba smiled but the smile left her face again. He was a genius…No, he will be a genius again, InshAllah!

Dr Danish had said that what look like disputes between the close borders could very well be the intrigues of the big powers. And in reality, they, too, are backed by the clout of the huge resources of wealth. The big powers dance to the tune played by these stone-hearted capitalists who are the owners of diamond fields. He had said that these countries who were sworn enemies till the last World War have now joined hands opportunistically to pursue their selfish motives. They make the smaller nations helpless, despite the fact that they do not want it to happen to them, as if under the influence of some force verging on the supernatural. These people want all the lands, and all the treasures hidden under their soil.

They want oil for their industry, and they crave the precious stones—no matter how many lives get destroyed in the process. It has become important for a machine to outlive a human being. But how can the lands which possess these riches said to be at fault? Sheba remembered all these words spoken by Professor Daanish in the past.

'Look at the many lives these greedy powers snatch away on various pretexts. They attack and fight with each other. They break apart entire countries. They separate the ones who love each other. These are the heinous acts committed by the power hungry, and who rely on their feeling of superior strength. They have defiled and disfigured the pages of history, covering them with their abominable black deeds splattered in blood. They have put their parents in prison for the sake of power, murdered their brothers, widowed their sisters and killed little babies. They are creatures of a different kind, and until the poison reaches their own veins, they will have no pity for anyone else.' They are the aliens, she thought to herself.

'Mayuri, man is actually an alien,' Sheba called Mayuri's name softly. Mayuri lay motionless.

Man is an alien. An unknown being from an unknown world. Made out of some weird stuff. A creature different from the woman in its very essence. He can turn emotions into torture. He can force himself physically on a woman in vengeance. He can violate the sanctity of a body to satisfy his vindictiveness. A woman does not tarnish her instincts with torture. That is something foreign to her nature. She just cannot indulge in such base acts. She just cannot relate the negativity of anger, a desire for revenge, or ego-centricity with her body. All these emotions are poles apart for her. The concept of relationships for her is based upon the feelings of motherhood, humaneness, nurturing and compassion. She is far away from all this. Her ego does not demand offerings of blood and gore. She wants peace.

The world should be handed over to women or, at least, no political decisions should be taken without consulting them. She is capable of taking care of the politics of her country, the nation, the whole world, just as she is the anchor in the household—whose stability is endangered without her. Only, she should not be led astray by the ruse of love; her behest should be honoured without letting the ego be a hindrance, and this will suffice for making the world a better place for humanity. She is the procreator of life, and has nothing to do with death and destruction. And so, only she can solve the problems and usher peace in the world. Sheba mused confidently.

Perhaps till the time that some great leader, chosen unchallenged to have absolute sway over the whole world, and considering himself a God, will decide to take care of this planet. That is when there will be no borders. But will there be no strife when there will be no borders? The strong must have a victim as this best of all creation does not have the disposition to live peacefully. And history will repeat itself. There will be bloodshed then, borders will rise again and the cycle of creation and destruction will continue like they always have. Why is it so? Why?

Sheba looked at Mayuri's bed for her assent to these musings. No, that simpleton will ridicule me, alleging that

I have become a feminist instead of a humanist, and will threaten to tell on me to Daanish sir. Sheba took a deep breath and changed her side. She had some respite from her gloom, but thoughts still kept plaguing her. What is happening to this world, where everyone of any age suffers from insecurities? The so-called globalization has stupefied the world. The cable TV culture has taken away the peace of mind from the young. The internet is a positive development, but has so many negative aspects as well. And all this has created total confusion by mixing up the very concepts of day and night. Science is a blessing, and is being used to make great advances. But then, besides developing horrible means for destruction, divinely created beings are mutated into strange creatures. Their bodies as well as their emotions suffer a change. Sheba opened her eyes and then closed them again.

She remembered Sonia's puppy. Mayuri's teenage cousin Sonia was gifted an expensive dog by her mother, a single parent; it was a toy dog, a tiny one, which hung on to Mayuri's dupatta, barking whenever it saw her. But then, getting scared, it hid behind the bed, became breathless and had much trouble regaining it. The veterinary doctor later told them that this was a genetically mutated breed which had smaller nostrils, and thus, enough oxygen did not reach its lungs. That makes the poor creatures breathless, and can even becoming life threatening. Humankind—the creature born with destruction on his mind—carries out weird experiments. Most grievous things are happening in the world because it has become a vast marketplace—a huge arena of commercial dealings. A soulless place, really. Sheba changed her side again.

Markets rise and slump, prices rise and fall. 'Get some sleep, oh God's dear creature!' she said to herself in her head, and began to caress her hair softly with her fingers. Soon enough, she fell asleep.

The Daffodils Behind the Dry Leaves

Sheba waited in the science block cafeteria for her friends as they had planned to go shopping for Diljeet's forthcoming engagement. When no one arrived at the agreed time, she sent them a message from her phone. Seeing a banner for a seminar nearby, she entered the seminar hall, since wasting time made her tense. Moreover, she had already spoiled her mood with a cup of bad coffee after some good tea.

There were five people sitting on the stage. A round-faced man sat in the corner chair, near the dais. He glanced at the audience and began to speak. Before that, he looked at a paper, at which he would glance every now and then during his speech too. When he looked at the front rows, his deep black eyes appeared to be speaking a singular truth. Sheba had never ever seen such truthful eyes before. He was wearing a black shirt. His round face could not be called handsome, as a chubby face at his age does not look good, but it was not unattractive either. And there was something pleasantly unusual in his common face, which made it somehow outstanding among others and added a touch of dignity to it. These thoughts kept occurring to Sheba while she listened to his speech. When the session was over, he rose with the others. Some students approached him and he sat back in his chair, pleasantly answering their questions. His smile, like him, spoke of an innate truthfulness. His black eyes, which matched his shirt, kept closing while he laughed. Sitting in the corner chair of the third row, Sheba laughed at this thought, and continued looking at him more keenly.

When he stood up for a second, she saw that he was tall and well-built. Always an astute observer, Sheba concluded that he was a beautiful person.

She smiled and bent her neck, looking at the other side. 'Well!' she said to herself and rose from her seat. She proceeded towards the gallery for the tea break; she had got a message from her friends that they were in the cafeteria. She mentally rehearsed the words she was going to use to show her anger to her friends for keeping her waiting for so long. In the five-member group, she was the only one who was particular about punctuality. But when she saw them approaching her with smiles and laughter, she forgot all her angry words and joined in the music of their laughter. At the same moment, he also began walking. Sheba saw that he walked in a lopsided manner; he bent to his left while walking. Something was wrong with his feet. Sheba looked at them for some moments and then smiled at her conclusion. He is still a beautiful person, she thought, pressing her lips together, and went to the cafeteria to meet her friends.

Sheba had to submit her thesis the following month and was very busy, forgetting everything other than Daanish

Kadah. She was under tremendous pressure, and was mostly in the library collecting all the material. It looked like making Xerox copies and finalizing the paperwork would take more than a month but she cut her sleep to three or four hours a day, and submitted her thesis on time. Her friends called it a miracle and she smiled happily. That day, she slept peacefully after a long time.

Sheba waited for her viva in the department's lobby. As usual, professors from other universities had been invited for the students' viva voce. When her turn came, she entered the room and saw only one expert sitting there. When he raised his head from the papers in front of him, she looked at him and was surprised to find that he was the same person she had seen already, the man who smiled with his dark, half-open eyes in the seminar hall. It was Professor…Professor… what was his name? She tried, but could not recall what it was, and then she woke up. She looked at the ceiling for a few moments. When she was free of what she had seen in her dream, a smile appeared on her lips and stayed there. Who was that beautiful person? Where had he come from? She did not know and had never thought of enquiring about him. Where had these thoughts been hiding till now? Perhaps they were lodged somewhere deep in her mind without her knowledge, and had now entered her dream like a reality. If she could remember the topic of the seminar, she could find out about him as well, she thought, changing her side.

But why?

Because!

Because?

Because he was a beautiful person.

A beautiful personality...and...

And?

And she missed him badly at that moment. Thinking about this, she was surprised at the sense of loss at being unable to experience a glance from those truthful, dark eyes, and her own eyes filled with tears. What has happened to me? I...how can this happen?

She got up and sat on her bed. Tying her loose hair in a bun, she walked out to the veranda. The deep blue light of early morning rendered the surroundings magical. Most birds were still asleep. However, some far away bird's whistle-like chirp could be heard faintly. The morning breeze was blowing the crinkled frill of her nightgown's collar towards her right cheek, and it stayed there for some moments. Sheba felt the soft touch of the frill and closing her eyes, she thanked the breeze. The wind blew again and entered the room through the door which she had left open, waving her gown-like nightdress swiftly. The pages of Mayuri's book, on the table between two beds, began to flutter. Mayuri covered her head with the white sheet she was lying under, but the next moment she pulled it away from her face and looked around.

'What is disturbing your sleep now? Woke me up too!' said Mayuri, looking towards the open door where Sheba was standing.

'Sheba!' Mayuri said loudly when she did not get any answer.

'Yes, ma'am, have you woken up?'

'Woken up? What do you mean? Has anybody slept here for last few nights? Your exams are tests of my patience too. But today you should have slept peacefully. What is it that is not letting you sleep now?'

'Nothing, my dear. I woke up suddenly. Sorry to disturb your sleep too.'

'Yes, that's what you did,' said Mayuri, pretending to be angry.

'Now sing me a song and lull me back to sleep! That is your punishment.'

'I do not know how to sing, but I can give you a head massage,' Sheba reached across the small dressing table to pick up a bottle of oil.

'No, please! I shampooed my hair just yesterday. And please do not make a noise. But you may sing. I know full well that you can sing. I want to sleep for at least another two hours.'

Mayuri lay on the bed again and covered her face with the sheet. Sheba looked at her for some moments. Then she moved the bed sheet from her face and looked at her closed eyes. Mayuri did not open her eyes.

'Mayuri' she said softly, 'Stop pretending to be asleep!'

'What sleep? You do not let me!'

'May God spare even my worst enemy from having a friend like you.'

'Why? Oh Lord, what have I done?' Mayuri sat up on the bed.

'You could have done this before,' said Sheba reaching her own bed.

'You could have told me before that I should not sleep. Now tell me, what you have on your mind that won't let you sleep.'

'I miss someone without any reason.'

'O Ram! You are in love. With whom? Since when?' screamed Mayuri, and jumping down, sat on Sheba's bed.

'Tell me his name and I will bring him here at your service, right away.' She put her hands on Sheba's shoulders.

'Name…I do not know his name,' said Sheba softly.

'What does he do? Does he live on campus or outside?'

'I do not know where he lives.'

'Phone number?'

'I do not know his phone number, but he is a professor.'

'In which department?'

'In the Sciences, perhaps.'

'Which science? There are so many sciences.'

'Maybe in Physics.'

'Maybe? Then, yes I have got it,' Mayuri nodded enthusiastically. 'His name is Newton and he is fondly called Sir Isaac Newton. He is a scientist as well as a mathematician. He does not have a telephone, but I can give you his address,' said Mayuri seriously, trying to hide her smile. Sheba looked at her naughty, bright eyes. Sheba's eyes danced around in disbelief and her delicate nostrils, resembling the petals of wild flowers in the grass, trembled. She had inherited these nostrils from Suraya Begum. The next moment, a smile appeared on her lips.

'He has been resting in the royal graveyard of the famous building called Westminster Abbey in England for some centuries now. But he is not of marriageable age anymore as he was born in the early 1700s, and is older to you by almost 300 years.'

Sheba burst into a loud laughter even before the completion of Mayuri's sentence. She held Mayuri's throat with both her hands. 'I will kill you if you say another word.'

Mayuri laughed uncontrollably. 'Hey, it is not fair when one's good deeds are not appreciated.'

Mayuri, trying to put on a serious expression, caught both of Sheba's hands. 'Should we seek help from friends?' asked Mayuri affectionately, and the smile on Sheba's lips dimmed.

'Oh no, they will make fun of me.'

'Tell me the whole story. Where did you meet him?'

'I never met him. I've seen him only once. I don't know whether he belongs to this place or came from some other town,' said Sheba in a serious tone.

'Oh Lord! Is that also a possibility?'

'Yes it is, and all this happened because of you latecomers. Had you not made me wait outside the Science Block cafeteria, I would not have entered the seminar hall to escape the boredom and...'

'Oh, then the matter is so old that he must have got married by now and gone on his honeymoon. No, he must be about to return from his honeymoon!'

'I swear, Mayuri. I…I came to know of it only today that…that I love him.' Sheba looked at the fingers of her hands.

'Today? How come? Did he appear to you in your dreams to tell you that you began liking him?'

'It's not a joke Mayuri. It happened exactly like that. I saw him in my dream today and lost my peace of mind. Actually, that day I did like him, but I did not think much about it. Then I got busy with my thesis soon after. I have found some time only now. Only God knows in which partition of its memory my mind's computer had stored it for all these days, and then displayed it to me only today. And, you know something Mayuri? I am dying to see him.'

'Well, that sounds serious. But I feel that the situation is still under control, though it is critical.'

'No, it's not under control. I did not tear up my clothes like a crazed one. That's why the intensity of my feelings is not…'

'Oh no! Please do not tear up your clothes, my beautiful!'

'Can't you take me seriously?' Sheba's face looked grave.

'Do not say that, sweetheart! We will do something about it.' Mayuri glanced at Sheba's face and then looked at her own feet hanging down from the bed. 'Something should be done immediately in this case. We have to go to the Sciences Block.'

'Thanks, Mayuri. I was sure you would find a way out.

***

Shahaab stood on the balcony of the bungalow looking at the greenery, freshly washed with the rain. He was deep in thought. His youngest paternal cousin was calling him for quite some time now.

'Sha (Shahaab) Bhai jaan! Sha-aa-aa-aa-aa-aa-aa Bhai-e-ye-ye-ye-ye ja-aa-aa-aa-aa-aan! Sha Bhaayeejaa-aa-aa-aa-aa-aa-aan!'

Calling him loudly and by now getting tired of shouting, he started calling him softly while climbing the stairs. He placed his feet on the steps one by one and kept one hand on his left knee while holding the varnished, round and chiselled pillars of the wooden railing with the right hand. He climbed the stairs calling 'Sha Bhai Jaan' quietly; in fact, he was just humming 'Sha Bhai Jaan'.

He had put his little shoes made of a fur-like material in the lowest shelf of the shoe rack on the ground floor, and had glanced at them a couple of times. The shoes were not supposed to be brought inside the house because it was covered with soft flooring. The wooden stairs made a loud sound with the lightest step, but his feet could not make as loud a sound as he wanted them to. He hit his heel forcefully at every step but the stairs, which were covered with green carpet-like thick material, didn't make any sound resembling the thud when Sha Bhai Jaan sped up the stairs.

He was upset because his feet were not making the loud sound on the stairs. While crossing the second floor he hummed the same 'Sha Bhai Jaan' song, when he suddenly happened to see something interesting that made his mood better. The thought of stopping for a while to look at the interesting spectacle seemed to make him very happy, and so, he squatted on the floor. There was a huge flowerpot in the corner. A small branch of the plant growing in it hung outwards, and there was a small creature crawling on it. His teacher had shown them a picture of an insect resembling it, and had told them that it was called a caterpillar; and also, that it would turn into a butterfly when fully grown. Imaad looked at the insect keenly for some time and then got up. Trying to contort his body like the insect, he tried to bend his knees backwards and walk a couple of steps but could not do it. To walk like the insect was as difficult as climbing the stairs making a loud sound. While he was doing it, the tune of 'Sha Bhai Jaan' sometimes rose. On the last step of the stairs, Sha Bhai Jaan was resting his elbow on the window sill looking out. When Shahaab heard the familiar low gasping in the big room, he turned his head.

'Oh, I am so tired.'

Imaad was about to sit on the floor when Shahaab reached him. He picked him up in his longish muscular arms and while at it, held the child close to him.

'Why do you have to climb so high? I was on my way home from school.' He put his arms around Sha Bhai Jaan's neck.

'Do you know something, Imaad? I have been so lonely since the day you started school. I get bored here in the house,' Shahaab said, touching Imaad's ear with his cheek.

'When are you going back to college? You are fine now. You picked me up like superman. Does your foot still hurt?

Is your sprain better?' He raised his head from the curve of Shahaab's neck and looked at his face. 'Sha Bhai Jaan, I have twisted my foot too. Please tell Ammi that I cannot go to school, and cannot walk either.'

'Oh no, God forbid! You know, a sprain is so disabling it makes you absolutely miserable. That's why I went to the conference even in this condition last week, do you remember?' Shahaab asked seriously. He talked to Imaad as if he were talking to someone his own age. Sha Bhai Jaan did not laugh at what Imaad said, thinking him a child; he rather gave him importance and asked for suggestions. Shahaab had found this easy way to enjoy his innocent talk, and that's why Imaad was more frank with him than with others. Shahaab always felt a deep pleasure when Imaad spoke his innocent heart out in a serious manner.

'Oh, yes,' Imaad nodded seriously.

'And then your mother…You know these mother-father type people never listen to anyone. Do you know that I myself am so agitated?' He brought Imaad down from his lap and made him sit near him.

Imaad made as serious a face as Sha Bhai Jaan had, a short while back when he had said 'God forbid'. They had a long discussion after that, and Shahaab enjoyed the conversation despite being lost in his own thoughts many a time.

***

Shams-u-din Shairwaani and Sharf-u-din Shairwaani continued as business partners, even after the death of their father Shafi-u-din Shairwaani. The three timber factories and fruit orchards at various places were still in their father's name. The ancestral house was not spacious enough to live in anymore though. So, they built two houses with an identical plan near a big garden just outside the city, where both their families lived separately. The two houses were joined by a lawn in which the kids grew into adolescents and then adults, though some were still little children. Their ages were such that there could be no match among the cousins who could inter-marry to keep the property within the family. But the Shairwaani brothers, like most of the business class people, were not gentle-hearted. And so, Sharif-udin Shairwaani's 17-year-old son Shaheer-u-din Shairwaani was engaged to Shams-u-din Shairwaani's 21-one-year-old daughter, Shaista; and 26-year-old Shahaab-u-din Shairwaani to Sharf-u-din Shairwaani's 16-year-old-daughter, Raahat.

Shahaab had never thought about this match. Neither had Shaheer considered Shaista Baaji in that role. The cousins who freely enjoyed each other's company till a few days ago were not even looking at each other's face now. The lawn which linked the two houses together previously became the one separating them now instead, as the steps that led to their homes through it mostly stopped at their respective doors. The cemented narrow pathway dividing the lawn had no mud stains for many days now, and except for the small prints of little shoes, the passage mostly remained clean. The entire matter had become very complicated and the young felt ashamed and guilty, but the elders did not care about that; though the women of the house were not included among the elders.

The information Mayuri had collected was enough to upset Sheba. 'You are really late, Sheba. You should not have taken so long to open your heart.' Mayuri encircled Sheba's shoulders from behind, who was sitting in the lawn of Professor Daanish's house; she stood up, turning her back towards the gate.

'What are you saying, Mayuri? What happened?'Her sparkling eyes moved about restlessly on Mayuri's face. 'What are you talking about?' Sheba's voice became shaky and her eyes, that shone brightly, suddenly lost a little bit of sparkle because looking into Mayuri's eyes, she had understood what her friend was trying to say. Mayuri looked at her silently. 'You mean, you mean, he is…'

'Yes, he is married. And that too, just a few months ago—according to the wishes of his family, to his paternal cousin.'

'Married to his cousin?' asked Sheba, gasping a chair's arm and slowly sitting down.

'And the girl is younger than him by 10 years, and his younger sister is married to her cousin, who is three years younger than her.'

Mayuri also sat in a chair near her and looked at the sky. 'It must have been settled beforehand.'

Sheba tried to control the quivering in her voice; Mayuri looked at her face. Sheba had bent her head and was looking at her hands. Mayuri held her head close to her shoulder and Sheba started sobbing. She herself didn't understand how long she had kept all those tears to herself that she was crying so profusely now. Some moments passed like that. Sheba's sobbing saddened Mayuri too. Sheba suddenly became silent and raised her head from Mayuri's shoulder. She took a tissue paper from the box on the table and wiping her eyes, looked at Mayuri's eyes, sniffled and smiled. A faint smile appeared on Mayuri's face too.

'What did you think? That I would spend the rest of my life crying?' Sheba closed her eyes tightly for a second and blinked her eyelashes quickly.

'I don't know but I feel like that, and now he has the responsibility of someone else's life as well.'

'Yes, and I have no right to interfere in anybody's life—even if it is just thinking about him.'

'And we have nothing to do with someone else's husband,' said Mayuri, laughing, and Sheba smiled too. But she felt two fresh tears appearing in her eyes and Mayuri saw it too.'

'Let's go inside,' Mayuri said pleasantly.

'Yes,' Sheba gave her a broad smile and stood up.

***

Dr Daanish was eating very little since the day of the seminar on 'Globalization and Challenges in India'. And no one—neither Saleem Miyaan nor the other students—could motivate him to eat, except Sheba.

'Good morning, sir,' Sheba said pleasantly, entering the room. Dr Daanish did not react.

'Sir, do you know what happened today?' she said somewhat loudly.

She had guessed from the sad expression on Saleem Miyaan's face that Daanish sir had not eaten anything. It was confirmed when she saw the untouched glass of juice near the teapoy next to him. She pulled up a chair and sat close by.

'Today, they were considering the papers written for the seminar on globalization for publication!'

Professor Daanish was sitting motionless in his easy chair, looking at some distant object with a steady gaze. His pupils moved slightly and he slowly turned his head towards Sheba.

'You know, sir, there were no papers worth publishing as a book. A few portions of some could have been acceptable, but they were still not entirely up to the mark.' Sheba said.

'What…did you…say?' she heard Dr Daanish's voice and looked at him. She silently gestured Saleem Miyaan to get her the glass of juice.

'Yes, sir. I was talking about the standard set by you, since everyone in the department has been saying the same thing.'

Saleem Miyaan came to the table quickly and picked up the tray with the glass of juice. Daanish motionlessly stared outside the window. Saleem Miyaan put the tray on the table. Sheba picked up the napkin from the tray and tied it around the professor's neck. Noticing the expression of dislike on his face, Sheba smiled.

'What can we do, sir? The department will be at the mercy of such people till you recover. They will get any dud to write a paper, send him an air ticket and provide him the best accommodation using university funds and...' Sheba touched the edge of the glass to Daanish's lips and he sipped it, listening to her carefully.

'And students have to listen to all those worthless, outdated theories, and you know why?' She put the glass on the teapoy and looked at Saleem Miyaan. 'Saleem Miyaan, would you please toast a slice of bread very lightly?' she said, and wiped the moisture from Daanish's chin, holding up the glass again. 'Because after some time they return the favour and invite these mediocre duds to their cities, giving them the same treatment and keep exploiting the poor students...'

Sheba put the empty glass on the table and laughed softly. 'And this scandal continues, isn't it so?'

'Ye...Yes,' Daanish smiled too. His face looked quite peaceful.

'Wait *bitiya*, I am getting some tea for you.'

Saleem Miyaan went towards the kitchen, smiling. Sheba heard the sound of the main gate opening and came out to the veranda. Diljeet came through the gate smiling, Aaftab Aalam following her.

'Our guess that you would be at Daanish's place on a Sunday morning was correct. We were planning to come here with you but found your room locked. Mayuri was not there either, where could she be?'Diljeet quickly came to the veranda.

'Can we go inside?' Sheba said slowly. Diljeet suddenly noticed the seriousness of her tone and looked at Aaftab Aalam. Aaftab's face showed no surprise.

'What happened, Sheba, why are you so sad? Is sir all right?' asked Diljeet, putting her hands on Sheba's shoulder.

'Yes, everything is fine. Let us go inside,' she answered Diljeet quickly.

Going inside, Diljeet noticed that Sheba was all normal now. She was talking to Dr Daanish about something or the other.

Professor Daanish was given a proper bath every Sunday. The other days, he was just cleaned with a wet towel. Aaftab Aalam was about to go to the bathroom to check if the water was warm enough when Saleem Miyaan entered with tea.

'Let's have tea first,' Saleem Miyaan said, putting the dishes on the table.

'Sir, will you have some?' asked Diljeet, picking up a cup.

'No, Diljeet, he will have a bath first, isn't that so, sir?' Aaftab smiled. Professor Daanish smiled back faintly and looked at his students silently.

'I will also help Aaftab bhai today,' Saleem Miyaan said, as Saagar was still not there and the job was rather hard for only one person. Hearing this, Sheba looked at Saleem Miyaan appreciatively when she heard the main gate open.

'Your Saagar is here, and perhaps, Mayuri as well.'

Saagar and Mayuri had already entered the room before Diljeet finished her sentence. 'Good morning, sir,' they said.

Daanish sir looked somewhere far away, but Sheba had

seen his face changing colour again and again. This was so painful, she thought. A healthy brain, but a stuttering tongue, his sensitive intellectual mind must be so perturbed at the thought of not being able to speak normally. Sheba looked at Mayuri, who was also looking at her.

'Mayuri, I was thinking...' Sheba left her sentence incomplete. 'We can now take him for a bath.'

'Yes,' said the boys and they came forward and helped the professor out of his chair and walked him slowly to the bathroom.

'Mayuri, I was saying that if we could motivate Daanish sir to read the newspapers, he may recover his speech. He feels miserable, Mayuri, I can see that.'

'Yes, you are right, a sensitive person like him, if we all request him, he...'

'Yes, he has developed a somewhat resistant attitude just like a small child, and does not even easily agree to eat. The doctor said that he would recover fast if he was looked after properly. We should try our best and once he starts reading again, he will come back to life I hope.'

'Yes, I wish so.'

'And we will read to him from his books at times.'

'And sometimes other things of his interest as well?'

'Yes.'

When the voices of the boys taking Professor Daanish to the bathroom faded away, Mayuri looked at Sheba's face. 'Are you still sad?'

'No, Mayuri, to be sad is no solution to this situation.'

'Yes, I expected that from you, but your sadness is not genuine either, do you know why?'

'Why?'

'Because it was a one-sided love.'

'Yes, that is true. I myself did not know that; I don't know what happened to me…as…'

'How complex is the human mind! As to where all these emotions were hidden, you yourself did not…'

'But tell me, where did you get all the information from?'

'Shall I tell you the truth? You won't get angry, will you?'

'No, please tell me.'

'Do you remember that day we were going on a shopping spree for Diljeet's engagement, Aaftab Aalam had said that one of his relatives had come to attend a seminar?'

'Yes, I remember...'

'He was the one. His uncle's wife, now his mother-in-law, is the sister of Aaftab Aalam's mother. That means he is Aaftab Aalam's second cousin, got it?'

'So if he is Aaftab Aalam's second cousin that means everyone in our group knows about my stupidity.'

'No, not at all, it is only Aaftab Aalam. But he said that even if you had talked about this earlier, it would not have helped because in their family neither the daughters are married out of the family nor are the brides for their sons brought from outside. But have you not forgotten him, you lovelorn girl?'

'No, it is not that. Now that I think rationally, I feel like I was stupid.'

'Well, at least now you are thinking rationally.'

'Yes, they say that too much pain is a remedy in itself.'

'Oh Lord! That shows how painful it was, and you were not even aware of it. But could you be certain that you, I mean, that he would also like you? No darling, I am wrong, no one can help liking you, and he too would have been sincere.'

'Yes, he would have been. I saw how he treated and interacted with others. He is as good a person as can be. It is my firm belief…a good man can be a good teacher or a good…'

'Does that mean that a good politician would be a good person and a good businessman as well? I don't think so.'

'Why not?'

'Because a criminal can also be a good person, or even a very good person for certain people, but will the world accept him as a good man or will the law give him any concession or allowance on this basis?'

'No, but I think everyone's basic nature always remains the same, even if they're influenced by the environment. They can be better in positive surroundings, and in other cases, can behave negatively in opposite circumstances as well. But the basic thing is one's own nature, and he was a thorough gentleman, I know.'

'It seems that you are hellbent on not forgetting him! You are unnecessarily sad on this account and…'

'That is because I have never experienced anything like this before…You know everything.'

'Why? Were you not in love with your father's friend at the age of 11?' Mayuri asked quickly before getting up to run away but Sheba got hold of her. 'I will kill you today.'

At first, Sheba tried to understand what she said but when she realized, she burst into laughter. 'You infidel! I will never share anything with you anymore.' Sheba caught her hand and pressed it with both her hands. Mayuri tried to get it out of her grasp. Both were laughing uncontrollably.

'You, you callous-hearted feudal landowner, sucking the blood of poor tenants, you want to break the hand of a frail Brahmin girl! You will go to hell! Demons will feast on your blood. I will not let you do that!'

'Alright then, try and free your hand, you are no better either. You, too, have been stealing from the people for centuries to feed yourself, calling them inferiors, and you blame us, and we…'

Mayuri somehow freed her hand from Sheba and climbed onto her lap while she was sitting on a chair and began to tickle her knees. Sheba's knees were very ticklish and only Mayuri knew it, besides Sheba's sister Farkhanda.

Both of them felt tired but they laughed and laughed.

'Mayuri, please, I feel breathless, buddy.'

'No, there is nothing like that. You are not out of breath. I have been hearing this same excuse for three years by now (laughter). Why did you press my hand so hard, my poor delicate hand? And I remember, you told me that you wanted to sing songs with him in the meadows, that he looked like a famous film star, didn't you?' said Mayuri. laughing breathlessly. Hearing this, Sheba too laughed loudly.

'Tell me, didn't you say so?'

'Yes I did (laughter). And I think I was just 10 then, and he was 30!' Sheba's laughter brightened with the innocent memory from her childhood.

'So, that was your first love and you should admit it.' Mayuri said, drawing a deep breath in her laughter, and Sheba freed herself of her grip.

'I will not leave you today. I will kill you.'

Sheba was about to grab her when she heard the voice of Aaftab and Saagar, who were bringing Dr Daanish in after giving him a bath. The laughter gradually faded away and their shining faces resumed a serious expression.

Washed, clean-shaven and sitting in his chair in freshly pressed clothes, Professor Daanish did not look unwell at all. The doctor was expected for a check-up soon. Aaftab Aalam made him drink his tea. The rest of the students were busy chatting but kept in mind that their discussion should cheer their teacher up.

Dr Ghayi checked Professor Daanish's blood pressure and weight, and the movement of his limbs. Sheba and Saleem Miyaan served the tea and snacks. They all liked the way Dr Ghayi treated his patient.

'It seems as if a friend has come to see Daanish sir, isn't it Saleem Miyaan?' Sheba said, emerging from the kitchen.

'Yes, bitiya, and he never gives you medicines unnecessarily. Those medicine sellers visit these doctors to promote their medicines, but he does not prescribe medicines unnecessarily like other doctors; and sometimes, he does not even prescribe any. If I call him to say that I have caught a cold, or that I have a backache, he asks me to have some basil tea or hot fomentation with the water bottle, that I will be fine and there is no need to take medicines!' Saleem Miyaan left the room, smiling.

'How much sugar, doctor?' Sheba looked at the doctor, holding out a tea-spoonful of sugar.

'Yes, young lady. Now, Daanish, you have to eat healthy and try to walk,' said Dr Ghayi, taking the cup of tea from Sheba and putting it on the table. He looked into Professor Daanish's eyes and smiled. As Professor Daanish also looked at him, he had an amiable expression too.

'When will sir get back to how he was? Isn't he better than before?' Saagar was standing against the wall with his hands folded under his arms. He glanced at everyone's face before looking at the doctor. Everybody looked eagerly at the doctor.

'Yes, but now…' Dr Ghayi bent his head and raised his eyebrows. 'Look students, I must tell you now that the professor has to work hard himself. He has to use his will power. I am not very happy with his progress; it is too slow and he has also lost weight. I have prescribed some supplements, but good food is a must. And the physiotherapist must visit every day as well. Now don't get too worried, he is fine otherwise.'

'Doctor, your tea,' Aaftab said, putting his tea in front of him along with a boat-shaped glass bowl of biscuits.

'My mother has sent some mangoes from our orchards in Chandigarh. I will send you some in the evening, and you will see the difference. They are fertilizer and chemical-free. They are for you all!'

Dr Ghayi bent his head and nodded. The students smiled at him.

'Yes, doctor, sure,' two of them said. Saagar and Aaftab headed to see him off to his car; the girls also followed them.

'He has lost much weight…it is not a healthy sign,' Sheba thought to herself. She knew that when Dr Ghayi was worried about something and nodded repeatedly, it meant that something needed to be done.

'So, what should be done doctor?' Sheba's responsible voice had a touch of anxiety.

'How is his memory?'

'It seems fine,' Saagar said, looking at Aaftab.

'We did not think about that as nothing related to his memory has happened. But doctor, he usually looks sad, isn't it?' Diljeet said, looking at the others' faces for affirmation.

'Yes, doctor, if our conversation moves to some older events, he becomes sad and goes deep into thoughts for hours. It becomes difficult to feed him too,' Mayuri bent her neck.

'That means his memory is fine, isn't it doctor?' asked Saagar in a hopeful voice.

'I am not talking about that memory,' the doctor turned his head left and looked at his car. 'Well, I was eager to know…I mean, it is all right,' the doctor looked at their faces. 'I was actually asking about his short-term memory.'

'But doctor, is he making any progress? We cannot bear to see him sitting at one place like this, and we all love him so much that...'

'Yes, doctor, we owe him everything—all this knowledge, the manner in which he taught us to think about the societies we humans inhabit, these degrees—everything,' Saagar said with a touch of sadness in his voice.

'He taught us to be human. If we could at all be what he wanted us to be...We feel guilty, as if we have not looked after him properly. That is why he is still not...we...we are really worried, doctor.'

Aaftab looked down. Mayuri kept looking at some words written on the green wooden gate. The green paint had peeled off in patches at places, but the words 'Daanish Kadah' written with a coloured pen were still clearly visible despite having been washed by many rains.

'No, do not feel guilty about anything. This illness is like that. But I think if you read to him from his books, he will enjoy that and his sadness will reduce.'

'Yes, doctor.'

'And give him some newspapers, etc., to read. Put them on the table before him, and he may turn the pages and show some interest. Make him walk frequently. Everything will be fine. Anything else?'

'No doctor, thank you.'

Dr Ghayi headed towards the car and left. Although Dr Ghayi's driver was standing there, Aaftab opened the door for him and shut it after him.

A friend of Aaftab and Saagar was in the cricket team that was playing a match with another university. When they both left, the girls went inside.

Sitting on a tree in the biology faculty near professors' lodges, the screaming koel was now silent.

Entering the house, Sheba told Dr Daanish that he would have to read the newspaper every day. Diljeet came in with a newspaper and they adjusted the table in a way so that Dr Daanish could see the paper easily. He looked at the paper for some moments, then rested his head against the back of his chair and closed his eyes. The girls looked at each other. Some moments passed silently. Perhaps, he had fallen asleep.

Sheba stood up, and Mayuri also headed towards the door. 'Looking at him usually makes me think that Goddess Saraswati has come to bless us in his form.'

'The goddess of art and literature?'

Reaching the veranda, Sheba sat in a chair and put her arms on the table, looking at Mayuri. 'Yes, we have distributed the existence of God among many gods and goddesses. Isn't that better for us?'

Mayuri kept her elbows on the table and rested her chin on her hands. 'Yes.'

'Yes, how?'

Mayuri shook her head upwards.

'Yes, because one reason to feel content can be the belief in God too,' Sheba nodded.

'Does that mean man has created God?' Mayuri smiled. 'Or has God created man?'

'It depends on the thinking and beliefs of the people. God does not care whether people think him to be God or not, he will always remain God,' Sheba said, thinking something.

'If someone does not have the concept of God in his mind, how would they feel?'

'They would feel lonely and helpless.'

'Yes, we should leave everything to Him if we trust Him fully.'

'Yes. Do you know why I have a firm belief in God?' Sheba said to Mayuri.

'Why?'

'I will give you an example. If someone does something wrong, something bad will definitely happen to him. Does one need any more proof than this?'

'Yes, you are right. But sometimes people do not understand the logic of God's acts—like accidents, lightning, devastation wreaked by earthquakes, floods or by something else…'

'Yes, this thought does come to the mind. But how can we know what is in store for any of us in the future? The things we humans consider bad, or which seem like destruction to us, what effect it is going to have on the future, only He knows. But yes, man thinks about these things sometimes.'

'And sometimes, one becomes so helpless.'

'Yes, a human being is, after all, a human being; and he can only try to do his best. He cannot control anything.'

'So…man has no other choice than to trust Him? That means one really can't interfere with what God does.'

'Yes, one cannot. But one can have faith in him, in his kindness, and then leave everything to Him.'

'That means one can surrender to Him and become free of all worries.'

'Yes, when one does not know what is in store for him the next moment, why worry and lose one's peace of mind? I mean, what I am saying doesn't have religious overtones, I am just trying to explain it scientifically. There are so many reasons which strengthen man's belief in God.'

'I know…I am not an atheist, you know.'

'You should ask the atheists that if they can predict the future, since they think they are the masters of their existence. What would they say? Every atheist, at some point or the other, agrees with the fact that there is some supernatural power which is omnipresent.'

'Yes, everywhere on this earth and beyond—in every part of the universe, something or the other keeps happening. Who knows about that? How big is it, where it ends? And if it does not end then, O Lord, I will…' Mayuri focused on some distant object and seemed to speak to herself.

'Don't think about this.'

'Why, this is the most important thing to think about!'

'Yes, it is, but when human logic fails to provide an answer to them, these kind of questions can drive one to the verge of insanity.'

'That's true. Only, people shouldn't kill each other in the name of religion.'

'Then isn't religion the easiest thing to rely upon?'

'It has become so common everywhere. People keep killing each other in the name of their God, or because of politics or some other belief. This means that when one sect cannot accept another, that is a valid justification for doing away with them.'

'What will happen to this world? Where are we going?'

'A very difficult question! For the time being we should go inside. Isn't that a very good place to go to?'

'The best place…at the feet of our Guruji—our revered teacher,' said Mayuri, swaying her head pleasantly.

The Eyes Don't Think

The seminar was at Aligarh Muslim University. Sheba had to read her paper in the first session of the opening day. The paper was very well received, giving rise to much discussion. During the tea-break Sheba, Mayuri and some other participants kept discussing the same topic.

'The big powers keep hatching conspiracies; they see nothing wrong in genocides as long as their own people are safe and not in the way of any harm. Where are the Red Indians, the indigenous people of America who had been living there for centuries, now? You see them only in pictures.'

'Yes, these strong nations have their big plans. Remember, Mayuri, there was a movie some years ago about a "great white man" who had made some predictions. Books published in various languages said that every important event which took place since his time had been predicted by him, but many recent events had also been added to the new editions of the book as having been predicted by him.'

'Yes, I remember! He made predictions about some great man's assassination, of devastating earthquakes, a flood, etc. And in the end, he predicted that the most important city of the most powerful nation in the world would be destroyed by somebody pressing a button from one of the Arabian countries. And a lot of evidence to this effect had been made up so that the common man would just start believing it. But, in reality, they only wanted to control the huge riches buried under the soil of those countries.'

'But people are not so stupid now that they would not understand their hidden motives,' said a student.

Listening to him, an olive-skinned girl in jeans and a tank top came over to their table, widening her kohl lined, intelligent dark eyes, and started looking at them one by one. 'Yes, but you see, the voice of protest is also raised in those same countries, no matter what the political stance.'

'Yes, and the issue of human rights is also raised in the same countries, and it is again there that the masses take to the streets.'

'Yes, that is true,' the girl said, nodding, and took a sip of her tea, anxiously awaiting further arguments.

'That means the people who play these political games are not human?' A middle-aged professor passing by also joined in their conversation.

Another professor of rather short stature, whose paper was read in the morning session and was appreciated by everyone, also joined their discussion. 'No, it is not that. You can't place politics and humaneness on the same platform. The craving for power is a strong poison in itself.'

'It is a poison that does not kill the targeted person, but kills the others...'

'Drunk with arrogance of power, they are the ones propagating hatred against a particular religion as part of a huge conspiracy, with the objective of appropriating the riches hidden under the soil of those countries and controlling the whole world by using those resources. The same arrogance of power was the basis of the genocide of the Red Indians some five centuries ago. Even in the last century, they introduced AIDS, the dreaded disease, among the black people in a planned manner in order to eliminate them, and are now looking at their helplessness.'

'What?' a shocked Mayuri asked astonished. Others, too, had the same expression on their faces.

'Yes, but the gory tale just does not end there. They have the cure for this disease as well; however, they will not disclose it to the world so they can protect the same genocidal plans.'

'Oh no, sir!' Sheba said, shocked; others were totally shocked too.

'Oh yes, madam. But how will you prove all this? They will repeat their story so many times that their statements start sounding true. Such attacks are often planned. The innocent are put to blame and arrested…and it is all part of the game.' The professor smiled and headed to another table to put his empty cup away.

'But sir, I believe the world is changing, otherwise Obama would not have been elected President,' Sheba said seriously.

'Yes, you are right. Who could have imagined even a few years ago that an African-American will occupy the highest office in the White House? But you can't make any predictions; and you know, no miracles are going to happen...political strategies take a long time to change. But then working for a revolution always carries a danger to one's own life as well, and history affords ample evidence to this.'

'Yes, sir.'

'But the new generation, this well-informed generation, is quite honest. That is how racism has ebbed somewhat.'

'Yes, it has decreased but it has not stopped. People are still biased one way or the other.'

'Labelling a particular sect with certain ills will not do any good. This must be realized by those among us who do not understand this, and insist on treating minorities as enemies. We have to come forward for the minorities lest their faith in democracy is completely shattered.'

'I hope this does not happen. They have destroyed Iraq, and are unable to control the situation in Afghanistan. How will it end? These catastrophes are impacting the global economy. People are bewildered, you know.'

'I believe some day everyone will begin to think in the right manner.'

'Yes, let us cherish that dream.' The professor bowed, then raised his head up and went inside. The participants began to go in, and Sheba and Mayuri also headed to the hall. During the next session, Sheba could not concentrate. Professor Shrivastava's sentences echoed in her mind. A sort of helplessness had taken over her whole being for hours, and Mayuri also felt the same. The next speaker held the microphone, smiling.

'I am not tall, like Professor Shrivastava isn't either, so I need this wooden stand too!' the speaker joked. The wooden stand had been placed a little bit away from the podium. He pulled it over from the corner of the long dais with his foot and stood on it.

'Now I can see the first row!' he said in a very humourous manner. The serious faces of the audience softened somewhat.

'I am reading a couplet written by the famous Urdu poet Sheikh Ibrahim Zauq for you:

> *Aadmiat se haibaala Aadmi ka murtabah*
> (A man rises above himself for being human,)
> *Pasthhimat yeh nah ho, past quamat ho to ho*
> (One should not lack lofty ideals, even if he is
> short statured!)

People clapped in applause and smiles appeared on their faces. The speaker thanked them, bowing his head a couple of times. 'This means that my reading of the couplet was correct. It seems that we have a good gathering of people here who have good command over Urdu language. I am not a poet but I am a Kayastha, and that is why I have a smattering of this sweet language. It is a very serious topic that I am going to speak about today, so I wanted to lighten the grave mood of the audience a little.'

He began to read from his very interesting paper. Sheba regained her pleasant mood, and listened to all the following speakers with interest. In the evening, she went to see the university campus along with Mayuri, offered *fatiha* at Sir Syed Ahmad Khan's grave and looked at some precious manuscripts in the libraries, planning to use them. She thought about Ammi, whose face appeared in her mind at times, but the next moment her mind diverted to something else. She felt her tension releasing with the soft, dignified noise of the seminar hall and the peaceful silence outside every other hall in the vast university campus. Life seemed to be all about knowledge and learning. A mysterious and virtuous silence was spread all over, like it would have been in the ancient *pathshalas*—the traditional religious schools and educational institutes; like it would have been in shrines and in the company of Sufi saints. It was a whole world of learning, conveying the fact that learning was equal to worship. That is why, she thought, the *Hadees* (sayings of the Holy Prophet of Islam) states that one should even go to a distant place like China in pursuit of knowledge. It was such a peaceful evening, silent and serene.

Sheba and Mayuri decided to take a long walk in the quiet evening. A cold day's sun had added pleasant warmth to the air. Students could be seen moving around. A boy headed towards his hostel hurriedly, and some girls in rickshaws came back from their shopping. A man was looking at the building near the corner of the road, about a furlong away. Perhaps he had just got down from the rickshaw, which was coming from the opposite direction now. Sheba paused for a moment when she saw him. She slowed down a bit and Mayuri looked at her curiously.

'What is it?' Mayuri asked.

'He is…he is…Mayuri…he is standing there!' said Sheba hesitantly.

'Who he? You mean that…' Mayuri enquired but knew before even completing her question who Sheba was referring to.

'You mean that person you saw in the seminar hall?' Mayuri asked.

'Yes, the same…' Sheba replied.

'How can you recognize him from such a distance? It cannot be him. What would he be doing here?' said Mayuri thoughtfully.

'It is him, Mayuri. I can recognize him.' Sheba looked anxiously in that direction and did not walk a step further. The man looked at the building for some time and then went inside.

'You were right, Mayuri. It was not him,' Sheba looked at Mayuri for a few moments and moved her head in negation.

'Oh, God. That is good, but even if it was him you should have nothing to do with that. He is someone else's husband now. Why even think about him?'

'Thinking about him? Who is thinking about him? He just came to my mind when I saw that guy.'

'But how did you know from this distance whether it was him or not?'

'He looked like him, but then he did not walk like him.'

'What do you mean? Seeing him for a few hours, how can you know how he walks?'

'No, it is not that. I had only seen him walking a few steps,' Sheba shook her head lightly.

'Then what? Was he jumping while walking? And now you think it was not him because he was not jumping!' Mayuri said giggling.

'No! Just that he had a slight limp and…'

'You mean he limped, and you…you were not blind,' Mayuri said, surprised.

'Do not be so cruel, Mayuri. What does it matter? The main thing is to be humane, and he is a very good human being.'

'Yes, my dear, yes it is. He was a very good human being. Oh, Bhagwan!' Mayuri touched her ears in denial. 'This girl is…and do not give me a lecture! He, too, could have found a good girl who limped like him. God has created a match for everyone, and you—Bhagwan has made you with great effort!'

'Tell me one thing though…the villains who look good but play a bad role in the movies, don't we hate them? And what does it matter even if a person with good qualities is not really good-looking and doesn't meet all the requirements of being a hero?'

'Oh yes, you are right,' Mayuri smiled, nodding.

Sheba had selected a secluded corner table for dinner that evening but the participants were supposed to eat together. Some tables were set together end to end, with chairs at their sides in the centre of the dining hall. So they had to leave the corner table to go to the centre table. Mayuri was also about to sit after Sheba had taken her seat when Sheba quickly pulled her down to her chair.

'Look, Mayuri, there,' Sheba whispered, looking at a tall man entering the hall. Mayuri cast a quick glance at the entrance. A young man and a woman were coming in. The woman was as tall as the man and was dressed in a gaudy outfit. The man was dressed in a fine suit of a light shade.

'What an odd couple! Such a couple looks stupid here in India, doesn't it? She is too tall,' Mayuri whispered, seeing them approaching.

'Had she thought about the decorum of a university and not worn these colours, she would have looked good with this graceful man. And she should have been shorter by at least five inches.'

When they reached closer, Sheba pressed Mayuri's arm with her elbow to silence her.

'Did I say anything wrong?' Mayuri asked somewhat louder and looked at the dishes.

'No, no, yes, you want vegetarian food,' said Sheba hurriedly, and lightly pinched Mayuri's arm.

Mayuri suppressed her laughter and looked at Sheba. Some more people were entering the hall and the cafeteria staff guided them to the tables at the centre of the dining hall.

'Sir, please come this side, the food is hot. I am the only one serving and it can get cold by the time I reach the tables there,' the waiter said, and the new guest looked at him and smiled.

'We will sit wherever you would like us to,' he said looking at the people around in a friendly manner and pulling a chair towards him. The table was quite broad and the waiter moved the plates quickly towards the guests.

'I did not say anything wrong, I suppose, and then they are too far to hear us. Is it really a sin to have a little fun?' Mayuri took a little dal in a bowl and turned towards Sheba. Sheba was looking at the couple curiously. Mayuri also looked at them stealthily. Sheba glanced at Mayuri and looked at the man again. The man had deep black eyes and an angular face. The suit looked good on his slim physique. He had a pleasant smile on his face. The woman's face had no smile or expression. She was breaking small pieces from her chapati, stretching out her left nostril as if she did not like anything that was served. But her blank pretty face looked innocent.

'Look at her expression, it looks like she is doing us a favour eating this food,' Mayuri said softly.

Sheba glanced at them time and again, and seemed to be lost in thoughts.

'What is the matter with you? Do you have a crush on this young man now? After all, you start liking other women's husbands, whether it is your uncle's friend or Shahaabudin Sherwani,' said Mayuri. Sheba pressed her arm hard and Mayuri became quiet.

'Have you lost your mind?' Sheba asked.

'What is wrong? No one is listening.'

'Mayuri, that is his name, he is the same person.'

'You mean…but he is walking all right, and is quite good looking…' Mayuri left the sentence incomplete. 'Oh, God… So this was your choice! Good choice, sweetie.' Mayuri moved her head slightly in negation, as if regretting what had happened.

'But we can't do anything now,' Mayuri smiled and looked into Sheba's eyes. Clouds of sadness had engulfed Sheba's face.

'I mean, he is not handsome like a movie star, of course, but…' Mayuri tried to get busy eating; Sheba also did the same.

'But he was not like this before,' Sheba said, putting some rice on her plate and looking at Mayuri to show that she was not upset. 'He was a little fat and had a round face. He looks more handsome now.' Sheba tried to sound normal, and even smiled. But Mayuri knew she was very sad.

People around were talking and eating. Someone introduced them to other people. Shahaab happily participated in the conversation. His wife was eating silently.

On the second day of the seminar, he was not seen anywhere though both the faculties were close by, and lunch was also served in the opposite corners of the same lawn. By the time the participants for the sociology seminar came out to eat at 2:30 pm, the guests from the Sciences had already eaten and gone back to the hall.

'It looks like the scientists were really very hungry, as if they had eaten only after they had found solutions to all the problems in the world!' Mayuri said, looking at the empty tables across the lawn. The parrots on a tree with big leaves scattered flower petals on the grass and shrieked loudly every now and then.

'They were on time. We were late, wearing our brains out for that shallow discourse.' Sheba looked at the vast sky from one side to the other. A little distance away, small birds were flying in and out of a bougainvillea creeper with white flowers that had climbed onto the green wooden railing.

'Why, ma'am, are these lovelorn eyes longing for a glimpse of someone?' Mayuri asked pleasantly, observing the tension on Sheba's face and trying to lighten Sheba's sad mood, as she had a tendency to be miserable for hours and sometimes even for days altogether.

Sheba smiled suddenly. 'Yes, ma'am. A glimpse would give me some consolation and the seminar would be a success.'

'Why, ma'am, a glimpse of someone's hubby?'

'Yes, ma'am, because I loved him first and he became someone else's husband later.'

'But one must never do that. He belongs to someone else now.' Mayuri broke a small piece from the corner of a quarter-piece of a naan and without looking at Sheba's face, said, 'Isn't it morally wrong?'Mayuri's voice sounded somewhat serious.

'Yes, it is. That's why I did not even look at that hall where he can be seen,' said Sheba, and Mayuri suddenly looked at the building at a little distance.

'So, you saw him at such a distance?'

'No, I did not. He suddenly appeared before me when I turned my eyes back to the ground after looking at the sky, but...' Sheba sipped some water. 'But I know this is wrong and I will not do so again.'

'Yes, but he did not look very happy yesterday, isn't it?'Mayuri turned her face away towards the window.

'He was fine, but the woman with him didn't seem to be happy.'

'His wife,' said Mayuri as if correcting her.

'Yes, unfortunately,' Sheba's voice became sad. 'Had I been in her place, I would never be sad.'

'And he would have certainly been happy too.'

'I don't know whether he would have been happy or not, but I would have tried my best to make and keep him happy. But, there is no use talking about it now.'

'Yes, you are right.'

'How about going back today, can we?' Sheba said, putting her plate aside.

'We have the reservations for tomorrow, Sheba,' Mayuri said, suddenly looking at her and realizing her state of mind. Sheba looked away.

'And we are spending our time in the library tomorrow. Participating in the afternoon discussions is not very important, is it? We will have our lunch somewhere else, there will be no chance of facing him,' Mayuri said and bent her head to her left.

'Alright,' Sheba said, somewhat resigned.

The first paper of the session was being read when they reached the seminar hall. The chairperson who sat among the four participants nodded slowly with his eyes closed.

'Mr Chairperson is actually sleeping while pretending to be a good listener,' Mayuri whispered into Sheba's ear, and she laughed. They found two vacant chairs and quickly went over to the seats.

'You often see such sights in the sessions after lunch, many in the audience are sleepy after stuffing themselves!'

'They should have a light meal, like us.'

'Everyone is not a genius like us,' Sheba said, smiling.

A man from the front row turned his head towards them and stared at them sternly for a second before turning his head around. Following suit, a middle-aged woman with thick glasses and a bony girl also looked at them with the same expression. Mayuri and Sheba both assumed a serious expression.

'Don't you think we disturbed the gentleman who turned his head and looked at us because he himself had been sleeping, and got angry because we woke him up when we talked?' asked Mayuri, looking at the speaker seriously, as if commenting on the paper.

'And these two ladies?' Sheba controlled her smile with much effort.

'To be counted as intellectuals.'

Next day, in the afternoon, they saw a guy sitting on the fourth step of the broad staircase, with his long legs reaching the ground and thick hair covering his forehead. He looked up suddenly and smiled at the girls climbing the stairs as if he had been waiting for them. He bent his head back to his book and began to read but before they could reach the library, he once again looked up from the book.

'How was the seminar?' he asked them, blinking his eyes in the direct sunlight. Sheba was walking fast to get away from his presence, but was now standing at the door looking at Mayuri, who had stopped suddenly. The sunlight was bringing out the different shades in Shahaab's hair, making them look various shades of light brown, and very light brown, instead of black. Sheba closed her eyes as if to avoid seeing it all, but it had already imprinted itself in her brown eyes—the eyes she had inherited from Suraya Begum.

'What is all this?' she said to herself, shaking her head but could not stop a smile from appearing on her lips.

'It was good. And how about yours, is it over?' asked Mayuri, casting a look towards Sheba at the door and looking at Shahaab.

'This session was not very interesting, so I decided to come to the library instead,' he said, standing up.

'I have to return this book. I had taken permission to read it outside the library, and sat here in sight of the lady at the counter inside to save her any apprehensions that I may run away with the book!' He went in laughing, and Sheba moved aside. She did not feel bad about enjoying his good sense of humour for a moment or two.

'Aadab. You both are in the same varsity, aren't you? Someone had perhaps mentioned that yesterday?'

'Yes.' Sheba looked at Mayuri.

'Actually, they have such a congenial educational atmosphere here that you can't think of doing anything else. Sir Syed Ahmad Khan had certainly planned the university after much thought. He was a great man.'

'Yes, you are absolutely right. But in those days, many people did not understand this; and so, teaching them English language had become a huge controversy in itself,' Mayuri said, smiling.

'You are right, madam, but I think that people have started realizing by now what a crucial step it was and how important it was for our progress,' he said but stopped suddenly.

'Have you been looking for a particular book or did you just come to see the library? There is no one at the counter now, and the librarian has also turned her chair to the wall to convey that she is taking some time off. There is no one to help you with the catalogue since it's the lunch break. Shouldn't we, too, have some tea somewhere?' he looked inquiringly at the two ladies. There, that is the cafeteria.' He waved his arm covered with a sky-blue shirt with dark blue stripes.

'Yes, that would be fine,' Mayuri completed her sentence, looking at Sheba. Sheba's face had no clear expression.

'Is English really a necessity for us, I find myself wondering at times,' Mayuri asked.

'It depends. Many European countries have not adopted English to such a large extent. Japanese have all the technology in their language; Russia and China use their language as the medium of instruction too. Many countries prefer to use their native language. But our country was not free in those days. And apart from employment, knowing this language was necessary for many other reasons,' answered Shahaab.

'You mean English as a medium of education?' asked Mayuri.

'Yes, of course.' He began to walk ahead, smiling. Mayuri smiled as well.

'Where is ma'am, your wife?' asked Mayuri, following him down the stairs.

'She was too bored, so she went to sleep. There is nothing of interest for her here.' He turned his head back and smiled, climbing down the steps.

'You mean something like shopping malls, etc.?' asked Mayuri, smiling.

'Yes, shopping malls and cinema halls!' he laughed. 'What else should an almost new bride look for?'

'You should have taken her around somewhere,' Mayuri said. They were coming down the stairs and Sheba, who earlier walked down behind them, now walked alongside them.

'There is no place like that here, I already asked some people. But she is happy staying in the guesthouse and watching television between naps. Actually, she is very interested in theatre. I will take care of that when I go to Delhi after a month or so, hopefully.'

'Is she a playwright?' asked Mayuri.

'No, she just likes to watch people acting on the stage.'

'Better than watching them on screen, isn't it?' said Mayuri, looking at Sheba.

'I watch movies as well, but only if they are good,' Mayuri laughed, 'but I do not find much time.'

'Yes, time is precious.'

They entered the cafeteria. 'You are making good use of your time these days, I assume,' said Mayuri moving a chair near the window.

'Yes, I have been trying not to waste my time,' said Shahaab.

'Are you also studying sociology?' he asked, looking at Sheba.

'Yes,' she replied slowly.

'I went to your varsity last year, for a conference.'

'Oh yes, Sheba had seen you there, didn't you Sheba?' Mayuri said, but realized immediately that she should not have said that.

'Yes, I thought it was you. I told Mayuri last evening when I saw you that perhaps you had come to our university last year.'

Sheba had become nervous after Mayuri's faux-pas but recovered her composure and replied to him confidently; Mayuri relaxed. Shahaab noticed that Sheba's eyes were almond-shaped, like golden fish swimming in a spring, with light brown pupils that made a rare and beautiful combination, with her spotless, fair-skinned face and pink lips. Shahaab had noticed this casually, and had observed it objectively as if an interesting essay in a book had suddenly opened before him. But observing this made him concentrate for a moment, and Sheba felt that Shahaab had known that she had been thinking about him for a year. That he knew that she had cried many times when she came to know about his marriage, and that she had been sad for days, because of which her hair had started falling out.

'Yes, I had sprained my ankle but I had a commitment to keep.'

'Your paper was good and was liked by…' Sheba said quickly and then stopped suddenly. 'Everyone liked it, I still remember,' she continued confidently with a light smile on her face, pretending to be casual. Addressing Shahaab, she felt an emotion that combined nervousness with pleasure; Mayuri noticed this as well.

'Did you hear the paper? Are you also interested in sciences…but sociology?'

'Actually, I was waiting for some friends.'

'We were late that day and she had gone to the Science block. Sheba does not believe in wasting time,' Mayuri said abruptly. 'Losing a little time sometimes becomes a big loss,' continued Mayuri, looking at Sheba mischievously and Sheba wrinkled her nose to warn her. At some other time, this statement would have made Sheba sad, but in Shahaab's presence nothing was making her sorrowful, not even the grief of losing him.

'The tea is good but I must apologize for not inviting you ladies to a better place than this!' Inhaling deeply, Shahaab offered tea cups to Mayuri and Sheba one after the other.

'We have some common friends in the Sciences faculty. We will arrange someone to take you to Kamani, FICCI, Shri Ram Centre, etc., when you come to Delhi. All the best plays are staged there. After all, you served us such nice tea. In short, we Delhi people are good hosts, and we have a great variety of teas there too,' said Mayuri, smiling.

'Yes, thank you very much…InshAllah!' Shahaab laughed.

'These people put salt in the tea,' Mayuri said, looking at Sheba with a visibly bright smile. Sheba smiled as well.

'Oh, how is that?' Shahaab looked at Sheba and bent his neck slightly to his right.

'It is made with black tea leaves and has some health benefits. Sodium bicarbonate is also added to that tea, which again is good for mild stomach disorders.'

'OK, sodium bicarbonate, a weak alkaline salt. They make this tea in Lucknow too,' Shahaab nodded.

'Yes, they make it like us too, adding cream to it. Its aroma fills the whole house when it is boiling in the samovar. It is made in many countries of Central Asia, like Russia, and China as well. But those who do not have a taste for it may not like it.'

'You are very well-informed.'

'Her paper was on similarities of cultures in different societies.'

'I heard people praising it during the lunch break.'

'But that tea is really very delicious, Sheba has made me like it too!'

'And whoever tastes it, I mean even someone from another place visiting the Valley, has liked it very much.'

'Oh, then I must also come over someday!'

'We will invite you to Sheba's wedding.'

Listening to Mayuri, Sheba held her lips tightly closed and tried to appear happy.

'When is your wedding?'

'Not very soon, since she has a strange choice. She found someone she liked last year but she did not tell anyone. And by the time she was a bit free from her exams, we learned that he had already married,' said Mayuri.

Sheba looked at her, surprised, for a few moments and then laughed for a second, in the same threatening manner. 'What nonsense, you liar, that is all baseless!'

'If it is true, then the guy is very unfortunate not to have such a nice partner for life. I wish you good luck,' said Shahaab.

'She was joking, this friend of mine is crazy,' Sheba said, also smiling, the threatening spark was visible in her eyes. When her gaze met Mayuri's, she smiled too.

'That was a joke,' Mayuri said without smiling, and again looked at Sheba.

'Wasn't that a joke?' said Mayuri laughing, and Sheba held her arm and smiled, but her fingers were pressed tightly into her arm. Her grip was so hard that after smilingly tolerating it for some time, she suddenly got up to relieve her aching arm. Had it been some other occasion, both of them would have started in a friendly scuffle and would have ended up laughing uproariously.

'It has been a pleasure meeting you. Keep in touch. We will certainly give our students a chance to benefit from your presence,' he said pleasantly and stood up.

'Sure,' Mayuri nodded confidently.

'Khuda Hafiz,' said Sheba, pushing her chair back and stepping forward while turning her head to look at Shahaab.

'Khuda Hafiz, and see you both again.'

***

Sheba and Mayuri returned to Delhi and were back in their hostel. They relaxed for some time, and then left for Daanish Kadah.

At the same time, there was a call for Mayuri at the hostel reception. 'You go ahead, I will be right there,' Mayuri said, handing over the packet of bread they had brought for Dr Daanish. Sheba walked away at a fast pace. She went to the kitchen first, giving Saleem Miyaan the '*matree*', a special bread from Aligarh, before going to the professor's room. Daanish was an Aligarian—from Aligarh Muslim University, and loved *matree* from his hostel days—when it used to be an important item of breakfast.

Sheba picked up a famous book from Professor Daanish's writing table, saying, 'Sir, when did you write this book?' She opened the book and looked at his face. A faint gleam appeared in his eyes for a moment and then faded away.

'This…I…wrote…it…I…' he said slowly and was silent again. Sheba turned another page.

'Yes, in 1988,' she said, raising her head to look at him, and then looked down again.

'*The Impact of American Political Strategies on the Indian Socio-political Scenario*, what a vast topic, sir! You must have studied day and night, and consulted volumes of books to write it...' she said while continuing to turn the pages; she kept talking and raised her head occasionally to try and read his expression. His eyes lit up one moment, and were off in the next, like a flickering candle.

'Any developed nation can influence the economy of developing countries and exploit its peoples, and...,' Sheba read aloud and looked at Professor Danish to find out if he remembered the rest of the words.

Professor Daanish tried a couple of times to say something, but then moved his head in negation.

'Na...no...cannot...can...not...say it,' he said in an annoyed voice.

'You can, sir! I will read for you: Any developed nation can influence the economy of the developing countries and exploit its people...' Sheba stopped again for a moment and looked at him.

'And...and the resources...' Daanish said between the pauses, and his eyes filled with tears. He looked towards the window.

'Yes!' Sheba put the book in her lap and shouted, closing her fists tight.

'You did it, sir! You did it!' Sheba's voice got louder and hearing it, Mayuri, who had just entered the main gate, ran in.

'What is the matter, Sheba?'

'Mayuri! Sir can speak easily now. Sir remembers his important passages, Mayuri, yes, he is absolutely fine! He remembers, Mayuri, he is recovering, you know!' Sheba's voice was like the happy chirping of a bird.

'No…no…it is not true…' Professor Daanish said in a low tone and burst into tears.

Saleem Miyaan entered with the tea tray. Seeing Professor Daanish crying, he looked at the girls, shocked.

'All is well, Saleem Miyaan, give it to me, I will make the tea.' Mayuri took the tray from him.

Sheba closed the book, put it back on the rack and went to Professor Daanish.'Sir, believe me, you…you.'

Crying helplessly like a baby, Professor Daanish did not look at Sheba.

Sheba wiped his tears with a tissue paper.

'Sir, these truthful statements in your book are as real today as they were 20 years ago. That's why we have to save you for the world. You have to live and be healthy again. Why do you think you do not remember? Why don't you think that you can remember everything when you try to? This is an occasion to celebrate, sir, and not to grieve,' Sheba said, looking at Professor Daanish's face, wiping his tears. Professor looked at her in disbelief.

'Are…you…sure?' he said between pauses.

'Yes, I am sure!' Sheba smiled.

'Now,' she bent her head slightly and looked at Professor Daanish, raising her eyebrows the way Dr Ghayi did.

'You must have your tea,' she said. Mayuri laughed at this and Professor Daanish smiled too.

'Thank you, sir,' said Sheba, taking the cup from Mayuri's hand.

Returning to the hostel in the evening, Sheba seemed to be lost in thoughts again. Mayuri tried talking to her a few times hoping that she might say something, but Sheba walked ahead, taking her usual small steps, lost deep in her thoughts.

'What are you thinking, Sheba?' Mayuri ran the few steps to her.

'I am thinking about Daanish sir…perhaps his recovery is really very difficult.'

'But you looked very hopeful.'

'But looking at his depression makes me apprehensive. We have to try again and again; we have to read to him from his books like we did today. He may recall one thing or the other this way.'

'But how will you do this alone?'

'We all will do it together.'

'Everyone will have to give their time for this but…'

They reached their hostel. Mayuri stopped and left off her sentence half away.

'But what, Mayuri?' Sheba also stopped.

'I wanted to tell you about that telephone call from home. I am getting engaged,' Mayuri said slowly and began to unlock the door.

'When? You did not tell me a thing about it!' Sheba said, pleasantly surprised.

'I did not find any time to tell you. I told you earlier that they were talking about it during the vacations. My brother and sister-in-law had asked me if I liked anyone; I had told them I did not. So they made their decision, but he lives in London. He is coming to India during the Christmas holidays...' Mayuri said with no expression on her face.

'You must be happy about this engagement, you have to be!' Sheba removed the bed cover and sat on her bed. Mayuri, too, sat on hers.

'I am neither happy nor unhappy. I have no feelings, but since one has to get married someday...'

'But what about your studies, job, etc.?'

'They say I can get a job there, and those people would also like me to work. They actually were looking for a working woman.'

'That's good.'

'What good, Sheba? I am not in that headspace yet.'

'Who asked you to get into a headspace to marry!'

Mayuri lay down on her bed. Sheba felt as if her voice was coming from somewhere far away. 'What are you saying, Mayuri? You mean you will spend your life with him without even knowing anything about him?'

'Yes, my sister-in-law's folks know him for a long time, and one has to make some adjustments always. The basic thing is his general reputation. And specifically, what his relations know about him,' said Mayuri, yawning.

'Yes, you are right, that is a practical approach.'

'Yes, and then a love marriage isn't always successful either, whereas sometimes two strangers can lead a perfectly happy married life.'

'You are absolutely right. I wish you a very happy married life,' said Sheba in a voice full of affection.

'Thanks, dear. But let the marriage take place first. Do you want to throw me out of this room sooner?' Mayuri said, sounding less tired.

'No. I myself want to run away from all this.'

'Worried because of Daanish sir?'

'There are many reasons…'

'Ammi is worried about your marriage, isn't it?'

'Yes, she is, but she leaves it to me.'

'And you?'

'I have not given serious thought to getting married.'

'Is that so?' said Mayuri, somewhat sharply.

'Yes, it is.'

'Why so, should people not get married?'

'They should, those who want to. But those who do not want to, should not, provided they are not under any pressure from their families and the society.'

'And what about human urges?'

'Those depend upon one's priorities.'

'Is that so?' said Mayuri pleasantly.

'Yes, dear,' Sheba spoke warmly while lying on her bed.

'How?'

'God has given a human being so much energy. This small creature has huge potential, you know. When one realizes the path one would like to follow, all of one's energies get directed to that channel and one's whole being goes through such a transformation, making one rise above the common people to master the incredible, got it?'

'Yes.'

'Tell me of some great personality of such calibre then,' asked Sheba, like a school teacher, and Mayuri started laughing at that.

'Yes.'

'Who?'

'Mother Teresa.'

'Excellent, you have grown so wise. Name some others,' Sheba chirped like a lark.

'No, it's your turn now.'

'Me? OK...Qurat-ul-ain Hyder, and Lata Mangeshkar.'

'And the saints and yogis of the olden days, who had full control over their beings and wrote volumes on various aspects of life, right?'

'Yes, exactly. Everyone has a different interpretation for creativity. Some call one thing a creation, and some another.'

'But then, isn't it necessary to have a family and children?'

'Of course, it is, but again, priorities matter.'

'And what about old age? You will need someone, either a life partner or your children. Is it all useless?'

'No one takes anybody else's responsibility. People unnecessarily rely upon others mindlessly. Then one fine day, they suddenly come to know that everyone relies upon others for their own self-interest. Perhaps this happens subconsciously, but this is the truth. Being really dependable has nothing do with relations and duties. It is a kind of altruism!'

'You are absolutely right.'

'The basic reason for unhappiness in reality is reliance upon others. I am going to make tea, would you like some?' Sheba said, rising from her bed.

'All right, since my sleep has vanished altogether.'

'And the fatigue went away with the rest!'

'Yes, for example, you are sure that I will never forget your birthday but if I forget…'

'Then I will not talk to you,' said Mayuri, pretending to be angry.

'Exactly, and if you do not expect me to remember your birthday and I still wish you?'

'I shall be very glad,' said Mayuri, keeping her neck erect.

'Yes, you will be very happy!' said Sheba, waving her head to throw her hair back.

'Undoubtedly,' Mayuri set her pillow straight and rested her back against it as Sheba handed her the cup of tea.

'I made only a little, lest it robs us of our sleep. So, tell me…'

'Yes, I will be more than happy.'

'So, isn't the reason for being sad our expectations from others? Not expecting anything from anyone means not giving them any opportunity whatsoever to disappoint you or hurt you.'

'Fine, but the joy of having children?'

'There are so many orphans in the world. If they are loved, adoptive parents can experience the same emotions with them as one's own children. There is no difference between motherhood for an adopted child and for a biological one. Seemeen and Yasir are so dear to me, I love them as if they were my own. I am sure if I had any children, they would be as dear to me as these two are. To have peace in life you need to give love, and not necessarily receive love—and to love those who really need it. The love we share in relationships depends on our own selfish motives. If it goes against our need, the relationship breaks. Many wise people have mentioned such things so many times, but we foolishly rely on relationships and do not understand this fundamental truth.'

'Like?'

'I will give you an example. Don't you think that the death of the character Desdemona is because of her own father?'

'How? She is murdered by her own husband.'

'Yes, but initially, her father says a line to her husband, remember? "...Look to her (Moor) if thou hast eyes to see; she has deceived her father, and may thee". Remember?'

'Yes, Sheba, and this fact lodges in his mind somewhere and he suspects her. Had Shakespeare not wanted to reveal this to his readers or viewers, why would he put these words in her father's mouth?'

'That means all relationships are just a selfish need, for one's own self.'

'Human beings are instinctually selfish. And there is one more thing associated with this: it is a person's financial position which plays an important role in the stability of the relationship.'

'Of course, it does—it's the most important thing! Financial stability sustains relationships…'

'So, marriage is not important?'

'I did not say that but priorities are important.'

'Everything depends on luck, Sheba.'

'A person creates his destiny by using his brain, which is given by the God Almighty.'

'And yet, you feel there is nothing in our hands?'

'Yes, human beings are helpless.'

'You can call it destiny.'

Sheba finished her tea and lay down on her bed. 'I feel sleepy now…You did not lace the tea with some sedative, did you?'

'It's early dawn, this is the intoxicating effect of the morning breeze.' 'Oh God! It's 3 o'clock,' said Mayuri, looking at her watch. 'You are also sleepy, aren't you?' Mayuri said drowsily.

'Yes dear, I am. Let's to sleep, enough philosophizing!'

'Alright then, good night.'

The Swallows on the Lakes

Sitting in the veranda and yearning for some peace in the vastness of the evening, Sheba started thinking of friends who had drifted away so far apart from her. Mayuri had settled in a distant land; Diljeet and her Sukhi, Saagar and Aaftab... Aaftab Aalam and his second cousin—Sheba's heart beat fast for a moment. Aaftab had landed a senior government job and was in Bhopal, the city of his second cousin.

She had been to Bhopal once, for a seminar, and the city had appeared to her to resemble her own beloved city—Srinagar. The vast waters seen from the window of her hotel room looked like the Dal Lake, right down to the islands with trees like 'Chaar Chinaary in the Dal', 'Sone Lank' or 'Roppe Lank'—Golden Island or the Silver Island. There were four chinar trees on each island in the Dal Lake, though one of them had fallen recently. While having her morning tea in the veranda in front of her hotel room in Bhopal, she had seen swallows flying about in the vast sky above the waters—just the way they flew, round and round, and looking so busy and committed above the Dal Lake, the Wular or Manasbal Lakes. How she loved to enjoy her tea while watching those long-winged sleek birds with soft, white, tiny tummies flying low over the water! She loved their chirping, which sounded like a whistling toy of children.

That day, Mayuri had suddenly come over from the adjacent room, with a face pack on.

Sheba closed her eyes and rested her head against the back of the chair.

'You are ready to display your charm today, aren't you? And you better adorn yourself, and don't wear your glasses! Do you have your contact lenses with you, or did you leave them behind again? Why did you buy them at all if you were not going to wear them?' Mayuri had asked with her teeth slightly clenched while sitting on a chair facing her, in the hotel balcony that morning.

'You asked me to buy them, you demon! You look like a white-faced demon with that mask on! Now please stop scolding me so early in the morning!'

'Why, aren't you happy to see your love? Now don't force me to speak for I will end up with lines on my face if I do. I had thought of giving some respite to my suffering skin, but you compel me to speak!'

'Well, you are getting married after all. The desire to look beautiful as a bride is the greatest weakness of every woman! Will you have some tea?' said Sheba, laughing and removing the top of the teapot.

No, I just had some. And yes, I am getting married. Had I been lost in memories of one-sided love like you, I would have died a spinster!'

'Do not talk about that, Mayuri,' Sheba said in a sad tone.

'Why shouldn't I? Don't you long to see him? Aren't you tempted to see him at all?'

'I will feast my eyes on him for a long, long time today, my little devil,' Sheba's voice brightened suddenly. 'But then you will taunt me later saying that I had no right to.'

'No, I won't. You can look at him today to your heart's content.'

'But why? Isn't this against the norms of ethics?'

'You may look at him secretly today, because after today you may never have a chance like this. By the way, it is very interesting to have a combined seminar on sociology and science,' said Mayuri.

Sheba sighed sadly. 'Mayuri, how handsome he had looked last year! I wonder how he will look today. Will he be as handsome as the last time?'

'Yes, you can look at him, like you look at the fish in some of the springs in your Valley…about which you once told me that it is *halaal*—allowed according to a religious ruling—to look at them but non-*halal*—prohibited—to catch them.'

'Yes, you are right. It is like that for me. But listen, who will I talk to when you are gone to a foreign land, thousands of miles away?'

'Don't remind me of my impending departure, Sheba,' Mayuri said, and was suddenly very quiet but then smiled after a while.

'And what if he finds out?' Mayuri looked at Sheba.

'Let him. Who knows whether I will get such an opportunity in life again? But why are you asking me to adorn myself?'

'I don't know. Maybe because my heart wants to see you with him, looking gorgeous, with happiness on your face reflecting all your feelings and desires,' Mayuri laughed with clenched teeth.

'You have the pack on your face, otherwise I would have taught you a good lesson,! And what do you mean by desires, you bad girl? I did not just have a crush on him...I loved him with all my heart.'

'I know,' Mayuri said in a forlorn voice and got up, adding, 'I was just trying to cheer you up.'

'I keep thinking that you and I...all of us friends will soon be separated, and it will be death for me missing these days.'

'No, it will not be so. With the hard struggle ahead for a career, and settling down after getting a job...then family and children—we just won't have the time to reminisce about these days. And then after some years we will all be sad, and we will shed tears remembering these days.'

'Do the boys cry as well?'

'Yes, we have seen that. Saagar got so emotional that day when he saw tears in Professor Daanish's eyes; and seeing him, Aaftab had also started crying.'

'Yes, he wiped his nose again and again with his handkerchief! Poor thing.'

Professor Sherwaani did not show up for the first session. After the tea break, when people were getting back to their seats, Mayuri saw him entering the hall. She looked at him keenly. He had put on much weight, and had developed dark circles around his eyes. She pressed Sheba's arm with her elbow, who was sitting next to her.

'Sheba, isn't that him?'

Sheba's heart almost missed a beat. 'Yes, it's him but...'

'But what? Is this how he really looks!' Mayuri said, but seeing Sheba shocked, she jokingly added. 'He was about to get married those days, so he must have worked hard in the gym to look like he did then.'

Sheba laughed, 'He is fine. He looks somewhat dull but that doesn't lessen his charm.'

'What charm, you silly girl? He looks unattractive. He must have dyed his moustache.'

'But he is not that old that he needs to colour his moustache; see, his hair is so dark!' Sheba said softly.

'He must have dyed his hair too,' said Mayuri, putting both her hands on her lap.

'I will kill you today,' Sheba pressed her nails into Mayuri's arm and kept pressing it harder and harder.

'Sorry, I am sorry. I will not say anything anymore, I swear!'

The topic for the next session was very interesting. It was about the impact of science on the development of society. Professor Sherwaani had to chair the session. His name was announced and he walked to the stage. He delivered a wonderful address. Mayuri listened very carefully throughout, and Sheba was mesmerized by each and every expression on his face. They met during the lunch break; he seemed to be quieter than before.

'Your wife is not with you today?' asked Mayuri. She had picked two tiny pieces of salad with her fork. Swallows flew around the tall trees of the gorgeous Bharat Bhavan on the bank of the vast man-made lake.

Hearing Mayuri's question, Professor Sherwaani looked at her and then at his plate. 'This is her home town, so why should she come? Yes…that time in Aligarh, she was rather bored,' he laughed softly.

'You are an excellent speaker,' Mayuri said, 'Right, Sheba? But you were just looking, were you even listening?' Mayuri added with an innocent expression on her face. Sheba looked at her sternly. Smiles appeared on both their faces. Professor Sherwaani looked at their faces, somewhat puzzled, one after the other. Mayuri's mischievous looks and Sheba's shy smile reminded him of the meeting in the cafeteria in Aligarh last year. He had never thought about this before, but some similarity of the two situations somehow made him think about it.

'Your health?' asked Mayuri, suddenly noticing him looking at both of them.

'Don't I look in better health than before?' he asked, addressing them.

'No, it seems to have rather deteriorated.' Sheba said quickly and became silent again.

'Actually, after getting married, a man becomes careless about himself,' he said, and smiled.

'Is that so?' asked Mayuri.

'Or maybe he surrenders himself to the mercy of his wife, and she turns him into a fat lamb,' Professor Sherwaani said and laughed out loud.

Sheba kept listening to him laugh even after he had stopped.

What a lively laugh he has…and what a pleasant voice, thought Sheba, wearing a serious expression and picking a bite with her fork.

'And you have not been exercising, since you are in academics and have to work at a desk,' said Mayuri, walking two steps backwards and standing against a tree.

'Yes, that may be one of the reasons. Studying at night is not a good habit, but one feels so peaceful while studying at night—only God knows why!'

'Yes, that's true. One can concentrate without much effort,' said Mayuri.

'Only if the dogs do not make such a riotous uproar outside,' she added. Professor Sherwaani laughed and Sheba smiled.

'The night has its own ambience, which no one can disrupt,' Sheba said softly.

'Dogs definitely have all the liberty though,' Sherwaani laughed again.

'I don't even like the lights interfering with it.'

'You are right. Night has its own charms, its own grace. Science has turned everything topsy-turvy. People sleep during the day and are up at night,' said Sherwaani, putting his plate on the table next to the wall.

'Our next topic covers this as well.'

'Is that so?'

'Yes, "Science, Human Needs and Social Pressures"'.

'That sounds interesting,' Mayuri said.

'We gather piles of stuff without thinking if we really need all that. We get loans for things we don't use and then spend our working years paying off the same,' she added.

Sherwaani got some dessert in a small bowl and looked at the empty plates they were putting back on the table.

'Would you like some dessert?' he asked.

'It's a delicious *halwa* made of *moong dal* (green gram),' he added, picking up a raisin with his spoon.

'It must be so full of fat,' said Sheba.

'But it is good for one's health to have it once in a while,' said Mayuri smiling, and headed towards the dessert counter.

'And what about you?' he turned to Sheba.

'I…I will see if Mayuri likes it…'

'Don't you trust my opinion?'

'Yes, sure I do…this may be the secret of your health!' Sheba said smiling, and looked at him from head to toe.

'You are taunting me! You are casting an evil eye on my health! But I don't feel bad about it. It has saved me from jealousy of my middle-aged and overweight seniors, who would have really created problems for my being younger otherwise. Earlier, I looked younger than my age; but now, looking older than my years impresses people.'

Sherwaani laughed and proceeded to dispose his paper plate. Wiping his mouth with a tissue, he smiled and looked at Sheba for her reply before turning his head to the other side. His eyes were tired but his dark pupils looked bright. The grey collar of his coat with his white shirt contrasted well with the dark hair. Sheba felt a pang in the depth of her soul. She sorrowfully moved her eyes away. Mayuri returned with the halwa. Sheba looked at her intently. Wearing a black sari contrasting with her fair complexion, all of Mayuri's affection for Sheba was evident in her smiling face.

'Why are these beautiful eyes wet?' asked Mayuri, and Professor Sherwaani looked at Sheba, alarmed.

'I didn't do anything,' he said abruptly and frowned, and then smiled.

'No, you are not to blame. She must be feeling homesick,' said Mayuri.

'There are no tears, nothing of the sort,' said Sheba, and headed to the other side to have some water.

Sheba was lost deep in her thoughts. Hearing Professor Danish cough in his room, she returned to the present abruptly. She looked up; the stars had appeared in the sky.

'Those stars in the centre of the sky form so many different shapes.' Dinner had been arranged in the hotel lawn for the participants. Sitting at a table with a round white tablecloth, the three of them were talking about various things.

'Yes…that, there…that shape looks like a lion. It's for the zodiac sign of Leo. Isn't it?' Mayuri said, looking up at the sky.

'Oh, you are interested in astrology?' Sherwaani asked, looking at her. 'If it speaks,' he added.

He laughed, as Mayuri smiled pleasantly.

'That is a good line from some movie. But I know what you mean...the secrets of the stars.'

'Yes, in their secrets too. The study of the stars is a fascinating subject. I, too, am a star,' Sherwaani smiled.

'What do you mean?' asked Mayuri, curiously.

'*Shihab*, in his name, means a star,' Sheba said, looking up at the sky too.

'That is a nice name!' Mayuri said.

Pointing to the stars, Sherwaani showed them more shapes they made in the sky.

Sheba heard the professor cough again in his room. She lowered her eyes instead of looking up at the sky and got up from her chair. She moved her neck right and left a couple of times, and then went inside.

Professor Daanish woke up, and looking at Sheba, smiled vaguely.

'Would you like to drink something?' Sheba asked, going closer.

'Some juice?' she asked. The professor did not answer.

What is the matter with him? Sheba thought, looking at him. She suddenly realized that he had not spoken a single word since morning—he had not even tried to.

'Please tell me, sir.'

She leaned over the chair and held his shoulders. Professor looked at her closely. Sheba shook his shoulders gently.

'Please tell me, sir,' Sheba looked at his face; it was as blank as before. Sheba started thinking about the situation.

Dr Ghayi was away with his son in America. He visited him every summer but Sheba kept in touch with him. She got up to call him, but sat down again, realizing that it would be rather early in the morning in America. People sleep till late in the day on a Saturday morning. And this was not an emergency either, as Professor Daanish had only been silent. Thankfully, he was eating, she thought calmly and looked at him. He had dozed off again. Sheba went out to the veranda. She put her hands on the railing and looked up at the sky. It was dark now. She felt that she ought to go inside but she did not want to. Hearing the telephone ring, she went into the room. It was a call from home.

'When will you come home, my child?' Ammi asked Sheba between pauses; she was barely audible.

'Ammi, how are you? Are you OK?' she enquired anxiously.

I haven't seen you for a year and a half now.'

'I will come soon. Are you all right?'

'Yes, I am fine but what about you?' Suraya Begum asked quietly.

'Tell me the truth, please.'

'I am fine, my child. I just want to see you. When are you coming? Tell me the day…the date.'

Ammi sounded very sad and this pained Sheba.

'I will be leaving the day after tomorrow; I have made a reservation for that day,' said Sheba after a pause.

'Why did you not tell me before? Had you decided earlier or did you do so just now?'

Ammi sounded calm and Sheba relaxed.

'Yes, Ammi, I had planned already,' she said quietly.

'Alright, my little doll! What are you doing there in this terrible heat? God bless you and protect you always.'

'I will be home soon, Ammi! Khuda Hafiz.'

Your little doll has grown old now, Sheba thought to herself after putting the receiver back.

I have to go...but how would I manage everything over here? Sheba began to think. A nurse has to be arranged, no one else can be trusted. There should be no disturbance in sir's schedule. Sheba suddenly missed all her friends; none of them were in town.

By good chance, Dr Ghayi returned to India the next day for some important business. He called to enquire after Professor Daanish. Sheba told him about the new problem; Dr Ghayi's answer was reassuring to her. They also found a good nurse.

The Pain of Yellowing Leaves

Faheema and Farkhanda were already present when Sheba reached home. Ammi was not unwell, but she looked weaker than before. The garden was still in full bloom, and the apricots, plums and figs were ripening. Seemeen was not with Baaji; neither had Farkhi brought Yasir with her. Both of them might have been at college and school, Sheba thought. The dining table had been set with tea and other fare.

'Does anyone stay away from home so long?' Ammi asked, looking at her reproachfully, and pouring tea into her favourite mug.

'It was important, Ammi, otherwise why would I have stayed there?'

Ammi handed her another cup, which Sheba passed on to Farkhanda, who placed it before Faheema.

Ammi sat near Sheba. She poured out one more cup of tea, which Sheba placed before Farkhanda.

'I feel so good to see you all here sitting together,' said Sheba, smiling, and moved the mug towards herself.

'But you may not be happy hearing what we are going to talk about,' Faheema said, after clearing her throat.

'Oh please, do not start right away. She has just arrived,' Suraya Begum said helplessly.

'When Ammi, if not now? We have to return to our homes. We have responsibilities. We do not have the luxury of looking only after ourselves,' said Faheema, the taunt in her voice quite apparent.

'Are you living with someone?' asked Faheema, looking at Sheba sternly. Sheba was nervous for a moment but then she recovered her composure.

'I am living where I always did, earlier with Mayuri and then...'

Faheema interrupted her quickly, 'We are not talking about that. We are asking about that man you are living with. You have become very modern indeed, haven't you?'

'What happened? What have I done?'

'Sheba, Baaji has asked you something. We are also responsible for the honour and prestige of our family. Tell us the truth of the matter,' Farkhanda said, and shifted her glance from Sheba to Ammi.

'Why? Am I still a child? Don't I know that I have to uphold my prestige as well as that of the family?'

'You only have to put your hand on Ammi and swear that you are not living there with a man,' Faheema said, flaring her nostrils with a contemptuous smile on her face.

'Yes, I live with a person but...'

'What are you saying, Sheba?' Suraya Begum exclaimed, shocked.

'Yes, Ammi, but it is not what you all think.'

'What is it then?' Faheema asked in a relaxed manner. 'You are staying with a stranger and his servant,' she added.

'No, that flat is allotted to me. I am not living in anybody's house.'

'Oh, so that man is living in your house, is it?'

'Yes, but he is an invalid,' Sheba looked at Ammi, who was now sitting with her head lowered.

'If he is ill, he will recover. And anyway, it's the responsibility of his folks to look after him.'

'He has none.'

'What can we do about that?'

'He cannot be left alone to die. I cannot…'

'Fine, then marry him. You have rejected good proposals and now you live with a stranger immorally,' Faheema said.

'Baaji, please stop!' Sheba said firmly.

'Baaji has not said anything wrong,' Farkhanda interjected quickly.

'You don't know these in-laws. If someone gets to know, they will taunt us and make our life hell. It can even result in divorce. Today, Baaji found out and only Ammi and I came to know. What if our families find out?'

'Sheba…' said Ammi, raising her head. She knew her daughter. She knew about her high moral values, decisions and her firmness of character.

'This must be very important to you, but Baaji is not wrong. Call him over here and we will arrange a grand marriage,' Ammi added and Sheba looked at her.

'Alright,' Sheba said, after some moments. 'Is that what you called me for, Ammi?' she asked.

'No baby, I missed you! But I also wanted to talk to you about this. Whatever has happened is all for the best. Now, my only desire in life is to see you get married, my child. After that, God will take care of everything,' Ammi said peacefully.

Sheba had to return after four days. While she was there, she kept going aimlessly all over the house from one floor to another. Seemeen and Yasir also visited a couple of times, and Sheba realized how fast the time flown by—faster than a person can think or imagine. Seemeen was in college, and they were planning to send Yasir to a hostel. He had grown taller, but his eyes with their thick lashes looked charming in his still-innocent face. He was confused about going to the hostel, alternating between sadness and happiness. Seemeen was mostly silent.

'Our Seemeen does not visit us now,' Ammi said, hugging Seemeen and smiling.

'I don't get the time, Nanna Jaani, but I still come over often,' Seemeen said, getting out of her grandmother's arms. Sheba kept looking at her lovingly. She didn't know why but she had always held Seemeen very close to her heart. And she had always cherished this relationship, especially during the lonely days of her hostel life when she missed her home. She had always considered her to be her soul mate at some level of her consciousness, but this time Seemeen had not even looked at Sheba. She had tied her hair in a pigtail, and had hidden it under the dupatta that covered her head up to her forehead. When Sheba held her in her arms, Seemeen stood like a statue with her arms hanging on her sides.

'Did you hear the Azan, Nanna Jaani?' she asked, looking at the clock.

'No, sweetheart, but it is about time.'

'I am going for *wudu*. Mamma says that we should always remember God, and that doing anything against his commands is sinful. One should always save oneself from *Gunah-e-Kabir* (cardinal sin), whatever one's heart may say, since a sin is after all a sin,' she said with a downward gaze, and went to the bathroom.

'Sheba! Did you hear our Seemeen's wise words? She now prays regularly and offers every Namaz! *Ma Sha'a Allah* (by the grace of God),' Suraya Begum said, taking the jar full of *baqarkhanees* from the storage room to the kitchen.

Sheba did not say anything. She felt as if her chest was filled up with smoke and fumes. Her eyes would have been filled with tears had she not controlled herself. Her heart pounded fast for many moments. She exhaled deeply. A dialogue from Julius Caesar echoed in her mind.

'Et tu, Brute?' she had whispered, translating the Latin sentence into English, 'You, too, Brutus?'

Sheba heard the water flowing in the bathroom and got up to go out to the lawn. She spent most of the time during those four days with Ammi—in the garden, the kitchen, the drawing room, talking about her childhood, about Abbu, about the whole world. She would have even slept in Ammi's room, but she had gotten used to sleeping alone. Apart from those hours in the night, she had spent every moment with her Ammi, and had returned on the fifth day. That day, embracing her mother, she had cried a lot. She knew that she would not be able to visit her home for a long time to come, and would not have the privilege of being in Ammi's arms for a while. She had tried to tell her mother the reality during those four days, but had changed her mind because she knew she would be grieved at the fact that her daughter was living with an invalid and had no intention of leaving him before he recovered.

Ammi's face travelled with her, as always.

When she reached the university, she learnt that Professor Daanish had not eaten since the day she had left. Dr Ghayi had been giving him electrolytes through a drip. She ran to his room. Professor Daanish was lying in bed, sleeping perhaps. Dr Ghayi had visited him a short while ago. Sheba looked at Professor Daanish sleeping peacefully for a few moments. He looked weaker than before.

'He just went to sleep,' Saleem Miyaan said softly, offering a glass of water to Sheba. Hearing his voice, the professor opened his eyes; they brightened slightly when he saw Sheba and a child-like, innocent smile appeared on his face. Sheba went closer to him. Saleem Miyaan also came over.

'He looks happy today, but he has not talked since you left.'

'What?' Sheba was stunned for a moment but forced herself to smile.

'How are you, sir? I have brought some spinach for you from our kitchen garden. Saleem Miyaan is an expert in cooking it. Will you have some? Shall I ask him to make it?'

Sheba looked at the professor and then at Saleem Miyaan, who eagerly waited for his reply. No expression appeared on the professor's face. Sheba looked at his face for some time and he looked back at her silently.

'How do you feel, sir?' she asked, and gave him a bright smile. But the shadows of apprehension were apparent in her eyes. She was sure that the professor, who appeared to be unconcerned about everything, would smile back because he had smiled when she had entered the room. Sheba remembered that he had also smiled like this a couple of times before she had gone to the Valley. The smile of a baby who smiles readily at times, but does not smile at others, no matter how hard you try. Did that mean Daanish sir's mental health was also affected by now? Sheba looked at Saleem Miyaan in alarm.

'Saleem Miyaan, what did Dr Ghayi say when he came the first day?'

'He tried to talk to him for quite some time, but sahib did not even recognize him. The doctor was very concerned but said there was nothing to worry about as this was a temporary change, and that he would be fine, but *bitiya...*' Saleem Miyaan trailed off, looking at the floor, and then raised his head and looked at Sheba.

'But the doctor kept visiting and saying that there was no improvement. He injected some medicines into his arms as well, but sahib has been like this since that day.'

Hearing Saleem Miyaan's words, Sheba walked a few steps towards the chair and almost fell in it. She called Dr. Ghayi.

'Doctor, this is Sheba. What is happening to sir? He was recovering till last week and now suddenly...'

'No, it is not like that. When he smiled hearing his words being quoted by you and yet did not speak, that was no improvement actually.'

'What was it then?'

'We must accept the fact that he is not recovering, and I am afraid that he will not,' Dr Ghayi replied. He was silent for a few moments and then resumed, 'Now, he has Alzheimer's disease as well. His memory seems to be deteriorating fast, which happens in such cases. The body of a semi-paralyzed person deteriorates rather fast with age.'

Sheba listened to him, shocked. 'Then...is there no treatment for this? What will happen now?'

'I am giving him the best treatment I can. I have also consulted other doctors. We have to think of the best thing to do now, and how to make him more comfortable. I think you better call Mrs Daanish and let her know as well.'

'Is there anything to worry about?' Sheba asked.

'No, it is not that. He needs constant care; and let me tell you frankly, his progress towards health may be *very* slow.'

'You mean that the hope we had last time was false?'

'No, if you consider it and recall, for the last four-five years, I mean, since the stroke, his health was deteriorating steadily. But for about a year, his speech had improved slightly and that too...'

'But why did this happen so suddenly? Did it have something to do with reading him his books? Did that awaken a sense of loss which took a toll on his health, or some such?'

'No, no, it's not that....these things happen in this illness. You should not blame yourself. Science may have progressed a lot but there are still many things which it does not know, and cannot.'

'Yes, doctor,' Sheba said in a weak voice.

'We, at least, are taking good care of his physical health and treating his mental health. A physiotherapist also visits him to help him exercise. You should not worry. Miracles can happen. Who knows? Maybe he will recover with the care and concern he gets from you people and regains his health.'

'Yes, we will return him to health,' Sheba said with great determination.

'I do not need anyone else, just Saleem Miyaan and myself are enough,' she added.

'Count me in as well. I will always be with you in this mission,' Dr Ghayi said.

'You have always encouraged us, sir, you have been very kind.'

'But you will surely notice the change in him, since you are seeing him after four days.'

'Yes, Saleem Miyaan said that he had smiled when he saw me after many days.'

'Oh, really? That is a positive sign; it is an indication that he still recognizes you, which is very good,' Dr Ghayi said somewhat enthusiastically. 'Now, there is nothing to worry about and things are under control. You should also stop worrying and let us hope that everything will be fine.'

But nothing like that happened. The next day, Sheba discovered that the professor, who could earlier stroll with the support of Sheba's arm, was not even able to stand on his own. She and Saleem Miyaan tried to help him get out of his bed after seeing him smile a little the evening before. He could only sit up when he tried to stand. Even when they put his feet on the ground, he could not get up. Sheba and Saleem Miyaan looked at each other's face, alarmed. They called Dr Ghayi, but he was not surprised, and said that he had been apprehensive about it for some time.

A gentle, pleasant breeze was blowing that day when Sheba and Saleem Miyaan helped the professor in a wheelchair. He kept looking at the wheel chair, sitting in it impassively. A faint smile appeared on his lips when he reached the lawn, and seeing this, Sheba felt somewhat relieved. She relaxed, thinking that his smile indicated that he still loved life and may make a comeback.

Sheba started taking him out in the mornings and evenings, and advised the physiotherapist to come twice a day. She also consulted a dietician, and made changes in his diet after talking to Dr Ghayi. Life seemed to be moving on track and she began working hard on her D.Lit as well. She hoped that the professor would recover by the time she completed her D.Lit, and she would return to her city to be with her Ammi and work there...and do everything her

Ammi wanted her to. Shehla Daanish had not visited last year. She would surely visit this year during the Christmas holidays, as she had mentioned when Sheba had told her about her husband's condition.

Certain things happened just as Sheba had anticipated. Professor Daanish's life became more disciplined, and he began to look healthy. Dr Shehla Daanish also visited during the winter vacations, but Daanish's mental health did not show any improvement. He did not recognize anyone except Sheba, not even Shehla. Dr Ghayi was there when Dr Shehla had arrived. She drank a glass of water offered by Saleem Miyaan, sitting in a chair in the veranda. Sheba came out and greeted her.

'Would you like a cold drink?' Sheba asked with a smile.

'No, thank you. Where is he?' she asked, rising from her chair.

'He is inside, ma'am, in his room.'

While Shehla headed towards the room, Sheba looked at her from head to toe. Shehla was wearing a red sleeveless top and an off-white pair of trousers. She had very thin arms. Dr Ghayi introduced himself to her when she entered. Shehla looked surprised upon seeing her husband.

'He has grown very weak,' she said, sitting in a chair near the wall. She did not go near him. Professor Daanish kept looking at her with an expressionless face.

'Professor, do you recognize her?' asked Dr Ghayi, extending his arm towards Shehla; she stretched her lips in a smile, resembling the smile of a sales person. Sheba stood against the wall silently. No flicker of recognition appeared on Daanish's face.

'Sir, don't you recognize madam?' Sheba asked, going near him. Professor Daanish's face remained blank.

'How is he now, doctor?' Shehla asked, looking at Dr Ghayi.

'He is stable, but there is no improvement. We are hopeful though, of course,' said the doctor, looking at everyone.

'We have many facilities there,' Dr Shehla glanced at her hands and looked up. 'I don't know how you people manage here,' she added, curving her lips a little and swaying her head in negation.

'You can take him there if you want to. That is, of course, an advanced country and his treatment will be easier there—which may also help improve his condition,' Dr Ghayi suggested her.

'Yes, that is right but he will not be allowed there in this condition. Moreover, he is used to these surroundings. I think he is fine here. I was really apprehensive earlier. There are so many hassles…'

'But they might relax the rules for an intellectual like him. If the government here…' Sheba said slowly.

'Maybe, but it's very difficult. Moreover, I live in a studio apartment and till I can arrange for a hostel, or complete the formalities of an old-age home, where would I keep him?'

'Old-age home?' asked Sheba, incredulous.

'Yes, I do not have an attendant. Where else can he stay? I have a few more years left in my job. I, too, shall not stay alone; and will be looking for an old-age home or come back to India. But there is no one waiting for me here to stay with either. This is a really difficult situation,' Shehla sighed.

'But can sir be treated better there than here? What do they have there, which we do not have over here?' Sheba turned to Dr Ghayi.

'Nothing special, we have all the facilities here. I thought perhaps Dr Shehla might have some other plans for him.'

'No, Dr Ghayi, I am a teacher. You are the doctor. What can I do? It's very difficult.'

'Yes, I can understand that,' Dr Ghayi nodded.

'But I will leave all my contact numbers here. Please inform me whenever necessary,' Shehla bent her head to indicate her helplessness.

'Can I take a bath?' she looked at Sheba and got up.

'Yes, of course, the bathroom is across that room,' answered Sheba, pointing to her left.

Sheba looked at Dr Ghayi the moment Shehla left the room. 'Doctor, is it really important for sir to go there?'

'No, not exactly. But I did not expect this from her.'

'No doctor, we all knew it. But I thought she may spend some time with him knowing that he is so unwell. What did she come here for after all?' said Sheba, shaking her head.

'She has come for her own interest—money, property, etc.,' said Dr Ghayi dryly.

'What do you mean, doctor?' Sheba looked at him in disbelief and asked. 'You mean she…she thought, God forbid!'

'Yes, most people in the world are like that,' the doctor said, rising from his chair. 'But, don't worry. There are people like you and Saleem Miyaan too.'

'And like you, doctor,' Sheba said. 'We will not let him go anywhere. I will look after him till my last breath.'

'The world will respect you for your sacrifice, dear child.'

'No, doctor, it is no sacrifice. I am here just by chance. The others have work, jobs, etc., otherwise we all have been equally dedicated. Now that they are away, it is my responsibility to look after sir.'

'It's like worship,' the doctor said, heading to the door, and asked, 'How long is madam here?'

'I don't know, as long as she may like.'

'I had hoped that Daanish might remember something upon seeing her, but I was wrong.'

'Maybe, I hope seeing her stony face does not make him forget even my face. And those smiles which seem to be the only indication of his mental state do not disappear altogether.'

'No, that will not be so. God bless you.'

Sheba did not read the whole paper while having her morning tea and got up from her chair. She walked about in the small lawn and, returning to her chair, folded the paper and put it aside. She picked up the tea pot and shook it slightly. There was some tea left in it which meant that she could make a full cup of tea by adding some more milk to it. She poured out the golden drink into the cup.

Tea can cheer anyone up, she thought, and wanted to smile but no smile came to her lips. It only reached the stretched skin of her somewhat shrunken eyes and up to the line drawn between her eyebrows, which remained lost in deep thoughts. The other tense muscles of her face also relaxed a little. But till the spoonful of sugar had added some sweetness to her tea, her face had remained the same as it was before—silent and serious. She looked at the sky across the only tree in the lawn while sipping her tea. All her friends had gone away since she started teaching in her department. It was impossible for her to find mental compatibility with any of the other members of the faculty. The realization had dawned upon her slowly. A weird kind of political maneuvering went on in the department, but she thought it below her dignity to be a part of it, as every discussion would begin with bitching about one another. Be it with the middle-aged Dr Sharma who wore her sari above her ankles, or the very senior professor, Venkat, or a junior one, Dr Rizwana—or any of the others.

Actually, if one observes a person keenly, his or her nature becomes evident from many clues. Looking at a person from head to toe, his face, speech, walking—all of it can throw a light on his personality. Whenever Dr Sharma was asked about anything, she would begin her reply with a 'No'. She even walked with her neck and head moving sideways in little jerks. To save her sari from wear and tear, she tied it high so it won't touch the ground. She would wrap her sari many times around, onto the folds of her waist—making her stomach bulge out even more, leaving only a short length of it as '*anchal*', which she tucked in those folds too.

Looking across the tree and thinking about Dr Sharma's appearance, Sheba tried to smile but could not do so. She drew a deep breath. Professor Venkat, with his stiff neck, appeared near the top of the tree. He moved the whole of his body if he had to turn his neck because of his spondylitis. He would get angry over any trifling matter.

Ms Renu Chopra and Ms Priyanka Verma had been friends before joining the department, and were not concerned about anyone else except each other. The rest of them, too, were more or less the same. The students lived in a world of their own. Sheba's heart filled with love thinking about the students, and she tried to smile again. This time, the left corner of her lips stretched out slightly. She bent her head and looked to the other side where peacocks could be heard calling in the trees close to the imposing building of the Law Department, but neither the building nor the birds could be seen.

Hearing Professor Daanish coughing hard in the room, she picked up the newspaper from the corner of the tea tray and went in.

Professor Daanish's face wore the same expression for many days, and Saleem Miyaan and Sheba looked helplessly at each other. No one seemed to talk in the house. When Sheba entered the room, Saleem Miyaan had already helped Professor Daanish wash his face, and was tying a napkin around his neck. His breakfast was on the teapoy. Sheba added some milk to the cornflakes and went over to him, stirring it with a spoon. She wanted to smile while feeding him but no smile came to her lips, and merely ended up stretching her lips. Professor opened and closed his mouth six times like a robot, but finally shut it tight. Sheba returned the spoonful of cornflakes to the bowl.

'*Bitiya*, you please get ready for work. I will feed him later. You have a lot of work nowadays. I will manage it, please do not worry,' Saleem Miyaan said.

'Alright, Saleem Miyaan,' Sheba got up to go to her room.

'I will serve you breakfast in two minutes. I am making *gobi* (cauliflower) paratha for you,' said Saleem Miyaan, quickly collecting the dishes.

'Thank you, Saleem Miyaan,' Sheba tried but failed to smile, cleared her throat and went inside. This time, the attempt to smile was so unsuccessful that her lips did not even move.

Later that morning after walking some distance with small steps and glancing vaguely around, lost in her thoughts, Sheba headed towards the department. Someone called out her name and she turned her head and looked to her right. A young woman close to her age was walking towards her.

'Don't you recognize me? I…aren't you Sheba?'

'Yes, I am! Oh, I am sorry, I did not recognize you.' Sheba stopped and the girl came nearer.

'I recognized you from a good distance.' she said smiling, and Sheba remembered that when she and Mayuri were in the hostel, Angmo was in the corner room across the long corridor; they were not very close. She was from the far flung Ladakh province of Sheba's beloved Jammu and Kashmir.

Angmo hugged her. Sheba tried to smile, hugging her back like a childhood friend. She still could not smile and her eyes filled with tears, which crossed the barrier of her lids and rolled down her cheeks like summer rain. Angmo embraced her and Sheba wept profusely. A few moments passed. Sheba withdrew her arms slowly.

'Is everything fine, Sheba?' Angmo looked at her tearful eyes.

'Yes...yes,' Sheba said with a sniffle. 'Yes, everything is fine. I don't know, I am just tired. I...I mean...' she added, failing to make sense of her reaction. She wiped her tears quickly and a dull smile appeared and disappeared from her lips. 'How are you?' Sheba asked.

'I am good. My niece is here for admission today so I better run! You take good care of yourself, OK?'

'Yes, I will. Thank you.'

'Bye,' said Angmo, walking ahead.

Sheba felt her steps grow heavy; she was walking very slowly. What happened to me, Sheba thought to herself. Why did I start crying? Angmo was never one of my friends; we hardly even greeted each other. We only saw each other occasionally while entering or leaving the hostel rooms. Why did I cry like that, embracing Angmo? What had I shed so many tears for? What had I lost, that I cried for? Who did I cry for? Did I cry for myself or for somebody else? For whom? For what reason? Why? Was it because I had not cried for many days? Had I wanted to cry for many days?

Yes, she had wanted to cry for a long time, and that is why she was still crying. She wiped her tears with her dupatta the entire way and yet tears were still rolling down her cheeks. Reaching the department, she unlocked the door of her room and headed towards the bathroom. She looked at herself in the mirror. Her wet eyelashes stuck to each other, looking thicker but fewer in numbers. Her eyes were blood red. The tip of her nose was shining, and her cheeks looked red. Sheba stopped looking at the mirror and began washing her face. She took another look at her wet face in the mirror and sniffling, cried some more and then, splashed some more water on her face. Wiping it with the towel, she came back to the room.

The books, brought from the library the previous day, were lying on her table with tiny slips of paper sticking out between the pages. She opened a page with a slip in it and began to write in a notebook. She suddenly remembered that while in the hostel, after meeting Angmo, Mayuri had said to Sheba that she had never heard of Leh before, after which Sheba had told her about Ladakh in detail. The incredible landscape surrounded by mountains, once a Buddhist kingdom that included Baltistan and Aksai Chin—now in Pakistan and China respectively. Sheba had told her that the people living in the area now belonged to the great Mongol race but the ancient inhabitants of that region had been the Dards, an Indo-Aryan race. She also told her that migrants from Tibet, more than a 1,000 years ago, overwhelmed the culture of the Dards, and that the present inhabitants seemed mostly of Tibetan origin. Listening to her interesting account of the area, Mayuri was so fascinated that they had decided to visit the place sometime in the future. She unintentionally pressed the button of the bell fixed on the edge of her table, and heard the peon approaching.

'Madamji, shall I get you some tea?' he asked in a rustic accent, peeping from behind the curtain.

'Yes, some good tea,' said Sheba, raising her head from the table.

'Yes, Madamji.'

She bent her head again, smiling, and got busy with her work.

Mrs Daanish left for another city, after she had finished her shopping, two days later. That day, sitting in a corner of the lawn at Daanish Kadah, Sheba drank many cups of tea one after the other, and was engrossed in reading the newspaper when she saw the buttons of her recently bought silvery cell phone blinking like jewels from behind the newspaper. She had put it on silent mode, as it had a very loud and harsh ring, and she did not know how to turn it down. Professor Daanish was sleeping till late that day.

'Hello,' Sheba said softly.

'Could I please talk to Sheba Khanum?' a female voice speaking in a British accent came through.

'Speaking,' said Sheba, thinking it might be Mrs Daanish.

'Why do you sound so low?' asked the voice. Sheba did not reply for a few moments wondering how someone could ask her a personal question like that.

'May I know who is calling?' she asked without any shade of emotion.

'A well-wisher,' the voice said in the same tone, which made Sheba frown. She was in no mood for riddles so early in the morning. She removed the cell phone from her ear to hang up when the voice said, 'Are you missing your friends, Sheba?' The voice was placid this time.

'Yes, I am,' Sheba replied, and realized that she was actually thinking about her friends. Sitting in a corner of the lawn staring at the newspaper, Mayuri, Diljeet, Aaftab and a few others had appeared before her eyes, who had been with her until some four years back. She remembered many other faces with whom she had not been friends but still greeted them, smiled at them, or merely looked at them going to her classes as it was a part of the etiquette. Now, after all these years, her memories seemed to be incomplete without them and their images were a reason to remember the past: Mehek, who was rather short, and her tall friend Saahil, or the two close friends Srilata and Pritama. The group consisting of Raghav, Rahul and Gulshan Singh, who were laughing all the time and made others laugh as well. Mohit and Rohit, the twins who did not resemble each other at all and were active members of the students' union, creating problems every now and then—and then solving them too.

Sheba rose from her chair and began to stroll in the lawn. A smile appeared on her face.

'Do you miss your close friends or all of your friends?' another question was asked by the voice on the phone.

'I miss my close friends badly,' said Sheba slowly, holding the cell phone in her hand and walking in the lawn.

'So, who do you miss most?'

Hearing this question, Sheba's heart saddened at the thought of Mayuri who had been away from her for so long; the voice on the phone also seemed to sadden. 'I miss my roommate, she was a very good person,' said Sheba in a voice that had become heavier from the rush of memories about Mayuri.

'I miss you too, Sheba,' the foreign accent suddenly turned local.

'Mayuri? Mayuri! You…where are you? I am not talking to you! Where have you been? For such a long time, for one whole year, you did not bother to even call me? How could you be so…so…How could you be so inconsiderate?' Sheba kept speaking.

'Got busy with all the hassles of domestic life, but that does not mean I have forgotten you guys. Shifting house was a huge problem since I was doing it all by myself...So please don't say that I forgot you ever again.'

'What do I say then? I am so…so lonely…You…you…'

'I, too, am very lonely. I tried to talk to you so many times, but I don't know what happened. Something or the other kept coming up.'

'At least…at least once a year was not…,' Sheba complained painfully and her eyes filled with tears.

'Where are you? How are you? You forgot me, but I called you so many times!' added Sheba.

'Called me? On what number? My old number changed when we shifted and I did not have a mobile phone for a while!'

'But you have forgotten everything. Only God knows how you thought of calling even today. I wondered if I would ever hear from you again. You changed your house, your number, and you never called either. Is that friendship? You never cared to think how I might have been, Mayuri,' Sheba said sadly.

'No, that is not so. I called the department numbers many times. Thank God, I got your number today. You were never there and no one ever picked up Daanish sir's phone either. I lost contact with all our friends. Aaftab would call sometimes; he had my new number. I had asked him to give it to you also, but then he stopped calling me as well. Maybe he lost my number…he was going to Dubai. I called his home phone, but he was never there,' Mayuri said between pauses, 'Don't doubt my sincerity, Sheba,' she added.

'No, I will not. But don't you have any plans of coming to India? You said you would visit every six months when you left, and see how many…'

'I am coming to India,' said Mayuri at once.

'Really?' Sheba screamed with happiness.

'Yes, Sheba, I can hardly believe I'll see you all there again like in old days, under that same sky.'

'All of us, all who? No one else is here, it is only me, everyone else has drifted away.'

'We will find all of them. I am coming and you know, it will be a long visit.'

'That is great, Mayuri! Are you happy, Mayuri? You are not a mother yet…and…?'

'I am happy.'

'Swear to me that you are happy.'

'No, you stupid, if I had not been happy, could I have changed my voice and teased you? I have entrusted all to God and believe me, my friend, I have no care in the world anymore,' Mayuri laughed.

'Fine, come soon then. I shall be waiting for you.' Sheba did not read the rest of the newspaper after the call ended, and got up from her chair to go inside.

The Magician

Neel's pupils were exactly the colour of his caramel skin. His hair, moustache and eyebrows were black. He was tall and had a strong physique. Mayuri had thought all this casually, when she saw him for the first time. When Neel smilingly asked her for the dictionary lying on her table, Mayuri noticed that Neel had very white, even teeth. She had noticed that his hair did not move from their place when he had bent his head slightly to pick up the dictionary. Mayuri had also noticed that the deodorant or the cologne he wore lingered in her room even when he was gone.

She raised her head from her notebook and turned a little more to her right, and glanced at Neel who was sitting in one of the chairs hidden between the long tables; but the next moment, she shook her head and turned to the thick book lying before her. Prashant Patel had prompted her to get admission in this prestigious university for higher studies as it was so tedious for her just staying back at home. Prashant Patel's pleasant smile appeared on the notebook in front of Mayuri. His hairline had receded but his broader forehead looked good on his fair face. Prashant's nose, bent slightly towards his thick moustache, went well with his angular face. His upper lip was thin, but his thick moustache covered his upper lip and almost reached down to his lower lip, hiding the fact that his upper lip was much thinner than the lower one.

Mayuri closed her eyes for a few seconds, and then shaking her head, bent down to her notebook. But the next moment, she raised her head slightly and glanced at the other end of the big library hall, where Neel was busy writing something. He had no moustache at all. Mayuri returned to her notebook and began to turn the pages of the thick book in front of her more quickly than before. She was busily copying some paragraphs in her notebook when Neel put the dictionary back on her table gently and thanked her. Mayuri accepted his thanks with a slight nod of her bent head and kept writing, but the moment she realized that Neel had turned to leave, she lifted her head and looked at him. He looked as attractive going away as he appeared approaching the table. He had a very charming walk. Holding the pen in her teeth, Mayuri thought it looked as if he was enjoying his every step, bending and straightening his shoulders towards his right and left slightly; his right shoulder moving gaily with his left foot and the left with his right. What a walk, Mayuri thought to herself, and wondered that a person could have such a charming gait that one would just like to keep watching him walk. Almost immediately, she was surprised at her thoughts, and pulled the pen out of her mouth and was about to bend her head to the notebook when Neel suddenly turned around and approached her. Mayuri quickly pretended to turn her attention to her notebook. When his perfume reached her, she knew he stood near her table but did not raise her head.

'I left a slip of paper in the dictionary,' he said gently. Mayuri looked up at him and then at the dictionary. Neel bent down slightly, turned the pages and seeing a slip, took it out, pushing the dictionary slowly towards Mayuri's note book.

'I am sorry!' he said very politely.

'That's all right,' said Mayuri, softly.

'Thank you,' he said with a nod, looking at Mayuri's face. He did not smile this time, thought Mayuri briefly, but he was about to smile when he turned to leave. She knew this because his eyelids suddenly appeared puffy and partly hid his pupils—the way they had looked when he had earlier asked for the dictionary, flashing his pearly white teeth. Then too, she thought, there was no sign of a smile on his face but his eyelids suddenly became puffy and lowered over his eyes, in a way that even if a person tries hard to hide his smile, his eyes give it away. Mayuri shook her head again and started writing, but this time, another strange thing happened. Instead of copying the rest of the paragraph in English, she wrote something in Hindi that went like this: 'Bhagwan has created a face whose eyes reflect his smile exactly at the same time when the person is preparing to smile, yet pretending that he does not want to show his smile. His eyes disclose the fact that he was about to smile but did not. Bhagwan might have created other faces like this as well, with such wonderful and beautiful smiles.'

Mayuri finished and then read those lines. She had found the mystery of such a smile in her mature years merely by looking at his face. She smiled for a moment but was astonished on realizing what she had thought, and looked at her pen and then at her notebook, surprised. She got up from her chair and stood there for a few moments, then collected the books from her table to put them back into their shelves. She left the book she was taking notes from on the table as an indication that she would use this book tomorrow again, and that it should not be removed from the table. This was a privilege granted to all members of the library.

Reaching home, she wanted to talk to Prashant about those smiling eyes, and ask him if he had ever seen such eyes because she clearly had never seen such eyes, or rather such a smile ever before. Prashant was working the night shift as usual, and she knew that she would be asleep when he would return—and that when she would leave in the morning, he would be sleeping. Mayuri microwaved the pre-cooked food packets she had bought from the store, checked the mail, put the clothes in the washing machine and hung them to dry when they were done. Completing her other chores, she set Prashant's food on the dining table and went to bed.

She thought that if Prashant was at home, she would have talked to him about many other things as well. But she had to wait for the weekends to talk with Prashant. Mayuri tilted her head helplessly, pulled aside the soft quilt and slid into the soft mattress. She smelled the soft scent of Prashant's aftershave on his pillow beside her head. Prashant did not like synthetic perfumes much. Mayuri, too, did not like strong perfumes but she had always liked wearing soft, light fragrances. Prashant's light aftershave could be smelled from his clothes and the mild perfume filled the whole house. Mayuri smiled with her eyes closed, thinking that the strong perfume Neel wore was also enchanting; and even if one did not know his name, he could be located in the library by the fragrance. This meant that like her, even if someone who had not heard his name—like the girl at the library counter guiding him about the library membership—could still know his whereabouts. Mayuri took a deep breath, in order to sleep. She opened her eyes for a moment and looked at the room bathed in the dim blue light of the night lamp. She had not cleaned the room for a whole week. But the room was still clean because the windows were kept shut to keep the cold out. However, Mayuri still felt that if she touched the bookshelves fixed to the table with her finger tip, she would definitely have a smear of dust on it even if it was hard to see. But she could not help it, since she hardly had any time.

Prashant himself had suggested that she should go for further studies. She was alone at home from noon to midnight almost every day. They had been married for five years now but had no children. Earlier, Prashant had to work long hours, and trying to pursue a good career and have a comfortable home, they had decided to put it on hold. But it did not happen later either, and the doctors thought that she had little chance of becoming a mother. She had become pregnant twice, after her doctors had given her some recently developed medicines, but they had ended both times after one-and-a-half months. She had even quit her job for the sake of her pregnancy. Her general health had also deteriorated. The third time, they sought the help of a healthy woman but something happened with the surrogate too.

Mayuri had to undergo a minor surgery performed by a group of expert doctors. Prashant had arranged for a full-time maid so that she could rest at all times, but Mayuri got bored of inactivity after a few days. She sent the maid away and resumed the charge of her household, but she still had plenty of time, lonely time, on her hands.

In those days of hopelessness, Prashant got her—the girl his parents had chosen to be his wife, and who he later began liking a lot—admitted to a prestigious old university to keep her busy, and to fulfill one of her wishes. Resuming studies and looking after the home seemed to be somewhat tough for Mayuri for the first few weeks, but later on she felt that she was moving in the right direction and started liking the change.

Located near the confluence of the two rivers, Cherwell and Thames, the university was a unique city in its own right. It was a whole world of knowledge within the gorgeous buildings with their pillars and chimneys. A house of learning in the brown and white grand structures with tall pillars, numerous glass windows and slanting roofs. There were new futures, new aspirations at every hundred steps, people of all ages walking or occasionally riding bicycles, and gardens, restaurants and an abundance of natural beauty. It was a source of knowledge as well as entertainment for Mayuri. The plans of going out had always included Prashant but his busy schedule usually put a stop to them; and now, she could be out for many hours without him. However, despite all this, she still felt his absence and experienced a feeling of uneasiness. Spending time in the museum adjacent to the university gave her a deep sense of tranquility. The Christ Church Picture Gallery at Oxford was one of the oldest museums in the world, and the paintings of old churches as well as many other rare works were of great interest to Mayuri. Some of the paintings were in colour, others had only one shade, and some of them were drawn in ink. In the winter, the museum opened at 10:30 instead of 10 am, and Mayuri spent some time there, after sitting with her books for long hours, or during her lunch break between 2:00 and 4:00 pm.

She also went to other museums like the Ashmolean, the oldest public museum in Great Britain, which was a world of aesthetics in itself. This museum was opened for the public almost three-and-a-half centuries ago. It was located in a grand building constructed in old architectural style, the displays conveyed a sense of serenity; Mayuri found it interesting to even just look at the building. Its huge doors and gorgeous stature looked magnificent. Free entry to the place and cosy warmth in the afternoons on rainy days, where there were all kinds of works of art to feast one's eyes upon, was a great pleasure. Mayuri would be lost looking at the pictures from different angles for hours, but sometimes start laughing while trying to find meaning in modern art.

It had antiques from different places in the world—from the East and the West, the North and the South, from the earth and the seas, almost everything from everywhere. It had old coins, ornaments, Roman and Greek statues, antiques from the renaissance of Europe, terra cotta and stone figures, and artifacts from all over the world.

Mayuri felt as if history had come to life in the museum, and the thought gave her a sense of peace. But she soon recalled how sad all the students and other peace-loving people had felt on hearing the news of the wanton destruction of the archaeological inheritance and museums in Iraq during America's unprovoked attack. The headline in the newspapers had read: 'Missing 5000 years of history'.

There had been no example like that before. Baghdad, the third biggest city in Central Asia after Tehran and Cairo, as well as other cities in Iraq, had been destroyed and vandalized. Mayuri stopped near a long table, looked around and then upwards. When they started the attacks, no one could believe that such a thing could happen in this day and age. Shocked students would ask Dr Daanish time and again for confirmation in disbelief, and he would answer their questions sadly. Sheba had endless questions; she would brood for hours as if it was a personal loss for her. Helpless and gloomy, she talked to Mayuri only about this topic. Dr Daanish also looked lost in deep thoughts. All the members of their group as well as many others in the department were sad and upset. It was as if the grief had taken permanent and deep roots in their hearts. The news of every new attack would bring more grief to the sensitive souls but there were many others who were indifferent to all that and were lost in their own world, as usual. Mayuri took a deep breath, returned her glance from above and looked around.

Dr Daanish had said that Abu Ja'far Almansur had long discourses with top experts in the world in his days about the location, weather and environment for years before starting the construction of Baghdad in July 762. He named it Baagh-e-Daad which means The God-given Garden. Abu Almansur called it 'a city of peace'. He was certain that this city of peace would be the seat of power for his progeny, and that they would rule from here for all time to come. One of the seven wonders of the ancient world, The Hanging Gardens of Babylon, along with ancient Mesopotamian antiquities, the oldest relics from the beginning of civilization, the remains of the ancient northern Iraqi cities of Kirkuk and Mosul, and many other remnants of the past suffered irreparable damage. The national museum of Iraq was razed to the ground and plundered. Sensitive souls like artists, social scientists and anthropologists called it 'the black day for civilization'. Reference cards, catalogues and the computer systems were totally destroyed. The 7000-years-old past turned to rubble and ashes. The ancient manuscripts of Mesopotamia, the documents about mathematics and sciences from the dawn of civilization, old statues and artifacts that had been kept in the national museum for safe-keeping were all destroyed instead. The overthrow of Saddam Hussein's government was actually mankind destroying its own roots and origins.

All that the looters could lay their hands upon, including more than 17,000 priceless relics from the past, was stolen, emptying the great treasure house.

'Old cities are the common heritage of man and should be taken great care of,' Dr Daanish had sighed sadly, and continued, 'The old city of Beirut in Lebanon, Damascus of Syria, and other such places like our own old city, Banaras.' Mayuri looked about and headed forward, lost in her thoughts.

All museums have almost the same surroundings—the still objects, dim lights and a faint smell of preservatives, thought Mayuri bending her head, and are equally absorbing. Here, too, they had the full account of the discovery of the precious articles displayed, which was as interesting as the antiquities themselves.

It was beautiful all around the university. It was beautiful wherever one looked—the hotels, residential areas, the temporary and permanent homes, all looked like precious stones set along the clean grayish pathways in the lush green area. It seemed that the trees and plants had just been washed and one could look at it from any angle and spend many hours just thinking about the beautiful settings. But with the passage of time, as Mayuri became familiar with the names and sources of many of the articles on display, it started to be somewhat boring for her.

The next day, when Mayuri reached the reading room in the library, she had completely forgotten about Neel's smiling eyes, and his captivating perfume. She headed to the table she was working on the previous day, taking her usual short steps, passing long rows of tall bookshelves. She became aware of the same perfume and found Neel bent over the pages of a thick book on her table; he had spread his papers all around. Mayuri stopped in her steps, but not hearing her soft footsteps on the thick flooring anymore, Neel had probably become aware of her halting, and rose from his seat, collecting his papers and looking at her. When she started to walk slowly again, he quickly headed towards another table, looking at Mayuri and apologizing. She accepted his apology with a nod and reached her table. Neel had no smile on his face but his eyelids were puffy like ripe wheat heads, thought Mayuri, reaching her table. While sitting in her chair, she thought that Neel's day-old stubble, which gave something like a border to his face, made it strangely attractive. Mayuri was about to open the book after she took her seat but started looking towards the window instead. She saw that tiny flakes of snow had begun to fall, and a smile appeared on her face. It was raining when she came out of her flat. She had faintly heard thunder above the hum of the air conditioner in her bedroom in her sleep the night before. While changing sides in her sleep, she had wondered why there was thunder, as it was very unusual in the winter. She had opened her eyes to look towards the other pillow to see if Prashant, too, was disturbed by the noise and whether he had returned in the first place, and had found him deep asleep in the light of the blue night bulb. She looked at the shining hands of the wall clock; it was 4:00 am. She took a couple of deep breaths and went back to sleep. When she woke up in the morning, Prashant was still asleep as usual.

Sitting in the library, Mayuri stopped gazing at the falling snow she could see through the tall window glass and looked back at the table. Prashant had somewhat Mongolian features. He had a scanty beard and his moustache was not very thick either. Prashant had a slight growth of hair on his face in the mornings, and so, his beard did not have a greenish shade which shows a thick growth of hair on a wheatish complexion. Mayuri had put Prashant's breakfast on the table, and had caressed his hair softly so as to not disturb his sleep. Today, she resolved that she would not sleep till he returned home. They had not had the chance to speak a single word to each other for many days now. In the morning, he had said bye, opening only one eye, when she had tenderly stroked his hair, and had heard him snoring before she even reached the door. Mayuri smiled peacefully remembering that, but also thought that they had both become needlessly busy. Prashant had a reason, as he had to work to run the household, but why did she leave her job, and had taken up the burden of studying again after such a long time? And Prashant is busy on the weekends, too, as his company sends him out of town often. That's not fair, Mayuri thought; she shook her head and bent over her books. Maybe he would not have to go anywhere this weekend, she thought, raising her head and looking out. The snow was falling in bigger flakes now. It's Saturday tomorrow, she suddenly remembered. He should not be busy this weekend since he was out on the last two weekends, she said to herself with great conviction. She began to work, but instead found herself writing a note that read as follows:

> We have not had a chance to speak to each other for so many days. You will not have to go out this weekend, I hope. We will be together for a full 48 hours. I miss you so much.

She tore the slip of paper from her notebook carefully and put it in her handbag. She had actually promised herself that she would stay up at night till Prashant returned, but if she could not help falling asleep, she would put the note on the dining table under the corner of the casserole. She pursed her lips and looked at the window again. Prashant had promised her a long trip to Geneva. She loved to spend time on the shore of the big lake which looked as huge as an ocean. When she came to London for the first time with Prashant after getting married, he would take her to some country on the continent every weekend. How quickly time had changed since then! It was as if a handful of water had fallen through her fingers and the wet palm was the only sign that there had been water in the hand. Mayuri felt her heart overwhelmed with a dark void for a moment and her eyes became watery. She turned her head away from the window and sighed deeply. She bent her head over her notebook, but felt the fragrance that moved with Neel entering her mind, and a day-old, deep-green beard and marigold, petal-like, wheat-coloured eyelids appeared before her. That is a strange face, she thought, shaking her head—flowers, grass and wheat! Sheba would have laughed much at this. But how handsome! Though Sheba may have made fun of her notion of beauty, she thought.

'Where are you, Sheba? See what's happening in life... what strange things happen in life.'

'Nothing is happening, everything is fine...everything will be fine,' Mayuri's heart heard Sheba's voice and somehow, she felt at peace. I wish Bhagwan makes it true, Sheba!' said Mayuri to Sheba, in a language known only to her heart, closing her eyes.

Someone entered the reading room. A gust of cold wind also entered with the person and reached Mayuri. She raised her head and looked in that direction. Neel, too, raised his head and looked at the door. A tall girl had come through the glass door. She hung her overcoat on one of the hangers, fixed on the crimson coloured coat stand that was kept at the left of the entrance, and was removing her hoodie. She hung her jacket, and combing her blonde hair with her fingers and moving her blue eyes around, she headed towards the book racks. Mayuri saw that Neel was looking at her steadily and when she went behind a shelf, Neel quickly turned his head to look at Mayuri, and then bent over his books. Mayuri also bent her head over her notebook but Neel had seen her looking at him. Mayuri felt somewhat agitated. 'Why should she have looked at him?', she thought, vertical lines appearing on her brow. 'But that is of no importance,' she thought, and the long lines disappeared from her brow. She closed her lips somewhat into a circle, shaking her head, and got busy with her work.

Reaching home in the evening, she received Prashant's SMS from a place she did not know. It read: 'Was in a hurry… your phone did not connect. Have a two-day conference in Venice and I will have a very busy schedule. I will be back on Sunday, take care…'

Mayuri kept staring at the message for a few moments and took a deep breath. He could have taken me to Venice as well—the city on water. We would have enjoyed ourselves, looking at city lights reflected in the waters.

She did not reply. She did not eat, just had some cookies with coffee instead, and went to the bedroom to sleep. But she found the bedroom in complete disarray.

Prashant had pulled down the big suitcase from the top of the cupboard, as the smaller suitcase was inside the bigger one. It was lying on the floor along with some clothes. Mayuri began to put the room in some order. The top of the cupboard was rather high. Holding the suitcase in both hands, she raised her arms to put it on top of the cupboard but dropped it on the floor instead. Tears blurred her eyes and she switched on the night light, turning off all the other ones. Pulling the quilt away with a jerk, she picked up the TV remote control, but did not switch on the TV and threw it away on the sofa instead. She lay down on the bed and closed her eyes. Neel's green, bearded face appeared before her eyes and she thought that Neel might also have run short of time in the morning, and had not found the time to shave. But since he had gelled his hair the usual way, so it might be because the day-old stubble is in, thought Mayuri, turning over to her left side. 'He is somehow so artificial,' she thought, turning to her right again. 'But what is it to me…How he had looked at that girl…Let him, why should I bother?' She lay on her back and looked at the ceiling in the blue light for a moment and closed her eyes again. She recalled Prashant's SMS and pursed her lips tightly.

'I don't care!' she shouted, and turning to her side again, breathed unevenly a few times and drifted off to sleep after a while. That night, she had a dream in which she saw herself sitting unhappily amongst her university friends. They asked her the reason for her being so sad, but she did not tell them anything. She wanted Diljeet, Saagar and Aaftab to go away so that she could speak to Sheba for a long time, to laugh and to cry. But no one left; they kept chatting and enjoying each other's company. Then Sheba stood up pretending to remember something, and Mayuri got up too. Sheba was about to ask the reason for her feeling sad when Mayuri suddenly woke up. Prashant was calling her on her cell phone. She felt like disconnecting the call, but did not pick it up instead, and let it ring. The alarm clock also started ringing. She got up, made herself some coffee and went over to the table. Adding a spoonful of sugar to her mug, she sat motionless like a statue. After a few sips of coffee, she loosened up a little and began to dial Prashant's number but stopped halfway. She would talk to him when he called again, she thought. Drinking her coffee, she turned the pages of the newspaper, humming to herself.

There were fewer people in the library that day; she had arrived a little early. Mayuri looked at her watch and walked towards her spot. After some time, she became aware of the enchanting fragrance but did not raise her head. Neel had hung his jacket on the hanger near the entrance. Before going to his chair, he picked up a book from another rack and sat near a long table at a little distance from Mayuri. She had not looked at him; she had just sensed his presence without raising her head. After a while, the tall girl she had seen yesterday came in and sat at the same table. Mayuri later realized that all the other tables had already been occupied. Everyone was busy till the lunch hour. At lunch time, Neel went to the tall girl and said something to her, she stood up smiling and they both went out. Soon after, Mayuri also left for the cafeteria. She saw them sitting at a table, sipping soup with large burgers in front of them. Mayuri glanced around and headed towards the counter, and carrying a bowl of soup in a small tray, started looking around for a place to sit. Neel gestured with his hand, pointing towards a vacant chair at their table and the girl sitting with him also looked at her, smiling. Mayuri accepted the offer.

'I am Neel, Neel Biswas, from India.'

'Amelia Fernandes, from Ireland,' Amelia extended her hand.

'Mayuri Patel,' Mayuri looked at Amelia smiling. They made some small talk after that, as all three of them had met for the first time. Neel kept being humorous, which made all of them laugh, but Mayuri was somewhat reserved. She looked at them, surprised, as if trying to look into herself.

'Why am I so tense?', she asked herself and began to catch two pieces of carrot floating in her soup with her spoon. 'Because you are lonely,' her heart answered.

Neel's face had two days' stubble on it. 'How exceedingly handsome is this man, and he does not at all look good sitting with this girl who looks like a white bedsheet,' Mayuri thought. The girl had yellowish-white teeth, and the hand in which she held the burger had unclean nails. The girl wore a deep-cut pullover which had a pink collar, and her trousers were blue with a lot of mud around the hems. The fragrance coming from Neel surrounded them. He was clad in a black shirt made from some soft fabric, with many pockets, and khaki trousers. He had a black and khaki checkered muffler of heavy yet soft flannel around his neck. Mayuri had not lifted her head to see all this. She had seen it before they even got introduced to each other. She finished her soup quickly and made an excuse to leave the table. She went out of the hall and got busy with her work.

In the evening, when Mayuri was collecting her papers, she saw Neel and Amelia—through the tall glass windows—coming to the library, with their arms around each other's waists. Their heads were covered with snow; their caps were hanging on the coat hanger near the entrance. As to when they had come in and left with their coats, Mayuri had no idea. She recalled that she had looked at their chairs while she was working, and had found that they were not there.

Mayuri shook her head and got out hurriedly. She had to do some grocery shopping; she walked to a market close by. It was a very cold day. She entered a superstore located near the university, asked for some coffee and, pulling her gloves off and rubbing her hands against each other, sat at a table while glancing at the canned items.

After finishing her coffee she still sat there, looking at her cell phone and pressing some buttons on it. After a while she stood up and got busy with her shopping. When she left the shopping mall, evening had already set in and all the buildings were bright with lights. It was not snowing any more. She looked down the road and saw Neel going towards the hostel buildings with a girl of a somewhat dark complexion. He was holding her close and walking fast; the girl also had her head close to his shoulder, keeping pace with him. Mayuri waved to a cab passing by and got into it. At the same time, Prashant called her on her cell phone.

'You are angry with me, I know,' said Prashant, hearing her say hello. 'I did not want to go,' he continued, 'but two people in the office had already asked for leave and I had to decide about the dates for our channel. They are also paying me extra for this, so we can…'

'What will we do with that money?' We don't even have time for each other!' Mayuri interrupted. Neither spoke for a few moments.

'I may have to stay for a few more days, and you are there…'

'Who is stopping you from…'

'Please do not get mad at me, dear. It is not in my hands. This job is like this, you know that I do want to spend more time at home.'

'I am not angry. It is alright…I am alright, don't worry.'

'Thank God. I will call you tomorrow…eat well and take care,' Prashant said, and ended the call.

'Eat well! As if he cares,' Mayuri said to herself and looked out of the window.

The whole world seemed to be covered with snow and the whiteness pervaded the atmosphere peacefully. A lot of snow could be seen on the trees as well, though some thin branches still looked dark, which meant that they would take hours to get covered. Across the road, an old couple walked towards an apartment building at some distance, perhaps after their evening walk, wearing raincoats and holding each other's hands. They looked good, walking side by side with each other, wearing almost identical clothes, glasses, shoes and caps. Mayuri looked out from the opposite windows.

The girl walking with Neel also looked good. Neel made friends with girls very quickly. He had disappeared with Amelia for the whole day, and she had seen him going to the hostel in the evening. They might not even be allowed to visit hostels like this. They might be coming from some place or going somewhere. Mayuri shook her head. She had reached home.

Mayuri slept soundly that night, either because of the cold weather or because she was tired, and woke up half an hour before the alarm rang. She moved the curtain aside to look out. It was a sunny day. The melting snow slipped down the garage roof, the dripping melted water froze and hung like glass tubes, with more ice adding to their length by freezing the water at the end of the icicles. Some droplets were blown away when the wind blew hard, but some just froze on to the side of the icicles, giving them a twisted shape. Droplets of water fell from everywhere—the trees, roofs, walls and gates, and even from the tops of the cars. Water had frozen on the windscreens of the cars, fixing the wipers to them. Mayuri looked out for some time standing near the window. The rays of the sun gently touched her face, and the warmth of the soft winter sun brought a smile to her face.

Entering the main gate of the library, she had just walked a few steps when she heard someone calling her name. Turning around, she saw Neel approaching her quickly, smiling. 'Wait, Mayuri!' he said breathlessly, reaching her. Mayuri stopped. His belt had slipped out from one of the loops around his grey overcoat and was smeared in mud. Seeing this, Mayuri laughed suddenly. Her tops with three little diamonds in each ear glittered along with her teeth. Neel looked at her for a few seconds, and looked towards his left shoe to see what had made Mayuri laugh. He saw the muddy end of his belt and smiled a little.

'Oh, so this is it!' he said. He pulled the belt out from his left side and holding it in his hand, walked ahead of Mayuri, looking around.

'I need to wash it somewhere first.'

'In the cafeteria?' Mayuri suggested.

'I don't know how long it has been hanging like this. There is no mud here, it may have been earlier.'

'Oh, yes,' Mayuri agreed, and he shook his head and began to walk quickly, laughing.

'Excuse me,' Mayuri said and headed towards the library entrance.

'Oh God, you are leaving me alone in this crisis! I never expected this from you,' he stopped, smiling.

'Oh sorry, I will not,' Mayuri said and turned back and began to walk with him. The glass doors of the cafeteria were like dark mirrors. They could see their reflections. Neel stopped.

'Wait, Mayuri,' he said abruptly and Mayuri, somewhat surprised at this, stopped.

'We look so good together,' he said, looking at the images in the glass doors.

'I mean, you are very beautiful,' he said. Mayuri looked at him sternly, but did not reply. Her face reddened. Neel looked at her face.

'You look very pretty when you blush,' he smiled and looked into her eyes. Mayuri had not blushed because of shyness. She was actually annoyed at Neel's comment that they looked so good together. She was about to answer him when she saw his eyes peering from behind his puffy eyelids that reminded her of golden wheat buds when they are ripe and ready to be harvested. Feeling a sense of defeat, she looked into his enchanting eyes for a few moments. But there was no expression of softness on her face. She turned her face away.

'Should one forget one's morals, one's values and ethics, in a foreign land?' she said in a low tone.

'I did not say anything of the sort,' he said without stopping to look at her. 'I was just admiring your beauty.'

'You need not do that!'

'I am sorry. I will not do so again. Can we go inside now?' he asked, bending his head.

'I am going to the library,' Mayuri turned back and walked quickly to the library. Her heart was beating very fast.

Looking at her notebook on the table, Mayuri started thinking that Neel had not said anything that should have prompted such a harsh reaction. Is it bad to admire someone? But then, why did he say that we both looked so good together? Had I really become angry for this reason or do I fear something inside me which caused my face to turn red? Had I really blushed because of his comment, or was I feeling guilty about something regarding Neel, am I…am I?

When Mayuri's thoughts ran short of words, her image on the cafeteria door with Neel appeared on her notebook. With her slim, tall figure, kohl-rimmed dark eyes and her complexion like mustard flowers, she indeed looked so good standing with the tall, broad-chested and handsome Neel. A corner of Mayuri's lips rose in a faint smile, but before she could really smile she began to think whether she and Prashant made a good couple. Prashant was taller than her and Neel, by four or five inches, but so what? Prashant looked even better with her; his complexion was lovelier than her own. But still, she somehow looked perfect and complete standing with Neel. Neel's face was alive with smiles, mischief, jest, irony, curiosity and God knows what else, but Prashant's face was so peaceful. Prashant spoke less and stayed happily busy with his own world; but Neel was eager to make friends with people. Mayuri suddenly picked up a pen and began to write something when a gust of fragrant air reached her. She knew without raising her head that Neel had come back and had gotten into his chair. Had Prashant been home, she would never have gone to the library on the weekend, nor would she have been attracted to this fragrance. She started thinking and took a deep breath. She turned a page of her notebook while still attracted to this magical fragrance. Was it just the fragrance? Yes? No? It was Neel's enchanting eyes peering from behind his puffy eyelids, and the way he looked at her in the cafeteria mirrors after she had shown her anger, as if he knew that she, in fact, was not really angry at his comment, intrigued her.

But then, why had she left abruptly when he had said that they looked good together? She was not angry, but why did she leave hurriedly? It was because she was not running away from that place, she was trying to run from herself. When she had turned and looked angrily at Neel for a second, Neel had looked at her as if he knew everything. Oh Bhagwan, did Neel, did Neel, did she really, was she really in, in, no, this is crazy! Mayuri turned a few pages of her notebook hurriedly and began to write:

> Prashant...Prashant, you should...you should take some days off from your job as I am getting attracted to Neel because you are not with me. He is not a good man, Prashant, but... he...but I am...I am very lonely Prashant. I cannot conceal anything from you, you know that. Wake me up when you return at night, I will explain everything. You can surely save me from this, Prashant, otherwise if I follow this wrong path, I will be ruined.

She folded the paper and unzipped her handbag to put it inside when she saw that her cell phone, which she had put on silent, was blinking. It was an SMS from Prashant which said that instead of that day, he would be returning the day after, and that he would tell her all about it later.

Reading the message, Mayuri felt hot waves of fire going through her brain. She held her temples with the fingers of both her hands, closed her eyes and remained motionless for a few seconds. She then kept her hands on the table and turned her head slowly and looked at Neel's table. He was looking at her. Seeing her looking at him, he rose and walked towards Mayuri. His was silent but his eyes were smiling, which said that he was about to smile, and he did.

'You have a headache! Would you like some coffee?' he smiled and said, reaching her table. Mayuri kept looking at him. He had combed his hair backwards, bending it slightly towards his forehead with hair gel. Mayuri blinked her eyes.

A button had been left undone near the off-white collar of his shirt, which he wore under his bottle-green cardigan. He had no beard on his face today, else he would have looked much more attractive. Mayuri blinked her eyes twice. His pearly white smile looked exceedingly good against the off-white collar of his shirt. What should she do? Mayuri blinked her eyes again. His long arms under his broad shoulders were in the pockets of the blue jeans he was wearing. He was patiently standing and waiting for her reply, with his head bent sideways. 'Why is he so good-looking?', Mayuri thought, lines of helplessness appearing between her eyebrows. Neel bent his elbow near her chair, inclining his head in a respectful manner; and Mayuri, feeling weak as if under the influence of some unknown power, put her hand on his arm and stood up.

Neel told her that evening that he loved her passionately—since one month…'One month is not a long time,' she thought, but his magic has already worked, and she smiled.

When Neel was leaving Mayuri's apartment, he whispered to her that it was his birthday the next day and he was throwing a party at a restaurant in the evening.

'But you never told me,' said a surprised Mayuri, laughing softly.

'I am not very happy about my coming into the world!' he said expressionlessly, looking at the huge paintings on the walls on his right and left.

'But I am glad…I am very glad for it,' she said quickly and turned her head away.

'I have been thinking of gifting myself a guitar for my birthday for a long time, but...' Neel laughed and looked at the ceiling bathed in soft light from the bulbs concealed behind the crown of the ceiling. The nine-inch band of the crown of the sky-blue ceiling was decorated with flowers and vines carved in different colours. They were all in light colours, contrasting with the peacock blue frames of the large paintings on the wall, adding a solemn grace to the lobby. Mayuri looked at his Adam's apple, quivering with laughter, for a moment and looked back at the floor. Neel pulled his overcoat from the purple coat hanger and put it on his shoulder.

'Please do come to the party tomorrow,' he smiled.

'You never mentioned the venue!' Mayuri got the coat and went behind him, Neel stretched his arms back. Mayuri pulled the coat up to his shoulders and he turned towards her.

'Thank you. Oh, I forgot!' Neel looked like he was thinking.

'If you have not decided on the venue, then why not here at my home?' Mayuri looked into his eyes.

'Yes, that will be great!' he laughed.

'Fine, invite your friends...How many people will it be?' she smiled.

'Just two,' he also smiled.

'A couple?'

'Yes, you and I,' he laughed again.

Mayuri kept looking at him, smiling.

'See you tomorrow evening then,' Neel said and went out.

Mayuri decorated every nook and corner of her apartment that evening, ordered delicious food from a classy restaurant, served it in a fine porcelain dinner-set on the dining table and packed a gift for him. The big golden package shone bright along with the sparkling silvery cutlery. It was an expensive red guitar wrapped in golden paper.

Neel entered the house, along with a freezing gust of wind, but it was warm and cosy inside. Light music played and the house was redolent of the delectable lavender air freshener.

Mayuri never forgot that evening and the evening before her whole life. It was not because she never had an evening like that afterwards, nor because she never felt such warmth in Neel's expressions of love, and not even because ultimately Prashant had found out about Neel. But it was because Mayuri had asked for a divorce on his return the very next day, and Prashant had just kept silent. For many days, Mayuri kept insisting on a divorce, like an adamant child asking for the moon, and Prashant looked at her, wordless and shocked, and cried silently sometimes. This would have continued, but Prashant's friend Vinay arrived from India and things came to an end.

After the divorce of a flop singer and a not-too-famous actress, Neel Biswas was raised by his maternal grandmother. He was in primary school when his grandmother died, and his maternal uncle and aunt sent him to a missionary boarding school. His address changed frequently. The evening spent at Mayuri's house was not his birthday; in fact, he had only wanted gifts. Neel had trapped Mayuri after he had made a good guess of her being well off from her appearance and her nice apartment. And Mayuri had recklessly squandered away her passions and Prashant's hard-earned money on him. Even if Neel would not show his love for her like before, each new gift from Mayuri would bring a smile and a few sweet words for her to his lips. Mayuri had started realizing it as well, but she felt totally helpless. A vast distance had grown between Prashant and her at home. The truth of the matter had now strangely engulfed her whole being.

The day when Prashant and his friend told her about Neel's reality, she was not very surprised. She had told Vinay in a very low voice that Neel had got a ring gifted to her by her mother, and had then gone to the market to buy some groceries. On her way back she did not hire a taxi but walked a long way in the rain and snow, and reached home drenched and shivering. She would have fallen had she not caught hold of a chair after putting the bags on the table; she had passed out after that. When she regained consciousness, she had high fever. There were medicines for cold and fever on the side table. Prashant was working on his laptop at his writing table. He turned his head on hearing her move in the bed. Seeing Mayuri open her eyes, he went to her.

'Drink some water with glucose in it,' he said, picking up a glass from the table. Mayuri felt very weak trying to sit up.

'You had high fever. I gave you a tablet two hours ago, but you still have fever,' said Prashant, feeling the heat of her hands while handing over the glass to her. 'I called the doctor, but he is out. I will call him again in the evening.'

Mayuri took a couple of sips and handed the glass back to him.

'No, I am alright, it will go away,' she said weakly.

'Would you like to eat something?' Prashant asked. He remained standing even when he actually wanted to sit on the edge of the bed. Before this, Mayuri had insisted on getting a divorce in response to everything he asked her, which had assured him that she hated him. He blamed himself. Their marriage had been an arranged one, and he felt that a beautiful girl like Mayuri could never have liked an average-looking man like him. Neither had any relatives except each other in that city. Mayuri was still childless, and had recently had some surgery for the problem. Prashant's heart had always been full of sympathy for her on that account. When he found about Neel, he felt more sad than angry. He had always thought that he did not deserve a girl like Mayuri but their life had still been good before Neel. He felt sorry for her anguish and thought that Neel's deceit was to blame for this. Mayuri sat on the bed, looking at Prashant who was standing in front of her. Prashant saw that Mayuri's face was red with high fever. He looked towards his study table where a blue-capped thermometer was kept along with some pens of different colours in the pen stand. When Prashant turned towards Mayuri with the thermometer in his hand, he saw that Mayuri was sobbing with her face in her hands.

'Please, Mayuri, do not cry, please. I will do whatever you want, any time. You want a divorce? I will sign the papers whenever you want…We will go to India when you recover.

I will get the reservations for whenever you want…or even if you want it here in the court. You…you get well first… this thermometer,' said Prashant, controlling his tears which were choking his throat, and holding out the thermometer to Mayuri. She kept crying and hiding her face. She did not take the thermometer and Prashant, balancing himself at the edge of their bed, kept looking at her holding the thermometer in his hand.

'Alright Mayuri…I will ask the lawyer to come over here tomorrow and call your family…As you wish…I…' Prashant could not complete his sentence as his voice became very heavy with emotions. He stood up looking at her with the thermometer in his hand for some time. Mayuri wiped her eyes with a tissue paper and took the thermometer from Prashant's hand.

'Prashant,' she said softly. He kept looking at her silently.

'I want to go to India,' she said, folding the tissue paper.

'Fine, as you wish. I will get the reservations whenever you want!' Mayuri put the thermometer under her tongue and rested her tired head against the pillow, closing her eyes. Prashant turned towards his table. After a moment, tears rolled down Mayuri's face towards her ears. Prashant's hands were on the keyboard and his eyes on the monitor, but Mayuri's serious face and her words kept playing in his mind.

The first thing she had said after regaining consciousness was that she wanted to go to India. Prashant sighed deeply, thinking that Mayuri did not want to stay with him anymore even though he had not done anything wrong to her. On the other hand, he had even exposed the person who flirted with her for money and cheated her. That meant that he could not win her heart all these years, and so she got attracted to someone else. Prashant took another deep breath and began to type on his laptop. Mayuri opened her eyes and looked at Prashant. From the bed, she could see his back, shoulders, neck and head slightly bent over the screen of his laptop. His receding hairline reached only up to the middle, and he had no hair at the front of his head. His shoulders were not very broad and he was wearing a sky-blue night suit with vertical stripes. Mayuri saw Prashant's shoulders tremble slightly and her heart filled with emotions. She knew that Prashant was crying and thought that it was because he was married to a girl like her. This meant that Prashant regretted his relationship with her, cursing the moment when Mayuri entered his life. It meant that Prashant regretted being with a depraved woman like her, who had no moral values. Her heart began to beat fast. He had every right to leave a characterless woman like her, she thought, and was still looking after her only out of his gentle nature and the goodness of his heart. How could she have acted like this? How would she face her folks in India? How would she explain it to Sheba, whom she had called so happily just a few days ago? She had told her that she and Prashant were coming to India for a few days, and that she was looking forward to seeing all their friends; but now, Prashant was not going with her. She had left him alone while living with him, she had cheated on him, betrayed him, hurt his self-respect and he still looked after her so devotedly. She did not deserve to live with such a decent man. She could not give him the joy of being a father and yet he had looked at her infertility as if the problem was with him and not with her. She would free an angel like him from her presence, and then only would he be able to marry another woman and become a father. It was good that he hated her. An ordinary husband would kill his wife for something like this. It was his godliness that he chose to look after a fallen woman like her.

Mayuri took the thermometer out of her mouth and put it on the table. She slipped down on the silk bedsheet noiselessly and covered herself up to her shoulders with the quilt. She put her arm over her eyes as if she were sleeping, but she was actually crying silently. She did not know when Prashant picked up the thermometer, washed it and put it back. Mayuri wiped her tears, pretending to change sides. People back home would find out what had happened. Something in her soul had kept telling her that Neel's words of love had not been as true as they sounded. Why had she done this when her heart had known that Neel was a con artist? Why had she not stopped herself? She knew why… because Prashant had left her alone, all alone by herself. But it was not his fault, he had been busy with work. Then what was the reason? Yes, it was because…Neel Biswas was so handsome, so very good-looking, thought Mayuri. She sighed deeply, 'How madly I loved you, Neel Biswas!' Mayuri began to sob quietly. 'I loved you, but you were so selfish and such a mean person. You proved to be ugly, with a low mind, just the opposite of your looks. You do not know what beauty of the mind is, Neel Biswas. Beauty of the mind is in Prashant Patel. He has always loved me, but I lost him for this lapse. Prashant can never love me again. It is better that he should hate me, and remarry and become a father. What a fool I have been! Neel, who had no home, was pressing me to marry him. Yet why had I acted stupidly when I knew everything? What was he trying to prove by sounding so certain? I gave him the best gifts I could afford, spending my savings, even selling my jewellery! How artfully he let me know the list of things he wanted from me, one by one; and I, like a fool, was spending my money to meet his demands!' Mayuri heard the sound of the door being closed. She sat up on the bed and started crying again. That evening, when Prashant and his friend reached Amelia's home looking for him, Neel had asked her to a party. When Mayuri refused, he told her that he was asking her to go to a party for the first and the last time, adding that his friends had planned the party in her honour as they wanted to meet her. He told her that if she refused, he would never see her again. After that, he held her hand and pulled a ring off her finger, which she had worn for many years, saying that he would return it to her in the evening.

Mayuri shivered with apprehensions. Who knows what vicious plans he had made? Mentioning marriage often to win her confidence, he could have violated her honour, maybe even along with his friends. 'Oh God,' Mayuri trembled at the thought. He had known that Mayuri had already spent almost all her money and jewellery on him. How stupid she had been to doubt him one moment and to trust him in the next! She had planned to go to another town with him. She was about to leave when Prashant came and told her that Neel was leaving Amelia's place, when he and his friend had reached there, looking for him. Amelia was throwing her shoes at him telling him to get out. She was cursing at him for cheating on her, and for all the money he had borrowed from her but had never returned. She threatened to take him to court, when Prashant's friend Vinay got hold of him, pressing the fingers of his strong hand into his shoulder telling him that he was a friend of Mayuri's husband Prashant. Amelia's ex-boyfriend had punched him in the face with his big black fist, giving him a black-blue bruise on his cheek, and the police had also arrived soon.

Mayuri never asked what happened after that. She was shocked and threw herself on a chair. After a little while, she had got up and gone out with a big bag as if to buy groceries from the nearby market. She got the groceries but then she had been walking around dazed and bewildered. On her return, she had fainted on the floor because of the cold and fever.

Mayuri became peaceful the moment she decided that she would leave Prashant so that he could begin a new life. Her tears stopped but thinking about the reason behind what she had done made her sad, as she kept trying to solve the puzzle. She had been lonely, so very lonely. But was being lonely reason enough to cheat on her husband? She had not thought about that. But even if she had, could she have stopped herself from doing whatever she had done, when Prashant had left her alone? She made efforts to spend some time with him, but Prashant had no time for her.

But did that mean that she should have gone with that shady character after knowing him for hardly a month and leave her life companion, a man who had looked after her with such care and devotion even after knowing everything?

Yes, she had made a mistake. Why had she committed such a blunder? He was nobody to her; she had hardly known him. Only God knows why he was there and what he actually studied! Did he really study or did he just work somewhere around there? What business did a cheat like him have in such a varsity? God knows why this had happened! She had never been like this; she had been as innocent as a child in her teens, so reserved in college, and cautious and careful at the university. People had liked her, wanted to be in a relationship with her, marry her, be friends with her, but… but what just happened?

Perhaps she never found anyone she could like. 'Neel, Neel, I hate you,' she said murmuring to herself, 'I hate you.' She clenched her teeth and her lips quivered. 'I hate you, bastard,' she said in a voice trembling with rage.

Even after her fever was gone, Mayuri did not go out of the house for some days. One evening when Prashant was not at home, she went to the market and bought groceries for a few days so that Prashant would not have any problem when she was away. She was leaving for India the next day.

Footprints on the Grass

When Sheba first listened to Mayuri's story, she just could not believe her. But as Mayuri related each and every incident to her, one by one, Sheba believed her and was shocked. They were sipping coffee sitting in their chairs in the lawn of Daanish Kadah. They were lost in conversation, eating peanuts from small glass bowls and occasionally throwing them to the birds flying about. They heard Professor Daanish coughing inside the house and Sheba looked at her watch. Mayuri abruptly became quiet and looked down at the ground.

'Sheba, I know that I have fallen from grace in your eyes, but you are the most important person to me of all those from whom I want to seek pardon. My brother and his wife do not know anything about this but you are the judge sitting in the court of my conscience. I will not blame you if you end your friendship with me as a punishment, since I must be punished for my bad deeds,' Mayuri said, without raising her eyes. Sheba took a deep breath.

'No, Mayuri, all this is not that unlikely. Yes, it should not have happened, but sometimes a person does become helpless. You are a human being after all. You made a mistake and you repent it now. This in itself is your punishment. Friendship does not end so easily, my friend,' Sheba said, turning over the bowl of salty peanuts on her palm. Emptying her hand in Mayuri's hand, she picked up a few of them from her hand and put them in her mouth.

'Thanks, Sheba.'

'Don't be silly. What did you tell your brother about coming here all of a sudden?'

'I have not yet gone there.'

'Really, you came here straight?' Sheba asked.

'Yes, I presented myself in your court first.'

'And what are your plans for the future?'

'I will stay here for some time and look after Professor Daanish with you. I hope that will free me from my guilty feelings somewhat, and I may resume my studies and complete my D Lit. At present, I don't want to do anything. I will try to work without rest for some months to punish myself, I will not rest. And tell me, how is Ammi?'

'She is fine, but she is angry with me. You know, I have not gone home for almost a year now. They were all talking about my marriage the last time I had gone there. And you know, Mayuri, I will not leave Daanish sir until he recovers. I have not even thought about marrying yet,' said Sheba, looking at the top of the trees. They sat silent for some time.

'Sheba, you can...you can now, because I am here for now. You can take a trip to your home town without any worries. And sir is on the mend as well, isn't he?'

Sheba brought her gaze back from the trees and fixed it on Mayuri. 'You mean…you mean I can…' Sheba's face lit up with excitement.

'Yes, sweetie, go, don't you miss your home?'

'A lot, I miss it a lot!' a surprised smile appeared on her face.

'Go then.'

'Really?'

'Of course.'

'For how many days?'

'Look, I am not going anywhere for a while. I have enough money; I can manage easily. I am not an outsider either, and I too have some duty to Daanish sir.'

'He also has his pension that goes into his bank account. The management said that they would send it here, in cash, but I told them there is no need for that. We don't have many expenses except when we need to buy some costly medicines. But Mayuri, you shouldn't take this burden, that's my duty.'

'You mean I am a guest here?'

'No, not like that, but I don't think it is fair…'

'No, it is very fair and you can spend a month, two months, three or more. I will miss you, and I don't want you to go but I want to be of some help here by trying to ease your problems and sharing Daanish sir's blessings.'

Mayuri rose from her chair and Sheba put the mugs on the tray, and hearing the clatter, Saleem Miyaan came out to get the dishes.

'You both look like sisters, twin sisters! Either that or my eyes are getting weak.' Hearing this, both of them laughed heartily. Saleem Miyaan smiled and cleaned the table with a dusting cloth. Mayuri looked at Sheba wide-eyed.

'Weren't we told this before too?' Sheba asked.

'In the hostel, yes?'

'Yes.'

'It feels so good to hear that.'

'Sheba, you sure you will come back?' Mayuri asked suddenly.

'I was just thinking about the same thing. Ammi would not let me go, but I will come back…I will. I have a job here, sweetie, where would I go? Where else could I go?'

'What if you did not have a job?'

'I still have a responsibility here.'

'If you did not have that either?'

'What are you saying?'

'I do not know what I want to say, Sheba. Let us see how things turn out. You apply for leave first.'

'Yes, I will but I cannot hand over the responsibility of looking after Daanish sir to anyone in this world except you. But I don't want to burden you with this responsibility either.'

'I will let you know when I start feeling it as a burden, trust me.'

'I have grown accustomed to looking after him over all these years, and he has also become used to my care, that's why…I…'

'He is happy with me as well. Haven't you noticed this over the last two days?'

'Yes, that is true. Let us see, for a few days, for the time being. I mean I will apply for one-month leave, but let me talk to Dr Ghayi first.'

'Oh yes, of course.'

'Otherwise, everything seems fine.'

'Oh yes, don't worry.'

Sheba headed towards the door. Mayuri walked behind her. 'Had we not been so far away from each other, Sheba,' Mayuri said and Sheba stopped, 'I am sure I would never have faltered like I did. I have not done anything my whole life without talking to you. Except for this one thing…this one wrong thing,' Mayuri kept her hand on the wall near the door.

'Yes, I was lonely too; I never realized I had become so lonely. A kind of dismal mood had set over my life since you left.'

'And since then things have changed by and by, but this happens to everyone.'

'Yes, so it happens Mayuri, but I feel very sad about your home breaking down like this. This should never have happened.'

'It happened because of me. I wronged myself. I was so vile that Prashant stopped loving me,' Mayuri removed her hand from the wall and went inside.

'Now forget all this. Who knows what is in store for tomorrow except for God Almighty.'

'Yes, no one can change what Bhagwan does.'

Being together for many years, Mayuri and Sheba had developed many similar mannerisms. The way they spoke, their phrases, certain gestures like bending their head to the side and raising their eyebrows while shaking their head, these were all so similar. Perhaps adopting similar gestures and expressions for a long time leads to a similarity in the age lines developing on faces, the expressions of the eyes and the movement of the hands, which create a resemblance in married couples' faces over a long time, making them look alike in their old age. Sheba had not spent a very long time with Mayuri but still, the time spent in the college and university hostel together was long enough. Their natures had a similarity because of which they had a great respect and affection for each other. They were as close as sisters, and their trust had deep roots in their friendship. Mayuri smiled, satisfied seeing that Daanish sir's attitude towards her was the same as towards Sheba.

The last one month's events were still fresh in Mayuri's mind. Events that felt very pleasant earlier—somewhat doubtful and strongly emotional all at once, had become less pleasant, very doubtful and less emotional, and had led to sadness, gloom and distrust. But back in those new, or rather old, familiar surroundings with her understanding friend and mentor—and the unwell professor as well as the kind-hearted Saleem Miyaan looking after her—Mayuri felt wonderfully peaceful. In addition, the week before Sheba left for her home town, both of them were as cheerful and funny as before. Saleem Miyaan had only one complaint against Mayuri, which was that she strictly avoided all meat. He realized this the day when he had very fondly cooked biryani for her in pure ghee with spices, dry fruits, saffron and other ingredients added to the special basmati rice, and the meat from a leg of mutton.

'What is this, Saleem Miyaan?' asked Mayuri, sitting at the dining table. She widened her eyes and looked at Saleem Miyaan, raising her head slightly, exactly like Sheba, and Saleem Miyaan suddenly realized that he had made a mistake.

'Oh, I…forgot that you perhaps will not eat…'

'I am a strict vegetarian. I don't eat any meat and fish, but this is very well-cooked. It has such a delicious aroma, and I'm sure sir would love it!' Mayuri took some in a plate and added a little raita to the dish.

'But what will you eat then? I have not even cooked any dal or vegetables today.'

'You made some wheat-flour dough?'

'Yes, I did.'

'And do we have any vegetables?'

'A small head of cauliflower, some onions and potatoes.'

'Fine, chop the flower part of the cauliflower and mix some salt and some thinly sliced green chillies in it. Put the mixture between two flattened dough balls and fry it in a little ghee, and that's it!'

'Oh, you mean *gobi paratha*?'

'Yes, with this raita,' said Mayuri, pushing her chair back noiselessly, like Sheba, and stood up, smiling. That day, Professor Daanish relished his dinner though he ate very little. Sometimes he ate only a small portion. But Mayuri made him eat the raita made of boiled pumpkin and yogurt, and he had quite a few spoons. Sheba had brought the fragrant black cumin seed which grows in the Kishtwar area of the Kashmir Valley, a pinch of which Saleem Miyaan had rubbed between his palms before garnishing the raita with it—the thick cumin from the plains, which has big seeds, does not give out its aroma unless roasted. Watching Professor Daanish relish it, Saleem Miyaan smiled warmly. Mayuri fed him spoons of raita and kept smiling. The design on the small bowl of raita had small peacocks, painted in their original colours, against a white background. This dinner set was a part of the crockery Mayuri had brought with her as a gift. She had it wrapped in many folds of bubble wrap and held it carefully, until the 'fragile' sticker was put on the box. The spoons also had the same pattern of the peacock as it was a part of the same China set. The clinking of spoons against the bowl and the aroma of parathas from the kitchen, Professor Daanish's calm face, as well as something else which was unknowable had spread much serenity in the small Daanish Kadah located at the end of the campus, away from the city. In the beautiful foreign land, with the latest utilities in the apartment, she would often be sad for Prashant's absence. It was as if the grief had lodged somewhere deep in her soul. But, in this 66-year-old house—the good old Daanish Kadah—the presence of the two old men who were not related to her, she experienced a strange sense of peace. Did it mean that strife in life begins with agitation, she wondered. Mayuri wiped Dr Daanish's mouth with a napkin. She bent her head slightly and got up smiling with a great sense of satisfaction. Professor Daanish spoke little if at all, but was fine otherwise. Mayuri pondered over it for a few moments but then went back to her previous thoughts. Sheba had told her that she was now sad for many days. So, is it monotony that makes a person sad? And was it the breaking of that monotony which relaxed her in Daanish Kadah?

And for some days, Mayuri certainly remained at peace in Daanish Kadah. She had not informed her brother and his wife about her arrival.

It was a very pleasant morning. It had stopped raining and the birds began to chirp and sing. Mayuri was awake and looking at the bluish light. She got up, but feeling dizzy, sat down again on the bed. She tried to get up again, but still felt dizzy and dropped back onto the bed. She remained there with her eyes closed for some time. The next moment, she was better but still had a feeling as if she had not digested last night's dinner, and felt nauseous. Instead of going to the window, she headed to the bathroom and putting her hand on the sink, she began to throw up; only water came out. She washed her mouth and face and came out to the lawn. She heard Saleem Miyaan offering his prayers in his room, and looked towards the kitchen. Hearing the door being unbolted, he turned his head towards the window on his right and looked out. He saw Mayuri holding the door, trying to steady herself on her way out to the lawn. He continued reciting his prayers in a low tone for some time more. Hearing him, Mayuri looked at his window and wearily stepped ahead. Pulling out a chair, she sat on it. The pleasant morning breeze began to fan her hair. Her face was still wet with sweat from vomiting. Saleem Miyaan folded the *janamaaz*, put it on the teapoy near the window and came out.

'Are you alright, dear? I will make some tea for you,' said Saleem Miyaan, somewhat alarmed, looking at her pale face. 'What is the matter?'

'I feel like vomiting and sort of dizzy…' Mayuri wiped the sweat from her forehead with her cotton dupatta. She had purchased that salwar suit from a showroom of Khadigram Udyog. The soft dupatta dried off the sweat from her face.

'I will make you some ginger tea, but you did not eat anything hard to digest last night, and you ate very little,' said Saleem Miyaan, shaking his head in negation.

'That room freshener you sprayed yesterday, was that different? Its smell…'

'No, it is the same one that I have been using for the last one month since you have been here.' Saleem Miyaan bent his head towards his shoulder but suddenly his expression changed and he looked at Mayuri keenly.

'Bibi…Bibi…you…' he left the sentence incomplete.

'What Saleem Miyaan?'

'No…nothing…I…I will get you some tea….'

He went to the kitchen, but after some time, when the smell of ginger spread from the kitchen through the windows to the lawn and reached Mayuri, she felt nauseous again and reached for the tap in the corner of the lawn used for watering the plants. After throwing up a little water, when she returned to her chair, there was a surprised smile on her tired, sweaty face. She reached the chair walking wearily, and sat down, resting her head against its back and let out a deep breath.

'Oh Bhagwan, what are these secrets of yours? What do you do? I had never thought of it...' A smile came to her face. She realized that the surgery she had some four months ago was successful, and that she was not infertile. Saleem Miyaan appeared with the tea and she asked him to get her cell phone from inside the room.

'Saleem Miyaan, I will have lemon tea, you may drink this. The smell of ginger is also making me feel nauseated.'

'All right, dear, fine,' said Saleem Miyaan, nodding his head in a manner which said that he understood everything and he turned back with the cup and saucer. Mayuri had pressed Sheba's number but suddenly realized that it was too early in the morning there and she would be sleeping, so she dropped the line. After a moment, she got a call from Sheba.

'Good morning, so you are up.'

'Good morning. Sorry, my dear, I woke you up.'

'No, Ammi wakes me up early at 4:00 am. I am awake and shivering with cold.'

'Why, has shivering with cold been added as a part of the chores for you over there?'

'Madam, winter is right around the corner and mornings and evenings are very cold now.'

'Put on your woollies then.'

'All my woollens are there. I had only brought a flimsy shawl with me. I had not thought much about the cold.'

'Then buy some or put up with it for some more days, then you have to come here, right? Sheba I want to tell you something.'

'Please do, quickly! Is sir all right?'

'Everything is fine with him…What I wish to tell you is about me.'

'About you…is it a job?'

'Yes, I will also get a job perhaps, but Sheba I…I am pregnant.'

'What? Really? You…you mean…I mean you will be a mother?' Sheba asked in an incredulous and happy voice.

'Yes, my dear, I am indeed going to be a mother. I had told you about that surgery, right?'

'Yes, the one some months ago when after recovery, you and Prashant went to France on a long vacation?' Sheba giggled.

'Yes, you are more than a midwife,' Mayuri also laughed.

'Have you seen the doctor?'

'No, I realized it just now. It had all been so irregular since the surgery, I did not think much about it, I mean…'

'I feel so good hearing this. We will raise the baby together!'

'But Sheba, Prashant hates me. Who will help me in bringing this child up?'

'How can you say this, Mayuri? You, yourself! God has blessed you with something to live for.'

'Yes, that's why I feel happy. And I am also happy that I am not unable to bear a child, but will it be right to have this baby?'

'Do you have any plans of marrying again? You never said anything like that, did you?'

'No, I have not considered it. But my brother and sister-in-law will not let me remain single. They will marry me off some day or the other, and this option will not be there if I have a child. And that's why they won't let me have this baby.'

'They do not know anything yet, and this is your life, you know…Hello?'

'Yes, yes, I am listening.'

'Every girl is a born mother, Mayuri, and motherhood completes her existence. She feels complete in her being when the tidal waves of the ocean of her love inside get an outlet. I myself have longed for completion of love in me, Mayuri. Motherhood has always been every woman's weakness, not just mine.'

'Is that so?'

'Yes! And even a weak and disadvantaged child can be the completion of one's love…God Almighty has blessed you with a precious and priceless being and you…'

'No, Sheba, I am thinking that…'

'What are you thinking? Since when have you become so weak, you?'

'Since I weakened myself in my wrong deed. I want a perfect home, I mean, I want…I mean, a child should live with both parents. It's still very early and I can…'

'Mayuri, what you have done till now was a mistake. But now what you are thinking of is a sin. Do not do this, Mayuri, just do not.'

'What should I do then?'

'I think you should speak to Prashant once.'

'No, Sheba, only God knows what he might think.'

'Why should he think anything? He is the father of this child.'

'That is what I know. But, I don't know what he might...'

'But this is the truth, and it can be proved with a DNA test if, God forbid, we have to.'

'Yes, and it is also true that I completely agree with what you are saying,' Mayuri said.

'Sure? Thank you,' Sheba's voice was full of happiness.

'Yes, my dear, that's why I called you. I came to know about it only this morning—just a few minutes ago, in fact. I have not decided anything yet. I have been thinking while talking to you, that...'

'I know, and I told you what I think is proper, but this is your life. You have the right to think about it. Friends can only make suggestions. You should relax and think calmly about it.'

'I have thought about it, Sheba. You are right. Can there be anything better to live for other than this?'

'So many independent women are adopting children and raising them without any help. I mean, it's not that big an issue. It depends on the priorities you set for yourself.'

Both of them were silent for a while.

'What are you thinking?'

'Nothing, Sheba, only how different I have become, almost insane. I did not realize the sign given to me by Bhagwan when He blessed me with the child to make me independent. And I...I actually did not think anything. These thoughts have just now occurred to me. I think if I get that job, I will stay here.'

'Sure?'

'Absolutely. I have decided, and you know that when I take a decision, I stick to it. Alright, now tell me, what did your family say this time?'

'It is a long story, Mayuri.'

'If you marry, and leave Daanish sir in my hands, I will look after the children, the old as well as the little one! I was so engrossed in this that I forgot to ask you. You mentioned the day before that there was a new proposal for you and you are going to consider it. I know Daanish sir is important, but how can you bear this responsibility your whole life? As far as I am concerned, I have already decided.'

'Oh yes, Mayuri, I have to talk to you about something but I have to recharge my phone. I don't have a land line in my room. I'll call you later or send you a detailed e-mail.'

'In the evening or in the day?'

'In the evening. You must see your doctor during the day.'

'Yes.'

'Take care of yourself.'

'And you too, bye.'

Mayuri was waiting at Dr Bhawana Tilaang's clinic for her turn. She occasionally raised her head from a fertility-related magazine and looked at the women leaving or entering the doctor's room—and at the pictures of babies and expecting mothers on the wall. This was a famous clinic in the country. Dr Tilaang was invited for important cases outside the country as well. When the doctor came out to see a special patient off at the door, Mayuri found that she was one of the doctors who had done her surgery in London! Seeing the doctor, Mayuri got up but the doctor did not see her, and went back inside. It was Mayuri's turn after the next patient. She entered the chamber, smiling. The doctor gestured her to take a seat.

'Thank you, doctor,' she said and sat in the chair.

'Is this your first visit?' asked the doctor, extending her hand out for the prescription and pulling it back since she did not have any.

'Yes, doctor, the first time, but I am an old patient of yours,' Mayuri smiled.

'Is that so?' the doctor smiled as well, raising her head.

'Yes, you did my surgery in London…in May.'

'Oh, yes! Mrs Patel! I did, along with Dr Lara Fernandes. You are Mr Fernandes's friend, Mr Patel's wife, right?'

'Yes, doctor.'

'So you are pregnant?'

'Yes, doctor.'

'Excellent, what good news!' A pleasant look of surprise appeared on Dr Tilaang's face.

'Dr Fernandes informed me yesterday that six out of the 10 patients had shown positive results, and asked if I knew how our pretty Mrs Patel was. I will give her the good news today. Actually, ours is a research group and we keep track of our patients. Even the results for the patients we treated in our charity program were 100% positive. I feel great, and your family has also been so close to our colleague, Dr Fernandes.'

'Thank you, doctor.'

A south Indian nurse offered Mayuri a patient's gown. Mayuri went inside and changed into the gown. Dr Tilaang checked her blood pressure.

'Everything is fine. I am prescribing some calcium and iron tablets but a nutritious diet is more important than this.'

'Yes, doctor, and anything for the nausea?'

'I have prescribed something for that too, but you better try some home remedies for this. Granny's advice, you can say, such as lemons, smelling mint, fruits and vegetables. This is a precious baby, you know,' Dr Tilaang patted Mayuri's shoulder. The nurse helped her get up.

'Good luck, Mrs Patel. You are always welcome if you have any questions.'

'And any precautions, doctor?'

'Rest for the first four months, out of which about two months have already passed. Otherwise, there are no precautions. All the best!' The doctor returned to her office.

Returning to Daanish Kadah, Mayuri tried to call Sheba but could not contact her. She had some juice and went to

Professor Daanish's room. He was sitting in his easy chair, and was sleeping with his head on his shoulder. Mayuri went to her room and lay down, enjoying the silence of the long afternoon. She looked at the ceiling. A koel was calling somewhere faraway. She listened to it keenly as this was not the time of the year for a koel to sing. She did not mind the untimely call and smiled softly. She herself was becoming a mother untimely…No, not untimely...just a little late! What was wrong with that? Whatever Bhagwan does, He does it for our good.

Mayuri closed her eyes, thinking how the baby would look…like Prashant, a very fair little girl, or a caramel complexioned boy like Neel? Thinking this, Mayuri became agitated.

To hell with Neel! What have I to do with him? This is Prashant's baby. I wanted to divorce Prashant because of this issue. When I did not conceive even after the surgery, I thought that something was wrong with Prashant. I never knew that I had become pregnant. Maybe it was because of my pregnancy that I was hypersensitive and felt so insecure. And I did not do anything sinful in my relationship with Neel. My sin lies in hurting an angel like Prashant. In fact, I wanted to marry Neel to have a baby. This issue must have been deep in my subconscious when the charm of his good looks bewitched me…No…yes. He was handsome, but he was not a decent person…I have nothing to do with him. I don't want anything from anybody now. Mayuri turned to her left and closed her eyes. At the same moment, her phone rang. It was a call from London; it was Prashant's number. 'Who had given Prashant her new number in India?', she wondered, and kept looking at her phone. 'If Sheba had given this number to him, she would certainly have told her. Who then?' Mayuri thought for a few moments and then hit the reply button on her cell phone to answer the call.

The Birds of the Snows

Sheba inserted a classical music CD into her laptop. The very first song made her miss her father. This song was composed in the *Malkauns* raga, which was Abbu's favourite. It began with low notes and went up to the highest ones. *Malkauns* is sung at midnight. It has such a melodious tune that a sad song composed on this raga touches a person's very soul. It is a magnificent raga that Abbu would hum for days after listening to it on his record player, and Sheba would sing along with him.

In Sheba's CD, the raga had a different *bandish* (the traditional lyric for singing a raga). Seeing her interest in music, Abbu had allowed her to learn the sitar. A tutor was hired to give her lessons. Sheba had a melodious voice but singing was not considered appropriate for a girl of a respectable Muslim family. She would sing the ragas she learnt on the sitar to Abbu.

Sheba had learned many a *bandish* while studying in the university during her vacations at Gandharav Vidyalaya, where she had gone with Mayuri; her teacher was Guruji Ratna Bhardwaj from Karnataka. The girls would touch her feet as a mark of respect, and her dusky, smiling face looked like a mauve rose in the small garden of her lawn in the early evening. Guruji would bless them, putting her hand on their bowed heads, and all the faces would brighten as if with an inner peace.

Sheba increased the volume and came out into the lawn. The *bandish* Abbu used to sing only had five words: *Daar, daar, daaa aa aar, Koyaliya.*

Abbu used to listen to these ragas on his record player. Later, when audio cassettes replaced the record player, he would get the cassette if a film song was composed in that raga. He liked to take his children to good movies, besides visiting the Mughal Gardens, hill stations and lakes. His would tear up while watching a sad scene in a movie. In one of those movies, there was a scene about a Pathaan who had returned after a life term in jail and a little girl, as dear to him as his own daughter, and who had grown up meanwhile, just did not recognize him anymore. Abbu wept along with the Pathan, and so did Sheba. Only God knows whether Baaji and Farkhi also cried or not. Ammi, on the other hand, believed that watching a movie was sinful. Sheba suddenly realized that films also symbolized the impermanence of everything. Like everything else in this world, the flower fresh faces, the agile dancers, the actors who portrayed their emotions with their facial expressions, the artists who created sheer magic with their films, and K.L. Sehgal with his magically melodious voice—all of them had gone away.

Sheba took a deep breath. Abbu would hum Sehgal's songs like '*Do naina matware tihaare ham par julm karainn* (your enchanting looks treat me so cruelly)' and '*Saawan ke badalo un se ye ja kaho* (O' clouds of Sawan—the rainy month—carry my message to my love)'. Sometimes, listening to a song or a raga being played on the radio brought tears to Abbu's eyes. Why do tears sometimes appear in people's eyes without their being sad? No, it is not entirely about grief. When one achieves great happiness or deep peace of mind, the subconscious of an intellectual person starts dwelling on the transience of all things. And, perhaps, somewhere deep in the mind of every thinking person, there is always lurking the question: what this *gorakh dhanda*—this riddle of life—all about?

One has to go back centuries to find a musical genius like Ustad Nusrat Fateh Ali Khan. The divine force of music! Nusrat Fateh Ali Khan's *qawwalis*, his immortal music is unique and unparalleled. It moves one like the magical music of *Lehn-e-Dawoodi*—the sonorous songs of David.

Sheba hummed a qawwali '*Biba sadadil mor de*' by Ustad Nusrat Fateh Ali Khan, and drew a deep breath. How perfectly the master had sung this! With what great excellence the maestro had rendered his songs, one line in countless tunes—such a great musician! But, alas, he is no more. The grief of his early demise will always be there, lodged somewhere deep in one's heart. Sheba tilted her head and looked at the cherry tree near the compound wall, with its almond-shaped leaves of a greenish yellow hue. She wondered if every cell of the human body keeps changing, then where do memories live? They never go away and one just has to think for a moment and all of it comes to life and starts playing in one's imagination, just like on a computer screen. And if sometimes these thoughts go to a particular spot in the depth of the brain, like some particular partition in the memory of the computer, one can suddenly remember things which had been forgotten for years. So where do they keep hiding? Perhaps, somewhere deep in one's soul. Thinking is also an addiction...thinking before one goes to the valleys of repose. Thinking, while strolling, when you are not in a hurry to get somewhere. Getting lost in thoughts unconsciously while just sitting motionless. Not thinking with a conscious effort is not pointless either, as staring at an object and not thinking about it, one surrenders oneself at that point in time. At such times, one feels that they have become a part of the vast universe by harmonizing with its infinite movement towards an unknown destination, and the mind attains a deep sense of inner peace and tranquility.

Sitting on the swing, Sheba rested her feet on the ground and closed her eyes. She looked like a statue sitting still on the swing with her eyes closed; she took a deep breath, and a serene look came to her face. She had learnt to attain a feeling of complete peacefulness by surrendering her body and soul to the passage of time. When she needed to breathe again, she half opened her eyes and closed them again, trying to breathe without a stir; she felt like the Jhelum river flowing calmly on a snowy day. Something like a vague smile came to her face, but it was not really a smile—it was more like the glow of the morning sun on autumn flowers, it was a feeling as if one's tranquil soul had flown to some unknown world, and thus becoming a part of the vast universe.

Abbu would also become similarly lost sometimes, without listening to any music. As well as while listening to music, if it was in his favourite ragas like *Darbari, Bhairavi, Malhar, Deepak, Pilu, Tilak Kamod, Jaijaiwanti, Bhopali*, or raga *Desh*. He would close his eyes listening to the *thumri*, and sway his head with the song, being played on *sitar* or flute, or sung in some rare or well-known *bandish*.

Sitting on the swing, Sheba closed her eyes again. She, too, loved music, the same kind that Abbu liked! Had Abbu been alive, he would have loved Pakistani folk singer Reshma's voice, which is like the murmur of a mountain brook, an uncut diamond or the fragrance of wild flowers.

Ve pyarya
Saadewal mukhda mor

'Turn your face to me, my love, turn your face to me'—she translated the Punjabi verse mentally. She started thinking about the poetry of the Sufi saint Baba Bulleh Shah. Buried in a town across the border, this couplet from one of his verses is carved on his tombstone:

Bulleh Shah asaan marna naahee,
Gorpiya koyi hor

'Bulleh Shah, I will not die, it's somebody else who lies in the grave', Sheba thought of the translation again, and repeated the couplet. She then started humming the lines '*Sade wall mukhra more*' slightly louder, closing her eyes like her Abbu, in the same tune as Reshma had sung in her melodious, raw silk-like voice. When Baba Bulleh Shah's *murshid* (teacher) Shah Inayat was once unhappy with him, Baba composed many poems expressing his pain and agony. Abbu loved such poetry, as did Sheba.

She had similar taste in music, and liked songs sung by Rafi, Hemant Kumar and Mukesh. She also loved old black and white movies with enchanting music, in which Dilip Kumar, Raj Kapoor, Dev Anand and Joy Mukherji had acted with actresses like Madhubala, Vijayantimala, Suchitra Sen, Shakila and Asha Parekh.

Where had those beautiful faces gone with the passage of time? Just yesterday she had watched an old film song on the TV in which the dancer, holding a tambourine, was dancing in such an enchanting manner that everything around her seemed to be dancing as well. Sheba started laughing. Some of the films were so marvellous that they had become classic pieces of art. A few years ago, she and Mayuri had seen an old movie called *Taraana*; it was such a realistic portrayal of love and life, with Dilip Kumar and Madhubala giving an outstanding performance in it. The girl with the curly hair and an angelic smile was now buried under the earth, becoming a part of the dust. Shadows of sadness descended on Sheba's face at the thought. Where do all the people go? Abbu, too, was gone. Time has a way of changing everything. Faces like red poppy flowers become like dry marigolds. A dimple in one's chin, making a face enchantingly beautiful, later seems to divide it up in two. Dimples in the cheeks become deep wrinkles with age; the nose with a glittering nose pin looks so unseemly as it bends downwards; the holes pierced in the ears look like healed up wounds. Age degenerates the body over the course of time till one reaches a point when one ceases to live altogether. A shiver ran through Sheba as she quietly asked God, 'Allah Miyaan, why do you do all this?' Sheba looked at the sky, and verses from a poem came to her mind:

The winds will dance in the trees,
The birds will sing their melodies,
Crimson light will shine on the mountain peaks,
Waters will flow dancing the way they do,
Dew drops will fall on the grass like ever,
Children will play in the playgrounds as always,
Heers will meet their Raanjhaas, secretly,
Mothers will sing lullabies to their young ones,
The mere fistful of my earthly being,
Would be but a speck in the dust.

She kept looking up at the swallows flying in the blue sky for some time, and then looking downwards, she tilted her neck slightly sideways. 'Only Allah knows his secrets best,' as Abbu would say sometimes in Punjabi: '*Allah diyaan Allah hi jaaney*!' And Abbu would bend his head sideways, just as she had done. She stood up and walked towards the house.

This is the miracle of music, one of the greatest of fine arts. It can spread magic of its beauty just by raising or lowering the tune. Even a person who does not understand music, and even the souls of the animals and birds, become a part of it. That's why an artist lives in a world of his own, a world common with his kindred souls, a world where there is no place for falsehood and deceit. At the shrines of Sufi saints, the hearts mesmerized by the songs and music of qawwalis get connected to the spiritual world, and they seem to lose awareness of all material surroundings.

When Abbu sang those difficult tunes, the veins in his neck, which had the same almond complexion of his skin, became prominent, with one of the veins looking bigger than the other. Being asthmatic, Abbu would stop to regain his breath. So, even though Abbu was very fond of singing, he could not pursue learning music to fulfill his dreams of becoming a singer. He would suffer a bout of cough after singing with the children. Seeing Abbu coughing, the children would get busy with some other games, but Sheba would become apprehensive and would remain there, looking at him with concern. She would get him a drink of water, and ask him if he wanted some qehwa.

Sheba went to her bedroom, lay on her bed and closed her eyes. 'Where has my Abbu gone?' thought Sheba, suddenly missing her father badly after many years. She lowered the sound of her laptop which was playing raga *Malkauns,* and cried her heart out.

Sheba spent many weeks in her hometown with her mother. Ammi was cheerful at her being around, and her health seemed to have improved. Sheba spent hours sitting on the swing like she used to in her childhood. Gulla Bhai prepared her favourite dishes. Baaji and Farkhi visited them occasionally but Seemeen did not turn up.

Sheba had unknowingly started thinking of Seemeen and Yasir as her own children. Yasir was not in town—he was, in fact, out of the country, but Seemeen was still there. Last time when she had visited Ammi's place, Seemeen's attitude had hurt Sheba so much that she was sad for a long time—even while she was busy looking after Professor Daanish.

Sheba would swing slowly, like she used to do in her childhood, lost in the past. In those days, when she had returned to her hostel after rejecting two marriage proposals, she felt an unknown sense of loss at times. When she would lie down to rest after dealing with the university classes, the staff and the students, and even despite the sense of peace in looking after Professor Daanish, she remembered many things besides the events of the day. Sometimes she thought that her entire life would be spent just like that, though there was nothing wrong with that. But then some unknown fear would engulf her whole being. Then Ammi's affectionate face would flash in her mind, and she would recall Seemeen's innocent face and Yasir's mischievous expression, along with their love for her, strengthening her feeling of being loved. But everything seemed to have changed so fast in just a few years.

Two years ago, when Sheba had gone home, Seemeen had met her like a stranger. Sheba left the bedroom and came out into the garden again. Sitting on the swing, she was looking at her feet. But recalling that, she had suddenly raised her head and looked into the distance, as she had felt something shattering in her heart, as if something fragile made of glass had fallen down from a height. A grapevine had become entangled in the top branches of the fig tree growing in the corner of the garden near the main entrance of the house. They would just break if someone tried to separate them, she thought. Lines appeared on her forehead. Had the grapevine not climbed up on the tree, it would have grown over the wall, or just on the ground. The entangled and twisted branches would have grown a little higher and then gone back again on to the ground. But then its sweet and sour leaves and tender-looking tiny grapes would get sullied lying on the ground.

She looked at the grapevine with love, but then recalled that she was thinking of something stressful. She tried to get back to the sombre mood she had before she started thinking about the grapevine. Sometimes one wants to experience pain in spite of knowing it is hurtful. Sheba shook her head. No, it was not that. She was thinking about it because she wanted to find a way out of the unpleasant thoughts which kept returning to her mind, making her brood about those matters. So, where had she been? She closed her eyes and opened them again. Something had crashed and broken inside her at Seemeen treating her not only like a stranger, but also just like Baaji used to do. She had felt as if its jagged spikes were piercing through her heart. Sheba had wanted to pull those spikes out, but their fragments had travelled to her vessels and were running in her blood. And whenever her thoughts stopped at some point, those fragments would begin to lodge in the empty spaces in her heart, and all the incidents surfaced from the memory of her subconscious on to the monitor of her conscious mind.

She would then be angry with herself. In the days of her taking care of Professor Daanish, the thoughts of these incidents gave her a strange feeling of deprivation in her heart. Sheba was years older than Seemeen, so why would she feel strong from her relationship with her? She wondered if these emotional relations become one's strength as well as one's weakness at times. Later, after taking the professor out on his wheel chair, reading to him, putting oil in his hair and spending a hectic day at the university, the thought of losing Seemeen's support would entangle her in a web of helplessness at night. She would feel very lonely. Because during the time she was free after work, two faces appeared in her mind: Ammi's, who was her weakness, and Seemeen's, who was her strength. If Ammi's face was the past and the present, Seemeen's was the past, present and future. But after suffering mentally for a whole year because of her attitude, Sheba dissociated herself little by little, and then totally, from the feeling of reassurance she felt from her love for Seemeen—a relationship upon which she had relied for such a long time. In Yasir's absence, his memories would bring a smile to Sheba's face but he, too, had gone away to study. And after dwelling upon it for so many days, she freed herself from the painful limbo of expecting Yasir's call from Europe. He had also got busy in his own world. Now, in Sheba's world there was only herself, Ammi, Saleem Miyaan and Gulla Bhai.

Her relationship with Professor Daanish was only that of a caretaker, Sheba thought keenly for a moment and shook her head. What other relationship could she have with him? All the same, it was such a deep one. She looked at her feet again; her toe nails were uneven, they needed trimming and filing, she thought. But what for? She was not going anywhere or visiting anyone. But shouldn't one do things for oneself as well? 'Poor professor, such a great intellectual', thought Sheba, taking a deep breath. Who am I living for, she wondered. She looked at the sky; she was living for her mother, because no one else was there for her—not even Seemeen or Yasir. Sheba's heart was sad again. How long can I live for them? Seemeen will marry and go to her new home. Yasir, too, would get busy with his own family at some point. Sheba raised her eyes towards the grapevine again. Even if they were her children, they would have their own lives, their own plans. Which meant that she would have to spend her life all by herself. Sheba tilted her neck thinking about why she was engrossed in such thoughts. The reason could be because of what Ammi had said last night…

'How long will this most gifted of my daughters live her life alone?' Ammi had put a small lump of coconut oil which had frozen because of the cold on her hair, and had asked softly, caressing her hair with her fingers. Sheba had not said anything in reply.

'How long will I be with you, my child? You should realize that before everyone else, it would be your sisters who will be asking for their share of the property. We did not get anything from the property in the village. They never thought of him as their elder brother.'

'Why do you have any expectations, Ammi? They have already sold the other bungalow, and in exchange for this house they took away hundreds of acres of our share in the land saying that the land was not as valuable as this bungalow. And then, how cleverly they proved that in the court too! But why think about all that and be tense now?'

'Yes, sweetheart,' the lump of oil on Sheba's scalp had started to melt and Ammi moved her fingers in her hair, 'but we have to think about your life, my child.'

'Let my thesis get published as a book. We will think about all this after that.'

'About what?'

'About what you are saying. But Ammi, I don't want to marry. I want to keep reading, writing and studying like this.'

'No, my dear, don't talk like that. Every girl has to marry. And as for your job, you don't need it. What we have in the bank belongs to all three of you. You can work here too, if you decide to stay back.'

'I am here for a few weeks only. Once my book goes to press, you will see that your daughter will get a good job.'

'Have you left your job there?'

'No, I applied for leave to meet you, and also to attend a workshop and a seminar at the university here.'

'Who can understand you, my darling? But you should learn to live for yourself as well. The world is very cruel. I know everything in your heart.' Suraya Begum pulled her head down a little and started to put some more oil with gentle fingers near her neck.

'For example?'

'For example, you had loved Seemeen and Yasir dearly. You are a born mother and loved them just like a mother, more than any maternal aunt would. But look how Seemeen has changed.'

'Is her behaviour with you also...'

'No, she is fine with me. But whenever her mother accuses me of pampering and spoiling you and starts talking nonsense, I expect Seemeen, who is now grown up, to say something sensible. However, she does not. Instead, she just nods often at what her mother says.'

'Yes, Ammi, I feel very sad about her changed attitude... Ammi, I feel shattered, I...' Sheba said slowly, and started crying bitterly. Her mother held her oily head against her breast, staining her spotlessly clean dupatta.

'Don't be stupid, do not cry. You are not a weak girl; you are different from all the other common people. She is first Faheema's daughter and your niece only afterwards. She was your fan during her childhood and she liked you, but she naturally loves her mother much more,' Ammi said, patting Sheba's cheeks.

'As I love my mother much more than them,' Sheba said quickly and laughed.

'Of course, my sweetheart,' Suraya Begum smiled cheerfully.

Swaying slowly, Sheba smiled and then got down from the swing. She started walking along the compound wall but without going all the way, she returned to the swing and sat on it again. She had many memories connected to that lawn, and those memories in turn associated with many people. A pall of gloom descended on Sheba's heart. Seemeen turned out to be just like her mother. How strange are the relations of blood! She started thinking about Seemeen's mother as well. She became apprehensive about Baaji's well-being, or her being sad. Baaji, who shed tears in her childhood at losing in a game, may still be crying over trifles. Those emotions would only be satisfied by cruelly and sadistically torturing Sheba—who felt like a poor, trapped creature. But against whom would she have such feelings now, and if she had them, on whom could Baaji vent now, and how could she satisfy them? She felt satisfied only when the victim of her wrath suffered agonies like a mortally wounded, moribund creature. Sheba's heart felt a wave of sympathy as well as the pain. How could Baaji, a fragile person with a weak heart and subdued attitude, accept defeat? Wouldn't her ego be wounded now? Poor weakling Baaji, may God bless her with good health and keep her happy.

Why does this happen? Why did she not hate people like others? Since she could not make a change in their egocentric narcissistic ways, she would change her path instead, and this was perhaps the best way-out. Sheba put her feet on the ground and gave the swing a small push.

A kangri vendor shouted, selling his wares on the street outside. His figure appeared in Sheba's mind: wearing a long pheran over a heavy vest, coarse leather sandals handmade by some cobbler on his feet, and wearing his trousers higher than his ankles, wearing the kangris strung on a thick grass rope through their handles around his neck like a muffler, and walking slowly, holding his own kangri with the hot, earthen fire pot under his pheran.

She saw him pass on the street across the gate. The framework of the ordinary kangris was made with the thin branches of a certain bush. But better quality kangris were made with willow branches sliced lengthwise, though they had the same natural wood colour as the other ones. The kangris were painted in red, green and blueto look more attractive to customers.

The kangri vendor's face looked like it was encircled in flowers with the colourful kangris around his neck. When he removed them from around his neck and put them on the ground, Sheba found that he was not wearing a pheran; he was very good-looking, like a real native Kashmiri, and was wearing a jacket and comfortable sports shoes. Sheba had to discard her old image of a kangri vendor. He put the kangris on the ground, and began to search for something in his pockets. He took out a packet of cigarettes from an inner pocket of his jacket, pulled one out and then put the packet back in his pocket. He took out a small cinder from his own kangri with the iron spoon tied to its handle, lit his cigarette with it and put it back in the kangri. An expression of satisfaction came to his face, which was partially covered with strands of his curly hair. Blowing smoke through his mouth and nostrils, he bent over to pick up the kangris again. Sheba wrinkled her nose.

'Stupid smoker!' she said reflectively. How quickly people all over the world were getting addicted—in the Valley too! There were so many different types of intoxicants around. There were many drug dealers with bustling businesses, and any of these drugs could ruin a whole nation. One only had to introduce it to the new generation and then watch the destruction. They realize the devastating outcome only when it reaches the person himself or his near and dear ones, but by then, generations of others have reached the point of destruction. And then there are the rehabilitation centres, offering their services. It is like many doctors, just to promote some drug manufactured by a certain company would prescribe the medication indiscriminately—it is just like spreading harmful malware on the internet and then offering anti-virus programs for it, Sheba said to herself, shaking her head.

Who knows how many different types of intoxicants have been developed, and have played what havoc in the world—on the millions, rather billions of years old planet? Who knows how many people used them for vicarious pleasure, and were ruined by such drugs? Sheba pushed the swing lightly.

She spotted an unusual bird on her right side, sitting on a low branch of an apricot tree and looked at it with a surprised smile on her face. This bird had a large crown of black feathers on its head, which made it look like its hair was combed backwards! It moved frequently with its head bent down. It had brown feathers over the rest of its body, with a long black tail. Sheba did not see it fly to a higher branch, and it would not sit still at one place for more than 15 or 20 seconds. Looking around, it would swoop down to the ground, pick up some small insect from the grass quickly, and then fly back to a low branch of the tree. This bird did not chirp; it made a whistling sound once, and another bird which looked like it appeared from somewhere. Eager to see them better, Sheba thought of going close to them but they flew away as if sensing her intentions. She had never seen such a bird before. Who knows where it had come from, facing what changes in weather? Strange things were happening because of global warming. Crops were ripening somewhat earlier, lotuses that bloomed in August and September were now blooming in May and June.

She heard another Kangri vendor from somewhere far away. He was a different vendor, as the one before had shouted, *'Buy Kangris'*, but this one only cried *'Kangri... i...i...i!'* The winter is close, and then *Chila-e-kalaan*—the forty-day coldest spell of the winter, is not far behind. All the leaves of the trees in the garden were wearing autumn colours. They were in various shades of green already, and were slowly changing into different colours. The leaves of the poplar that look like peepal leaves but are not so pointed as they do not have a long tip, had turned light brown from light green, and their back which was dull off-white in summer, was now the shade of dry wood. Willow leaves that were a somewhat deeper green on one side and a dull off-white on the other were now deep brown, like the colour of almonds. The peach tree with its deep green leafy branches had turned reddish crimson, and from a distance looked like it was all covered with flowers. The triangular yellow leaves of the grape vine, that had climbed over the trees, had turned deep orange and seemed to be giving out an orange glow. The green grass of the lawn, turning yellow, looked golden like ripe paddy fields. The smallish apple leaves looked dark brown. Some of the needle-like fragrant leaves of the pine trees had attained the colour of dry peel of walnuts. In a few days, even these colours would be lost, and they would fall down from the branches. Soon, every tree and every branch, denuded of the leaves, would assume a shade of light or dark grey. Then, the snow would spread a white dupatta on all the trees. The garden, the paths, roads and the roofs would all be white. Sheba raised her head and looked at the roof of her house at some distance. She heard the vendor of Kangris shouting loudly again.

'*Kangri...i...i...i!*'

In the cold winter he would be dressed heavily in a *Pheran*—made of some thick fabric like *Pattu,* or tweed or blazer woven in the Bemina Mills in Bemina, Srinagar—over his jacket and would only venture out wearing a cap covering his curly hair and his forehead, ears and the neck. Years ago a poet had said,

> *'Wanddtsalle sheen galle, beyiyi Bahaar'*
> *(The winter will come to an end, the snows will melt away, and the spring will come again).*

Sheba took a deep breath and getting up from the swing, began to walk near the flower beds, looking at the flowers and plants. It had been a bright and sunny day. There were still a few of hours left for the sun to set. A pleasant, warm air surrounded the plants and flowers, which had been spreading their fragrance and absorbing the heat. Sheba inhaled deeply and a pleasant smile appeared on her face. She looked at the sky raising her head, and suddenly saw Shahaabuddin Sherwani's face with his deep black eyes in the clouds. She turned her gaze away from the sky. But she still saw him smiling in the rows of flowers next to the green of the grass. She closed her eyes; a wave of sadness surged in her heart, spreading over her whole being.

'No...no way, what a stupid thought!' Sheba said to herself. But why had this thought not occurred to her till now, for almost four or five years; he must be living happily with his family and small children by now. Suddenly, Sheba thought that if Shahaabudin Sherwani gave one of his lovely kids to her, what else could she wish for? She stopped with the thought rising somewhere deep in her mind. 'Did that mean that she had not forgotten Shahaab? Did she still have a soft corner for him?', she asked herself. It is not like she had; she still has it. 'Is that the truth? I am lying to myself, even to myself, I am now lying to myself...even to myself.' She went over to the grapevine. The parrots were making such a din from the top of the fig tree. Sheba shifted her eyes to look at the sky once more. Shahaabuddin Sherwaani! A wave of pain arose in her heart. In her agitation, she headed to the door but turned again towards another flower bed. 'It is all because I have nothing to do,' she thought. 'I am on such a long leave, and there are still a few days left for the workshop'.

She bent down and plucked a tiny white flower from a small plant growing in the grass. Twisting it between her thumb and index finger, she went towards the door. Shahaabuddin Sherwaani's image appeared on the flower and stayed there. 'Oh God! This is so dishonest! Thinking about someone else's husband…No, this is not right. You should not allow these thoughts to overwhelm you, Sheba Khanum!' she said to herself out loud.

She brought the tiny flower to her nose; it had no scent but its thin, delicate petals touched her nostrils softly and its orange centre coloured the tip of her nose yellow. Sheba threw the flower away towards the flower beds, opened the door and entered the house. The delicious smell of turnips permeated the whole house.

'What is cooking, Ammi?' asked Sheba, going near Ammi, who was heading to the other room after her *wudu* and was unfolding her sleeves down towards her wrists.

Sheba offered to close the tight buttons for her and the offer was accepted with a smile.

'Isn't it *shabdeg* (a Kashmiri mutton and turnip delicacy)?' she asked, and Ammi patted her head. 'But that will cook for the whole night, with turnips and spices and what not. I am asking about dinner.'

'It will be *shabdeg* for dinner too. It's your favourite, that's why,' Ammi brushed a peck on her cheeks.

'Yes, Ammi, but only when you cook it,' she said, entering the room behind her mother.

'We have not bothered to cook something nice like this for a very long time. I cooked on weekends when I expected your sisters, but mostly, nobody turned up for months. Poor Gulla had to put it in the refrigerator and eat it for days on end,' Ammi spread her *janamaaz,* saying, 'your being around has filled the house with happiness.' Ammi was about to begin namaz but stopped.

'You should at least offer *Fajr* (dawn prayer) and *Maghrib* (dusk prayer) in time; go make *wudu* and come over to pray.'

'I will offer it, Ammi, later...'

'Of course, you will, hurriedly; without your heart in it.'

'I am busy, Ammi, I hope for Allah's forgiveness. He is *shafeeq* (affectionate) and *habeeb* (loving) first, and *jabbaar* (hard in judging) and *qahaar* (wrathful) only afterwards!'

'Fine, but still...' Ammi was about to start praying, but stopped.

'But, my child, you are not busy with anything right now. And what have you just said about turnips? You should learn the recipe for *shabdeg*, you will need it when you go to your own home.'

'Is this not my home?'

'It is, my darling. May Allah send a suitable groom who will be ready to stay here with us,' Ammi said and got ready to start with her namaz.

'Good idea, now that is worth some thought,' Sheba said in a chirpy voice so that Ammi would hear it before beginning the namaz, and went out of the room, smiling. Reaching her room, she saw pieces of the bluish light of the evening spread on the glasses of the windows. She did not want to be insolent towards the evening by staying indoors. She climbed down the staircase quickly and came out into the garden.

It was not very cold yet and the weather was pleasant with the sun, when visible, being fairly hot. The State Secretariat had not been shifted to the winter capital yet. Students were taking their entrance tests, and interviews for new jobs were also being held. Applications for different posts were invited from all over the country, and like the rest of the country there were a number of candidates for very few jobs. Specialists in certain areas of study had been called in from other universities for the selection process as well.

Entering the vast university campus located in the spacious grounds of Nasim Bagh on the banks of the Dal Lake, and seeing the crowd of students, Sheba felt glad as well as a little jealous. She took a deep breath and walked down the narrow, grayish road, looking at the flower beds on each side along the path. The students in their colourful clothes under the chinars, behind the cypress trees and on the grassy lawns looked like flowers strewn around by some secret hand. One could see all the aspirations of life reflected in their young faces. Most of them looked happy, and some looked even happier than others. Some professors, too, were seen passing by. A strong sense of gloom filled her heart for a moment. All these faces were unfamiliar; no one knew her. She looked at her golden wrist watch and walked fast.

She could see the board on top of the sociology building now, which was some hundred steps away. Sheba looked at her watch again; she was a little early, so she crossed the pathway between the flower beds and went towards a rose bush. She put her bag on the ground and sat down on the grass and looked around. Some girls were sitting at a little distance with their faces half-covered with their dupattas pulled down their foreheads, like brides in veils.

The girls in front of them had not covered their faces as they were not facing the sun. A smile appeared on Sheba's face. But she quickly assumed a serious expression, lest the students passing by think her insane for smiling by herself. Sheba looked at the sky, lifting her head. The sun in the blue sky was beaming down pleasantly warm rays but she still did not face the sun, as even a little sun caused pigmentation spots at three points on her face. She adjusted her dupatta, covering the back of her neck and turning slightly away from the direct sun, and started looking at the road going in the opposite direction. She could wait in the department too, she thought after a moment, but why? She had just sat down a moment ago, then why? Because she suddenly felt very lonely. She was the only one sitting by herself near a wild rose bush. Till that day, she had never been to another university without Mayuri; and after Mayuri left, she had never gone to a seminar because she had to look after the professor.

'I came to a stop, while life went on ahead', thought Sheba. Pulling out a pen from her bag, she wrote some words on one of the few empty pages in a small notebook. She put the cap of the pen back on it, and took a deep breath. Her eyes became a little misty. The fragrance of the tiny wild flowers she inhaled seemed to have perfumed her whole being. She took a tissue paper out of her bag's outer pocket and wiped her teary eyes. Two spots appeared on the tissue paper that had two little stains of kohl as well. She had forgotten that she had put kohl in her eyes in the morning because she was going out of the house after many days. She thought about the fact that she had stopped using any make-up, and almost never dressed up. Trying to restore Dr Daanish's health, she had forgotten that it was important to have her own life and look after herself too. She was not so old that she should have given up dressing up and using light make-up now and then altogether. Looking after him, she went beyond being a dutiful nurse and a compassionate person, and had morphed somewhat into a mother—a 33-year-old mother to a 70-year-old man—who just gathered her hair in an unkempt bun, would put on any clothing hanging in the front in her wardrobe, and leave for the campus. It had occurred to her just that day while dressing to go out that she had not done any shopping in the last four or five years like she and Mayuri used to do. That morning, she had selected an old salwar kameez to wear, but the colour of the dupatta had faded. The black silk kurta had a thin strip of embroidery on its border. She had luckily found one of Ammi's old dupattas, still in excellent shape, that matched perfectly with her kameez. It was then that she had thought of putting kohl in her eyes to match with her attire.

She looked at her small-heeled sandals that sounded very graceful while walking, and saw that her salwar and the shirt had the same blue-green embroidery on the edges, and Ammi's dupatta had matching blue-green stripes on it. The sandals had a silver star near the toes, and her small feet looked very pretty in them. She quickly raised her head, wondering what someone would think seeing her looking at her own toes like that. These young students would think that this middle-aged woman had gone crazy. She frowned at the thought. No, she was young and had hidden under the guise of old age, forgetting that she was a young woman too. She was happy forgetting this, but professor was yet to recover. Sheba sighed deeply and got up. Reaching the department, she entered the students' washroom. One of the two girls in there was combing her hair and the other was applying lipstick. Sheba reached for the mirror and saw that she looked more beautiful than the two young, fair and rosy-cheeked girls. Her heart felt at ease. She did not let any expression appear on her face, but controlling her emotions made her smile. The kohl in her eyes had not spread. She stroked her hair backwards lightly and then came out of the bathroom. She looked at the vacant chair near the reception counter. A man with spectacles came and sat in it. She pulled a file from her bag and held it out in her hand.

'Is the sociology workshop going to be held here?' she asked.

'No, the venue has been changed because of renovation work here. It is in the education department now,' said the man, searching for something on his table.

'Where is that?'

'There, in that building with the green roof,' he gestured towards a building half visible through a window.

'Thank you,' Sheba said quickly and walked out fast. Once down the short staircase, she turned to her left and almost bumped into someone.

'Sorry, madam, very sorry,' a man with deep, dark eyes wearing a grey suit apologized profusely, even though it was none of his fault. Sheba did not answer but looked at him sheepishly.

'Sorry,' she said softly.

'Oh hello!' Professor Sherwani smiled, pleasantly surprised.

'Oh, Aadaab. It's you!'

'Aadaab! How is everything? What are you doing in this town and where is that friend of yours?'

'Mayuri is...she is there...' said Sheba, her heart beating fast. She looked around.

'Have you also come to attend the workshop?' he asked, stepping forward.

'Yes,' she said in a low tone, walking behind him.

She turned her head and looked at the flower bed along the concrete path leading through the garden. A nightingale perched on a rose bush with huge flowers turned her beak upwards, jerked her curved crown of feathers shaking her head twice, looked at Sheba for a second, and flew away. Sheba's eyes followed the bird, which went to a smaller tree nearby and began to sing loudly. That was a young pine tree with the countless needle-like leaves on its sturdy branches, spreading the peculiar pine scent. The scent did not reach Sheba but was so fresh in her heart and mind that her nose seemed to smell it. She loved the forests of her Valley dearly—the forests of pines with fragrant leaves, the evergreens and conifers with creepers spread over them like dupattas. She had loved running carefree at the edge of the forest with her cousins in her earlier days. Running barefoot, the needle-like pointed leaves often pricked the soft soles of her feet. She loved even that, there was pleasure in that pain too.

A faint smile appeared on her lips, a feeling rising from some remote corner of her consciousness deepened that smile, and made her fix her eyes on the man walking ahead steadily, filling her heart with more smiles—which she would not allow to reach her lips.

Professor Shahaab was the only person Sheba knew in that workshop. They would make small talk in the tea and lunch breaks, but it was very formal. At least it was formal on Sheba's part; she was very conscious about maintaining a reserved behaviour, but Shahaab's manner was relaxed and friendly.

Since the day Mayuri had told Sheba that she was pregnant and had resolved to spend her life with the child, Sheba found herself thinking about two things. One was that she had someone else who could share the responsibility of looking after Professor Daanish; and secondly, that she, too, could perhaps think about her own life now. She thought that the second thing was because of her mother's unhappiness at her rejection of all proposals, and also because in some remote corner of her being she was still sad about not being able to have a story with Shahaab.

Sheba got lost in her thoughts. Sitting in the hall she was mostly calm but still felt agitated occasionally, because it was a temporary happiness for a man who belonged to someone else. But she had neither expressed her emotions to Shahaab, nor been frank while talking to him. Yet, she kept thinking about him deep in her heart, her eyes wandering around his seat wondering whether he was among the audience or on the stage. And Sheba could not find a way out of this predicament, even though she felt that it was absolutely wrong. This was a pain with no cure, which she was all too willing to suffer. The day Mayuri told her with great confidence that she was not going back, she was sad too. That was because since there was someone to share the responsibility of caring for Dr Daanish now, the thought of spending her life with a nice person kept coming to her mind and she wished with all her heart for that person to be Shahaabuddin Sherwani. She was lost in her dreams and strange thoughts while looking at the speaker on the dais. Deep in those thoughts, she was unable to make sense of whatever he was saying when Shahaab turned up. He picked up her handbag from the chair next to her and sat down. Though lost in her thoughts, she was aware of the fact that Shahaab had not returned to the hall after lunch break. When she turned towards him, he smiled in a friendly manner and extended the handbag towards her.

'Oh, you had kept this seat for me, right?' he smilingly whispered.

'It was…Yes…I mean,' she fumbled and smiled.

'The speaker is so boring, isn't it?' he asked.

The speaker was delivering his address in a monotonous voice, droning on without any pause, with his hands in the pockets of his trousers.

'You are right,' she said impishly.

'What, that you had kept this seat reserved for me?'

'No, that the speaker is quite a bore,' she answered.

'Oh…and…so…so…?'

'So, we are just sitting like obedient students,' said Sheba looking straight.

'No, we will not just keep sitting silently like obedient students.'

'Shall we start shouting?'

'No! What we can do is get up and go; we will have tea outside and have a lively discussion,' Shahaab said with a serious face and stood up, heading towards the exit.

Sheba glanced at him but did not move from her seat. When he reached the door, he turned his head and looked at Sheba. He had such a surprised look on his face that

Sheba could not help laughing. With his hands spread out and his mouth wide open, Shahaab looked at her with his dark eyes rounded with astonishment. Sheba put her hand on her mouth, pretending as if she was scratching her nose to hide her laughter, and stood up. A couple of other people headed to the exit door as well, and this assured Sheba that her leaving the hall would not look odd.

Shahaab was standing against a pillar in the passage leading to the garden, looking away. She went to him and stopped at a little distance.

'Thank you. Had you not come, I was thinking of striking my head against this pillar because of how bored I was,' Shahaab finished the sentence seriously and then looked at Sheba's face, smiling, and began to walk slowly to the outer gate.

Sheba stood still for a few moments but seeing him walk, she followed him down the tiled floor too. But she was not seeing the big tiles, nor the pathway. Instead, she only saw the deep dark eyes, the naughty smile under the thick moustache, and the wheatish complexion of the neck one could see above the collar of his white shirt. He abruptly turned towards her.

'So, who is the next speaker?' she asked Shahaab.

'The next paper was by this humble servant,' he walked on calmly.

'Oh, you mean yours?'

'It was, but I got it changed to the last day just this morning.'

Sheba glanced at the sky as she came out in the open.

'I have not even written the paper actually, but I have some points in my mind. I will think about it in the evening. By the way, where are we going?'

Sheba was puzzled at this question.

He spoke softly again. 'This is your city. You would know where we can get a nice cup of tea here,' he began to walk with his head bent downwards.

'At my house,' Sheba replied quickly, surprised at this answer.

'You mean…what a good idea!' he said at once. Sheba thought for a few moments and added, 'and I can give you a book or two to read as well.'

'Is that so?'

'Yes, I mean I can lend them to you.'

Both suddenly laughed together. There were some cars waiting for the participants of the seminar near the entry gate. It was a distance of about a hundred steps; it was a straight path. Sheba looked at the far gate. A gust of wind blew the end of her dupatta on to Shahaab's arm. She pulled it back quickly and wrapped it around her shoulders twice, and smiled to herself. How kind was the wind and how lucky her dupatta! How good Shahaab looked walking with her to the gate! How pleasant was the afternoon! How good is Mayuri!

Mayuri said she would stay back in India after the birth of the baby. Otherwise how could she free herself of Dr Daanish's responsibility long enough to attend the workshop and the seminar, and walk so far—Sheba looked at the gate, so far—she turned her neck stealthily and looked at Shahaab's shoulder—with Shahaab, a person she liked. She felt her heart smile at these thoughts. But then she suddenly became serious, thinking about the fact that he was someone else's husband, stopped in her tracks, and looked at Shahaab's face.

'Yes?' he said becoming attentive.

'No, nothing,' said Sheba, quickly fixing her gaze back at the path. The vehicles seemed to draw closer. If Ammi asked, she would just tell her that she was lending him a book, as no one had ever come with her to her house.

Gulla Bhai opened the door and greeted them, moving aside to let them enter. Shahaab turned to him and returned his greeting. A wooden staircase at a short distance from the entrance led to the upper floor. The small passage with the drawing room on the right, and the dining room on the left, led further on to the kitchen. Near the western wall of the drawing room there were a couple of sofa sets made of intricately carved walnut wood and thick rubber foam seats with their covers of old fashioned densely embroidered crewel in walnut brown shade, indicating that they had been in this place for years with the same dignity, and many graceful personalities had sat on them. In the eastern corner of the room, there was a triangular almirah made of walnut wood with an arched back, and the doors with bubbled flowers on their semicircular glasses. The droplet-shaped petals near their branches reflected the light from the bulbs fixed in the candle stand-shaped holders of the old-fashioned grand chandelier hanging in the centre of the ceiling. A 20 feet square carpet was spread in the huge room of the same dimensions. Lifesize oil portraits of two gentlemen hung on the wall; Sheba's father and her grandfather perhaps, Shahaab had thought looking at them. Above the fireplace on the shelf in the next wall, there was a photograph—perhaps of Sheba's father again, Shahaab thought, of a man wearing a necktie, and with the straps of the case with a pistol around his neck, standing with children. He had placed his foot on a mounted lion and was smiling at the camera, holding a pair of sunglasses in his hand.

'Smart,' said Shahaab to himself, and went closer to the wall to see if he could find Sheba among the children. Sheba entered the room with Gulla Bhai, who was carrying a tray with tea and snacks, behind her.

'Why all this formality?'

'What formality?' Sheba said in a questioning tone.

'Where is that pistol now?' Shahaab smiled.

'It was sold a few years ago, but I burnt the case during the days of militancy.'

Sheba was pouring the tea into a cup when Suraya Begum entered the room and Shahaab stood up.

'This is Professor Shahaab, Ammi.'

'*Assalam-ul-alikum,*' Shahaab kept standing.

'*WaAlaikum-assalam,*' Suraya Begum said, sitting at the far edge of the other sofa. She was a graceful figure in a mauve silk salwar and a fine cotton dupatta with sequined work on it. Shahaab suddenly felt that he had seen this face somewhere before as well, a face exactly like this—full of grace and simplicity as well as authority—the sitting posture of a winner, but the slight bend of the neck indicating great humility as well. The face was almost without any expression, except a faint smile, and the complexion of an off-white flower. Shahaab remembered that he had seen a face like this a few years ago at a seminar in Aligarh and later, at a conference in Bhopal. Now, he had also met it in the university in this city and there was not much difference between the two faces except for their age.

This face was that of a guardian angel and the other one of an angel with the same humility, grace and gravity, the same grandeur and magnificence in the movement of the neck while looking at something, with skin like flowers or milk with saffron stirred in it. Lines of thought appeared on Shahaab's forehead. Why had he not noticed, when he saw her with Mayuri for the first time, that Sheba's personality was magnificent…simple and yet graceful. Did it mean that in order to realize her elegance, he needed an ambience different from the chairs in a cafeteria, seats in seminar halls or the surroundings of lawns? That he needed an old-style bungalow and a drawing room with almond-coloured, walnut wood sofas, and a mother with a mauve dupatta seated near the guest, to understand that beauty is passed from generation to generation? And Shahaab, too, would be happy to relate himself to this noble family, and to maintain the class of his family. Shahaab looked keenly at the ladies in the room. Had this thought occurred to him just now or did he already have a liking for Sheba but was not aware of it? Or had that risen from some obscure corner of his mind before, too, but had then vanished because of the circumstances? Or was it that he was in a relationship and to secure it, particularly for the sake of his sister, he could not have thought of being disloyal but in the changed circumstances, it had become important to think about it now? Shahaab looked at Sheba, who held out the cup of tea to him, and then looked at the cup. 'Thank you very much.'

Gul Mohammed entered the room holding a tray with a big bowl of kebabs and some plates, and put it on the dining table at a little distance from the entrance. Sheba began to serve.

'The tea is very good,' he remarked politely, looking towards Suraya Begum.

'Earl Grey, a company of long standing,' Sheba replied, smiling.

'It smells like flowers,' he smiled.

'Yes, we make it since my grandfather's time,' Sheba said turning to him, 'Or it is the salted tea!'

'Salted tea, very interesting, but may be some other time…' Shahaab stirred the sugar in his cup with a silvery white metal spoon, and watched the tea getting darker in colour. He strongly felt that the relationship with Sheba was very important.

Till that day, no one had ever come to their house with Sheba, nor had she talked about anyone except about the sick professor. Suraya Begum thought that Shahaab was the person whom Sheba had been looking after so attentively, forgetting even her own self. She looked at Shahaab.

'How are you now?' Suraya Begum enquired in a soft tone.

'Me? I am fine," Shahaab said, after a moment's thought.

'I mean, your health problem, now you can walk all right, I hope?'

'Oh, yes…that fracture, yes, yes,' he stammered. 'She remembers,' Shahaab said looking at Sheba, surprised and happy. 'Now, I am fine!' he answered with a smile.

Sheba looked puzzled for a moment but seeing this turn in the conversation, she relaxed and began to make tea for herself. Suraya Begum cast an affectionate glance at Shahaab's face. Last year when Sheba had come home, Ammi had asked her to marry the sick professor, as it was not appropriate otherwise for her daughter to be living with a man without being married. Faheema and Farkhanda, too, had strongly supported it. Suraya Begum was very apprehensive, wondering about the sick person with whom her beautiful daughter wanted to spend her life. But she was very happy upon seeing Shahaab now.

'Sheba did not tell us that you were coming, otherwise we could have offered you some good tea at least,' Suraya Begum said with a little smile. Sheba turned her face to look at her mother and then at Shahaab.

'We met by chance; and he wanted a book for his paper tomorrow, which is in our library. Let me first get it from upstairs,' Sheba glanced at the ceiling.

'I would like to see the library too if you don't mind.'

'Certainly, but you will mainly find books on literature in different languages. Abbu was very fond of…'

'Do you mean that I don't know anything about literature?'

Hearing Shahaab's answer, Suraya Begum laughed. 'Who else is there in your family, son?'

'There were many people but they are going to be less now,' Shahaab said in a low voice.

'I do not understand,' Suraya Begum smiled, somewhat confused. Shahaab had just moved his lips to say something when they heard the telephone ring. Suraya Begum turned her head towards the door and Gul Mohammad appeared with the cordless phone.

'Begum Sahiba, it's *badi bitiya* (elder daughter),' he said, holding out the phone. Suraya Begum got up and walked towards the door.

'I will just be back,' she said quickly, turning her head.

'Why did you say that there will be less people there?' Sheba offered a bowl of dry fruit to the guest, looked at his face for a moment, and put the bowl near his cup of tea.

'I meant that our parents had married my elder sister and me off to our cousins, but the marriage is now ending,' said Shahaab with an expressionless face.

She was silent, somewhat surprised. She bent her head slightly and looked at the sofa on which Shahaab sat.

'I know you are surprised; actually it was all in connection with the family property. They wanted to keep all the property within the family and made these faulty matches. There were age differences, and the lady married to me was not willing to compromise at all. She was unhappy with me for these three or four years for everything, and her folks retaliated, and our resentment…I mean her resentment was, in return, vented out on my sister. My uncle does not say anything but my wife and aunt were always annoyed with her, while my brother-in-law would just keep silent…And over such frivolous things that…' Shahaab shook his head and sighed deeply.

Sheba controlled her tremulous voice and cast a glance at Shahaab's face. 'Things like?'

'Like, they said that the dishes cooked at our home were never of their daughter's liking, or that she had unnecessary restrictions imposed upon her. Whereas, in fact, she asked the cook to make the food of her choice. And I never put any restrictions whatsoever on her, so I just don't know what that one was all about!'

'Then why was it so?' asked Sheba, thinking something.

'Only God knows, maybe she wanted to marry someone else. Who knows where and to whom the four of us would have got married if we didn't have elders who, without talking to their children…'

'Yes, maybe…'

Suraya Begum entered the room and Sheba put a cup of tea before her. She stirred it with the spoon.

'Shall I get the book from upstairs?' Sheba got up from the sofa.

'You mean we should go to the library?' asked Shahaab, sitting up.

'You better have your tea while I look for the book. Rearranging the racks has upset the order totally and I have to search for it.'

'Oh, let it be another time then; let me know when you have arranged them, I will come to see it.'

'You will come to Srinagar all the way from Bhopal to see them?' Sheba smiled.

'I will, most certainly,' he said laughing.

Suraya Begum laughed too, and Sheba hurried to the staircase.

The slight rustle of Sheba's dress and the low creaking of the wooden stairs created a kind of music in the silent house. Reaching upstairs, she went to her room instead of the library. Standing in front of the mirror, she looked at her face and saw that her cheeks were a glowing crimson, with stars twinkling in her eyes. She laughed suddenly with her lips lightly closed. She turned back and ran to the library upstairs.

When Sheba returned to the drawing room, Shahaab was saying goodbye to Suraya Begum. Sheba offered the book to him.

'Many, many thanks!' Shahaab bowed his head slightly.

'If you ever come to Bhopal, you will not feel away from home. We have a lake with an island and a few trees too. My parents would be pleased to meet you,' he said, looking at Suraya Begum.

'Let us see, InshaAllah,' Suraya Begum smiled.

'You mean the one called the Big Tank? It was constructed by Raja Bhoj of Malwa. But that is man-made, and was perhaps designed in imitation of our lake, the Dal,' Sheba said mischievously; Suraya Begum also smiled at that.

'Oh, yes…' Shahaab said, smiling at that, 'Yes. That must be so. I was only trying to say that we are self-sufficient in this respect too. I will take your leave now. I will always remember your hospitality in this unfamiliar place.'

'God bless you,' Suraya Begum said, and he walked towards the door. Gul Mohammad stood alert near the wall, opening the door and holding it out. Sheba also came to the door.

'Khuda Hafiz,' Shahaab said, and touching his forehead with his right hand, bent his head too. He looked at Sheba, and then at Suraya Begum standing near the entrance of the drawing room, and turned to go to the gate. Gulla Bhai walked fast, past him to the gate. When he opened it for him, Sheba quickly turned her head and looked back to the room. Ammi went to the washroom for *wudu*. Sheba climbed the stairs hurriedly and went to her room.

Shahaab was one of the speakers in the first session on the next day, and was sitting in a corner chair with a serious expression. Sheba was not there yet. He looked every now and then towards the entrance. Her absence was odd as she was representing her university; and on this last day, her participation in the group discussion sessions after lunch at the conclusion of the seminar was very important. He also had to return the book to her. What if she did not come? Then he would to go to her home to return the book. No, he would call her and ask her why she had not come. Did she not know that he had been thinking about her the whole night and had not slept well? He had seen her in his dreams as well, and as soon as the divorce was finalized, he would send his parents to her house with the marriage proposal. There was nothing wrong with the fact that he had been married since he had no children, and then there was not a big age difference between him and Sheba either. Shahaab took a deep breath. She might have decided to settle her career first and that is why she is not married till now.

But still, marrying a divorcée? So what? He was not inferior in social status compared her family, and then it is hard to find a decent family like his these days. But would Sheba's mother agree to this? Shahaab heard the clapping and came out of his reverie. The lecture had been interesting, but his glances again went to the doors. He began to think whether Sheba's mother and relatives would agree to the marriage of an unmarried girl to a divorcée? Yes, perhaps... because he…he was a perfect match for her, and liked her, and would keep her happy.

But…first of all, she should be asked about it too. I do not want to repeat history, and…and he glanced at the entrance again. But Sheba had already come and sat in the first chair of the second row where a bald, bearded man was napping a short while ago; he had just missed that as he was lost in his thoughts about her. Sheba looked at him. Shahaab smiled and bending his head, closed his eyes once and opened them again to greet her. Sheba touched her forehead with her hand to return his greeting and started looking towards the speaker. Shahaab was the next speaker; he delivered a nice lecture. He had noted some points on a small slip of paper and was looking at the audience and speaking, trying to make them grasp his views fully. With every glance he cast at Sheba, she noted that he had never looked at her like that before. Sheba shook her head quickly and turned her gaze to her hands placed on her lap. While delivering his speech, Shahaab noticed her bending her head suddenly, and remembered that during the last four or five years when they had met by chance, he had seen her averting her glances from him like that many times. So, did that mean that she had liked him before? If yes, then since when?

The audience started clapping and he returned to his chair, lost in these thoughts. When Sheba saw Shahaab looking at her again, she raised her head slightly to look at the new speaker as if she was listening to him very attentively. Seeing her becoming aware of him, Shahaab turned his attention towards the speaker to show his interest too. After a few moments, both of them looked at each other from the corner of their eyes.

Sheba's cell phone was on silent throughout the sessions. The first thing she did after the sessions were over was switch her phone on. She checked her missed calls and found one from Mayuri's number. A smile appeared on her lips at the thought of the dear would-be mother. Sheba was about to call her when she saw Shahaab coming towards her. She expected that he would come to see her as he was leaving the next day and had been looking at her time and again from the stage, and also because he still had the book.

Naseem Bagh, with some 12,000 chinars, had been built by the Mughal Emperor Akbar the Great centuries ago in 1586, on the shore of Dal Lake. The university was located next to the garden, and some of the university offices and a few departments were on the grounds of the Bagh. About a dozen wooden huts had been built near its boundary.

'The first garden ever planted in Kashmir Valley by the Mughals is this one, this is the west bank of Dal Lake,' Sheba said, looking at the ground. 'That…there, that green railing…' Sheba pointed with her hand while walking and Shahaab looked in that direction.

'Yes?'

'The first education minister of free India, Maulana Abul Kalam Azad, had stayed there. He has mentioned this in his letters.'

Shahaab looked at the huts surrounded by the chinar trees. The trees were casting thick shadows all around. Autumn had set in and the leaves of the chinars had turned crimson.

'These leaves will be on the ground a few days from now,' Sheba said, seeing Shahaab raising his head to look at the chinars.

'All the grounds would look orange then.'

'Yes, and it is so good to walk on the leaves.'

'The grass has already turned yellow, see?'

'In our area, every season is green.'

'Are you visiting Srinagar for the first time?'

'First time during this season…and this, too, is no less beautiful,' Shahaab looked at Sheba and then across the trees, towards the lake where children were playing and laughing in the garden near its bank.

'There, in that corner rests the greatest freedom fighter of Kashmir, Sher-e-Kashmir, and his wife.'

'Is that so?'

'Oh yes.'

'I will visit this place tomorrow before leaving. It's a blessing to offer *fatiha* at the mazars of such great people.'

They were walking slowly among the trees. Further away, near the trunk of a chinar close to the wall, some boys and girls were studying with their books spread out before them. Another boy and a girl were looking for something in a huge ledger-like notebook on the other side. Some students sitting near a tree on another side burst out laughing over something.

'Should we sit here for some time?' Shahaab stopped near another chinar tree and looked at Sheba for an answer.

'Yes, I am also tired because of these shoes,' Sheba stopped and pulled them off. Putting them away, she sat on the grass.

'What is wrong with these shoes?' Shahaab asked, sitting.

'Nothing wrong, they just pinch a little,' she pulled down the hem of her salwar, which had moved up slightly while sitting, over her ankles. 'Mayuri got these shoes for me from Punjab.'

'Oh, I see,' Shahaab smiled and suddenly said, 'Sheba.'

'Yes,' Sheba became somewhat alert at the way he had said her name. He had never addressed her like that.

'I wanted to ask you if…you will not refuse, if my family elders go to your place with a proposal?' Shahaab said, looking into her eyes directly. Sheba looked at his face for a few moments, somewhat puzzled. But because of Shahaab's presence, her joyful heart became somewhat mischievous and she put on a surprised look.

'But for whom? Do you have a younger brother?' Her nostrils quivered at the question she had asked him in jest.

'No…no…I mean…' Shahaab fumbled.

'You are already married, so then?' asked Sheba, seriously controlling the laughter tickling at her heart.

Shahaab had just opened his lips to say something when Sheba's cell phone rang.

'It is Mayuri!' Sheba's voice was full of happiness. 'Hello, Mayuri!'

'Hi, how are you?'

'I am fine, and how are you?'

'I can guess that from your voice. I am calling to share some good news with you.'

'Really? Tell me quickly! Is it some good news about sir?'

'No, this time the good news is about me.'

'Is it an offer for the job or…tell me quickly!' chirped Sheba. Shahaab picked a chinar leaf from the ground and looked at it keenly, twirling it in his fingers. The hand-shaped leaf had turned crimson but was still green at the edge.

'Sheba, Prashant is not angry with me, he called me!' Mayuri said in a happy voice.

'Oh really? That's very good indeed!'

'Dr Tilaang, my doctor here, was the same one who did my surgery in London. She must have told her colleague, Dr Fernandes, about my pregnancy; she was in the surgical team in London too. She is a family friend. She then called Prashant to congratulate him, and he got my number from her.'

'Oh God, that's so good!' Sheba said happily but on completing the sentence, she realized that everything was going to change now.

'Yes, Sheba, isn't that such a good thing to happen to me? My home will not break now, and my child will have his father! Prashant is coming here to take me with him,' Mayuri's voice was full with all the peace in the world, which brought a smile to Sheba's lips. But within a fraction of a second, something seemed to break into pieces inside her and her eyes suddenly rose towards Shahaab. A smile played at the corner of Shahaab's lips. He knew that Sheba was only teasing him. He kept playing with the leaf with his head bent down.

'Congrats Mayuri, when are you leaving?'

'Prashant has asked for leave, but don't worry. I am here for quite a few days. I will ask Prashant to come back here, to his own country. I am with you, Sheba, don't feel alone. Daanish sir is my responsibility too. By the way, what are your plans...for here?'

'Me...me...I...not sure yet. I will tell you when... when...'

'When are you coming back? It's so lonely here without you.'

'I will be with you soon, very soon,' there was a slight tremor in Sheba's voice, and Shahaab looked at her alarmed. Her chin was trembling. She turned her face away from Shahaab.

'How is Daanish sir?' asked Sheba hurriedly.

'He is fine. I will call you later. Take care, bye,' Mayuri said.

'Alright, bye,' Sheba said, hanging up, and looked the other side.

'You did not answer my question,' said Shahaab with his gaze still on the leaf. Sheba could not speak even after trying for some time. Shahaab moved a little to face her. Sheba's face had reddened and her eyes were full of tears. She was looking far away with her teeth clenched tight. Looking at Shahaab in front of her, she quickly covered her face with her dupatta.

'What is it, Sheba? Is everything alright?' Shahaab asked, slightly worried. She kept trying to control her sobbing as if she was swallowing her breath. Drops of sweat appeared on her throat.

'Please share it with me…please! Can I do anything?' Shahaab said with great concern. Sheba looked at Shahaab; she had wiped her tears by then, and moved her dupatta away from her eyes.

'Our Professor Daanish is…is very ill. I have to go back to Delhi soon. I cannot leave him alone. Mayuri had said that she would stay back here but now her husband is coming to take her with him. I have to stay with Daanish sir now. Mayuri will go back to London. I could come home only because she was here.'

Sheba took a tissue paper out of her handbag, and pressed it against her eyes a couple of times and wiped the sweat on her throat. 'He is our teacher. He made the lives of his students, of all of us, and there is no one to take care of him now except me. We have all been looking after him for some years, but now, it's just me. He will be...when he is fine...and then...' Sheba became silent and looked at the ground. Shahaab kept looking at her eyes. Some students sitting near the fence kept laughing merrily. The young man and the girl kept turning the pages of the big notebook sitting near the trunk of a chinar. A strong gust of wind blew and the leaves of the trees began to fall to the ground. Sheba raised her face up to the branches of the trees, sitting still and gazing at them while Shahaab kept looking at her.

Close to the Heart

Resting her gaze on a *sheesham* (rosewood) tree that looked grayish-blue in the darkening shadows of the evening, Sheba was lost deep in her thoughts. It was an evening like this on that day too; Sheba was watching Professor Danish intently. She turned her head towards the kitchen.

'Saleem Miyaan,' Sheba had called out softly.

Saleem Miyaan entered the room noiselessly. 'Add some more water to the kettle,' she told him.

'Really dear, did...has the doctor asked for more tea ?' Saleem Miyaan left the sentence incomplete and looked at Sheba. Sheba turned to the professor, whose eyes expressed an urge for tea.

'Drinking a cup or a half extra sometimes will do no harm, I hope,' said Sheba, as if asking for Saleem Miyaan's opinion.

'Yes, alright. I will get it,' Saleem Miyaan looked at the professor and smiled. 'Should I get it, sir?' he bent his head respectfully. Professor kept looking at him without any expression.

'You would like some tea sir, won't you?' Sheba left her chair and went close to him. 'Tea, yes?' she said, looking at his two-day old stubble, and caressed his cheek with the back of her hand. 'The barber will be here tomorrow; you need a haircut.' Professor kept looking at Sheba's face. Sheba looked into his eyes, smiling. 'Isn't that so?' she asked, nodding. Professor's lips moved slightly but no sound came out. He kept looking at her silently. Sheba moved her hand softly from his brow to his head. 'You will have a bath tomorrow, and you will look good and feel well then,' Sheba laughed a little louder and returned to her chair. Saleem Miyaan put the tea tray on the table and started making tea.

'I will help him with it, *bitiya*, you drink your tea,' Saleem Miyaan put Sheba's cup of tea before her. He put the tea and some biscuits in a smaller tray for the professor, moved a teapoy from his side to his front and put the tray on it. He got a napkin from the top of a small triangular closet in the corner and tucked it in the professor's collar under his chin. He tried to make him drink his tea with the help of a spoon but the professor did not open his mouth. Saleem Miyaan tried a couple of times, but in vain. Sheba kept looking at both of them.

'I will help him with the tea, don't you worry. He drinks it from me sometimes!'

'Alright then, try your bit. Though he seems to be in a different mood today...'

'Sir, please accept it from your Saleem Miyaan. Sheba is drinking her tea, grant me this honour today too...' Saleem

Miyaan picked a French fry with the fork and took it to the professor's mouth. He sat on the floor in such a way as if he will not move till he ate it, but the professor kept looking at him expressionlessly. Sheba went over to the professor, leaving her cup of tea on the table as she had drunk only half of it.

'One has to eat to live. Not eating means a slow death. Please, sir, you have to live,' saying that, Sheba held the mug in her hand and patted his shoulder. 'The physiotherapist will come tomorrow to help you exercise,' Sheba said, filling a spoon from the mug and touching it to his lips. Professor Daanish looked at her blankly, but as soon as the spoon touched his lips, he opened his mouth. Sheba fed him the tea slowly. He ate two French fries and two biscuits, and shut his mouth again. This was something new for Saleem Miyaan and Sheba, because even though the professor had almost stopped talking for many days by now, they could still guess his reaction from his expressions. Sheba looked at Saleem Miyaan standing by the door. He was looking silently at the professor, who was looking out of the window. But that was perhaps because he was sitting facing the window, and so seemed to be looking out through it.

'He smiled a little while ago, please read him something. Maybe he will nod the way he did yesterday. How happy he looked! Then what has...'

'Yes, Saleem Miyaan, yesterday he seemed to be recovering. He was smiling. He even seemed to be thinking about a sentence sometimes, he seemed to understand everything, though he did not speak. But now…' Sheba wearily returned to her chair. 'Only God knows what he has in store for…'

'Your tea is cold, dear child,' Saleem Miyaan touched the cup softly, 'I will make you another…'

Sheba felt the sadness in Saleem Miyaan's voice in the depth of her own heart. 'No, Saleem Miyaan, I don't feel like drinking it anymore.'

Sheba stood up again. Professor Daanish had continuously been looking out of the window. Saleem Miyaan started to pick up the dishes. Bent down, he looked somewhat hunchbacked to Sheba. While standing up, his shoulders were projecting out from under his black waistcoat, and looked bent forward. When he went towards the door, Sheba looked at his face. Saleem Miyaan's salt and pepper beard had grown completely grey in the last five years. Sheba shifted her gaze from Saleem Miyaan to Professor Daanish.

'Shall we go out to the lawn, sir?' Sheba removed his arm from his lap and put it again on the arm rest. Professor looked at her face. Looking at the *sheesham* leaves, Sheba sighed deeply. She remembered that when she had moved the professor's arm slightly that day, he had smiled a little and had looked at her for a few moments. 'Don't you want to go out?' Sheba asked, with much affection in her words, the way Suraya Begum would ask Sheba. A child-like smile spread on his lips. Sheba caressed his head and held it against her left shoulder with her right hand. Suddenly, she felt that she could give her life for this child-like smile. Her eyes became a little wet.

That smile had made her feel a strange sort of completeness. What else other than a sense of completeness in one's life did one need, Sheba thought. She did not try to find his reactions anymore and went to the kitchen, smiling peacefully.

'Everything is fine, Saleem Miyaan, he just smiled,' Sheba said with a bright face.

'Really? Thank God!'

When Sheba returned to the lobby, the professor was already sleeping with his ear resting on his shoulder. A smile came to Sheba's face. She slowed down the ceiling fan and came out into the lawn. It was almost evening. An airplane was flying in the sky, high above the deer park, towards the airport. It had lights of different colours on its front and back—on the wings, and on its upper and lower sides. Sheba looked at the plane, turning her head up for some time. When she brought her head down, she felt a light wave of pain at the back of her head. She turned her head right and left, and moved it a few times in a semi-circular motion. Sitting with her head bent on the table had been making her neck ache for the last few months. Her doctor had advised her to move her head in different directions to ease the neck muscles. Sheba rose from the chair, and moving her head slowly clockwise and anti-clockwise, began to think again… One does not fall ill during student days. She was reaching her mid-thirties...All her friends were married and had settled down—some of them even had children. Mayuri, too, was busy with her family abroad, and was perhaps trying to come back to India. Time was passing on.

The leaves of the *sheesham* were already turning into vague, dark spots by now. But the sky was not as dark as it had been the other night, a night darkest of all the nights. It had been all dark from the earth to the sky, from the very depths of the earth to the farthest point in the sky—even in the universe beyond the skies.

That night, she was sitting on a stone bench, staring into the silent, deep darkness. At the far end of the enclosure with the stone bench, there was a high, rectangular building with white walls and brightly shining lights. The last room on the eighth floor of that building was the Intensive Care Unit where a frail human being was struggling to survive with some water and air reaching him through the tubes. Sheba sat on the stone bench facing the opposite side, from where no light could be seen. At a small distance, there was a high compound wall near a honeysuckle vine in flower. It was pitch dark on the other three sides. Sheba turned her head and looked at the building.

Sheba's heart ached. It was just yesterday that while she was giving Dr Daanish some juice through a plastic straw from a glass, he had smiled twice, sipping the juice effortlessly through his toothless mouth; caressing his head, Sheba had kissed his forehead. 'My baby,' Sheba said, looking at his face...and he had smiled for the third time. It was strange because he had hardly smiled lately. Seeing him smile for the third time, Sheba's eyes filled with tears.

'Happy?' Sheba looked at him and asked hopefully, but he did not answer, nor did he smile again. She had looked into his eyes and he, too, had looked back. The effect of the long illness and old age seemed to have shrunk his bones, and his body had grown smaller. He had lost his teeth but the barber had been coming daily to give him a shave. The physiotherapist would help him do some exercises. Saleem Miyaan and Sheba bathed him, and changed his side many times a day.

'My baby,' Sheba smiled with teary eyes. People thought that this patient was very lucky to have such good care; Sheba had felt proud that she had succeeded in bringing a person back to the path of life every time he seemed to be slipping away from it. Though he was not as well as he used to be, he still managed to smile. He could not write scholarly books like before, but the knowledge was stored safe in his mind somewhere. He did not recall quotations from his books as before but listened to them when they were read out to him; he did not speak like before but he was still alive. And it was a matter of great happiness for Sheba that he was alive, and that she had a role to play in that. It made Sheba feel closer to God. It was because of her efforts that a person who was about to lose the struggle of life had made a comeback.

During the evenings, when it was time for Sheba to return from work, an urge lodged somewhere deep in the consciousness of the innocent, old, toothless man, and made him edgy. But his face would shine with happiness when she arrived. This was such a pleasurable feeling for Sheba that it helped to relieve her sadness over not talking to Ammi for months. I will explain the situation to Ammi to make her understand, Sheba would think, I will ask Ammi to come over here. She will know that her daughter is not doing anything wrong, that this old man is her baby, the reason for her being, her biggest responsibility, the completion of her existence, and a testament of her humanity. But all this held true only until yesterday. He was now in the ICU. Sheba rose from the stone bench. 'My poor baby,' she murmured and burst into tears.

When the professor had lost his battle for life in the ICU, Sheba had felt that she had no reason to live anymore. A few days after the funeral rites, when people stopped visiting her to offer their condolences, she walked through each and every room in utter bewilderment. The three-bedroom flat seemed to her more like a cemetery with thousands of graves. She ran towards the balcony, walked a few steps, and walked back inside again. Seeing the professor's wheelchair in a corner, she would utter such a loud scream, wildly running towards the lobby, that it was hard even for her to recognize her own voice. She lost track of the time. She never knew how long she kept sitting against the wall, crying. After a long time, she got up from the floor and went to the gate.

Evening was about to set in. The two words, Daanish Kadah, written on the outside of the gate still stood out against the faded green background. She stood there for a long time. There was no one in the compound. A dim light could be seen in the veranda of the small cafeteria next to a faraway wall. Resting her back against the gate, she looked to that side. After a few moments, she saw a group of some five or six girls walking towards the hostel, talking and giggling. She ran over and joined them. It was Diljeet, Mayuri and some other unfamiliar faces. A bird emerged from the hollow of a big broken branch of a leafless tree, and flapping its white wings in the background of the blue evening light, it flew towards the sky. '*Uloo da patha*,' Diljeet said, raising her long neck to look at the sky. Seeing Sukhvinder with Aaftab and Saagar coming towards them, Sheba poked her elbow on Diljeet's side saying loudly, 'Look, here is your...'

'Your Sukhi,' Aaftab, too said aloud, joining in the chorus with Mayuri and Saagar. All of them laughed.

'Hey, hurry up, Daanish sir will be waiting,' one of the students said loudly. Something shattered deep inside Sheba's heart. Her face was drenched with tears and she was standing all alone close to the gate with the faded green paint. It was getting dark. The big lights on the campus posts were shining brightly. Someone carrying his tired head on his bent shoulders was coming towards the gate, walking slowly, at a distance of some 50 yards or so. Sheba walked a few steps towards him, the wet smell of the gloomy dirt of the grave climbed up her nose.

'Saleem Miyaan, what shall we do now?' she had asked blankly. 'Who do I live for now? Why should I live?' She sat on the ground and Saleem Miyaan wiped the tears that had drenched his beard, and cleared his throat.

'For your own sake, *beta*. Please get up, life is a gift. It's one's duty to respect it as long as one lives.'

The deadly silence she had brought with her from the stone bench in the hospital was deep inside her being somewhere. She thought of visiting her home but did not want to leave Saleem Miyaan alone during these sad days either. It was becoming hard to distinguish the rosewood, cluster fig, parrot tree, peepal, banyan and, neem as well as the other trees one from the other because of the darkness. Myriads of stars had appeared in the sky…the dark night was taking over the bluish evening light in the campus. The dogs were barking somewhere far away, and the red glowing tip of the incense stick to keep the mosquitoes away was the only thing visible in the dark. Sheba opened her eyes. Although the sun had set a short while ago, the sky still looked somewhat bluish. The edges of the far horizon were not crimson but deep pink, as the rain had washed all the dust and smoke from the air and one could see its real colours. Sheba closed her eyes again, and the blue of the sky disappeared.

Birds in flocks were returning to their nests in the numerous branches of the trees in the Deer Park. The noisy parrots and little sparrows darted like missiles, flapping their wings, and the swallows floated in the air like swimmers doing a round or two in the open sky, going to their homes for the night. There were so many different birds—big, small, tall, fat, smart and lazy, but all of them had now disappeared. Not a chirp or flapping of wings could be heard anymore. Small bats began to fly across the dark sky. The colour of the sky was somewhat lighter in the spreading darkness of the evening, where the sun had set behind the rosewood tree, in a corner of the front park. Sheba rested her eyes on the sky, appearing and disappearing through the leaves fluttering in the light wind. After a few moments, she rose from her chair and walking wearily, went inside. Food had been laid out on the dining table. A few bowls, some small and big spoons, and only one plate. Sheba's heart started beating fast suddenly. She clenched her teeth and inhaled deeply, cleared her throat softly, as if announcing her presence to herself and went towards the kitchen. Saleem Miyaan was asleep sitting in a wooden chair, with his elbow on the arm rest and his chin on his palm. Sheba looked at him for a second or two, he woke up and stood up quickly. 'I have laid out the food, beta…you…' he said quickly.

'Yes, Saleem Miyaan, you should also have your food,' Sheba replied slowly and turned back.

For all these days someone or other had been visiting them. Often, one of the students from the hostel visiting her stayed with her for the night. This was the first night when Sheba was all alone. Going towards the dining table, Sheba switched on all the lights and sat in her chair. She repeatedly cleared her throat, feeling tears welling up in her eyes. As if swallowing something that felt hard to swallow, she lifted the top of a bowl. Coriander leaves sprinkled on the dish of cauliflower emanated fragrance.

Saleem Miyaan had cooked her favourite vegetable dish. The steam above the dal, garnished with fried garlic, could clearly be seen through the double glass cover of the casserole. Long-grained basmati rice bloomed like split cotton balls in a small rice bowl. A faint smile appeared on Sheba's lips and her eyes filled with tears. Till yesterday, people visited them and someone would make her eat a bite or two. Otherwise she just did not feel hungry. Only God knew if Saleem Miyaan had eaten or not. Perhaps nobody had even asked him to eat. Saleem Miyaan, like Sheba, was no relative of the professor but held him as dear as Sheba did. Saleem Miyaan had prepared everything of her choice that day, as if to convey the message that one should value the gift of life. Sheba took a deep breath. And what would Saleem Miyaan do?

She rose from her chair and went to the kitchen again. Saleem Miyaan was napping with his plate on his lap. Around his wrinkled eyes, the lower lid of one eye still looked wet. Saleem Miyaan was still crying, or had been crying recently, Sheba thought painfully. Saleem Miyaan was so sad too. 'Saleem Miyaan,' Sheba called his name.

He opened his eyes and sat up in an attentive manner, saying, 'Yes, *beta*?'

'Saleem Miyaan, we will go to Srinagar.'

Saleem Miyaan stood up and Sheba turned towards the room. 'You…is it…when are you…?'

'No, not just me, you too.'

'Me? And your job here?' Saleem Miyaan asked.

'I do not want to work here anymore, Saleem Miyaan,' Sheba stopped in the middle of her sentence and Saleem Miyaan pushed a chair near the table so that Sheba could sit down.

'I can apply for leave without pay for some months,' Sheba sat on the chair. 'You don't want to go to your village, Saleem Miyaan, do you?'

'No *beta*, go to whom? My son did not care to ask after me even once in this whole year.' Saleem Miyaan put some rice in Sheba's plate. 'If I go back, my daughter-in-law will resent my return, and that will upset my son too.'

'OK, fine, Saleem Miyaan. We will write a letter to tell him our Srinagar address.'

Saleem Miyaan moved a plate before her and started serving some vegetables. 'Have you made up your mind?' Saleem Miyaan moved another dish towards her plate.

'Yes, Saleem Miyaan, I have made the decision. I can get a job there as well. And in case I don't, I could do some tutoring, and stay with Ammi now. That will make her happy. Then we will see what to do next.' Sheba became silent for some time and looked at the plate. What did she say, what will she have to look for, what was there to see next? She bent her head sideways and looked at the window, lost deep in thought. Yes, she will see, there with Ammi…her Ammi will think about what next. She moved her gaze from the window and looked at the table.

Saleem Miyaan added a spoonful of dal to her plate. 'Yes, that's fine, but you have servants there *beta*.' Saleem Miyaan brought the bowl of yogurt, seasoned with chopped onions and cucumber, to her plate and looked at Sheba.

'It is only Gulla Bhai, as I told you before,' Sheba said, staring at her plate blankly.

'You and Begum Sahiba...' Saleem Miyaan picked up the plate with the spoons and forks, and put it before Sheba. Sheba picked up a fork and Saleem Miyaan poured some yoghurt into a small bowl and kept it near Sheba's plate.

'Gulla Bhai and you will look after the house and the garden. We have enough by the grace of God, Saleem Miyaan, you will be happy there.'

Saleem Miyaan kept looking at Sheba's face and then at the plate, hearing what she was saying. Sheba saw him looking at her like this and picked a small piece of cauliflower with the fork. She put it into her mouth. Saleem Miyaan's face seemed to relax. He added a spoonful of vegetables to Sheba's plate. 'It is good, isn't it?' he asked her, like always. It was unintentional perhaps, but he had a slight smile as well.

'Yes, Saleem Miyaan, it is delicious,' Sheba replied, somewhat thoughtlessly.

'You should have eaten, your food must be cold by now,' Sheba smiled lightly.

'Yes, of course,' Saleem Miyaan nodded and uncovering the jug, poured some hot water into Sheba's glass.

'Did you add lemon and ginger to it, Saleem Miyaan?' Sheba said, showing her interest like always.

'Yes, yes, it has settled to the bottom because it has been sitting there for some time now. I will just pour it back to mix it.' Saleem Miyaan poured the water back into the jug.

A motorbike was heard on the street; it was making a terrible din. The news was blaring loudly from a TV in the flat behind theirs. Saleem Miyaan helped Sheba eat for some time, serving her dishes one after the other. Although most of the food stayed on the plate, Saleem Miyaan had a satisfied expression on his face. He walked towards the kitchen slowly, as if no one had been sad a little while ago, as if none of them had teary eyes, as if no one had visited them to offer their condolences for the professor's demise, and as if their lives had returned back on track even after he was gone.

The moment Saleem Miyaan was out of sight, Sheba held her elbows with her hands, resting them on the table, and put her head on her arms. She should book the tickets to Srinagar tomorrow on reaching the department. She raised her head, and realized that it was Saturday the next day. She took a deep breath, and when the light clatter from the kitchen stopped, she rose from her chair. Pushing it back, she looked towards the kitchen and moved the chair again with more force to make the sound heard. She cleared her throat twice and walked towards her room.

There was some mail on the long table next to the bedroom wall; it was a weekly magazine and a plain envelope. Sheba sliced open the edge of the envelope. It was a short invitation card from Bhopal, the simple function for Shahaab-u-din Sherwani's second nikah ceremony was to be held in Lucknow after two days.